A Rendezvous with Death

DE MICHAEL MYER

iUniverse, Inc.
Bloomington

A Rendezvous with Death

iUniverse books may be ordered through booksellers or by contacting:

iUniverse
1663 Liberty Drive
Bloomington, IN 47403
www.iuniverse.com
1-800-Authors (1-800-288-4677)

ISBN: 978-1-4759-4691-8 (sc)
ISBN: 978-1-4759-4692-5 (hc)
ISBN: 978-1-4759-4771-7 (e)

Library of Congress Control Number: 2012915999

Printed in the United States of America

iUniverse rev. date: 8/31/2012

Other books by deMichael Myer
File 871 (2011)

IN MEMORY
TO MY FRIEND,
KAREN ANDERSON, WHO INSPIRED
ME TO WRITE THIS BOOK.
MAY SHE REST IN PEACE.

*   *   *

I WANT TO THANK MY BOOK EDITOR NIKKI MANDILE
FOR ALL HER HARD WORK IN MAKING THIS NOVEL
A MUCH BETTER PIECE OF WORK.

ALSO I WANT TO ACKNOWLEDGE BILL BOFENKAMP
AND TOM CUSHING FOR THEIR TECHNICAL INPUT.

AND A VERY SPECIAL THANKS GOES OUT TO THE LOVE
OF MY LIFE, LORI FOR PUTTING UP WITH
ME WHILE I SPEND HOURS BEHIND
A COMPUTER AS I WORK ON
MY LIFE'S DREAM OF
BEING AN AUTHOR.

*   *   *

FRONT COVER PHOTO BY DENI BILLMYER.

Chapter 1

A tall, rugged-looking blond-haired man was standing motionless and beleaguered, completely absorbed in thought as he gazed out the window of his sunny office on the tenth floor of the IDS Center. As he leaned against the glass, he looked down and saw people scampering about on Eighth Street in the heart of downtown Minneapolis. He watched intently as the swirling wind caught several unsuspecting women as they rushed from one store to the next, trying vainly to hold their skirts from lifting up and exposing themselves to the elements. It was on days like these that the man wished he had an office on the bottom floor, so he could have an up close and personal view of the sidewalk entertainment.

The man was Ian Christian, an army veteran who served in Vietnam from October 1968 to the same month in 1969. He had been an infantry sergeant with the Fourth Division in the Pleiku Highlands and was now working as an account executive for the Williams Agency.

As Ian stood there, he thought back to the phone message he had received a day earlier. It was troublesome. The message was from Benita Cummings, the wife of an old Vietnam buddy of his. Her husband, Roland "The Snake" Cummings, along with Paul Fisher and Ian, had been the lone survivors of an ambush at Fu

Pin, a small hamlet on the Cambodian border back in late spring of '69. The rest of his platoon had been killed by the Vietcong. That wasn't totally accurate. Actually, Ian had shot and killed James Wilson that very same day as he ran from the hamlet. At the time it had seemed the right thing to do because Wilson was a coward and he didn't deserve to live. Wilson could have stood his ground and fought his way out of the village; instead he turned and ran, so Ian had no choice but to put three nicely placed bullets in his back. Getting out of the ambush alive had been pure magic; one that would have even challenged the great Houdini. After Fish and Ian fought their way out, Ian picked up a wounded Corporal Cummings and carried him to safety. Shortly after that, Roland was discharged from the army with a very pronounced limp caused by a bullet from a Vietcong, whom Ian also sent to the hereafter. And Roland had been grateful to him ever since.

The lengthy message had been about Roland. Apparently, Roland had taken a header off of an office building in downtown Atlanta, causing his brains to splatter all over Peachtree Boulevard. Roland had been a night security guard at the Hawthorn Building, and for some reason, he went to the rooftop and took his life. Benita said his death was far too suspicious, as the two of them were living a great life together. They had recently made plans to visit Las Vegas and to stop at the Grand Canyon on their way. They'd even planned a vacation to Hawaii in the following year. So killing himself didn't make any sense. The police said it looked like a suicide, as they found no evidence that would lead them to think otherwise. Still, Benita couldn't fathom why a happy man, with no known vices, would up and kill himself.

Ian could tell by her message that Benita was still shaken by the incident and was desperately seeking answers. He couldn't think of a single reason why Roland would kill himself. The two of them spoke often, and Ian had never gotten the impression Roland was depressed or unhappy. To the contrary, Roland was elated to be alive, and he said he owed it all to Ian. So why did he do it? No one would probably ever know, but Ian thought it would be appropriate to place a call to Benita to see if he could help her with her grief.

On a brighter note, Ian was excited because he was going to meet up with his brother Eugene this evening. The two of them were getting together after work to have some drinks at Duffy's, which was located within walking distance of his office. It was on the corner of Eighth Street and La Salle. Ian hadn't seen his brother for almost a year and he was looking forward to hearing what was happening in his life.

*   *   *

Judy, a lovely young assistant who worked for Jack Evans, chose the moment to step into my office and interrupt the wonderful images I was having of Eugene and his family. She informed me there was a four thirty meeting in the conference room to discuss the Gustafson account, which would only take fifteen to twenty minutes. That was total bullshit, I thought. No meeting with the CFO and Jack Evans would ever take that short of time. I made a mental note to call my brother and delay our rendezvous until six thirty this evening.

An impending afternoon meeting meant only one thing…it was time to quit fucking around and get to work on a strategy for my business cohorts. The two men were typical Hugo Boss types: uptight, white shirt and plain tie, stick-up-the-ass kind of dicks with a boring sense of fashion. Never once had I seen them wear a colored shirt or even a tie with some kind of abstract print… just gray, black, or blue pin-striped suits. That was the extent of their wardrobe.

After wasting the first hour of the morning daydreaming, I decided to retreat to the confines of my desk to ponder what the two men wanted. I tossed a variety of ideas around in my head, but I just couldn't get my hands around anything. Nothing was clicking, so I decided to place a call to Judy to find out if she could give me a little insight as to what the two men wanted. She couldn't tell me squat, just said they were in the final planning stage of something very important for the agency.

Williams was a huge agricultural agency with many medium to large-size accounts. I had several; one being Gustafson, Inc. of Dallas, Texas, of which my brother Eugene happened to be the president and CEO. John Deere, Northrup-King, Monsanto, Land-O-Lakes and General Mills were among the rest, as well as a number of smaller implement, seed, and chemical companies.

I spent the rest of the day in my office reviewing notes on Gustafson, the newest of all the accounts I managed. Being an account executive was a steppingstone to bigger and better things within the agency. I eventually wanted to run the place, but who in their right mind wouldn't. That would mean big-time cash, luxury items, and a lifestyle that was only a dream, coming from my meager background. I was on the fast track to upper management, but if I was to make it to the top, I had to bide my time, put in the hours, and kiss ass with guys like CFO Jeff Barnes and the president of the agency. And kissing ass and following rules were two things I didn't do well.

Four thirty eventually came around faster than I had anticipated, so I gathered my file and took the stairs down to the meeting room on the ninth floor where I found Jeff Barnes and Jack Evans seated at a conference table in the middle of the room. Spreadsheets were out in front of them and a small timeline chart was just to their left. Speaking about stick-up-the-ass dicks, these two were still in their suits; neither of them had even loosened their collars. They were talking quietly, then stopped and kind of gazed at me with half-open mouths as I stood in the doorway. I was out of my sports coat, wearing a bright, purple-striped shirt and a tie with a Tasmanian devil at full rage. Needless to say, it wasn't the attire of an up and coming executive.

I exhaled slightly and entered the room. The two men greeted me from their chairs, urging me to have a seat between them where we could talk without interruption. They had some good news they wanted to share with me. They knew I'd been working with Gustafson on a promotional campaign, in this particular case it was a corporate video, some sales brochures, four or five direct mail pieces, and an island trade show display. It was a large portfolio of work that would consume much of my time for the next half year. The video was to be shot at three locations; two in the United States and one in Brazil. I had worked long and hard trying to sell this package and it seemed my efforts had finally paid off. It meant huge dollars for the agency and a large bonus for me. Jeff and Jack had worked out the cost projections, and they brought me here to tell me it was a go to get the project rolling. I was informed I had six months to put together a script and have Gustafson sign off on it. During that time I would need to get a camera crew together, as well as coordinate all the other details right on down to hotel and airline tickets. Wow! That was all I could say. I was so excited to be a major player in this game. I only hoped, when the project was completed, that I got full recognition for its plan and execution. But then again, who knows, I wouldn't bet against Jack Evans taking all the accolades for the finished product. He was a sneaky asshole whom other colleagues had warned me about.

We spent the better part of an hour going over the numbers to make sure they worked. The Williams Agency hadn't been one of the top agencies in the country for nothing. They were a stickler for having all the projections down to a gnat's ass. They asked my thoughts for the writing, art, and filming team, and that was it. It was a short meeting that lasted over the allotted time, but I wasn't a bit upset when the day ended like this.

When the meeting concluded, I went back to my office to check for messages and collect my things. There had been no calls from anyone, so I left to go meet up with Eugene. It was going to be a fantastic evening, one that would be filled with lots of vodka and tequila, and an expensive cab ride home.

I emerged from my office with coat in hand and took the elevator to the bottom floor of the IDS. Before leaving, I buttoned up my coat to keep the chilly Minnesota wind from causing my dick to disappear faster than money on a craps table. The half-block walk to the bar was an invigorating one to say the least. I was still congratulating myself as I walked through the front door at Duffy's.

Once inside, I looked right and came face-to-face with a seventies rock band called Frank Kohler and the Allies. The rather buff-looking lead singer, whom I assumed was Frank, had a Hendrix-looking Afro and was sporting a T-shirt that read: The Wet Spots are Coming. I believed the reference to be both a sexual aspiration and an aspersion toward women in general, but by the way he was screaming - *Big Ten Inch* - by Aerosmith, it might just have been more of wishful thinking than anything else. The band's loud music was drowning out this side of the bar, which meant Eugene wouldn't be in this section of the establishment. He hated loud music; thought it was unnecessary. So I walked around the actual bar and found him in a smaller room out back. As I approached, I saw Eugene and Dan Liberty, an old friend of his, sitting as bookends to a gorgeous woman I knew from my distant childhood. Her name was Kate Anderson, Kate Rutan or Kate Peterson...it was Kate something, that I knew for sure. I wasn't certain of which last name she was going by these days. The one thing I did know was that her face and body were as beautiful as the last time I'd seen her, which was when I was thirteen years old. Kate had coal-black hair, a rather long nose that had an ever-so-slight bend to the left, and a wicked smile that was inviting me to the party.

The three of them were nowhere near being sober. They were all major friends during their high school days and at least five years older than me. And there was Kate; licking her moist, red lips like a lioness does when she's anticipating her prey. I remember my brother telling me once that every guy in high school made a run at her with little to no success. She wound up dating a point guard on the basketball team her senior year and married him shortly after they graduated. That was the Anderson guy, I was sure of that. She then married another guy, and then another guy and, well, was divorced for the third time at age thirty-nine. And she was sitting right in front of me with those hungry eyes. Believe me; I had no plans on being husband number four.

It dawned on me at that moment as to why my brother was in town. He was here with friends to celebrate sealing the Gustafson deal. A was a great surprise, with some delicious cake for dessert. I really loved dessert, especially when it came in the form of voluptuous breasts that were stuffed into a size-two dress.

I shivered a little with delight at the sight of Kate and said, "So, you people started without me?"

"That's right," replied Eugene. "We've been here for a couple of rounds at happy hour."

I said, "Bullshit! It looks to me like you've been here for more than a couple of drinks."

Eugene blew that off and said, "I'll bet you never guessed why I was coming to town? I told the boys at Williams not to say a word about anything until the end of the day. I didn't want them to spoil the surprise. You know Dan Liberty, and do you remember who this beautiful young lady is?"

Eugene didn't have to introduce Kate: I knew her from all the wet dreams I'd had had of her up until the time I was sixteen years old. I hadn't stopped staring at her or her at me since I came into the bar. Those large, brown eyes were alive with anticipation and they were fixed on me. It was as if Eugene and Dan didn't exist.

Then Kate spoke. "Ian, it has been ages since we last met. If my recollection is correct, I believe it was at a party in your parents' basement. You probably won't believe this, but I always thought you were the cutest little brother of all of my friends. You were so inquisitive, always wanting to come down to the party and see what was going on. I remember your brother running you off on a couple of occasions. All the girls wanted you to stay, but your brother had other ideas."

"What's not to believe? I was always cute," I said with a grin. *But not so little anymore as Big Ian was telling me at this very moment.* "You know, I think it was pure inquisitiveness that brought me to the basement in those days." *No it was the desire to see you naked.* "So brother, do you plan on running me off again tonight?"

That brought laughter from everyone as I ordered the first of many cocktails for the evening. The four of us spent the next couple of hours catching up on old times. Eugene told me Kate worked in the same building as I did down in the Crystal Court, so they went over and invited her to the party. I could sense the two men still had hard-ons for her after all these years. I assumed they would have liked to be with her if they could. But I, on the other hand, could tell she wanted to be with me, as all of her conversations gravitated in my direction. She wanted to know what I'd been up to all these years. I told her I had gone to Vietnam and graduated from St. Cloud State University after I returned from the war. I had a couple of failed marriages, a four-year-old daughter named Alisa and a great job at the agency. And I still liked playing hockey on occasions and was thinking about coaching a bantam team if time allowed.

She informed me she had three kids under the age of twelve and said she was happy, but lonely. I doubted that. A woman as beautiful as her would never be lonely unless she wanted it that way. She continued by saying her second husband, who was an FBI or CIA agent, had been killed in a car accident. That I knew had been a lie; her second husband had been brain damaged in some kind of accident and she divorced him. I think that was the Peterson guy. Anyway, she was a wolf in sheep's clothing, and I could see where this conversation was leading.

Eugene spoke again and said to me, "I want to congratulate you on the great job you've been doing with the company project. I spoke to Ted Nevins before I left the office, and he confirmed that you did a super job on selling the whole package. I think our in-house agency in Dallas thought I approved this project because you were my brother, but they soon learned you were a very capable project manager. Ted seemed impressed with your proposals and timelines, so it's a go. I'm proud of you and the folks will be too."

"Thanks," I beamed. "I spent many hours making sure everything was correct. I didn't want to embarrass you or the agency. I believe this is a good fit for both of us, that being Gustafson and Williams. Let's drink!"

So we drank and drank some more. It wasn't long before I saw Dan make a pass at Kate out of the corner of my eye, as well as overhearing his suggestion that she go home with him after the party was over. Kate made light of the innuendo, suggesting maybe he'd had a little too much to drink. Dan assured her he was fine; in fact, good enough to drive her home and give her the big red weasel. That was Dan's way of saying he wanted to fuck her. He had the worst pick-up lines in the world. Plus he had names for body parts that were nonexistent and sexual activities that were downright repugnant. After several more drinks, Dan decided it was finally time to leave. We said our good-byes and moved the party from our table to the bar. I ordered a couple of tequila shots for me and Eugene, and that was it for my brother.

He said with a slur in his voice, "It's time for me to go to the hotel and find my pillow."

I looked over at Kate and asked, "Would you like to help me walk him down the Nicollet Avenue Mall, so we can get to the Hilton before he falls over?"

"Sure, why not," she said as she checked her watch. "It's early and it's Friday night. And I don't have anything planned for tomorrow morning."

The three of us eventually left the bar with my brother in tow. Kate and I put our arms around him, and Eugene staggered us down Eight Street toward Nicollet Avenue. We hadn't walked more than thirty feet when Kate said to me, "I heard you say that you had been in Vietnam. Do you talk about it much?"

"I do, with mute people."

"So, I should shut up then?"

I changed the subject and said, "Don't you think my brother is getting heavy?"

She giggled and replied, "I think that's supposed to be, he ain't heavy, he's my brother."

"No, that's a song. I mean he's getting a little chubby, don't you think?"

"Oh yeah, I guess he's put on a few pounds since high school, but that's not what we were talking about. I asked if you talked much about the war because I was wondering if you were alright."

"Well, I think I might be coming down with the plague."

"No, I mean are you alright from the war?"

"Define alright."

"Like, are you okay mentally?"

"I'm certifiable."

"And physically?"

"Physically I had my dick shot off, but outside of that I'm doing dandy."

"How could that be?" she said with a perplexed look.

"Well, it's like this. You just stand up when the enemy is shooting at you and bang, a bullet goes through you..."

"No. Not that. You said you had a daughter."

"Oh yeah. That would be Alisa. She was left on our doorstep in a basket."

"Is that so? On your doorstep, huh?"

"Yup. With a note that read, don't float me down the Nile, the basket isn't waterproof."

"So this means I should shut up?"

"Well, Eugene and I could always gag you."

"Okay. I get the hint."

Kate kept to small talk from that point on as we meandered our way down to the Hilton. She indicated her son Tony liked playing hockey too. She even went as far as to suggest I come to one of her son's practices this winter so I could help coach his team. I thought that would be a terrible idea, as I could hear wedding bells ringing as she spoke.

We finally arrived at the Hilton after a fifteen-minute walk. Kate and I held onto Eugene tightly as we moved through the revolving doors to the lobby and then on to the elevators. I pushed the wall button, and when the doors opened, we deposited him inside, sending him on his way to the sixth floor.

Kate said, "That was kind of cruel to send him up the elevator by himself. What if he doesn't find his room?"

"There's always the hallway floor."

"Ian..."

"Don't worry Kate. I'm sure someone would eventually come along and help him to his room. Besides, I know my brother. He can do the most incredible things when he's drunk. And speaking of cruel, he once tried to kill me by putting a spoonful of peanut butter in my mouth just so he could see my throat swell up. I believe your first husband and Dan were there to watch it happen. I got the hives, swelled up like a blowfish and started scratching my skin until it was raw. Now, that's cruel!"

"What do you mean tried to kill you?"

"You've obviously never seen anyone with a severe peanut allergy, have you? They could just as easily die from that as an overdose of drugs. That never crossed my brother's mind. He just liked being an ass for the sake of being an ass."

Our next move was to head to the hotel bar for a couple more drinks and some interesting conversation. We were about to sit down when she stopped. She turned toward me and said, "He really forced you to eat peanut butter as a joke?"

"Yeah. What don't you understand about older brothers? It's their job to fuck with their younger brothers. Kate, enough with the peanut butter talk. It's starting to make me itch. Let's order drinks."

We both took chairs at the bar and Kate said, "You know, once upon a time I knew a little boy who grew up to be a handsome man. I believe he's someone that the right woman could get to like."

"Hold on, is this a fairy tale because fairies scare me."

"No. No. It's not a fairy tale; it's about a kid I once knew."

"And do I know this guy?"

She looked back at me, winked and said, "As a matter of fact you do. As luck would have it he's sitting right next to me at this very moment."

I looked around her and said, "That's strange. The seat next to you is empty."

"You have such a great sense of humor Ian, but you must know I'm speaking of you."

"You know I've heard that before. My second ex-wife said the same thing about me. She said I was a real jokester right up until the time I had her committed because she was a fuckin' wacko. I must say a very good and bad idea on my part. I know what you're getting at Kate. I could see it in your eyes when I first walked into Duffy's tonight. You weren't hiding it from anyone. I also saw you blow Dan off in a nice way, and well, here you are with me. That sums it up pretty well. Correct?"

"So, I've been that obvious have I?"

"Let's put it this way. The licking of your lips while you stared into my eyes was definitely a dead giveaway. You did almost everything but take off your panties and toss them at me."

There was silence for a moment and then she said in a sly voice, "Did you want me to do that because it can be arranged easily, even here in the bar."

The bartender must have been eavesdropping because he immediately stopped what he was doing and shifted his eyes in our direction, curious to make sure the latter wasn't happening in this hotel.

She continued looking at me and chuckled while she played with the lime in her gin and tonic. I could sense she was contemplating something. There was a short pause in the conversation. Then she moved toward me and planted a long, wet kiss on my lips. She followed that up by slipping her tongue down my throat, retracting it, and whispering something in my ear that I couldn't clearly understand. I believe it had something to do with what she wanted to do to me, or was it she had no qualms about me doing whatever I wanted to her? Either way, it was clearly an invitation to ravish her in any way I saw fit. It was at that instant that I thought my wet dreams might actually come true.

I leaned back in my chair as I contemplated my next move. Some guy behind us and to our rear suggested we get a room. I ignored his comment and took a long sip from my Stoli martini. I never dreamt when I got up this morning I would meet a beautiful woman who was going to ask me to have sex with her tonight. Life was getting better by the moment. "So let me get this straight.

You want to go home with me tonight? Is that correct? Is this proposition supposed to be the beginning of a relationship or just a jump for the night?"

"You tell me," she said with a smile.

"Well Kate, I have to say I'm flattered you want to sleep with me, but I recently got over a bad marriage, and I'm not ready for any kind of commitment right now." What the fuck did I just say? I must be nuts. In front of me sits a version of a Playboy centerfold and I'm saying no to her. To boot, she doesn't care if I call her or not. I must be coming down with malaria again! This was one for the books. I'm not even sure if I could tell this story to my friends. They might think I'm out of my mind or just plain lying. "Let me say this Kate. I must be sick or something, but I'm going to pass on your invitation tonight. I'll take your home phone number though, if that's okay with you? I've got something coming up next weekend and I might like you to join me. I think you'll like what I have in mind."

"I know I will. All you have to do is pick up the phone and call me. You know Ian, I don't make this offer to many men, and I can't say I've ever been turned down by anyone. Not even once. That just makes me want you even more. So the answer is yes, call me anytime day or night and I'll be available."

Kate opened her purse and found a - Get Out of Jail Free - card from the Monopoly game. She wrote her name, phone number and a little note on the back side of the card that read, "What's mine is yours, and I hope you take everything soon!!!"

Getting the card and reading it left me with the feeling I was in the middle of a surreal porn movie, which would have been apropos for the evening's events. I had the feeling she had been keeping the card in her purse for a long time, just waiting for the right moment to use it. As I looked down at it I could see the corners were dog-eared, and it contained a wine stain or two. I had met many people in my career and we exchanged business cards all the time, but I never, ever remember getting one as forward or to the point as this one.

We finished our drinks and walked out of the bar with our arms around each other. The guy who was sitting behind us said in passing that we finally made the right decision. He wrongly assumed we were heading up the elevator to our hotel room. He would have lost his life's savings tonight if he had made that bet. I smiled as we passed, thinking to myself that I had the phone number of this fabulous woman and the invitation to Pass Go and Collect…whatever I wanted. Oh my God, who would have thought by evening's end that this would wind up being one of the most unpredictable and delightful days of my life.

Chapter 2

It was a chilly autumn Saturday morning in Ham Lake. There was a definite tinge of fall in the air. My head was still buzzing from the alcohol I had consumed the night before, so I choked down a couple of aspirins with a can of Coke to see if that would break me out of the funk I was in. If it hadn't of been for Kate's invitation, my whole being would have said…kill me now and put me out of my misery forever. But as it was, I was quite sure this was the best hangover I'd ever had in my entire life, if such things even existed. The delight of last night's sexual invitation far overshadowed the pain in my head.

Looking outside I could see the lawns were turning brown and the leaves from the crimson maple tree in the front yard were beginning to drop, most likely caused by the heavy overnight frost that had fallen on the area. From my vantage point, I could see the neighbors across the street getting ready for Halloween. The third of October seemed a little early to be decorating for the upcoming festivity, but when kids get antsy their parents have to pick up the torch and run with it. Bud Best was helping his two young twin boys, Shane and Shawn, with a very fat scarecrow filled with hay. It looked nothing like it should have…more like Oliver Hardy than Stan Laurel. The couple's younger daughter was running around the yard in a pink princess costume, tapping her brothers on their heads with a magic wand. I could hear her squeal with delight as she said, "You're a frog," and then scamper away as the boys tried to grab her. Bud's wife was inside their house standing on a ladder decorating the windows with paper pumpkins and witches. The skirt which she was wearing was hiked up almost to her crotch, and her small, but firm breasts were pressed tightly against the glass, which would be cause for idle chitchat at a later date in this well-manicured, tight-ass suburban neighborhood.

It was now four Saturdays and counting before the neighborhood kids would be roaming the streets to trick or treat. My daughter Alisa wouldn't be around this year for Halloween, so I would most likely stay at home and hand out goodies by myself to all the little ghosts and goblins as they came around with their parents. I thought for a fleeting second that I should invite Kate to come over and dress up like a naughty nurse to help me pass out treats. I should be more specific. She would be dressed up in some sort of nursing outfit with sexy undergarments that included crotchless panties and a push-up bra. Not that she needed a push-up bra as she seemed to have more than ample breasts for a woman her size. As a matter of fact, I thought they looked magnificent just the way they were. And to complete the ensemble, she would need to have a stethoscope to check the irregular heartbeat I would definitely be having. Wouldn't that have been a sight for the neighborhood parents? I believe the mothers would raise an eyebrow or two, and the fathers would stand at the curb with their hands deep into their pockets wishing they were me. I'm not sure if that would have qualified as a trick or a treat on my behalf. Oh well, it would have been my version of a Wal-Mart greeter…something like, "Have a nice night Joey, and hide that little erection from your parents if at all possible."

It didn't take a genius to realize the daylight was getting shorter by the week. And before long it would be the middle of November, which meant I needed to spend some time working on layouts for the Gustafson video script. I needed to start soon in case the ensuing holidays took more of my time than expected.

There was something else I needed to do. I had to make a phone call to Benita Cummings. It was the one thing I promised myself I would do to help the widow in her time of need. I had been going over Roland's suicide in my head, asking myself why someone would do such a thing. And each time I came up empty. It would have been understandable if he had come home from the war and killed himself because that was what a lot of vets did early on. But it had been more than thirteen years since Vietnam and I thought Roland had gotten over the hump like I had. Oh yeah, Roland would periodically get a little emotional and talk to me about the ambush and thank me from the bottom of his heart for saving his life, but he seemed to have everything under control. I would have thought a person contemplating suicide would have said something like; I would rather you had left me for dead, or I wished I'd died that day. But no, he never indicated he wasn't grateful for still being on this earth. Something had gone wrong in his ordinarily sane world. Again, two plus two didn't equal four. At least in this case it didn't.

I listened as the phone rang on the other end of the Atlanta exchange. A young boy picked up the phone and said, "Hello."

I asked, "Who am I speaking to?"

"Who are you?" he replied.

"I was a good friend of Roland's. Is Mrs. Cummings at home?"

Screaming through the receiver the boy yelled, "Mom, it's for you!"

There was a pause in the conversation as I listened to the sound of footsteps echoing off what I suspected was a wooden staircase. I could hear a woman ask as she approached, "Who is it?" And the boy replying, "I don't know. He didn't tell me his name."

The woman took the phone from the boy and said, "Hello. This is Benita."

"Benita. This is Ian Christian. How are you doing?"

She broke down at that point and began sobbing. I couldn't make out a single word she said for the next couple of minutes, and when she finally regained her composure she spoke in a soft, garbled tone. "Ian. I'm so glad you called. I was hoping you would. I have a thousand questions. I simply don't know where to begin."

"Well Benita, I'm sure this has been very difficult for you, but let's take it slowly by starting at the beginning. When exactly did this happen?"

"It was last Monday evening around nine o'clock."

"I understood from your message that this happened at his place of employment. Is that right?"

"Yes, that's correct."

"And did anyone know he was going up to the rooftop?"

"No, I don't think so. The police asked the night crew that question and no one said they heard from him. And he didn't leave a message with the security desk either."

"Then let me ask you this. Were the two of you getting along okay? You know what I mean, were you two at each other's throats lately or anything like that?"

"No, we hadn't had an argument for a very long time. As a matter of fact, the two of us were getting along better than any time in our lives."

"Was Roland in trouble with gambling or drugs?"

"Absolutely not. He came home every night after work and I never saw him do any drugs except for the pain pills he got from the VA."

"Could it be possible he may have been taking too many of those pills and felt the pain was too much to bear?"

"I don't think so, but then again Roland never complained about anything. He always said he was happy he made it through the war and went to church every Sunday to thank God for having you there to get him out alive."

"Then could it have been alcohol?"

"No, I don't think so Ian. I mean, Roland did drink a bit too much over the years, but that only seemed natural for him and the vets he hung around with. He did go to the VFW every once in a while, but he only did that when I was with him. He told me a few drinks were his lone release from the pain of the war. The emotional pain, that is."

"Okay, you're not going to like this next question Benita, but I have to ask it. Could he have had another woman on the side that you didn't know about?"

"How could you even think of asking me a question like that Ian? From what you knew about Roland and what I've told you, how could you even think he was capable of doing something like that?"

"It's tough to have to ask a question like that, but you know it had to be asked. Then is there anything in your past that could have caused this, like a jealous boyfriend or an ex-husband who wanted to get back at you?"

"I don't have any ex-husbands and I've never cheated on Roland. Not even when he was in the military. I loved him too much, and respected what he was doing to cause anything to come between the two of us."

"You know Benita, I had to ask you these kinds of questions. I'm sure the police did the same thing." I took the silence on the other end of the line as a yes to that question. "Then tell me this. What is the one thing that could make him do what he did? Something, anything at all; there has to be an answer."

"I've run it back and forth in my mind a hundred times and all I can come up with is that someone either lured him or forced him to the top of that building."

I asked with hesitation, "Then what?"

"Then someone hit him over the head and tossed him off the roof to make it look like a suicide."

Astounded, I replied, "You mean you think he was murdered?"

"He must have been because he had vertigo. He would have passed out and fallen to the ground long before he ever reached the edge of the roof. What I'm saying is he couldn't have jumped if he wanted to."

"What did the police say?"

"Let me put it this way: Holmes and Watson they are not. And with all the crime down here in Atlanta, they probably thought it was best to sweep it under the carpet and leave it at that."

"So they ruled it a suicide and stopped working on the case. Is that it?

"Yup, that's about the long and the short of it. I have no place else to go for answers Ian. I just thought you should know he had died and the circumstances surrounding his death."

"Is there anything else you want to tell me?"

"The only other thing I know is Roland had told me a couple weeks back that he had heard from his office manager that a man with an Asian accent called asking if he worked for them at the Hawthorn Building. They told him he did, but wouldn't tell him anything else. I'm assuming the guy wanted to stop by and say hello."

"Did Roland know any Asian men outside of work?"

"Not that I knew of."

"Did you tell the police that?"

"Yes, but they can't make any connection between Roland and the Asian man. They said they had no real way of finding out the man's identity. Let me ask you this Ian. Did something happen during the war that would have caused this to happen to my husband? I mean, did he do something dreadfully wrong that he wouldn't or couldn't tell me about?"

"I don't think so Benita, but he was with another platoon before I met up with him. He'd been in country for three months before I got there, so I couldn't tell you. I think this is all just a big coincidence to a mystery we may never be able to unravel. There must have been something down deep inside him that he never let on to you, me, or any of his friends. You know, people live with family and friends all their lives and still never completely know them. I could say I thought I knew my second wife, but I would never have guessed she was mentally ill. So there you have it. People surprise us all the time, and we seem stunned when something like this happens. I'll make a follow-up call to the Atlanta Police Department in a month or so and let you know if I find out any other information. In the meantime, keep your head up and spend a lot of time with your son. He's going to need you now more than ever."

"Thanks for calling Ian, and you take care. Bye."

Chapter 3

The slightly built assassin sat across the table from his friend, silently congratulating himself on his first victim. That person had been a trusting, Mexican-American security guard from Atlanta whom he had killed six days earlier. The assassin, posing as a maintenance man, tricked the guard into going to the roof of the Hawthorn Building to check on a faulty air-conditioning unit. He had found the security guard on the third floor and got him to open the door to the roof so he could check out the problem. The assassin had actually hidden in the building until closing time. Then he went and found the guard as he was doing his security rounds after the building had been locked up for the evening. The two men went to the roof and the rest was simple. He used blunt force to subdue the man then tossed him off the roof, which ended years of pain and frustration over an incident that took place over a decade earlier. It had been pitch-dark that evening and almost impossible for anyone to see what he had done. The height of the building, which was taller than most, was also an important factor in pulling the murder off. When the police arrived, the assassin quietly slipped out one of the back doors near the loading dock and vanished into the night. It had gone down quite easily. In fact, it seemed far too easy. No one noticed him and the lack of security from the guard was even more dumbfounding. The guard hadn't asked him for his identification, called the front desk for confirmation, or viewed the situation as something unusual. The guard simply took it for granted the air-conditioning unit needed fixing and that cost him his life.

The assassin's friend had given him all the vital information on the security guard, and confirmation as to where he worked was all that was needed to set the plan in motion. This had been his first kill since Vietnam, and it signaled the beginning of a long line of many that would follow. There would be seven or eight victims in all. Some would die in a similar manner as his two brothers, and others would be killed by whatever means possible. He liked the idea of getting back at these Americans. They were the type of people that lived by the motto "an eye for an eye," and that is exactly what he set forth to accomplish.

The next phase of the plan would quickly move on to Florida. The whole killing spree should take no longer than five, possibly six weeks if everything went according to plan. Of course, a number of things could happen along the way to change the situation, but the plan was a good one and he was confident everything would fall into place. If any of the individuals happened to be on vacation or out of town on business, then the order of the murders would change, and the time line might have to be altered. The assassin had special plans for the second to the last of his victims. This particular individual was the platoon sergeant who had captured him and his brothers, and set this whole plan in motion nearly ten years ago. The assassin hated him almost as much as the men who actually killed his two brothers because the sergeant failed to have his commanding officer turn the three of them over to the authorities at the American fortress at Camp Enarie. But killing him was a ways down the line, and the assassin would have to use extreme caution in dealing with him because he was the only one of the targets who was a true soldier. That sacred individual was also half a continent away from his beginning destination of Atlanta. If the assassin should happen to make any mistakes along the way, then he was sure the police would put two and two together and warn the sergeant that someone was out there who might be trying to kill him. That would put a major wrench in the plan. So he would have to act swiftly and precisely if he wanted to get to that individual.

Today's meeting was more about security measures than anything else. It wasn't about high fives or slaps on the back, but rather a time to sit and listen to his friend talk about the precautions that needed to be taken as he moved about the country. He was told to drive the truck his friend had gotten him to all the destinations. Under no circumstances was he to use an airplane to travel because that would create a paper trail, as the airlines kept manifests of their passengers. And if his name happened to show up on one of those flights, then it would be traced back to him by the police or the FBI. And in a worst case scenario, the authorities could put an APB out on him, which would send his description to every police station in the country in a flash.

As they sat there at the table eating lunch, his friend said to him, "Always remember to change the license plates on the truck as often as possible, especially when you're in a state that's more than two hundred miles away from the ones on your truck. It's extremely important to change the plates when you head north. Those people in the Midwest are an inquisitive bunch. They're definitely much more on their toes than the people or police down here in the south. Those northerners would think it strange that a truck with Florida or Georgia plates would be driving around later this month, especially in Iowa or Minnesota. It would be a different story if you were there in the summer because a lot people from the southern states vacation up there to avoid the oppressive heat the south produces from June through August. And I urge you to stay on major highways and drive the speed limit. A ticket could mean trouble if a cop really wanted to check you out. The most important thing I can tell you is to keep to yourself and blend in whenever possible. Remember, Asians stand out like a sore thumb, especially in the Midwest. I want to remind you that people all over this country have a distinct hatred for any Asian in the wake of the Vietnam War. They think your race is sneaky and can't be trusted, so use caution when confronting them."

He went on to say there were several military organizations he was to stay clear of like the VFW, DAV, and the American Legion. Those drunken war veterans would be all over him in a minute to start a fight, which could lead to some serious trouble. He should think of wearing some kind of baseball cap. Having a John Deere or a seed-dealer cap would be an asset in the Northern Plains States. And he was always to look and act like an American. He was to use cash and live in his truck until he had completed his task, then drive a couple hundred miles and stop at a motel to clean up. He was told not to forget to use gloves whenever he was in a situation where he could leave fingerprints. That had been easy when he posed as a maintenance man, as they were standard gear for someone in that profession. But gloves would seem strangely out of place at other times, especially if the weather was warm. If and when he used a gun, he was to pick up all the spent ammunition and take it with him and dispose of it as soon as possible where no one would ever find it. And he was to make sure he was in a rural area if he should happen to use his gun without the silencer, as gun shots summon the police in a hurry.

Each and every tip his friend had given him was done to keep the assassin's identity a secret and to ensure his complete success. To waver from the plan or to do something out of the ordinary could prove disastrous. His friend assured him he was the only person who could cause his plan to fail, and if he stayed the course he would be a happy man in Southern California in a couple of months. He could then be proud of what he had accomplished, and have the satisfaction that he had gotten revenge for his brothers.

Ah yes, there was vengeance to be had, and he was excited because he would be the one wielding the sword. He had all the financial backing he needed for a successful journey. He had gotten that prior to setting his plan in motion in Atlanta, and everything was beginning to take shape. The assassin would work his way through the Southern States, head north along the East Coast to the Carolinas, and then on to New Jersey. If he was successful at that point, he could move on to Illinois. From there he had options of where he could go in the Midwest. His final destination would take him to Laguna Beach, California. If he was lucky and cautious, then life would be worth living again.

Chapter 4

The assassin had been keeping a close eye on the helicopter pad and hangar, which were located at the far end of the Cross City Airport in Dixie County. The bright-red neon sign on the outside of the hangar read Florida State Police Helicopter Service. He had already been there on and off for a day and a half, watching from the cab of his dark blue 1974 Ford Bronco. The truck showed all the signs of having been a well-traveled vehicle. There was a deep puncture dent in the back right corner panel, a broken antenna on the left front fender, and a partially smashed grill in front from where a deer had been hit. By looking at the truck, no one would have suspected there was a new, overhauled six-cylinder engine under its hood. The Bronco was nondescript; no one would take notice of it setting off to the side of the road for the short period of time it would be in the vicinity of the airport. The assassin watched closely as former U.S. Army Warrant Officer Grayson Meeks went about his daily routine of checking maintenance logs while waiting for a call from the state or local authorities. Grayson was an ex-Vietnam pilot who flew helicopters in the five-county area. He would occasionally travel to other parts of Florida, but that was only in cases of emergency. His main job was to shuttle individuals to and from remote locations when there had been catastrophes like a plane crash, a major highway accident, or one of the frequent natural disasters that plagued this Panhandle Region of Northern Florida. He had been in Vietnam for two tours, the last one being in 1968-1969, and being back in the United States where it was safe was something he relished.

Grayson still kept his appearance extremely meticulous, like he had when he was an officer in the military. He always wore neatly pressed slacks with polished shoes, had manicured nails, and got a haircut every two weeks. He could be found at the airport from eight to five daily and at the barber every other Saturday at ten o'clock in the morning. Other than that, Grayson would frequent the American Legion on Tuesday evenings to play some poker with the boys, and be in bed by no later than ten thirty every weekday night except for Friday. He lived alone with his cat Maxx in a small house in Shamrock, a city which was within a stone's throw of the airport. Meeks had been married only once, which ended in divorce shortly after his last tour of Vietnam. He had extreme emotional problems from what he saw and did in the Pleiku Highlands of South Vietnam, and that's why he and his wife June had split in late 1970. Grayson had one vice and that was gambling, so he could be found at the casino playing blackjack every Saturday night.

These quirks were all routines the assassin's friend had told him would happen like clockwork; Grayson it seems was a creature of habit. If the assassin wanted a convenient place to kill him, then the casino would be an excellent location to do it. And the casino would have been the most explainable place for the killing, as the police would have thought it was a botched robbery and the victim had been stabbed to death. But the assassin knew he could easily have been seen by any number of gamblers that came and went, and besides, he wanted to corner him in the hangar and take his time killing ex-Warrant Officer Grayson Meeks.

So there he was, sitting in his truck in the sweltering heat watching the man who had been the pilot at the helm in his brother's death. The death had been swift. His brother had been taken for a ride by Grayson and an American intelligence officer who worked for the CIA. The officer had grabbed his brother by the throat and pushed him out of a helicopter, much like the assassin had done to the security guard in Atlanta. It had been a heartless act of cowardice by the colonel, who disposed of his brother from an altitude of several hundred feet. His brother was just another VC to the colonel, who knew nothing and said nothing right up until the time he exited the door on that fateful day at Dak Sen Luc. That brother had been the youngest of the three of them who had been assigned to fight the Americans and the South Vietnamese in a war between divided countries. The assassin and his brothers were from a small province about fifty miles west of Hanoi, and they were all captured at the same time in a night ambush by a platoon of American soldiers.

The assassin hadn't decided yet on how he was going to kill Meeks. His plan was to wait until Grayson went into the hangar to do his daily log inspection and then approach him at around four thirty this very afternoon, posing as a mechanic looking for work. After that he would wing it. The airport was open, as were many of the county ones here in the United States. There were no security guards or people patrolling the place, just a fence line surrounding the area to keep out stray dogs and wild animals. He also figured the fence was there to keep out unwanted people like him, but there was no one around to enforce that. There were a number of small planes arriving and departing daily, and those planes would go directly to the hangars on the other side of the tower. From his point of observation, no one seemed to venture to the north end where the helicopter pad was located. Therefore, the assassin would be free to do as he pleased with Mr. Meeks. It was nearing noon and the assassin had been parked for almost three hours. He knew he had been sitting there far too long, and thought it would be a good idea to leave for a while. So, to keep his visibility to a minimum, he decided he should go and return later in the day to dispose of his second victim.

The rest of the afternoon went by at a snail's pace. The assassin wanted to kill Meeks as soon as possible, but the timing wasn't right. He would have to wait for hours before executing his plan. There was time to waste, so he drove out the main gate and headed toward the freeway. The traffic was rather light at the noon hour as he drove the Ford Bronco downtown to a McDonald's where he would order a cheeseburger, fries, and a small vanilla shake. He had frequented McDonald's many times since coming to this country. It was a treat to be able to go to such a place and get something ready-made to his liking. He used to live on rice and anything else he could find to eat, but now he could eat what he wanted, and the sweet taste of a vanilla shake was something he thought came straight from the hands of Buddha.

It didn't take long to place his order once he got to McDonald's. He gave the pimply-faced kid in the strange white hat the exact amount of money and went directly to a nearby park where he could eat in peace and not be noticed by dozens of people. His friend told him that eating away from the mainstream of society would be better for him. The only time he should stay in a restaurant was when he went out to eat Asian food, as he would surely blend in at a place like that.

As he sat and ate, the assassin thought how similar, but different, the family of his first victim had been to that of his own. Roland Cummings, the security guard in Atlanta, had been one of the soldiers in the patrol that had captured him and his brothers. Roland hadn't actually been involved in his brothers' killings, but he was one of their captors and that's how he made the list of targets to be taken out by the assassin. Roland had a wife and young son, and that's what made his mission so difficult. Roland was now dead with loved ones left behind. That made him think of his parents and how they had lost two boys in the Vietnam War, and now they were without their loved ones. He was sure their deaths was a bitter pill for his parents to swallow, just like it must have been for Roland's wife and son. And that pill was extended to the assassin when he sent them a letter, telling his parents of what had happened to his two younger brothers. It was especially hard to have to tell them he was there at the time of their deaths, but was unable to do anything to prevent them from dying. He was actually too ashamed to face his father, and that was one of the two reasons why he never went home after the war. The other one stemmed from the new regime which unified the two Vietnams after the war had ended in 1975. The new government, which was now known as the Socialist Republic of Vietnam, didn't take kindly to traitors, even if he had been a double-agent during the war. So, with the help of the U.S. Government, he applied for immigration into the United States and was granted entrance prior to the end of the war. That meant he would never see his parents or his homeland again.

When the assassin was finished eating, he stuffed all his food wrappers and empty cup into the McDonald's bag and deposited it into a trash container near the entrance to the park. He knew enough not to do something stupid like litter, which would have drawn attention, and possibly gotten him a ticket or into a confrontation with one of the local people. He made sure he did what was expected of him by disposing of things properly. He had been schooled well by his friend, listening attentively to all the dos and don'ts of living in an American society.

He was heading back to his truck when he noticed a police car patrolling the street close to where he had parked his vehicle. He stopped abruptly and headed in the opposite direction. He knelt behind a tree and watched closely as the patrol car rolled by his truck moving like a turtle out of water. The car came to a halt next to the driver's door, then pulled in front of the vehicle to look at the license plate. He was in luck, as he still had the original Georgia plates on the Bronco. It was better he had them than some stolen ones from Florida. If that were the case, he would have lost his vehicle with some very damaging evidence contained inside. A minute went by, presumably to run the plates, before the police car went down the street and drove away.

Sweat beads had formed on his brow during the watch, and they were now running down the assassin's face. He took a few seconds to wipe his face dry with his sleeve; then he put his cap back on and headed to the truck. He knew there would be times like this where his identity may be compromised, yet he wasn't actually ready for it to happen right before he was about to face his next victim. It was a little too close for comfort, he thought.

He quickly opened the door to the truck, got inside, and hurriedly exited the park. He made a sharp right turn at the corner, squealing his tires as he sped down the road. His friend had taught him not to do such things, as it might draw attention. Yet he thought the hell with that because he needed to get far away from there as fast as he could. He took a couple of right turns and found an entrance to the interstate which sent him back toward the airport. He began breathing easier and settled down by the second mile, keeping the Bronco just under the posted sixty-five mile per hour speed limit.

He had been driving down the interstate for about ten minutes when he came upon the exit sign for the Cross City Airport. He took it and drove down the narrow, tree-lined road, turning left as he approached the entrance gate. The dirt road that went by the hangar was flanked on his left by a massive forest and an eight-foot-high fence that went from the entrance to a small parking lot at the end of the road. On the right were a number of tall, tightly spaced Italian cypress trees that shaped the landscape. There were a number of places along the way where he could park the Bronco and walk the short distance of less than three hundred feet to get to the hangar. It would be easy to park the truck and slip across the road to hide behind one of the large trees while en route to the hangar. The area was open for view and there would be no one to notice him unless Grayson Meeks would have been looking out at the road. The assassin drove down the road slowly to keep from kicking up the dust.

He looked over his right shoulder at the hangar, and what he saw next threw him into a rage. Grayson's bright-red Chevy Camaro was parked next to the hangar and so were two Florida State Police cars. At first he had a thought the police might be looking for him, but then he remembered what his friend had told him about Meeks being a pilot for the state. This put an immediately end to his plan for the day. The assassin would have to leave the area quietly and come back tomorrow. He didn't like waiting; it flat-out pissed him off. The longer it took, the more likely he might do something wrong and be identified.

Nevertheless, he had no other choice but to leave. So he continued to drive the Bronco down to the parking area, where he turned the truck around and left by the front gate.

He decided he would drive to Jacksonville on the coast and stay overnight. He knew driving to the ocean would take some time, but he wanted to be as far away from the airport as possible for the rest of the day. Besides, he wouldn't be able to take care of business for another twenty-four hours and that made him nervous. Once he made it to Jacksonville, he might get a room or just drive to the beach and take a long walk. He needed a distraction and the ocean would afford him that. Once there, he could spend the time daydreaming he was back in Vietnam at the ocean he had visited a number of times during his training. As a matter of fact, Florida seemed to resemble his home country for a number of reasons.

It took him a little under three hours to reach the coast. It was pitch-black by the time he pulled up on Ocean Road, which was about fifteen minutes from downtown Jacksonville. The evening was cool. He liked the cool weather; it kept his temper to a minimum. This stalking of victims was nerve-racking. It made him continuously uneasy. He seemed to be constantly looking over his shoulder for the police, which was a habit he couldn't seem to break. That's when the assassin did something out of character, something he would never have done if the killing had gone off like it was supposed to. He drove to a liquor store to purchase a bottle of rice wine. It was the only alcoholic beverage he would allow himself to drink. He parked the truck around the side, checked his surroundings, and walked into the store to check the place out. There were no other customers in the store which made him feel a little more at ease. It took him four to five minutes to locate the wine, but eventually he found the right one and took it to the check-out counter. A surly-looking store manager stared him in the eyes as he stood in front of the cash register. That greatly annoyed the assassin. When the manager finally spoke he said, "May I see your identification sir?" At first the assassin didn't understand the man. He didn't have an identification card and told the manager so. He was kind of panicking, so he slowly reached around his backside to get at his pistol which was tucked away in the back of his pants. He put his hand firmly on the handle and slid it a couple of inches out from beneath his belt. The manager instinctively sensed this may be a robbery and put his right hand under the counter where it found the handle of a Winchester, twelve-gauge sawed-off shotgun. The manager had the shotgun mounted in place on a swivel a few years back after a couple of Cubans came in and robbed him. He had it placed forward and tilted up toward the top of the counter, which meant it would be pointed directly at his assailant's balls. One pull from the trigger would disembowel him, not to say what it would do to the rest of his torso. Staying calm, the manager asked the customer if he had a driver's license. That's when the light went on in the assassin's head. His identification was his driver's license. He calmly slid the Beretta down his backside and slowly moved his right hand to his rear pocket to remove his wallet. There was a moment during the conversation that the assassin thought he might have to pull out his gun and kill the store manager. Little did the assassin know he would have wound up dead before he even got the gun out of his belt. Instead, he settled down, took a deep breath, and paid the man for the wine.

The assassin exited the store, quickly got in his truck, and drove directly back to the beach. Dear Buddha, he said to himself, thank you for giving me the patience to restrain myself in such a difficult time. Your guidance and love will lead me in my endeavors to kill all those who are responsible for the deaths of my brothers. He prayed often to Buddha for strength, a strength that would have made his father proud. But this false sense of humility was actually bullshit, as he had gained his life and freedom at the cost of his brothers. He could have saved both of them, but that would have meant he would have had to betray his country in front of his brothers, and they would have known that for the rest of their lives. So as it was, he felt justified in killing those who were responsible, and that made things right in his mind. He thought, if everyone involved were dead, then he would have set everything right, and the burden of what he let happen would be lifted from him forever.

He had a peaceful evening as he drifted off to sleep. The rice wine had done its trick. He slept well, dreaming of his childhood back in North Vietnam. He remembered how wonderful it was living in a small hamlet with his family. His father was a school teacher, and that's where the three boys spent their afternoons after working the rice fields. Then one day a group of soldiers came from Hanoi and took them away. All three of them were sent to a training facility, and they began working with the Vietcong shortly after that. They had survived two and a half years of the war until they were captured by the Americans. The rest was history. And here he was, well and alive, sleeping on a beautiful sandy beach on the Atlantic Ocean.

He awoke the following morning to the sound of seagulls flying overhead. He had passed out on the beach the night before after emptying the bottle of rice wine that he found laying next to him. It was seven o'clock, and he could hear the motor of a dune buggy in the distance. He figured he'd better get moving in case it was the beach patrol. He didn't want a citation, nor did he want to be recognized. So he got up, brushed off the sand, and headed to his truck. He had a good feeling as he drove away. This was the day that Mr. Grayson Meeks would meet his maker, and it wasn't going to be a pretty sight. As a matter of fact, the assassin was going to make sure the murder scene was something spectacular that the police from Dixie County would be talking about for years to come.

He had been driving down the highway for about an hour and three-quarters when he decided to stop and have some lunch. He found a little Chinese restaurant off the main drag in Lake City where ordered a pot of tea. Tea relaxed him. As he sat at the table near the kitchen he made a mental note of everything he needed to bring to the hangar...rope, knife, chloroform, hand towel, tape, a hammer, and his silenced Beretta pistol. Yup, it was all there according to his recollection, placed neatly in a small gym bag he had stuffed behind the seat in his Bronco. The gym bag wouldn't seem like something out of the ordinary if Grayson Meeks inquired about it. He would say it held some of the tools of his trade and move on with the conversation.

It was nearing a quarter past four in the afternoon when he once again began the slow drive down the dirt road past the hangar. He could see Grayson's Chevy parked next to it. This time there were no other cars in sight but Grayson's. So he parked the Ford at the far end of the road in the parking lot and got out while fetching the gym bag from behind the front seat. He moved quickly down the road for about one hundred and fifty feet, stopping only once to hide behind one of the cypress trees. A second tree found him in a position directly across from the hangar. He looked down and checked his watch. It was now four thirty-three and he was within striking distance of the man he wanted. He couldn't see Meeks from this vantage point or anything in the hangar, as the main doors were closed tight, so he assumed Meeks was inside finishing up on his day's work. He wasn't sure if that was good or bad, but decided the element of surprise would be his biggest asset. His next move was to take the claw hammer from its bag and slide its handle down his butt, concealing it from view with the help of his shirttail. He then walked across the open area at a normal pace, as not to attract attention. When he reached the service door, he stood patiently and listened for any sound that might indicate where Meeks was. He heard nothing, so he slowly nudged the service door open to move inside the hangar. The old metal door squeaked loudly for ten or eleven inches and stopped. The assassin then slid in undetected, walked to the middle of the hangar, and asked, "Is anyone here?"

He heard a voice reply from behind a door to his left. The person said, "Yes. I'm in the bathroom over here between the two workbenches getting cleaned up and changed. I'll be with you in a minute."

The assassin's heartbeat accelerated with anticipation as he listened to the sound of running water and the opening and closing of a locker door. He thought what a wonderful situation he had Mr. Meeks in. He rushed over to the bathroom door, unzipped the gym bag, set it on the floor, and removed the bottle of chloroform he had hidden inside. He opened the bottle and poured some of the potent liquid onto a small, white hand towel. The fumes nearly overwhelmed him, so he quickly closed the bottle and put it back in his gym bag. He then turned his head away from the towel, while holding one hand over his mouth and nose and the other tightly onto the towel.

Within a few seconds the door swung open as Meeks stepped out onto the concrete floor of the hangar. It couldn't have been more than a split second before Grayson noticed the smell, but by that time it was too late. His fate had already been sealed. The assassin sprang forth from behind the door. He clamped the chloroform towel down tightly on Grayson's face with his right hand and put his left arm around the man's chest, while holding on with all his might. There was a brief skirmish, which was all over in five or six seconds. Grayson tried in vain to throw a couple of elbows at his attacker, but his knees buckled as he lost his balance and fell forward onto the floor with help from the assassin. The assassin let him drop, continuing to cover Grayson's mouth and nose with the chloroform towel. Grayson would be out for a short period of time, and that gave the assassin time to survey the inside of the hangar.

There were two helicopters parked side by side and facing parallel to the hangar doors. They had been moved close to adjoining workbenches, assisted by the aid of large electric, chain-driven hoists that were attached to the ceiling by long, steel tracks.

This had been way more than the assassin could have ever hoped for. He could now use one of the hoists to actually lift Meeks up by his arms. The first thing he did was wrap both of Grayson's ankles tightly together with duct tape. He then removed the rope from his bag, quickly cutting a three-foot piece. He tied each end of the rope to Grayson's wrists and reinforced the knots with more duct tape. There was no way Meeks was going to escape. When the assassin had completed his task, he removed the chloroform towel and dragged Meeks over to a position directly beneath the first hoist. The assassin then dashed the twenty-some feet to the wall switch to push the down button. The automatic hoist slowly inched its way to the floor, as Grayson began to regain consciousness. He moaned and struggled a little as he was waking up, which meant the assassin would have to move swiftly if he wanted Meeks to be hanging in the air when he was fully coherent. When the hoist reached the floor, the assassin went over to his captive and gave him another small dose of the chloroform. He then attached the loop end of the rope onto the hook latch at the bottom of the hoist's chain. Again he moved quickly to the wall and began to hoist Meeks up into the air. He now had him positioned where he wanted...controlled and helpless, just like he and his two brothers had been back in Vietnam.

The assassin took the next few minutes to contemplate how he was going to kill Meeks before the pilot regained consciousness. He could simply shoot Meeks, or he could cut him and leave him to bleed to death hanging from the hoist. Maybe gut him just a little and let him die a slow death. Then there was the possibility of taking him down and hanging him by his neck, and watching as Grayson breathed his last breath. There were several scenarios the assassin could choose from, but none of them seemed to be the appropriate punishment. What was it his friend had said? Oh yeah, the punishment or sentence as he called it, should fit the crime. In other words, he should do something to Meeks that befits his brother's execution. The assassin only wished he could fly a helicopter and take Meeks for a ride so he could push him out the door like the colonel had done to his brother. But that was not within the realm of possibilities. No, there was no way he could kill the ex-warrant officer in the same manner as his brother, so that left only one way to get the job done that would meet his satisfaction.

The assassin heard Meeks cough and moan, and watched him wriggle as he dangled from the hoist. He heard him moan again and saw his eyes as they rolled around in their sockets. He knew Grayson was regaining consciousness. The assassin outwardly cheered to himself as he saw Meeks coming around because he knew he had the man in a compromising position.

Grayson looked down at the assassin and said, "What in the fuck am I doing up here?"

"All in good time Mr. Meeks…all in good time."

Meeks shouted back at the assassin, "Let me down immediately, you son of a bitch!"

"I don't think that's going to happen. Look at me, look into my eyes Mr. Meeks. It took me a long time to get you to where you are, and I have no intention of letting you go, now or ever."

Meeks screamed and swore at his assailant. He shouted for help, but it was pointless with all the air-traffic noise surrounding the field. The assassin knew Meeks' arms must be aching. He thought for a second that the man's arms would rip out of their sockets at any moment, so he told Meeks to quit squirming. He told him there was no way out of this situation. He wasn't going to give Meeks any hope he would survive the day.

The assassin smiled back at him and said, "You can yell all you want or squirm as much as you like Mr. Meeks, but as you know, no one will be able to hear you or come to your rescue. You must simply stay there awhile longer as we have this conversation and then…"

Meeks interrupted and asked, "Then what?"

"Well Mr. Meeks, then you will die."

He immediately saw panic race across Grayson's face, as the man began to twist and wriggle once again. He screamed at the top of his lungs. And then he screamed once again out of frustration and pain. Then Meeks let his body go limp. The assassin assumed Grayson had momentarily calmed himself to try and think of a way out of the mess he was in.

Meeks eventually tilted his head down toward his captor and said, "For what reason are you going to kill me?"

"Take a good look at me Grayson. Don't you recognize me? Think back to your past and ask yourself what possible reason could I have to want you dead?"

"I can't think of a single one," he replied angrily. "Maybe if I knew who you are and what your name is, then I'd have an idea what this was all about. Or is it possible that you have the wrong man?"

"No Mr. Meeks. I do not have the wrong man. In fact, I know I have the right man, especially because you're still doing the same job as you did in Vietnam, and your face has hardly changed since I last saw you."

"And where was that?"

"Well, first of all I should tell you my name. It's Throng Chu and my brother's name was Throng Ho. He was the young boy whom you let die in Dak Sen Luc."

"What boy? Where did you say this happened?"

"It was in Dak Sen Luc. A small Montagnard village located near Pleiku in the Gia Lai Province of Vietnam. Do you remember that?"

"No. I can't say I do. As you might imagine, I flew many missions while I was in Vietnam, and at this point in my life they're all a blur."

"Then let me refresh your memory. This particular mission was one you did with Colonel Robert Foss. You took him, me, and my brother Ho for a ride one day and only three of us came back."

Grayson's eyes widened in terror. That told Chu that Meeks now fully understood the reason for the attack. His motionless body once again began struggling with the rope.

Chu said, "Stop trying to escape. It's useless, as useless as Throng Ho's pleas had been as he was being tossed out of the helicopter."

"Okay. Okay." Meeks said. "I never wanted to take the two of you for the ride, but the colonel insisted. I had many jobs during the war. One was to fly intel missions for the brass and follow orders. I never flew one combat mission the whole time I was in country. Just intel and a few medical evacuations, that's all. I never used my guns or rockets on a single enemy soldier. I swear!"

"You can swear all you want and scream and yell, but there's nothing that can save you. I was there, Grayson, and you were the pilot who let my brother die. You are just as responsible as the colonel. Do you know how old my brother Ho was?"

"No, but I suspect he was quite young."

"Young!" Chu shouted back. "He was barely seventeen years old, just one year younger than my other brother who died the same day at the hands of another one of your officers."

"I'm sorry for your loss Chu, but you can't blame me for obeying orders. I had a job to do and the war is over. A lot of men, women, and children died in that war, but it is over. There was a peace agreement between our countries, and that put an end to all the killing. You have to understand."

"Understand what?" Chu yelled back in disgust.

"You must understand that people just can't go around taking revenge on others because of something that happened during a war. And the war has been over for a long time. Nothing you can do will bring your brothers back."

Chu saw that Grayson was sweating profusely. He could tell by his body language that Meeks was giving up the fight. Chu was positive Meeks couldn't take the pain much longer or the strain on his arms. But it didn't really matter at this point because Chu was all but done conversing with his captive.

"Listen to me Chu. I had a cousin who died in Vietnam, but I haven't gone around taking it out on all the Vietnamese in this country."

"That's because there aren't any enemy soldiers in this country except for me, or you just might think about taking your revenge. Enough of this chitchat Mr. Meeks. I need to get going. If I stay much longer someone is bound to come by to see why your car is still parked outside. And then I would have to kill an innocent person, and I wouldn't want to do that, would I?"

"But you're about to do just that. Kill an innocent person."

"You're not innocent Mr. Meeks. Just because you didn't pull the trigger on my one brother, or push the other out of your helicopter, doesn't mean you're not at fault. So you must pay for your sin and hope your God will forgive you in the hereafter."

With that, Chu went to the wall and hoisted Grayson Meeks up to the height of the rotary blades on the top of the helicopter. He positioned him about mid-torso to the blades and approximately fifteen feet from the furthermost point of the helicopter. He then entered the cockpit of the aircraft and started looking for the Pilot Operating Handbook his friend had said he would need to locate if he wanted to know how to run a helicopter. He never had a need to operate one until now, but he was sure he could figure out how they worked once he located the manual and read the checklist.

Grayson was screaming at the top of his lungs, "Please stop this now, you crazy fucker," but Chu had no intention of doing that. He was there for one thing and one thing only: to kill Meeks.

Chu quickly found the manual in a metal pocket located at the bottom of the control panel. He paged though it for a few seconds, but knew almost immediately that it would take him a long time to read through the POH to learn the initial start-up procedure. Looking further, he saw a hard-card instruction list attached to a chain near the starter button. He ripped the card from its location. The instructions on the card indicated that he needed to follow a sequence of three easy steps, and the turbine would eventually get up to maximum speed. Actually, start-up wasn't as difficult as he thought it would be. All he had to do was push the start button to let the engine spool up on the turbine. Then he had to turn on the igniter, and when he accomplished that, he had to turn on the fuel. It was a pretty simple operation, as all the buttons and switches were clearly marked. He did step one, and the huge turboshaft engine began to wind. It didn't take long before the twin blades on the main rotor began to reach maximum velocity. He followed with steps two and three, and in an instant, the place resembled a wind storm as log sheets, rags, and other small debris began to fly around the room. An engine blueprint flew up from one of the workbenches and landed flat against Meeks' face. His sweat held it there for a few seconds; then it dropped and blew away. Chu got the helicopter to full acceleration and stepped out of the cockpit.

Grayson, now in the state of complete and total panic, screamed out and said, "And now what do you expect to accomplish? You can't move or fly this thing."

"You're right. I can't, but I can let the hoist do the job for me. Then I'll be just like you. I'll be able to say I hadn't been the one who killed Grayson Meeks. It was the chopper that did it. What do you think of that Mr. Meeks?"

"I think you're totally mad!"

Chu snickered at Grayson, moved around the outside of the cockpit and headed to the wall switch. As he activated the forward button he said, "There's one for you my brother." The chain on the hoist moved slow enough for Chu to make his escape before the blades cut Meeks into little bite-size pieces. He turned his back on the scene and exited through the service door. Chu left the hangar without being able to hear the screams of his victim above the howl of the helicopter engine and the whirl of its blades. He was totally happy with himself, even though he had not personally witnessed the last moments of Grayson Meeks. He maintained a slow walk from the hangar back to his truck so he could absorb every second of his triumph. In the end, he was satisfied knowing the sound of an engaged helicopter inside a closed hangar would bring someone to investigate. Or the helicopter would run out of fuel, and Meeks would be discovered when the mechanic came to work tomorrow on his weekly Friday rounds. No matter what, the authorities would find a hanging Grayson Meeks cut in half about mid-chest and realize immediately it wasn't a suicide. There would be pieces of flesh all over the hangar and parts of bones strewn about like the inside of a slaughter house. And the blood; it would be splattered everywhere, resembling a macabre version of a Jackson Pollock canvas.

Chu got in his truck, pulled a map from the glove compartment and found the quickest route to South Carolina. It was Highway 95. To do that, he would have to retrace his drive to Jacksonville where he would pick up the interstate. From there he would drive north for as long as possible before stopping for the night. He was headed to Columbia to reacquaint himself with former U.S. Army Colonel Robert Foss.

Chapter 5

It was somewhere around three thirty in the morning, a day and a half after the murder, when Chu began falling asleep behind the wheel of his Ford Bronco. He had recently passed over the Savannah River and was now on the outskirts of Hardeeville in South Carolina. The assassin had been trying his best to make it to the intersection of Interstates 95 and 26 when the Bronco snagged some loose gravel on the shoulder of the road. The truck's rear end started sliding toward a small marshy area adjacent to the highway. Chu shook his head vigorously, instantly snapping him out of the haze he was in. He made a strong right and then a left, saving the Bronco from rolling over and going into the swamp. He fought hard to keep the truck on the road and was about to get it back on the highway when its right rear tire hit something hard causing the truck to leap nearly a foot and a half off the ground. He eventually got control of the vehicle and slowed it to a stop. Chu had avoided a disaster, but managed to blow the truck's rear tire in the process. Chu instantly knew this meant trouble; as his disabled truck would surely be investigated by a cruising highway patrolman.

He was now out of the truck, kicking the flat tire in disgust. He was extremely disappointed with himself. To do what he had done in Florida and not gotten caught made what he had just done totally unacceptable. Chu couldn't chance staying around for the morning's light, so he popped open the rear door on the Bronco to access the spare tire and jack. He muttered to himself, what would his friend do in a situation like this? He thought for a moment and concluded that the most important thing to do was to remove his gym bag from the truck and hide it somewhere until he had finished changing the tire. If a patrolman should happen to stop, he would surely want to look in the bag, and when he found the gun, knife, and other stuff, he would most likely be taken in for questioning. So he hid the bag, but not before removing the knife. He put the knife in a familiar location in the back of his pants and stuffed the rest of the bag's contents into a high grassy area a couple of yards off the roadside.

Chu wasn't five minutes into changing the tire when a highway patrol car passed him traveling south on the other side of the divided road. The patrolman immediately turned on his red light and drove the Chrysler a little further down the highway. From there he made a sharp left turn going down through the median that separated the two roadways. It wasn't long before he had the car up and moving in the northbound lane of the interstate. The officer then drove the big V8 cruiser to a position directly behind the Bronco so its headlights would shine directly into Chu's face. The patrolman stayed in the car while he called his dispatch. Chu could hear the officer ask someone on the other end of the line if there were any outstanding warrants on a Ford Bronco with Georgia plates. There was a long silence and then a small return conversation. Chu knew there weren't any violations posted against his truck, and unless he had been seen at the murder site in Florida, he should have no problem with the officer. The patrolman eventually stepped out of his car, put his Smokey the Bear hat on, and approached Chu.

The ageing, gray-haired patrolman looked down at Chu to assess the situation and said in a thick southern drawl, "Looks like you have a flat tire, son."

Chu could barely understand the man. So he paused for a second to make sure he responded correctly and replied, "That's right officer. I was driving down the highway when I must have hit something on the road that blew my rear tire."

The patrolman looked down at Chu who now had all but one of the bolts removed from the truck's rim and said, "May I see your driver's license, son?"

Chu handed the patrolman his license and said, "Certainly officer. Is there anything wrong?"

The patrolman didn't respond. Instead he took his flashlight from his belt and looked at the license, then flashed the light into Chu's eyes and replied, "Have you been drinking tonight, Mr. Chu?"

Chu was upset at what the officer had called him, but he kept his composure and replied, "Excuse me officer, but my last name is Throng. It's Mr. Throng. Not Mr. Chu." He knew right away it had been a mistake to tell the patrolman his correct last name. The officer had insulted him by not knowing his last name, and the miscue came out in a momentary lapse in judgment.

Browbeating Throng, the patrolman responded, "Sorry Mr. Throng, but that is the way your driver's license has it spelled. You may want to have that corrected the next time you return to Georgia. Here in the United States we put the first name in front of the last name. Do you understand what I'm trying to tell you?"

Chu acknowledged him with a nod and thought to himself that this roadside stop was getting a little too informational for his liking. He also didn't particularly care for the patrolman's attitude. It was arrogant. The highway patrolman now had a real grasp of his true name, the truck license plate number, and his full description. He wasn't worried about the Ford Bronco because it was listed as being owned by a corporation in Atlanta, and he could get rid of it any time he saw fit. What bothered him was the officer now had his name and description. And with that information the authorities might be able to put things together. He could be arrested before completing his mission, and the rest of his potential victims would live for many more years. He couldn't let that happen. He needed to stay calm and ride out the storm.

Nothing was wrong yet, but he was ready if something should happen.

The patrolman continued the conversation by asking, "Then you'll have that changed the next time you return home?"

"Oh, yes officer. That will be the first thing I do later next week when I return to Atlanta."

"May I inquire as to what you are doing out here, Mr. Throng? I mean, what's your reason for being in South Carolina and why are you on the road this late at night?"

Chu hesitated and thought to himself...I'm here to cut your throat if you don't stop asking so many questions, but instead he replied, "I...ah-ah...worked Monday through Thursday and left Atlanta yesterday a little before noon. I've been driving straight through the night on my way to Charleston to visit my brother. I had planned on staying at his place for the next four or five days. I got a late start and that's why I'm out here at this time of night."

"Are you sure that's all you've been doing? You didn't stop for a drink or two, did you?"

The patrolman was really starting to annoy Chu. He had already asked that question and now he was at it again. He should've been able to see and smell that Chu hadn't been drinking. It took all his composure to keep from lashing out at the man.

"Oh no officer, I hardly ever drink alcohol."

"Okay. Then you won't mind if I take a look in your truck?"

"No, I don't mind. Go ahead and look all you want."

The officer went to check the truck, and Chu went back to changing the tire.

Meanwhile, the patrolman used his flashlight to see what was in the rear of the vehicle. It was empty except for the spare tire. He noted that and moved around to the driver's side of the vehicle to look into the back seat. The only thing visible through the window was a suitcase. The officer then moved away from the window and proceeded forward to the front of the truck. He opened the driver's door and saw a Rand McNally road map on the dash. It was open to the state of South Carolina. There was a half-drunk can of soda on the council, which he sniffed, and a notepad on the passenger's seat. He checked the ashtray. It was empty. Everything seemed normal, no physical signs of alcohol or drugs. He was about to back out of the front seat when he noticed a small slip of paper sticking out from under the passenger's seat. He slid himself over the hump in the middle and took the piece of paper in his left hand. On it was scratched the name Cross City Airport – Florida. The patrolman eased himself back out of the truck and looked at the slip of paper again. On the bottom of it was written, need to be there no later than Wednesday, October seventh. It was now Friday the ninth…actually it was early Saturday morning on the tenth.

The officer closed the door and began walking back toward the rear of the vehicle. That name, Cross City Airport. Where had he heard that name before? And why had Chu written it down on a piece of paper if he'd been working in Atlanta on Wednesday? He tugged at his chin and frowned as he turned left around the rear fender of the Bronco. He stopped and thought again…Cross City Airport. Then it dawned on him. He had gotten a report yesterday of a murder in Cross City, Florida from the dispatcher. It was something about a murdered pilot. It wasn't often he got such reports, especially when the crime was committed a couple of states away. Therefore, he had placed the murder in the back of his mind, and it was just now coming back to him. If Chu was in Cross City on Wednesday, then he was lying about working in Atlanta until Thursday. All this might have been a coincidence, but he wasn't taking any chances. So the patrolman unsnapped the safety strap on his holster as he moved around to where Chu had been changing the tire.

Chu heard the officer unbuckle the snap and immediately knew he was in trouble. He made a quick quarter-turn to his left and moved into a crouched position behind the rear fender. The officer came around the back corner of the tailgate as he began to pull his revolver, but Chu was on him before he was able to get the gun out of his holster. And in a split second, Chu came down hard on the patrolman's right hand with a mighty blow from the tire iron. Chu could hear the wrist snap like a twig. The officer dropped his revolver and screamed in pain as he staggered two to three steps to his right. The patrolman instinctively went for his gun again, but Chu kicked it into the stubble grass before it could be retrieved. Chu raised the tire iron again and tried to deliver a knockout blow to the officer's head, but the patrolman blocked it with his left arm while kneeing Chu in the solar plexus. Chu doubled over and slid to his right to catch his breath. He stayed down on one knee as the two men momentarily ceased fighting to size each other up.

The patrolman looked at Chu and said, "You can drop that weapon Mr. Throng, or whatever the fuck your name is, and we can go quietly back to the station."

Chu blurted back at the patrolman, "And then what?"

"We'll straighten all this out, and if you have nothing to do with the murder at Cross City, then you aren't in any real trouble."

"But I am in trouble." Chu replied. "Even if I hadn't killed that pilot I would still be going to jail, at the very least for assaulting a police officer. Is that not right? Then there's that murder charge I would get, and it would mean death for me. No, I don't think I'm going to drop my weapon."

So they both stood as Chu moved the tire iron back and forth in constant motion from his right hand to his left. He was trying to think how he was going to get out of this without being arrested. He realized the answer without a second thought. He would have to kill the patrolman.

His hesitation grew second by second until the he patrolman finally said, "Then I guess I have no other choice but to take you down." He then rushed Chu.

Chu swiftly drew the knife from its sheath that was tucked in the back of his belt and caught the patrolman firmly in his inner thigh, just to the right of his genitals. The patrolman let out a torturous scream as both men fell to the ground. But unlike the first time Chu had struck him, he was now close to blacking out from the excruciating pain of the blade. The two men rolled around on the ground and continued to fight until the patrolman loosened his grip. That's when Chu landed the fatal blow. He quickly got to one knee and came down with the knife, slashing it across the patrolman's throat. It opened a gaping wound, but to Chu's amazement there had been no blood splatter. Chu stood up, looked down at the man, and saw his leg had been flowing blood like a spigot. Chu had severed the patrolman's femoral artery when he stabbed him in the thigh. Cutting his throat hadn't been necessary, as the patrolman was already dead with the first thrust of his blade.

Chu had to work fast. He had only seen two vehicles pass by during the stop, but none had been on his side of the highway and none since the beginning of the altercation with the patrolman. He retrieved the tire iron, which had landed under the car during the fight. He then tightened down the last two bolts on the spare tire. He lowered the jack and tossed it with the tire iron into the rear of the truck. The flat tire followed. After everything was done he went to the high grass to retrieve his bag. It took him almost a minute to locate it as the altercation with the patrolman had momentarily disoriented him. He quickly ran back to the truck and stopped for a second to wipe the knife clean on the patrolman's jacket as he lie dead in the ditch. He placed the knife and sheath back in the bag and tossed it into the rear of the truck. Chu closed the tailgate and went for the driver's door. He stopped before entering and went back to the patrol car. Using his jacket, he opened the door and carefully turned off the red revolving light along with the car's headlights and ignition. He thought that might gain him some extra time. He finished by closing the cruiser's door and tossing its keys into the pond before getting his truck back on the road heading north.

Chu drove away from the crime scene at an accelerated speed, even though he knew he shouldn't. The truck purred as the speedometer reached seventy-five to eighty miles per hour. He made several checks in his rearview mirror to make sure there was no one following him. He eventually returned his focus back to the main highway when he felt he was safe. Chu knew he had to get off the highway to change his clothes, but that was not his top priority, as he needed to put some distance between himself and the dead patrolman. He weaved back and forth across the white lines a couple of times, almost losing control of the Bronco. At this point he really didn't care if someone saw him, as long as it wasn't another highway patrolman. His adrenalin was pumping so hard he thought his heart would burst. Chu slowly began to gain his composure and the speed of his vehicle. He slowed down as he passed the exits for Hardeeville and sped up again when he was clear of them, looking all the while for the first road that would take him to the east. He found one minutes after Hardeeville. There was a sign that said Intracoastal Waterway and Highway 170 to the right. That was a good idea he thought. He should get off the interstate and find someplace where he could change his clothes. They were blood-soaked from the fight. He also knew he had to do a little cleaning on the inside of the truck. His hands were bloody, and it had transferred onto the steering wheel. He could see that from the lights on the dashboard.

His first thought, after calming down, was to turn on the radio, which he felt would help him relax. All he could find were country stations and he hated that squawky music. He never understood these American country western people. They wrote way too many songs about their trucks or their dogs, or their wives who left them for another man. Chu even thought he heard a song once about a dog that left his master for another dog, or something like that. Every song was about someone dyin'. No wonder all those people were so depressed all the time. No matter what, all these songs were just downright stupid, if you asked him. He moved from one station to the next looking for something soothing. Finally he found a station playing classical music. He left that one on. At least they weren't singing some crazy nonsense.

He had been traveling a short distance down Highway 170 when he came to a stop sign at the intersection of Highway 278. The sign on the other side of the road said Chelsea - 12 miles. He made a left turn there and kept driving north. He figured he'd better not get too far up the road before pulling off and taking care of some critical business. He also needed to change the truck's license plates as soon as possible because once the authorities found the dead patrolman they would surely put two and two together and start looking for a blue Ford Bronco with Georgia plates.

He flashed his high beams and noticed a dirt road up ahead that looked like it ran up to a house a couple hundred feet off the road. He decided he would stop there to change his clothes and clean up the best he could. He turned left off the road and shut off his headlights as the Ford crawled up the road toward the house. There was an old pickup truck under a carport in the yard to his right. The lights in the house were out, so he stopped the truck, turned the ignition off, and got out. He made a quick assessment of the property as he looked around for signs of life, but didn't see or hear any. No dogs, no people, no lights inside the house. It looked as if no one lived there. The only sound that could be heard was the buzz of an illuminated light on top of a lamppost in the backyard. Chu found the outside faucet to the house where he washed the blood off of his hands and face. When he had finished, he dried himself with the clean, backside of his bloody shirt. He then removed his pants and swiftly dressed in new clothes. He took the bloody, stained ones and stuffed them under the old house where no one would find them. It took him less than five minutes to change the plates from the old truck to his and clean the bloody steering wheel, then off he went down the road with a new vehicle identity.

He thought to himself he had just killed an innocent man and that was really bad karma. It was not in the plan. He never intended to kill anyone who didn't have something to do with the deaths of his family members, unless it was unavoidable. Buddha, he prayed, please forgive me, and get me back on the path I need to be. He then turned off the radio and headed back toward the interstate in dead silence.

Chapter 6

Watching the leaves turn color in Minnesota was just an expression to those who lived here. You couldn't actually watch them turn color, but rather you had to view their palette, and the best place to do that was to go to northern Minnesota in the fall. It was a tradition like no other...something you had to personally experience every couple of years to sense its splendor. To see the deciduous forest erupt in brilliant shades of red, yellow, purple and rustic brown, as it blended together with the pines, was like being in an actual painting.

From early September to the second weekend in October, cars would line the highways as they drove north from Minneapolis to small towns between Duluth and Grand Marais. People flocked to this so-called wilderness to paint, photograph, sightsee, eat, and even put down a few glasses of barley malt. My taste was more along the lines of smoking a joint and having a frequent tug off of my wine sack, which on most occasions was filled with cabernet. But for most people it was the connection with nature that brought them to this haven in the northland. For me, it was a return to Gooseberry Falls or Split Rock Lighthouse that made the long journey worthwhile. It was in places like these that one could be up close with nature to view the passing of the season firsthand. Fall was like experiencing the cycle of life. It was beautiful as well as exhilarating to have the opportunity to see nature change once every twelve months.

I had planned this weekend back in early June. The main purpose of the trip was to view the colors, but I also wanted to see my old friends Tim and Ginny Hauser who owned the Loft in Grand Marais. The couple had been living in the Minneapolis area for most of their lives, then one day they up and decided to leave the hustle and bustle of the Twin Cities for a more tranquil life in the Arrowhead Region. I thought they were crazy to move to a small town and be broke for a lifetime, but who was I to voice my opinion. They were happy and that was all that mattered. They lived a simpler life up there, one which included eight to ten feet of snow in real bad winters and a growing season that was over in a blink of an eye. Hell, frost up there was on the pumpkin even before it was fully mature. Yes, this lovely young couple was happy and they had invited me, along with other guests, for a long weekend of fun and relaxation.

Tim and I were Vietnam vets who had seen more than our share of the ugly side of war. The two of us had made it back to the States several years ago, but we both still had a difficult time dealing with the psychological effects of what had happened. When you peeled back our layers you found a couple of men who had some very profound attitudes about our government in Washington, and drugs and alcohol seemed the only way to subdue our tempers. Life was getting better as the years passed, but I still had many issues, especially those that dealt with the Veterans Administration. In the past, the VA had denied my claims on several occasions to disability I thought I deserved. They said, "Prove it," every time I went to see a doctor, which was damn near impossible to do with those assholes. I went to the VA hospital at least a dozen times with a host of ailments and asked them to confirm my suspicions. I had a number of problems, most of which were in my head. Life since my discharge had seen its ups and downs, but I wasn't going to let something like the war ruin the wonderful weekend that I had on tap.

I was making this run with Kate, the lovely and seductive woman whom I had vowed never to start up a relationship with. A last-minute phone call was all that was needed to make her available, which was exactly what I was counting on. Kate Rutan was exquisite to say the least, but I think it was the air of mystery surrounding her that made me want to be with her. That fascination and my desire to show her off were probably the main reasons why she was sitting next to me. I guess you could say I was flaunting Kate, but that would have meant I was vain, and that was one thing I was not. So, in hindsight, bringing her to the Hauser home for the long weekend was more for show than it was a sexual getaway.

I looked over at Kate and saw she was staring out the side window of the 911, watching the foliage as I ran the candy-apple-red Porsche through its gears down the road that was made famous in a Bob Dylan tune. Highway 61 had several winding and twisting turns, which was ideal for Porsches. But if you didn't pay strict attention to the road, it was quite possible you would crash into a rock wall on one side or go off the cliff on the other into Lake Superior, or Gitche Gumee as the locals liked to refer to it. The lake was eerily calm today, which made the leaves even more vivid as they floated lazily through the landscape and onto the ground. I could see from the expression on her face that the scene was mesmerizing. I smiled at her, patted her lightly on the thigh, and returned my attention back to the road. I would have preferred we had made the trip with the top down, but Kate insisted we leave it up so her hair wouldn't become an entangled mess. I always thought she had black hair, but I just now noticed it was dark auburn in this tantalizing Lake Superior autumn sunlight. She was wearing a V-neck, turquoise sweater and tight-fitting Guess jeans. Except for her cheap running shoes, you would have thought I had a model in the front seat of my car. She was perfect in every way, and that was the part of the mystique I was presenting to my friends when we finally made our stop at Grand Marais.

I looked back at her once again and said, "Wake up Kate, you're daydreaming. So are you enjoying the ride or is the sun putting you asleep?"

"No, I'm not sleeping," she replied. "I'm just sitting here enjoying one of the nicest getaways I've been on in years. I can't tell you how welcome your call was. I was hoping we would get together and here I am. What else can I say?"

"Well, let me think. I guess you could tell me what you'd like to see before we stop for lunch. The falls or the lighthouse, either one of them is an excellent place to view the colors. The falls gets you up close to foliage and the lighthouse lets you see the forest in its entire splendor. Or maybe we could just ride, and you could tell me a little more about your life. Like, what happened that all your marriages ended in divorce?"

"Wow. You certainly don't give a girl much of a choice, do you? So let me get this straight, my two options are we either see the good, or discuss the bad. How much time do we have because either way, the two are probably going to take a while? And talking about my divorces will take more than this trip to explain."

"I tell you what, why don't we stop at Gooseberry Falls where we can take a walk, and you can give me the shortened version. If you feel like filling in the blanks at a later date, then I'll be glad to listen."

"So there's going to be a second date?"

"I'll let you know after I confer with my shrink."

I drove for another ten minutes and pulled off the road at the falls. The walk would take us down to the river, and from there we could either go west to the larger falls or sit in the park near the lake to the east and relax. Kate decided she needed to take some pictures, so we hiked up to a place where the rest of the tourists stopped to get the best view of the falls. The walk was easy and it afforded us the time to talk a little more about our lives.

"So what do you think Kate?"

"You mean about the landscape?"

"Well that too, but I was thinking more along the lines of what happened to all the husbands in your life. Do you feel like talking about that?"

"Oh them," she replied with hesitation. "Well, for that to happen I'll need to go way back to when I was seventeen. That's when I met my first husband. We got married right out of high school like a lot of young people did in those days; we really didn't know each other at all. I think it was the sex thing. You know, we wanted to do it, and the sexual revolution was in the infancy stage. Birth control was sort of taboo in those days, so not wanting to get pregnant out of wedlock, we decided to get married. And I think the reason we got divorced was we were too young and immature, so we simply drifted apart after a few years of marriage. And that was my first bad decision in life. Hold that thought, Ian. I want to take some pictures of us with the falls."

Kate removed the camera from her purse and took a few shots of me as the river cascaded down from the hillside. Then she asked a younger couple if they could take some photos of the two of us. Shit, I felt like I was at the prom all over again.

"And my second marriage was to Bill Peterson. He was originally an FBI agent in the mid-sixties, and when he left the Feds he worked as a CIA operative in Europe for seven more years after that. I got pregnant in between one of his visits home. That's where Tony, my eleven-year-old comes from."

"So what's the deal with Bill? What really happened to him?"

"What do you mean?"

"I was wondering where he is these days. Is he dead or alive?"

"The truth is I really don't know. At the time of the accident I simply wanted to put it out of my mind. Not knowing meant he was still alive."

"So you don't know? Is he or isn't he? I heard he was in a real bad accident and you sort of pushed him out of your life instead of taking care of him."

"Trust me Ian; it wasn't like that at all. Bill was on assignment in Turkey in '73, at least that's what I was told by the government. He was on some sort of secret mission. He was a spook. That's what he called himself, but to the common person he was a spy. Anyway, I was informed by the State Department that he had been in an accident in Istanbul, which had occurred some six weeks prior to the acknowledgement. And that was it. There were no other details. I was never privy to what he did, nor did I want to know, and the U.S. Government is very tight-lipped about any activity of their foreign agents. For all I knew he was over there fucking his way through Eastern Europe, and that was his assignment. I figured he had a lot of women on the side, but I could never prove it. He would come back to the States periodically, get debriefed in Washington, and then come home until the next time they needed him. They used him, Ian, and he wasn't a very pleasant person to be around. When the call came about the accident I had to make a life-changing decision. I eventually learned he was in a hospital in Germany and mostly brain dead. I was told he was in a car accident, but I'll never know if that was the truth or not. I think he'd been shot by God knows who. Maybe it was the Russians or maybe it was the Americans. I'll never know. So, I told the government what they could do with him, and I divorced him a year later. I didn't think I had a choice. I was still young, and I needed to raise my boy with someone to help with discipline and guidance. Does that make me out to be a monster?"

"You're talking to the wrong guy if you want an answer to that question. I divorce a mentally ill person, which could be construed as doing the same thing as you did. My ex-wife was a nut case and still is, but some people said I should have lived with the situation. You know those that say, 'until death do you part'."

We both got a chuckle out of that. Here we were standing in the middle of a beautiful forest on a warm autumn day, and all we could come up with was we both had divorced a couple of people that we couldn't handle in our lives. I guess you could say we were bad, but at least we were happy. The conversation kind of ended there, so we walked back to the car and continued our journey northward.

We drove down the road in silence for the next half hour while watching the leaves fall from the sugar maples and aspen trees. I think we had shared a little more information about ourselves than what we wanted, so quiet was the word of the hour.

I glanced at my watch and said, "Did you know it's two o'clock, Kate? I'm hungry, how about you?"

"I could eat. Where do you want to stop?"

"There's a little place up ahead that I've always wanted to go to. Let's see if we can get a table."

The next thing I knew, I was pulling the Porsche over at the Goats Head Inn. It was a landmark restaurant on an overlook to the lake and literally in the middle of nowhere. The place was like Marthas Vineyard meets Wall Drug. The outside façade was well-manicured. It resembled one of those old English pubs with a wooden cutout of a goats head positioned above the front entrance. The inside was much different. The dining area was filled with numerous signs and decorative crap. There was shit all over the place, and it was so tiny that mice would have had a hard time maneuvering around. So we decided to eat outside in the garden. It contained three miniature waterfalls, some lovely natural flowers, and mums dotted in here and there. The temperature was warm for this time of the year, about sixty-eight to seventy degrees according to the patio thermometer. Warm enough to sit outside and have a nice lunch without wearing a jacket. We looked over the menus and ordered a couple of glasses of Duckhorn cabernet and the shepherd's pie from a skinny little waitress who couldn't have been more than sixteen years old.

"So where were we, Ian?" Kate asked.

"I believe we were reassuring ourselves we were right in doing what we did to our spouses. At least I think that was the bullshit we were selling ourselves."

"That's a good one Ian. No matter what, right or wrong, we have to be happy with our lives. We can't stand still or we'll find ourselves going backwards at some point in time. Sometimes we have no other choice but to move on with our lives because if we don't we'll find ourselves old and hating our decision, even if it wasn't the right one."

"I suppose you're right. I am happy now, and I like my life the way is."

"Does that mean you don't want to be with someone? Don't you want to get married again?"

"Marriage? That would be Armageddon! No, not at this point in my life I don't. You know Kate; I told you before that this trip was strictly for fun. If I remember correctly, I said to you on the phone that this was not going to go any further than just a friendship. I want no ties and that's the way it's going to stay. For now anyway...Comprendes?"

I looked at her from across the table and saw in her eyes that what I said hurt her, but it needed to be said. I knew if I even indicated I liked her everything would change and that wasn't in the cards. So I changed the subject, suggesting we eat our meal before it got cold. The wine was actually the best part of lunch. I guess the Goats Head Inn's idea of shepherd's pie was something from Birds Eye. That's what it should have said on the menu... Birds Eye Shepherd's Pie, not a delicious mixture of vegetables in rich beef gravy, made in the old-fashioned English style. Oh well, we were in Scandinavian territory, and I guess that's the way the Swedes made it.

We were back in the Porsche and gaining ground on our destination when Kate said to me, "So don't you want to know what happened to my third marriage?"

"Yeah, I kind of figured we would eventually get around to that. So as long as we're on the subject, what did happen to you and Mr. Rutan?"

"I married Doug a year after I divorced Bill and had a couple more children with him, but couldn't stand his drug abuse. He did a lot of heroin, and I didn't need my children getting messed up with that shit, so I decided to leave and we finally got divorced two years ago. He's dead now. He died of a drug overdose. That's it, and that brings you right up-to-date on this ride on a wonderful fall afternoon. There isn't anything else, but a handful of boyfriends."

"Were any of those handfuls serious?"

"They'd like to think so."

"You mean they weren't the right material?"

She said with a snicker, "Something like that."

"You know, we're almost there. One more hill and you'll be able to see the city. So where do you want to stop first? Do you want to go shopping, have a drink, or go directly to Tim and Ginny's store?"

"Oh, so now you're giving me options? I tell you what, why don't we find a seedy motel and start practicing on being great friends?"

"That's a very tempting thought, but all the motels and cabins around here at this time of the season are booked solid for months in advance. I'm sorry to say, but you're SOL, honey."

She giggled and gave me one of those pouty little-girl looks and said, "That's really unfortunate because I had just the right outfit for the fall."

"And what's that?"

With her best Marilyn Monroe impression she replied, "It has lots of beautiful colors and falls off onto the ground quite easily."

I believe it was at that moment my friendship with Kate became more involved than I had anticipated. Little Ian was becoming Big Ian again, and all I could do was squirm in my seat as the Porsche roared into Grand Marais.

Chapter 7

I thought it best we make the Loft our first stop, so we could visit with Tim and Ginny. The Hauser's shop was located on Front Street facing the harbor, which featured a small lighthouse at the very tip of the inlet to the bay. It was an older building with potted geraniums out front in a single, ten-foot-long window box. The place was touted as a Gallery of American Crafts, as they sold everything from high-end Indian art to inexpensive trinkets. They purchased the shop three years ago, and sales had been slow except during the selling season that ran from early spring through the fall-color season, which meant they were getting to the end of their yearly payday. It was nice to be here. Grand Marais often reminded me of a smaller Cape Cod with all the gulls and fishing boats that lined the harbor. It made a beautiful place for a sunset. I couldn't help but notice as I parked the car that the sky was still a deep blue, but it was changing rapidly. The sun had begun to fall behind the hills, leaving the entire city encompassed in a halo of colors.

We exited the vehicle and dodged several cars while making our way across the street to the Loft. The traffic was still quite busy for this time of year, even now during the dinner hour. We entered the shop and found Ginny behind the cash register. Tim was helping some obnoxiously loud lady who was trying her best to get a two-for-one on a pair of moccasins. Tim told her he would think about it and let her know before she left. He then made his way across the room to the front counter to say hi. I took the opportunity to introduce Kate to the Hausers, as other thrifty shoppers looked around for late-season bargains. Kate and I meandered about the place for a while, as we waited for the Hausers to decide who would be the one to close up the shop for the evening. The two of them flipped a coin and Tim won. So the three of us left Ginny behind, and Kate and I got in the Porsche to follow Tim to the house. Tim told us to stay close to him because he didn't want to go looking for us if we got lost. He said the other guests, the Bankes and Thompsons, had already made their way to the house and they were waiting for us to arrive.

Their house was located on the top of the hill above the city and about fifteen miles to the west. It was situated nicely at the end of a long dirt road, about three hundred feet off the main blacktop. The only thing visible on the ride in was a couple of rough grouse that were on the road eating gravel. As we got closer to the property, I could see the actual house was in the middle of a large poplar and aspen forest. It had a large, four-car garage on the right that was semi-surrounded by tamarack trees. The sparsely covered yard held a three-bedroom rambler on the left, with a huge deck on the backside that included a fire pit at the end. It was just the right place for the eight of us to get together for the weekend. I pulled in and parked the car next to Tim's truck, and the three of us exited the vehicles to join the party that was already in progress. The Bankes and Thompsons were out on the deck drinking when we drove up and most likely at least three or four drinks ahead of us. So we joined the group and began the weekend with a toast to the guests.

Ginny arrived sometime around eight o'clock and found the group well on their way to being drunk. She walked into the party room, lit a cigarette, and said in a loud, sarcastic voice, "So I see everyone found the liquor cabinet without any problem."

Tim replied, "Well dear, we couldn't wait for you, but we did save you some dinner. There's chicken and coleslaw in the refrigerator."

Ginny, again in a low, sarcastic tone replied, "I'm actually not hungry honey. I had something to eat back at the shop before I closed up the place. I think I'm going to pass on the food and drink some wine." With that, she opened a bottle of red and the party was on.

A half hour had gone by when Reggie Banks stumbled his way across the room and cornered me. He wanted to make a few inquiries about Kate. I could tell by his slurred speech and his stumbling feet that he was beyond drunk, so he had no problem asking some very personal questions. Like, where did you meet this babe? And how did you get her to go out with you? And have you done her yet? And the most important thing: was she open to having sex with more than one guy? All I could do was shake my head in disgust and tell him he needed to go over and ask Kate that last question.

"So Reggie, you want to know how I met her. Well, I've known her since I was a young boy, and we just got reacquainted about a week ago. But I'm only going out with her as a friend. She's kind of a lost sheep in need of some guidance, and you know I'm all about that. She wants me bad, but I'm not interested in having sex with her at this point. I'm just waiting for the right moment to do that." Actually, I was interested in having sex with her at some point in time. And I wasn't lying when I said I was waiting for the right moment, especially after the ride up here when she told me about her fall outfit. But first things first, as I needed to get the furnace lit to see if he would eventually heat the place up. And he did that like a champion.

Reggie was also a veteran like Tim and me. He had been in the same division in Vietnam at the same time I was. His helicopter squadron came into our village one night and saved everyone's life, including mine. It wasn't until years later that I made the connection between Reggie and the Ace of Spades. That was the insignia he had on his Huey gunship back in 1969. You had to know Reggie to understand his outward confidence. It was very distinct, which I believe came from alcohol and reading *Penthouse* forums. He was slender, a bit too slender. He wasn't what I'd consider handsome for a mulatto, and the gold tooth on his front central, combined with his total baldness made for an unattractive thirty-three-year-old man. I could understand his inquisitiveness, as he had a wife only a mother could love. Becky Banks was fat, loud, and a bad drunk. No, she was an ugly drunk. She had a tendency to slobber all over men when she had too much to drink. She sent signals nobody wanted and advances no one would take. So Reggie tried his best to pick up women whenever possible. I knew he was going to strike out with Kate, but I wanted to be amused for the evening, so I let him think he might have a shot.

I said to him, "Now play it cool when you talk to Kate. Like the time we were in that nightclub in Prescott, Wisconsin. You kept the place open until four in the morning tending bar while the old guy who was supposed to be working took a nap. You do remember that, don't you?"

"Oh fuck yeah! That was the same night our kleptomaniac friend Bob stole all those steaks from the restaurant freezer."

"So you do remember? Good, then be smooth like you and Bob were that night, and don't get me into any trouble with Kate or your wife."

That put an end to a very stimulating conversation, one I wished had never occurred. So I finished my cocktail and walked over to see Tim. He was standing at the bar in the dining room making a drink when I walked up and shook my glass to let him know I needed a refill. He poured me another Stoli martini and told me to move over to the hallway so we could have a chat in private. Our conversation hadn't been more than ten seconds old, and sure enough, Reggie made a direct move toward Kate. He immediately began to cozy up to her. He tried to charm her; even offered to get her another drink. Tim and I looked on and watched as the drunken lout tried to work his way into Kate's affection.

Tim said, "Take a look at Reggie."

"I know, and look at his wife. She's getting madder by the moment. And look at Brooke Thompson; she is getting pissed at Reggie too. I think there is going to be some fireworks tonight. Don't you just love it?" I said with shivering delight.

We both laughed and headed outside to smoke a joint. Ten minutes had passed when Ginny came out and said the two of us needed to come back in the house. And would I please go and get between Kate and Reggie.

"So what's the problem?" I asked.

"You know very well what the problem is. The problem is you brought that woman up here, knowing all along Reggie wouldn't be able to control himself."

"Wait a minute Ginny, are you saying Kate's a problem?"

"No. I'm not saying that at all. She's beautiful and nice, but far too sexy to have around a hound dog like Reggie."

"Hold on Ginny. The reason I brought her up here was to see the leaves and have some fun. Don't blame me for wanting to go out with a beautiful woman. After all, you were the Aquatennial queen once upon a time, so does that mean Tim should keep you away from other men?"

"I guess you're right, but get back in there and spend some time with your friend before we have to separate some people."

Ginny left and went back inside. Tim had one last drag off the joint. He snorted the smoke out his nose as he exhaled and said, "God that was funny."

"What do you mean?"

"Seeing my wife get jealous of your girlfriend."

"Don't you mean my friend?"

"Hold on Ian. If that's your friend, then I'm a fuckin' gay circus clown. Men don't have friends like her, Ian. She is totally hot and into you. She told me that earlier this evening. And if you aren't fuckin' her, then you must be an idiot."

Tim was right. What was I doing with this woman? I guess I did want to flaunt her a little, but what else did I want from her? I did like her and I did want to sleep with her, but that was as far as I wanted it to go. I knew for sure I didn't want this woman to wind up being a permanent fixture in my life. I needed answers, and I wasn't going to come up with any by standing out here in this chilly autumn night. I needed to go back in the house and have a few drinks with Kate. I had been neglecting her all evening, and it was about time I got to the bottom of how I felt about her.

I could sense the tension between the women as I entered the living room; the women being Brooke, Becky, and Ginny. Kate seemed fine and so did Reggie. He was just too drunk and stupid to see he was causing a commotion. So I walked over to Kate, put my free arm around her waist and gave her a kiss on the bottom of her neck just behind her left ear. She shivered a bit as she looked back at me in amazement. I asked Reggie to excuse us as I had something I wanted to discuss with Kate. He got the hint and moved back to the party.

I looked Kate in the eyes and said, "Are you having a good time?"

"Of course I am. I can't say the same thing for some of the other women in this place, but I'm having a great time."

"I see. And are you and Reggie getting along well?"

"We were doing fine, but I'm not sure about his wife. She seems a little pissed at me. She keeps sending me those dagger-eyes. There is a good possibility she could be pissed with Reggie and me. I'm not sure which one it is. I can't seem to read her. Then there's Reggie; he's a little on the immature side for a man his age. Don't you think? He fancies himself as a ladies' man, but I can't imagine where that comes from after seeing his wife. I'm sure he didn't need to be Prince Charming to get her." She laughed at that notion and took another sip of her drink. "You know Ian; you could be such a ladies' man if you wanted to be. You have charm, wit, looks, and your body is something I want to have draped all over me. Don't get a big head because you do have some flaws. I mean, just look at those cowboy boots you're wearing. Do you see any horses around here?"

"No, but there's certainly a lot of shit floating around in this room, and I believe I see a cow standing over there by the fireplace,"

I replied while damn near spitting my Stoli martini all over Kate's blouse. "By the way, did Reggie try to hit on you?"

She stood there staring me down and said, "You know he did. I saw you plant the bug in his ear while watching the two of you talk on the other side of the room. Then I knew my assumption was correct when he made a beeline to me after your conversation was over. I might add that what you told him wasn't very nice. All I'm saying is you didn't have to make me feel like a slut. I'm not here for your friends' amusement or for their extracurricular sexual activity. Do you understand what I'm saying?"

She was right. I was the one being an ass tonight. My inner child was coming out, and the room was beginning to sense it. It was time to pay some attention to my friend and let the party go back to being fun for all.

I said so the whole room could hear, "Excuse me everyone, it's time for Tim to cut the pie so we can have dessert. Kate and I stopped at Betty's Pies in Two Harbors on our ride up and got Tim's favorite, blueberry crumble."

Tim got up in the middle of the night the last time I was here and ate the remaining half pie that was leftover from dinner. The next day we got up and found pie and whipped cream all over the floor, on chairs, and even on the inside of the refrigerator. The place was a mess, and Tim had no recollection of ever having a single bite during the night. Tim, as one might guess, liked the booze. His favorite was Windsor and that's why he was known as the whiskey pig by his friends.

I said, "So listen up people. Make sure you eat up all the pie or Tim will be wearing it in the morning when we get up."

Tim just smiled back and gave me the middle finger.

When we finished eating, I grabbed Kate and a bottle of wine, and the two of us took a nice leisurely five-minute walk through the woods to the far rear of the property. The path we were on would end at a clearing facing a ten-acre pond and a bunkhouse Tim and his son had built last summer. It was a comfortable single-room structure with a small front porch. The inside was sparsely furnished with a single table and two chairs, a couch, a rocking chair, gas lanterns, and a bed that slept two comfortably. There was a small cast-iron, potbelly wood-burning stove in the corner that would make the room cozy on cool nights like tonight.

We took our time walking the distance, while stopping periodically to drink some wine straight out of the bottle and have a kiss or three. Those kisses were sweet now, more so than the time before when I was with her at the bar in downtown Minneapolis. I would say it had something to do with the marijuana, coupled with the chilly night air and, oh yeah, all the drinks and wine that I had consumed. We eventually made it to the end of the path. A sliver-sized moon was now up above the tree-line and it was glistening off the pond. The air was brisk and the landscape was quiet except for a few frogs that were settling in for the winter. We kissed and held each other for a long time. I could feel myself coming alive. I stopped for a moment to step back and look at Kate in the glow of the moonlight. She was shivering and her nipples were showing right through that thin V-neck sweater.

I said stupidly, "Kate, are you cold?"

"What was your first clue, genius? Of course I am, but not just from the cold. I'm shivering from your touch. I knew I would feel this way if I ever got this close to you."

"I too have been thinking about this moment since I saw you talking to Reggie. I've wanted to keep you out of my life because I felt you would complicate things. You know I have a young daughter, and I don't want to share her with anyone else at this time. I want to give her all my love and to make sure she knows I'm the only one in her life when she comes to visit."

"I feel the same way, Ian. I have small children too, and I don't want them to be hurt. That's why I haven't dated any of those guys who want more from me than what I want to give in return."

That's when I heard a twig snap and some rustling in the brush about thirty feet to the rear of the bunkhouse. It came from the direction of the main house. At first I thought it was Reggie trying to see if we were having a little sex in the woods, or maybe it was another couple that decided they too would come down to bunkhouse to stay the night. It hadn't been decided where people were going to sleep, so it could have been anyone.

I whispered to Kate, "Shush, be quiet for a moment. Did you hear something?"

"Hear what?"

"That noise coming from the direction of the main house? There it is again, did you hear that?"

"You're starting to scare me, Ian."

I could feel her shivering in my arms. Then I heard something that made me freeze. It was a snort. Not a human snort, but rather an animal one. I looked down the path and saw the silhouette of a black bear standing on its hind legs. He was sniffing the air trying to locate us. They had notoriously bad eyesight, and it was nearly impossible for them to see us even in this dimly lit moonlight. Bears are usually not nocturnal, but this was fall and that meant feeding season. They ate three times their normal amount of food at this time of year, and humans weren't on their diet. At least not tonight they weren't.

"Okay, listen to me and stay calm. There's a bear behind you out back beyond the bunkhouse."

"Yeah right," she said in a disbelieving tone of voice.

"No. I mean it. It really is a bear. Just don't panic or run unless I tell you to. First of all, I'm going to slide around you. Then I want you to turn and be at my back. From there we're going to walk slowly to the porch and go into the bunkhouse. If the bear should attack, I want you to run as fast as you can to the door and get inside. Lock it behind you. I don't care what happens. Do you understand me?"

"Yes."

I could hear Kate breathing hard and felt her tremble as she got around to my backside. The bear was still standing up on its haunches, sniffing away. Lucky for us the wind was coming from the side as the bear still hadn't located the two of us. Step by step we headed for the bunkhouse. We were within ten feet of the porch when the bear dropped to all fours and began to saunter toward us. I think it heard our footsteps or maybe a branch cracked beneath our feet. No matter, we had to move quickly now to ensure we made it to the door before it got to us. I grabbed her hand and pulled as we dashed to the door. Kate stumbled a few feet from the porch steps and went down. The bear had located us now and it was moving quickly toward our position. I yelled to Kate to get up and run for the door. I saw a shovel leaning up against the railing and grabbed it as Kate dashed by me on her way up the steps. I raised the shovel far above my head and hit the bear as hard as I could with a blow to the side of his head. That was all I needed, as it rolled to its side and scampered into the woods. I took a cue from the bear and ran up the stairs to the bunkhouse. Lucky for me Kate was still shaking beyond control and fucking around with the lock when I arrived. I burst through the door, knocking her to the floor as I slammed and locked it behind me.

A shaken and exhausted Kate said to me, "God Ian, are you alright?"

"I am," I replied as I helped her to her feet. "That was a close call. I thought for a second it was going to get me, even after I hit it."

"You hit it? With what?"

"My fist," I said proudly.

"Your fist?"

"Yup, just call me Superman. No Kate, I only wish I could do that. I hit it with a shovel that was leaning on the railing. I don't know what I would have done if it hadn't been there. Probably would have rolled to the left and jumped up on the porch. I think I could have escaped it in the dark. It would have been far easier than if it had been in the daytime."

Kate said, "I'm just glad you're okay. That sure sobered me up in a hurry. I need a drink. Where's that bottle of wine you had?"

"It's out there by the pond. I dropped it when we ran for the bunkhouse. You're welcome to go out and retrieve it if you like."

"Hell no! I think we'll just stay in and keep the place locked up tight for the rest of the evening. I'm really cold. Do you think you could make a fire in the stove?"

I lit my lighter and looked around the ten-by-twelve-foot room. There was an oil-burning lantern hanging from the wall, which I lit. There was also a pile of chopped wood, some old newspapers, and a bottle of Windsor in the corner on a ledge by the kitchen table. I said out loud, "Thank you Mr. Whiskey Pig!" I started the stove and poured a couple of glasses of whiskey for the two of us. The place got warm in a hurry and I could see Kate was fading fast. The heat and the liquor were finally telling us it was time for bed. I was sitting in the recliner when Kate came over and straddled me. She looked me in the eyes and said, "You're my fucking hero Superman and now it's time to prove it." And with that she kissed me deep and hard. That wasn't the only thing that was hard. Kate had decided to take measures into her own hands. She felt if this romance was to get going she would have to be the one to move it down the road. She stood up, pulled her sweater over the top of her head and tossed it on the bed. Next, she unsnapped her jeans and slid them ever so slowly down to the floor. Stepping out of them she stood there with legs spread and hands on hips. She was exquisite! Like a monument to the angels. There wasn't a single flaw on her, except for a small scar that went down the length of her right kneecap.

I asked, "How did you get that scar?"

"Oh that. It was a skiing accident."

"Downhill or cross-country?"

"Chalet," she said with a grin. "I don't ski, but I do go to ski resorts. I had a couple of drinks in Vail three years back and slipped on some ice and tore the ligaments in my knee."

She then motioned me to the bed. And what she said about her outfit was true. It was very colorful and it fell off without any help from me.

I woke the next morning to the sound of mallards squawking in the pond. I had a headache that just wouldn't quit, but it didn't matter because I just had some of the best sex of my life. Kate was awesome! I had never been with such an experienced woman. I thought I knew it all, but she taught me a thing or two. We kissed for a few minutes and decided we needed to head back to the house to get a couple of aspirins and have some food. We dressed without saying a word and walked outside, half expecting a big black bear to be waiting to have us for breakfast. There was no bear, just bright sunlight. Kate even looked ravishing in the early morning with messy hair and old makeup.

We walked back to the main house hand in hand. As we got closer I could smell bacon cooking in the kitchen and fresh coffee, which was something I never drank. It was good to be back in the fold after the emotional experience we had the night before, and I wasn't talking about the sex. I opened the front door, and the two of us stepped into the living room.

"Good morning sleepy-heads," said Ginny. "Did the two of you have a good sleep?"

"It was great, except for the black bear that tried to attack us after we left here." I replied.

"Bullshit," Reggie said.

"No, he's not joking," replied Kate. "There was actually a real bear that came after us down by the pond. We barely escaped getting mauled. If it wasn't for Ian, we both might not be talking to you this morning."

"You're shitting us," said Tim.

"No we're not," I replied. "And I think I owe you a new shovel."

"Why's that?" he asked.

"I seem to have broken it when I bashed it over the bear's head. I must have startled it just enough to make our escape. It ran harmlessly into the woods."

Reggie asked Kate, "So did you reward Ian for his heroics?"

Kate smiled and said, "I sure did, all…night…long." Then she winked at him.

I could see Reggie was getting a hard-on right there in the kitchen. He damn near dropped his cup of coffee.

His wife looked at him and said, "Your mouth is open Reggie and so is your fly. You look ridiculous."

Chapter 8

Chu had resisted the desire to drive all the way to Columbia after his roadside encounter with the patrolman, so he stopped just shy of the capital at Cayce, and got a room where he could clean up and get his mind in order. It had been a rough few nights, but the assassin was still on course to complete his mission. He would continue his quest to kill Judge Foss in a couple of days after he got some much needed rest.

Robert Foss, his next victim, had been posing as a lieutenant colonel in the CID during the Vietnam War, but actually it was a front for being in the CIA. It was the colonel's responsibility to be present when his intelligence officers interrogated prisoners and to turn a blind eye when those interrogations became more violent in nature. And that's exactly what he had done. He had watched patiently as his two intel officers failed to get what they needed from Chu and his two brothers, so he took matters into his own hands by taking Ho and Chu for a ride in a helicopter piloted by Grayson Meeks. When the helicopter leveled off at three hundred feet, Foss asked Ho one last time for information, and when the kid didn't give him any he was pushed out the door while Chu watched on helplessly. Ho fell to his death and that was the last time Chu had seen his brother. As far as he knew, Ho was still lying there dead in that very spot in the jungle in the South

Vietnamese Highlands. Foss had almost done the same thing to Chu, but he spoke up just before it was his turn to exit the aircraft. Yes, Chu had spilled his guts to what he had known and that's what saved his life, but in turn it was that same information that led to the deaths of many more of his country's comrades.

Chu learned from his friend in Atlanta that Foss had been a lawyer in private life before he was inducted into the military and that's why he was placed in the U.S. Army CID. As a CID officer, his assignment was to prosecute offenders, but the colonel, it seemed, had more of mind to be an executioner. That's what made the killings at Dak Sen Luc even more disturbing. Chu actually thought he and his brothers were going to be interrogated, and when they didn't give any answers, they'd be sent to prison. He never thought any of them would be killed. He expected the three of them would spend time in prison until they were liberated by the Peoples' Republic of North Vietnam. But that day never came. Instead, he was incarcerated and given a choice to either rot in jail or become a Kit Carson Scout for the American invaders.

He chose the latter and became a traitor. That wasn't completely true. He had become a scout for the Americans, but was also a double-agent and worked for the Vietcong underground. Working for the Americans actually turned out to be a good thing, as it eventually led to a successful immigration into the United States.

Chu settled in for the evening with his favorite bottle of rice wine. He sat thinking about his parents for a long time and wondered how they were getting along these days. He let himself daydream of a life he could have had with his childhood love, who he presumed was still back in his village in North Vietnam. Ma Lau was all of fourteen when he left for the war and would be a full-grown woman by now. She wanted to be a school teacher like his father. Chu wondered if she still had those aspirations or if she married and was working in the rice fields. None of these questions would ever be answered, as Chu was sure he would never return to his homeland. Chu knew somehow the authorities would eventually track him down, but by that time it would be too late. He would have had his vengeance and the corpses of all of his victims would be scattered across this new land he called home.

A week and six days had passed since he started his trek across the country. He had made only one call to his friend in that time period to get updated information on his targets. The latest info on Judge Foss was he would be in town on the second and third weeks of October. Chu was told there were a number of places where he could possibly abduct Foss, but most of them were dangerous. The best bet was to follow him for a day or two and track him to his home. If it came right down to it, Chu could strike out at Foss in the place he lived. That would be difficult, but not impossible. Foss had one son and a wife whom Chu would have to contend with and that was okay because Chu would do whatever was necessary to carry out his plan. He didn't want to hurt the colonel's family, but no one was exempt when it came to the killing of Foss. Chu would not be cheated out of his revenge for the man who had killed his brother, even if it meant killing his enemy's whole family in the process.

Chu was vulnerable at this time in his life. He needed someone to talk with to help him sort things out. But Chu was a loner. He had never dated nor had a girlfriend since coming to this country. He never felt the need for one as his one true love was still back in North Vietnam. There was no one to guide him except for his friend in Atlanta, and it wasn't a good idea for Chu to have too many conversations with him. So Chu went off to sleep for the night dreaming of how he was going to kill Colonel Foss.

Chu felt refreshed when he woke up the following morning. He had only drunk a couple of glasses of wine, so his mind was clear and his will as strong as ever. He took a shower, got things together, and headed to the capital building for a rekindling of two wayward spirits.

The old Ford Bronco came to a rest in front of a sign that said: VISITORS…Welcome to the great state of South Carolina. Two-hour parking limit, violators will be towed at their own expense. What a mixed message, Chu thought. On one hand they welcomed you, and on the other they said they would make you pay. These Americans and their signs; they were obsessed with them. Chu checked his watch for the correct time. It was exactly ten thirty-three. He could ill afford to have his truck towed, so he would have to be back by no later than twelve thirty. Chu stepped out of his truck, pulled his Pete's Trucking ball cap down to the top of his eyebrows, and headed straight for the capital, stopping only once to check the building's index of offices. He perused it up and down, but he couldn't find any listing for federal judges. So he went to the office of information to ask where he could go to see a judge. The perky young lady in a plaid dress, who was standing behind the counter, told him that judges were in the federal building located on Tenth Avenue and Madison Street, which was five blocks east of the capital in the center of town.

Chu turned around and stormed out of the building in a huff. He was damn mad at his friend for not telling him Colonel Foss was in the federal building. It was a waste of his time, and it meant more direct contact with people who could identify him at a later date.

Five minutes later he was back in his truck to go look for Foss in the federal building. This time there weren't any of those welcome signs. Instead, he encountered nothing but state and local police cars. He drove around awhile until he eventually found a parking place on the street which was within walking distance of the federal building. It included a city parking meter limiting him to one hour. This wasn't going to work as it would take him the better part of an hour to locate Foss, and that didn't give him enough time to get back and put more money in the meter. He needed a different plan. One that would allow him to take all the time he needed. He left the parking space and drove around until he found a parking lot. It said. - All Day Parking $2.00 - It was just what the assassin needed to check up on the colonel. He paid the attendant and walked briskly to the courthouse.

The place was ancient. From the brick front that was beginning to crumble to the worn granite steps inside, the building was in bad need of repair. He noticed some of the light fixtures were broken, and paint and plaster was flaking off the walls and ceiling.

There were cops everywhere. They terrified Chu, especially since he had recently killed one of them.

He wasn't sure how to go about his task, so once again he looked up the name Judge Robert Foss on the information index in the lobby, and sure enough his name was right there. It indicated he had an office in room three forty-eight. Chu looked around and decided he had two options: the stairs or the elevator. If he climbed the stairs no one would pay any attention to him, but if he took the elevator he might have to make eye contact with a policeman and that was the one thing he didn't want to do. Chu thought he might lose it altogether if he had any direct contact with one of them. So he chose the stairs where he accidently bumped into a patrolman at the top of the second floor. He excused himself, as he continued to move quickly up the next flight of stairs. When he made it to the third floor he straightened up, unzipped his jacket, and walked directly to the nearest men's room. He could feel the sweat running down his face, which meant that it was time to stop the hunt while he regained his composure. Chu took off his cap and splashed fresh water on his face. He looked in the mirror and saw panic in his eyes. He knew immediately he had to pull himself together or he would never complete this phase of his plan. He wiped his face dry with a paper towel, took a deep breath, and positioned the cap back on his head to conceal his eyes.

It took him no more than two minutes to find the judge's office. He went for the handle, but the door was locked. He looked up and saw there was a message on the glass window saying that Judge Foss was in court. Damn, he thought. He was being blocked at every turn, and it was beginning to frustrate him. So back down the stairs he went and found the information office. This time he encountered an older, gray-haired woman with a bit of a hunch in her posture.

Chu said to the woman, "Excuse me ma'am. I'm a college law student, and one of my professors suggested I take in a few sessions that were being presided over by Judge Robert Foss. Could you please tell me where the judge is holding court?"

"Oh, so you want to be a Perry Mason do you?"

Chu didn't understand her. Was this humor or just her being old and senile? Whatever, he wasn't sure what she meant, so he asked again. "Ma'am, could you please direct me to the room where Judge Foss is holding court?"

"Young man," she said. "You'll never win a case if you aren't patient and neglect to study the great ones like Perry Mason or Clarence Darrow. They never lost and I'm guessing you don't want to either. Am I right?"

"Why yes you are ma'am. Now could you please tell me which court he's in?"

"Let's see, I'll have to look that up. Okay, it says here he's in Court Room E. That's down the hall to the…"

And before she could complete the directions he was out the door and on his way to find his old nemesis.

Chu entered the courtroom which was being guarded by two state policemen. He took a short breath as he passed them; walked two-thirds of the way down the center aisle, and found a seat to the right of the judge. From his position he had a clear view of the bench where Foss was sitting. Chu thought to himself the judge looked so high and mighty sitting there in his black robe. He wondered how this man could be impartial to such proceedings. Just how could he sentence someone to jail or death when he had killed young, innocent men himself?

As the day progressed, Chu thought about how much the colonel had aged from the last time he saw him. Foss now had a short, salt-and-pepper beard and wore glasses. He seemed much heavier than his days in Vietnam, at least twenty-five to thirty pounds more. That could work to Chu's advantage if he had to elude him in a struggle. In fact, Foss didn't look good at all. His skin was pale, almost gray and pasty in texture. And his eyes seemed distant and tired, but that would only be natural for a federal judge who stayed up most nights past midnight while looking over case files. He also looked uninterested as Chu caught him staring into space on numerous occasions. That would seem to fit the colonel's personality. He didn't much care about the victim or the defendant in this case, just like he hadn't cared what happened to either of his brothers back in 1969. Yes, the colonel and the judge were one in the same...judge, jury and executioner.

Foss interrupted the hearing at four thirty and said the court would continue on the following day at eight thirty. "All rise," a man said and the court stood while Judge Foss left the courtroom. Chu wasn't ready for this. He had assumed the judge would conclude business for the day and walk out of the court and back to his office. He did not. Instead, he left the bench and exited by a rear door. Chu beat a hasty retreat from the courtroom and went back up to Foss's office on the third floor, but it was still locked. He knocked, but no one answered. Instinctively, Chu knew the judge must be heading to his car in the private parking garage located below the federal building. So he left the building and waited at the rear exit to see if he could see Foss as he drove out. He waited twenty minutes before Foss came out of the garage in a big, black Lincoln Continental. The judge looked at Chu briefly then turned his attention to the oncoming traffic. He hesitated a few seconds at the edge of the curb before taking a right turn, presumably to head home for dinner. Chu made a mental note of his license plate and headed back to the Bronco.

Chu spent the next several hours doing some canvassing work. By nine o'clock he realized he couldn't do anything more for the rest of the night, so he decided to drive his truck out into the countryside. He would find a small road that led to some sort of nature site or a dead-end road to some farmer's land and sleep in his truck. He would drink some of his leftover rice wine and be ready for the judge at the garage exit the next evening.

Chapter 9

Chu had made his way to Tenth Avenue by noon. He figured lunch time would be the best time to find an open parking space on the street. He had stopped at a Seven Eleven to get some chips and a sandwich, and a bunch of nickels to put in the parking meter. He was prepared to wait all afternoon, so he could follow Foss home as he left the courthouse.

The phone book had six listings for a Robert Foss and R. Foss, but none of them was the one Chu was looking for. He had spent the night before checking them out and it was no surprise to Chu that the colonel was unlisted. He figured such a high-profile person and a state official wouldn't be printed in the phone book. If they had been listed, then people would be coming after them left and right to do something awful…the kind of things Chu had in store for the colonel.

Finally, the garage doors opened at five-fifteen and Chu saw the black Lincoln with the colonel's plates enter the street. Foss turned right like he had the night before and continued down Tenth Avenue. Chu followed, but not too closely as to create suspicion. He stayed two or three car lengths behind the Lincoln until they made their way out of the city. Ten minutes went by before the Lincoln made its way to the parkway heading south, where it jumped the speed limit by twenty miles per hour. Chu followed at a distance, letting a car or two pull in front of him. The caravan kept moving until the Lincoln took a left off of the parkway onto Dasher Boulevard. From there Foss drove a half mile or so and turned left into a driveway to an old colonial home.

The house was painted white, with eight Gothic pillars on the first two levels. There was a porch on the second level with two connecting doors to the house. On top of that was an attic with dormer windows facing out on all four sides of the roof. This grand two-story home must have been at least one hundred and fifty years old if it was a day. It was nicely kept with well-groomed shrubbery and lovely old Magnolia trees filled the yard. The house sat on what looked to be four to five acres of land and it was completely surrounded by a six-foot honeysuckle hedge. There was a double-wide carport to the left of the house and a detached double-car garage at the rear of the property. Above the garage was a smaller room which Chu knew to be a mother-in-law's room or servant's quarters in another era.

Foss exited the car, took his briefcase and suit jacket, and locked the car behind him. He walked to the side entrance of the house and opened the door. It seemed a bit odd that the door to the house wasn't locked, but maybe it was too early in the day to do that, especially in this neighborhood. Chu made a mental note of this as he parked his truck down the street and out of sight.

He sat in the Bronco until the sun went down then left to do a little reconnaissance work. He knew just how to go about this tactic. It was an easy task for an ex-Vietcong and Kit Carson Scout to do recon. Chu would simply have to move about, staying low and quiet as he checked things out. It was a must to avoid dogs as they would begin barking and send off an alarm. Most of all he had to stay put after he surveyed the lay of the land then observe from a distance. He needed to take notes so he could come back tomorrow night and conclude his business.

He kept his eyes sharply focused on the house and watched as lights went on and off at random. He could see the second-floor bedroom light come on at nine o'clock. Then, a few minutes later, a light came on in the backyard, which startled Chu who had taken refuge in a large pile of leaves near the back of the property. He saw a young man go out the back door and head to the room above the garage. That must have been the son, he thought. Good, that meant there would be one less person to deal with when he made his attack on the colonel. Chu's next move was to go over to a window on the south side of the main house. He peeked in through the glass and saw Foss at his desk attending to some paperwork. Chu figured it might have had something to do with the hearing the colonel had presided over that afternoon. Chu didn't stay long; as he did not want the colonel or anyone else to accidently see him.

Chu retreated to his truck and sat in the front seat to watch the house until all the lights went out. He saw the lights in the room above the garage go off at ten o'clock as well as the ones in the colonel's bedroom. He then saw the ones in the colonel's office extinguish at eleven forty-five. All was dark by midnight.

Chu didn't have all week to sit and watch to make sure this ritual happened night after night. He would have to assume it was a routine the family followed closely every weekday night. For now, he was content on knowing that Colonel Robert Foss would not be alive in another twenty-four hours.

Chapter 10

The assassin sat patiently in his truck at a distance down road from the Foss home at 325 Dasher Boulevard. He had arrived at six twenty in the morning, as not to miss the family members as each one exited the property. He saw the colonel leave at seven fifteen and his son about twenty minutes later. Chu figured the woman of the house didn't work like most of the rich wives in this country. They were all lazy women in his mind. They either stayed at home or went out to lunch with other rich wives to plan charity events, which he did think was admirable.

Fifteen minutes had passed since Chu last saw any activity coming from the Foss home. So he exited the Ford, walked up the driveway, and went to the backside of the house. He looked through the windows and listened, but he couldn't locate Mrs. Foss. As far as he knew she wasn't on the lower level. He then moved to the side door next to the carport and tried the knob. To his astonishment it wasn't locked. These Americans were all alike. They were too trusting; they never seemed to lock their doors. Chu opened the door, slipped inside, and made his way into the kitchen area where he stopped and listened for any sign of life. Again, there was none. He knew there wasn't a family dog or they would have let it out the night before, but they could have a cat or a bird that could sound some type of alarm.

He neither heard nor saw anything on the first floor, so he took out his knife and ascended the staircase to the second floor. The staircase was long and curved to the left as it extended to the next level. The ceilings on the main floor must have been at least twelve feet tall, which made getting to the second level much more difficult without being noticed. Again, he stopped and listened for any indication of where Mrs. Foss might be.

He didn't hear anything. So he continued to move down the hallway until he came to a room with the door ajar. He stopped abruptly and eased the door open ever so carefully with his left hand as he held the knife in his right, ready to strike without hesitation. Chu had opened the door to the master bedroom, but no one was in the big, four-poster bed. He looked around the room. It was beautifully decorated with lavender wallpaper, a table with daylilies and family pictures, and identical his and hers armoires to each side of the bed. She must be in the bathroom he thought. Chu then entered the room and tiptoed ever so quietly over to the bathroom where he heard water running. She was in the shower. That was perfect he thought. He had hoped he would find Mrs. Foss in a compromising position.

He inched his way into the bathroom as he listened to the colonel's wife humming a tune he wasn't familiar with. He moved closer and closer into the steam-filled shower. It was decision time. Chu said to himself, do I kill the wife or do I let her live? A dead wife would spoil his plan and it would be all over for him here in South Carolina. The son or the judge would discover her body and that would be it. Or Chu could kill her and leave her in the shower with a broken neck. It might look like an accident, but that meant he might have to kill the son too, and that wasn't part of his plan. No matter what the colonel had done during the war, it didn't warrant killing his whole family, unless they got in the way. They were not responsible for his actions, and therefore, shouldn't suffer the consequences. He was carefully weighing his options when Mrs. Foss shut the water off, causing Chu to back away a step or two. Startled, Chu bid a hasty retreat and scrambled out the bathroom door.

Ten seconds later he was on the lower level. He had a plan and felt the best way to have it unfold was to secure entrance to the house now, so he could reenter it later in the evening. He surveyed the layout of the first level where he found an office, a huge living room and formal dining room, a bathroom, the kitchen, and a large walk-in pantry at the back of the house.

The pantry had a window in the room, so Chu went over and unlocked it. He moved the window up and down to see if it would be difficult to open. It squeaked like fingernails on a chalkboard. That's when Chu decided it needed some type of lubricant like butter or oil to make it move smoother and quieter. He found some butter in the refrigerator and greased the metal tracks. Chu had been lucky as someone had replaced the original windows with a newer style or he would never have been able to use it as an entrance to the house. The window was now working fine, so he closed it almost all the way to the bottom and left the pantry the way he found it.

He had just stepped out into the kitchen when he heard Mrs. Foss coming down the stairway. There was no time to make a run for the back door nor was there any place to hide, so he went back in the pantry and closed the door. From his location he could hear Mrs. Foss banging cupboard doors as she wondered aloud if there was any coffee in the house. She must have looked in a couple of places and given up. Chu then heard footsteps on the wooden floor as they got closer and closer to the pantry. He took out his knife once again as he hid behind the door. It opened as the colonel's wife took two steps into the pantry and said, "Good, I thought we had an extra can." She exited the room with a new can of Maxwell House and closed the door behind her. She made coffee and went back upstairs, presumably to finish getting dressed for the day.

Chu was trembling as he left by the side door. He walked directly around the back of the house to check on the window from the outside. It looked fine; all he needed was a stool or something to stand on, and he could get into the pantry easily. Having done all he could to prepare for the evening, Chu walked to the front of the property and out onto Dasher. He got in his truck and headed to his favorite place – McDonald's.

All the Foss family members were home by six o'clock that evening. They ate dinner and went about their nightly ritual. The colonel's wife did the dishes, then sat in the living room to read an autobiography by Amelia Earhart. Her son went to his room above the garage for a while and then came back in the house to speak with his father. He sat in the colonel's office for over an hour before he said good night. After that he went into the living room, kissed his mother on the cheek, and said good night to her. He was back in his room by nine o'clock. Except for the office, the house and the rooms above the garage were dark by the usual 10:00 p.m.

Chu waited another half hour to make his move. That afternoon he had found an old, empty five-gallon bucket by some dumpsters and figured it would be an excellent stepstool to use to get in through the pantry window. He grabbed it, along with some rope, his knife, a flashlight, and his Beretta, and moved to the backside of the house. He placed the bucket directly below the pantry window and took one step up. Using his knife he cut the screen from its frame.

The next move was easy. He quickly slid open the window and slipped into the pantry. He closed the window behind him and turned on his flashlight. He went to the door and opened it slowly. Once inside the kitchen he moved quickly to the staircase, making sure the colonel was still in his office. Chu shot up the stairs in a matter of seconds and was at the entrance to the Foss bedroom when he heard a cough from the downstairs area. His blood pressure rose as he thought for a moment the colonel may be on his way upstairs, but then he heard some footsteps crossing the wooden floor below and the sound of a man urinating in the toilet. Chu was as relieved as the colonel to know he had time to take care of Mrs. Foss.

Chu snuck inside the bedroom and crept over to the side of the bed where Mrs. Foss lie sleeping. He took the knife and placed it next to her throat. When she woke he placed the other hand over her mouth and said, "Be quiet." She began to struggle, so Chu went right up close to her ear and whispered, "Don't make a sound or I'll cut your throat. Do you understand me Mrs. Foss?"

She nodded in reply.

"Okay, now I'm going to remove my hand, but if you even twitch I'll kill you. Do we understand each other?"

Again she nodded. So Chu, ever so cautiously removed his hand from her mouth. He could hear her let out a gasp and then she said, "Who are you?"

"Never mind who I am. You just keep quiet and still and I might let you live. Okay?"

"Okay. Okay. I get it. You're here to rob us, but you must know my husband is a federal judge, and he is downstairs in the study. He could be up here at any moment."

"I'm not here to rob you ma'am. I'm here for the colonel."

"For whom?" she said with some confusion. She hadn't heard the name colonel in almost ten years.

"Yes, I am here for your husband. Colonel Robert Foss of the CID."

"My husband is no longer in the military."

"I know that ma'am, but nonetheless I am here for him. Now I'm going to put a gag over your mouth, so keep still and this will all be over in a short period of time."

Chu worked swiftly to gag and bind the woman. First he tied her ankles with one end of the rope then cinched them tightly to her wrists. She wasn't going anywhere until morning when the police or her son would find her. When he was done he covered her with blankets and left the bedroom. He closed the door behind him, so she wouldn't hear any of his and the colonel's conversation. She had not been able to see his face, and the less she knew the harder it would be for the authorities to identify him.

Chu descended the staircase and went directly to the colonel's office. He could see the colonel sitting in his chair looking down at some sort of document. He pulled out his Beretta and entered the room. At first, Foss didn't notice him, so Chu cleared his throat forcing the colonel to look up from his work. Foss calmly set the documents down on the desk and stared at Chu in bewilderment. He said, "What are you doing in my home young man?"

Chu replied by saying, "Just keep your hands on the table colonel and don't make any sudden moves."

"Again, I ask, who are you and what are you doing in my home?"

"You don't recognize me, do you colonel?"

"Why do you keep calling me colonel?"

"Well, that's what you are, aren't you? An ex-CID colonel in the United States Army. At least that's what you pretended to be the last time I saw you."

Confusion and fear could be seen in the judge's face as he stared back at someone whose identity eluded him.

"Now colonel, listen to me carefully. I want you to put your hands straight out on the desk in front of you and put your head down in between them. Just so you know, I have your wife tied up in the bedroom, and we both know your son is asleep in his bedroom above the garage for the night. But if you don't do exactly what I say, I'll kill both of them after we have our little talk. Do you understand?"

"Yes. I do. And just to make this clear, you will not hurt my family if I do what you ask of me. Is that correct?"

"That's correct, colonel."

"And why do you keep calling me colonel? I'm a judge, and I might add that you're going to be in serious trouble if you don't stop this nonsense immediately."

"Save that for the court, colonel. You don't have any bargaining power at this hearing. You're not the judge or the jury in this matter. I am, and unless you do what I say immediately, I'm going to shoot you in the head and kill the rest of your family. So quit fucking around and do what I say."

Foss then extended his hands out onto the table and went facedown on his desk as Chu had requested. Chu worked like a surgeon to tie the colonel's hands behind him. Then he looped the rope around his waist and neck for good measure.

"Stand up colonel. We're going upstairs to further our conversation. I don't want to hear a peep out of you unless I ask for it. Do you understand me?"

"I do," said Foss.

Chu stuck his pistol in the colonel's back and pushed him up the stairs to the second level.

"Colonel, where is the door to the attic?"

The colonel tilted his head to the left and said, "It's down that back hallway."

So once again Chu forced Foss up the stairs to the attic on the top floor. Chu opened the door and pushed him in. He said, "We have some catching up to do colonel. Are you ready for a walk down memory lane?"

Chu followed the colonel into the room and closed the door behind him. He shone the flashlight in the colonel's face. He could see the man was sweating and sensed his frustration about who his assailant was.

"So colonel, have you figured out who I am yet? I'll give you a hint. We met in May of 1969 in a small village called Dak Sen Luc. Does that ring a bell?"

Acting stupid, Foss replied, "No. I've never heard of the place."

"You don't mind if I open the window, do you colonel? It's a little stuffy and musty up here for me." With that Chu opened the window and kicked out the screen which slid down the roof and landed somewhere on the ground below. "I wanted to make sure we were going to get a good breeze in here, and I thought maybe you might want to look at the stars later if we have the time."

Judge Foss said angrily, "So let's get to the point. Who are you and what do you want with me?"

"Ah, spoken like a true minister of justice. You want answers and you want them now, don't you? You're still so demanding colonel and arrogant too, but you're in no position to expect I'll do what you ask simply because you're a colonel or a judge or a killer."

"What are you talking about? I've killed no one."

"Now you are starting to upset me and make me mad, colonel. I saw the lies in your eyes when I spoke before about Dak Sen Luc. You know damn well what happened that day. You killed one man and were about to kill another, but I stopped you. Now do you remember colonel?"

"That was a long time ago son, and I've put it behind me. I'm sorry for what I had to do during the war, but that's war. Things happen that can't be undone. Yes, I had to take some lives for the betterment of the war, but I never murdered anyone."

"First of all colonel, my name is not son. It's Captain Throng Chu of the Vietcong. And the man you killed that day was Throng Ho. Do you remember tossing him out of a helicopter like a sack of potatoes? Don't bother answering because all you'll do is lie. Ho was my younger brother. You never knew that did you? You never bothered to ask. You just accepted that he was a useless young boy and you killed him with your hands. Is this all coming back now colonel?"

"Again, I can't say I do. There were many situations like that during the war. So, you can't be sure if that was me or another colonel I'm being mistaken for."

With that, Chu took the lamp from the corner of the room and ripped the cord from its base. He split the ends to expose the wires and shoved it down the colonel's shorts. He plugged the other end into the wall outlet and let the 120 volts electrify his testicles.

"So how does it feel to be tortured, colonel? My brothers and I didn't like it much either. You beat us, and choked us, and did everything to make us talk. Why don't you scream colonel? Then your son may come and I'll have to kill him along with you. No colonel, you're not going to do that because it probably means I'll have to kill your wife too, and you'll do anything to make sure that doesn't happen. Am I right, colonel?"

The colonel couldn't speak, as the electricity that surrounded his balls made it nearly impossible. He stood there looking back at Chu with a clinched jaw as he forced himself to take the pain. Chu then took two steps toward Foss and kicked him in the balls, sending the colonel to his knees. The cord came out of the colonel's pants as he let out a large groan. Chu replaced the Beretta with his knife and stuck the blade next to the colonel's throat. He made the colonel feel the steel. He quickly moved the blade to a position below the colonel's left ear and cut him diagonally down his neck. Foss knew better than to scream out, as he had been in interrogations like this many times during the war. Yelling out only gave power to the inflictor and showed weakness from the victim. So Foss took the cut, knowing all too well what was to follow.

"Colonel, you surprise me. I thought that you would cry out like a little child."

"Then you don't know me Chu. I know how these things go and I'm ready for anything you have for me."

"Does that include death, colonel?"

"It includes whatever. But whatever you do here tonight is not going to bring back your brother."

"It's plural colonel, it's brothers. One of your other intel officers shot my other brother that day, so you see I'm here to get justice for Ho and Nye. They both died that day and they didn't have to. You could have taken us to your base camp and we would have eventually told you what you wanted. But no, you had to terrify us individually and still you planned all the while to kill us. So what do you think, colonel? Am I right, or do you need some air to refresh your memory?"

Chu grabbed Foss by his right ear and belt, and dragged him over to the window. "Look out there colonel. Look up at all those stars. They're very bright tonight. My two brothers can't see them because you executed them, and now it is my turn to be the judge and jury. I find you guilty colonel, and just what should your punishment be? I'm thinking it's death!" With that, Chu struggled, but still managed to pick up the overweight Foss and push him headfirst through the window. Foss slid down the eight feet of roofing and landed face-first onto the concrete sidewalk at the base of the front door. Chu heard a thump and a snap, and all was quiet. He knew instantly that the fall had broken the colonel's neck and he was dead.

Chu worked frantically to gather all his things. He wanted to make sure he didn't leave anything behind that could help the authorities identify him. He then went down the stairway and exited by the back patio door. He retrieved his bucket and went around to the front of the house. The last thing he did was check Foss for a pulse. When he found none, he turned his back and headed for his truck. His next stop was to be somewhere in New Jersey.

Chapter 11

"So how was dinner, Kate?"

"It was fantastic. Where did you learn to cook duck like that?"

"From Chef Tell," I said with a grin.

"You mean the Chef Tell on television?"

"That's him...the one and only."

"How in the world do you know him?"

"That's a funny story. How should I explain it? Tell and my parents were good friends back when I was a child, and he and my mother used to have sex quite often whenever my father was working out of town. I caught them doing the dirty deed one afternoon, so he bribed me with great food and taught me how to cook at the same time. I have dozens of tasty recipes on file and to think, I owe it all to Tell, my mother, and I guess to some extent my father too."

Kate seemed to know me well enough by now to know when to stop asking questions. Like the one she had just asked. She knew I had a quick wit that I liked to use whenever the opportunity afforded itself. I never give anyone a straight answer; I'm the master of the unexpected. I remember telling her a number of wild stories and anecdotes while we were on that little three-day excursion to the northland. I had actually made her cry a number of times; tears of joy that is. She had begged me for mercy on two or three occasions, but I just wouldn't let up. Yes, Kate had been with me for only a short period of time, but I could sense she was beginning to fall for me. From what I knew about Kate, I was like no other man who had ever been in her life. I'm sure my sarcastic nature intrigued her, but it was the, "I'm not interested in a relationship" attitude that had her hooked. Kate after all, had been pursued by men all her life. Rich ones…handsome ones… clever ones, they all went after her. But those men all had one thing in common; they wanted Kate as a possession, which was the furthest thing from my mind. I was in it for the ride and that was it in a nutshell. She knew where I was coming from, but she was still bound and determined to change that.

"It's time to change the subject again, isn't it?" she asked. "In that case, do you think we could do a little bear hunting later tonight?"

"Oh? Was that like in b-a-r-e or b-e-a-r? I think I need more details before I can commit to any such request."

"Spell it however you like, but it means the same thing," she replied. "Just to let you know, I have another one of those special outfits on tonight like the one I wore last weekend and it has a Halloween theme to it. I thought you might like to see if you could scare it off of me this time."

"Wait. Do I have to wear a mask to do that?"

"Only if you want," she said.

"Oh, in that case do I have time for dessert? You know how I love dessert?"

She laughed and said, "I'm the dessert, dummy."

"Well, in that case I probably can grant your request. By the way, are you staying over for the evening?"

"That depends, how long do you plan on bear hunting tonight?"

"Wait a minute. Are we both talking about the same thing, or do I need to get my gun?"

With that, we both laughed and headed to the living room to relax and watch some television. I opened a bottle of California red and asked Kate what she would like to watch before the news came on. I knew it was a mistake to ask that question. Kate told me once that she never really liked to watch TV. She thought the time after dinner was best spent with her children or going out with friends for drinks.

"So what do you prefer, Taxi or Cheers?" I asked. "I would actually like to watch Magnum, P. I. or Simon & Simon after that if it's okay with you. I kind of like Tom Selleck; he sort of reminds me of myself."

"And why is that?"

"Well, we're both about the same age, tall and rugged-looking with a chiseled chin and we both have a taste for adventure. Not to mention that we both drive expensive, hot red sports cars and we seem to have beautiful women who like to hang around all the time."

"So you think I'm beautiful?"

"That, and the fact that you like to hang around a lot, which, I might add, is what I like best about you."

"So you like me?"

"I didn't say that. I said I liked you hanging around. It makes my evenings very pleasant."

"That's it. I quit," she said. "Pour me another glass of wine and put Taxi on. I'm beginning to think I like Danny DeVito better than you."

"DeVito? Are you shitting me? He's short. Hell, my dick has to be almost as long as he is tall."

Kate shook her head and said, "Give it a rest Ian."

For the next two and a half hours we watched a comedy, followed by a couple of who-done-it mysteries, while finishing off two bottles of wine and a half pint of strawberry ice cream. My dessert actually came twice tonight; one was hot and one was cold.

"I'm tired. Let's go to bed," said Kate.

"Not yet. I need to watch the news to see what the weather is going to be for this weekend. I have some yard work planned and I need to find out if it's going to rain. Just hang in there for another fifteen minutes and I promise you a treat afterwards."

"Okay, but that's it. No Johnny Carson."

"I promise, no Carson or Late Night David Letterman or..."

"There you go again, stretching TV until after midnight. At this rate I'll never be able to go home tonight."

"Yup, you have now fallen into my trap. I guess it's TV and scary Halloween outfits for me."

Kate went and got a blanket during commercial break, as we had some time to waste before the WCCO newscast began. Just as she was returning, an anchorman came on the screen and said, "Good evening and welcome to the 10:00 p.m. news. I'm Dave Moore. As we reported in an earlier broadcast, a federal judge has been found dead in Columbia, South Carolina. We now take you to James Sims at our CBS affiliate station WLTX in Columbia. James, are you there?"

"Yes Dave, I am."

"What can you tell us James?"

Standing under an umbrella in the pouring rain, he said, "Well Dave, I just spoke to Sheriff Roy Alters of the Columbia Police Department, and he has informed me that Judge Robert Foss was indeed found dead earlier this morning at his home. According to the sheriff, the judge was murdered. Local police and FBI agents are on the scene looking for evidence. What we know so far is the judge's son found him dead around six forty-five this morning. We understand the son came in the house for breakfast from his apartment above the garage at the rear of the property. He looked for his parents, but they were nowhere to be found. He then went upstairs to their bedroom where he found his mother gagged and bound. She informed her son and the police that an intruder had entered the house around ten thirty the night before, looking for her husband. The rest of the information is still a little sketchy as to what happened and why. We have also learned the intruder knew the judge, but from where they're not sure."

"James, do you know how the judge was murdered?"

"Yes Dave. The judge's hands were tied behind him and he was pushed out of the third-story window of their home that's behind me here on Dasher Boulevard, which is located on the west end of the city. He died of a massive skull fracture and a broken neck."

"Tell me James, do they have any suspects yet?"

"No Dave, they do not. The FBI is here because this was a federal judge and they aren't saying much. I think we'll know more in a couple of days, but for now the Feds are keeping a lid on the case. The only thing I can tell you is the judge's wife told the police she could not see her attacker as it was dark in the bedroom at the time of the attack, but she spoke with him. She said he was a male and he was definitely an Asian from his accent. I can add one thing, and that is the son is beside himself. He had to be taken to the hospital along with his mother because he was so distraught to think he was right there when it all happened, and he didn't and couldn't do anything to stop the crime. As you can imagine, he and his mother are two very troubled individuals at this time. Now back to you Dave."

"Well, there you have it, one dead federal judge and no suspects. We'll keep you up-to-date on further information as it comes in. Now to the local news."

"Wow, can you believe that," I said.

"Yeah, now go and lock all the doors and windows. That's creepy."

"That's not creepy. It happens every day in this country."

"Not to a federal judge it doesn't."

"That's true. Not to a federal judge and in his home nonetheless. I think the Feds are in on the case because there is more to the killing than meets the eye."

"Like what?"

"I'm not sure. I'm not a cop, but I do remember an officer in Vietnam who had the same name as the judge. His name was Colonel Robert Foss and I had a couple of encounters with him during the war. He was CID, but smelt like CIA all the way down to his stinky feet. And didn't they say it was most probably an Asian who did the killing?"

"I believe they did. But what's that got to do with anything?"

"That could explain a lot of things. The Colonel Foss I knew was the head CID officer of interrogations in the Fourth Division and a killer to boot. The man and his team left a number of bodies strewn all across the Pleiku Highlands. I wouldn't be surprised if someone from back there was connected to this murder. It's a stretch, but there's always a possibility that that might be the case."

"You're beginning to sound like my ex-husband. He talked like that. He never spoke in length about specifics, but he always seemed to know the real meaning behind political or law-enforcement rhetoric."

"You mean bullshit, don't you?"

"Yeah, that's another way of putting it."

"I've had my share of military bullshit and I saw it first-hand from Colonel Foss. We'll just have to follow the murder and read the paper to see if I'm correct."

"You know Ian, I could probably get you that information if you're truly interested. I still keep in touch with one or two of the FBI agents whom Bill used to work with. One of them is the regional director for the Midwest."

"And how come you're still good friends with him?"

"Oh? It sounds like you might be a little bit jealous."

"Me? Not at all. The only thing I'm jealous of in this whole world is a guy who can tie his dick in a knot. Otherwise, I couldn't care less about anyone whom you were married to or went out with."

"Not to worry."

"Okay, then why does he keep in touch with you?"

"I think you know why, but I'm not interested in him the way I'm interested in you. He always tried to hit on me, even when Bill went over to the CIA. We went out to dinner a couple of times after I divorced Bill, but that's as far as it went. He still calls, but I blow him off. He's harmless."

"You know half of me would like to know if the judge and colonel are one in the same, and the other half says who gives a shit. I really don't want to help the FBI, but if you want to give the agent a call you could say you have a friend who knew a Colonel Foss during the war and was curious to know if it was the same man as the judge. I don't want to get involved with the Feds, so keep my name out of it.

There's another reason I might like to know more about this murder. I haven't told you about a friend of mine who committed suicide a couple of weeks ago because you didn't know him. It happened in Atlanta. The guy was a Vietnam buddy of mine. His widow called me the day before I met up with you and my brother to tell me he was dead. My friend either jumped or was pushed off the roof of a high-rise office building. And get this; there was an Asian man looking for him just a few days before he died. Strange coincidence you say; maybe, maybe not. This is what I can tell you. The Colonel Foss whom I knew was with his team at a small village back in '69. They were there to interrogate three VC prisoners we had captured and brought in the night before. My dead friend, Roland Cummings, was also there at that interrogation and he witnessed the same things I did. He saw Colonel Robert Foss and another intel officer murder two of the VC soldiers. They left by helicopter with the third VC who later became a scout for the army. That's a lot of coincidental happenings and maybe that's all it is."

"You mean you saw this guy Foss murder another guy? If the judge and the colonel are one in the same, then how did he become a federal judge in this country?"

"Don't be so naïve, Kate. I don't think his Vietnam activities were common knowledge or part of any platform for public office. I'm assuming only a handful of people know about his past. He kept it that way, but maybe, just maybe, there is someone out there who knew about his past and killed him for it."

"That may be true Ian, but then how does that connect your friend with the judge's murder?"

"I'm not sure, but with your looks and connections you might possibly find that out for me. You might even put a bug in the agent's ear and he can connect the dots. I told Roland's widow I would talk to the Atlanta Police Department to see if I could get any more answers for her, but this may be a better way of finding them out."

"God Ian, all of this is kind of wild. I think I've had enough of this murder talk for one night. Let's go to bed and see if you like my two jack-o'-lanterns."

"And are they scary pumpkins?"

"No, and neither is my bag of candy," as she stood up and shook her hips.

"Wait a minute, I need to go and find my Zorro costume."

"And does it come with a sword?" she asked.

"That's right."

"Well, I hope it doesn't get in the way."

"Oh yeah? That's not what you said last weekend."

Chapter 12

"Detective Ryan, this is Agent Patrick Hines of the FBI," said CID officer Walter May from the Provost Marshal Office at Ft. Dix.

"Good evening. It's nice to meet you. Do we know the name of the victim yet?" asked Agent Hines.

"Yes," said Ryan. "His name is Warrant Officer Dave Gunderson."

"Has the crime scene been investigated yet?"

"No. Not yet. We're still gathering evidence and the medical examiners from the city of Mount Holly and the CID are inside the house examining the body. I believe we'll have this wrapped up in the next hour or two."

Walter May interrupted and said, "Excuse me gentlemen, I'm going to talk to some of the neighbors and see if they know anything that might be of help to us."

"Okay Walter. I'll get back with you when I'm finished here. So tell me Ryan, are you okay working together with the CID and the FBI?"

"Yeah. The local police don't have any problem with that. We've actually done it before on a number of occasions. As you would probably guess, being this close to Ft. Dix has caused our paths to cross more than once. There are a lot of soldiers who live off-base here in Mount Holly. It's the biggest city in all directions, so there are several incidents that occur from time to time. Usually they're limited to domestic assaults and a few bar fights here and there. Once in a great while someone is killed, but that's usually from a drunk driver or a fight that went bad. But a murder involving a military individual is something we haven't seen in over a decade."

"It's good your department feels that way about working with all of us. I've been in situations where the police think they have all the authority and want to proceed without consulting us. When it comes right down to it, I find it nice to have different agencies working together. The crimes seem to get solved that much faster."

"I hear you," said Detective Joe Ryan.

"So tell me detective, who discovered the body?"

"It was actually the local fire department. They found the body, and we called the base when we learned the victim was on active duty in the military. The fire wasn't very big, so the call didn't come into the fire station until around midnight. They actually stumbled upon body when they went in the house to put the fire out. That was around one thirty this morning."

"So what do you know about the crime so far?"

"At this point I can confirm it was definitely a murder. The victim was shot in the head. And there was some mutilation to the body, which suggests it was something more than a simple shooting or robbery. The killer also tried to burn the place down, presumably to hide any evidence. The gunman must have been an amateur, or he didn't have the time to stay around to make sure the fire was in full force. It was started in the dining room with some towels and a pile of wooden chairs. We think he used cooking oil to fuel the fire, but it burned out before it ever got going. It could have been a lot worse. The place could have caught fire and we wouldn't have been able to gather as much evidence as we have. It also would have taken us much longer to process the scene. As it is, we have a head start on the killer. "

"Did you find the murder weapon?"

"No. We did not. The killer must have taken the gun with him."

"And you said there was a mutilation. What kind are we talking about?"

"Why don't you come inside and see for yourself."

The two men then crossed over the crime scene tape and walked to the front door.

"Here, put these gloves on, Agent Hines, and these plastic bags over your shoes. And be careful where you step because there's blood all over the carpet and on the linoleum in the kitchen. There are still several good footprints left on the floor and we don't want to accidentally smear any of them. We haven't got photos of them yet."

The two men entered the front door, and from his vantage point Agent Hines could see Gunderson's body sitting upright in a chair in the living room. The place smelled of smoke and it had been trashed as if the killer had been enraged.

"As you can see, there's a single-bullet wound to Gunderson's forehead. The ME from your agency believes that's what killed him. He won't be sure until he gets him back to the lab."

"Then what's that blood coming from his mouth?"

"That's the mutilation part of the crime I spoke of earlier. It seems the killer cut Gunderson's tongue out after he shot him."

"Are they sure he was dead before the killer cut out his tongue?"

"Yes. They're sure. Otherwise there would have been evidence of a struggle and there would have been a lot more blood. The examiner said it was done postmortem. As you can see, there's a large pool of blood on the carpet, directly behind the door where Gunderson fell after he was shot. That blood came from the large hole in the back of his skull. The body was lifted up sometime after that and placed in the chair by the killer. By that time Gustafson had bled out and the tongue was an afterthought. The examiner is just about done, but he's sure those two wounds are the only ones on the body. There may be other marks, but again he won't be sure until he gets him back to the lab and cleaned up."

"Do we know the time of death?"

"Yes. The examiner said he put the preliminary time of death as sometime around ten to eleven o'clock last night."

"So he's been dead a long time. That means our killer is long gone by now."

"Maybe not," said Detective Ryan. "Maybe he's a local and still in the area."

"That's a possibility, detective. Tell me, was Gunderson married or living with anyone?"

"No. The CID officer said he lived here alone. He has never been married as far as they know."

"What else have you found?"

"We're fingerprinting the place now. We'll know more when we've run the prints against the ones we have on file in the federal database."

"Make sure you talk to May and have the prints run through the military database too."

"I'll make sure that happens. We do have a couple of other pieces of evidence that I'm sure will be of help. They're over here in the kitchen. Besides the bloody shoe prints, there are some bloody glove prints on the countertop and the walls by the phone. No actual fingerprints. It looks like the killer was wearing latex gloves. The prints lead us to believe they're from a small man or a boy. Also, the trajectory of the bullet would suggest the killer was very short because the bullet entered the victim's forehead at an upward angle and exited out through to top rear of his skull. I'm betting the killer was a short male."

"What else is there?"

"Well, we have the slug. We dug it out of the wall up there by the entrance to the kitchen. It went through Gunderson's skull and lodged there. We got lucky, as it was in clear sight after we got all the smoke cleared out. It looks like it's from a 9mm hand gun. We'll know for sure if that's correct after we run it through ballistics. There's not much more we can tell you at this time. Check with the coroner at the Provost Marshal's Office at Dix tomorrow for an update."

"Will do, and thanks detective. Here's my card. Call me with any other information you find. I need to talk to May and I'll let you know if he finds anything that can help us solve the killing."

Agent Hines left the murder scene to find Walter May. Hines was willing to work with the local authorities, but there were some things that were strictly off limits when it came to the murder of a federal employee. This may have looked like a simple murder, but then, it could be much more. Like something involving national security.

"Oh, there you are Walter. I've been looking all over for you. Did you find out anything?"

"I spoke to a woman who lives across the street and she said she saw an older Ford truck parked in front of the victim's house last night. She thought it had New Jersey plates, but couldn't be certain. She never saw the man who was driving it."

"Did she say what color the truck was?"

"Dark blue she thought, but it was dark outside at the time. She only knew it was blue because of the light that was shining from the corner lamppost."

"Did she say what kind of truck it was? The make or model? Was it a pickup or Bronco?"

"It must have been a Bronco from the details she gave me, but we'll know for sure after we show her photos back at the station."

"Good. Stay on top of that witness and let me know the minute she identifies the vehicle. Did you talk to anyone else on either side of the street?"

"Yeah, I spoke to another woman who lives to the left of the victim's house and a guy who lives next door to the woman who saw the truck. I asked them if they heard a gunshot last night and neither of them said they had. No one else was at home last night or they aren't talking. That's all I have for now."

"Great work. I'll have my assistant run Gunderson's name through the system to see if he comes up with anything that might help. It's now six thirty. Could you get his complete military file and meet me back in your office on-base by ten o'clock tonight?"

"That will work. But why do you need to move on this tonight?"

"Well, I'm no profiler. I'll leave that up to one of my colleagues. I'll have her there with me later on tonight. It's the tongue thing that has me thinking. I'm guessing it might have been removed because Gunderson may have known too much about something. Let's see what the profiler has to say."

Agent Hines bid Walter May a good-bye and made a call to his office to make sure Marsha Hall, his profiler, would be able to make the ten o'clock meeting tonight. This wasn't a random killing. It had all the markings of something more, something evil. Maybe even a Mafia killing. Hines wanted to make sure the FBI closed the gap between the murder and the lead time of the assailant. It had been a little over twenty hours since the killing, and he needed a quick connection to help him solve the murder or it could quickly become a cold case.

The taskforce met in the office of Walter May at exactly10:00 p.m. Detective Ryan was not invited as Hines didn't think he was needed at the present time and he could be filled in later when they had a better idea whom they were up against.

"Walter, this is Marsha Hall, the FBI's profiler here in the East Coast Region. She's from the Philadelphia area. And this is my assistant Peter Dunn, who ran a background check on Dave Gunderson. I also asked him to see if there had been any other crimes of this sort in the last month or so. Let's start with Marsha. Have you had time to work up a profile on the killer?

"It was kind of short notice, but I've given it some thought and here's what I've come up with. I concur, after looking at the crime scene photos, that it was more than likely a male who did this. First of all, women aren't usually cold-blooded killers and very few mutilate their victims. So that says it is probably a man and a short one by the size of his shoe print. See here in the photos, the shoe print looks like it's a size seven, but it's definitely not as large as a size eight. The guy probably isn't very tall either. He's probably no more than five-two, maybe five-four at the most. I'd put his age somewhere between twenty-four and thirty-eight years old. The age is a little hard to define, but if the victim knew the killer then I would say he was closer to his age. I would definitely rule out that it could have been a boy. Boys can obviously kill, but the tongue being cut out suggests it was not a young kid who did this. Then there's the mutilation of the victim. That had me confused at first."

Walter May said, "What do you mean, confused?"

"Well, someone who would do this to a person would usually incapacitate the victim first, then cut their tongue out while he or she was still alive. That way the victim would know it was coming and why it was being done to them. It's all part of the retribution process. But the killer did not do that. He killed Mr. Gunderson as soon as the door opened to the house, and then cut his tongue out. That would suggest a couple of things. One, he didn't have enough time to do it while the victim was still alive or two, it would have caused too much noise and drawn attention to the murder scene. Either way, he did it as a statement. The killer wanted to leave us a message."

"Like what?" Hines asked.

"Like tongues have consequences. In this case, the consequence was mutilation or specifically the tongue being cut out. Mutilation or the removal of one's tongue goes way back to the ancient world of the Assyrians. There are also many bible passages on the subject spoken from Jesus to a number of his apostles. God was quoted as saying 'Devious tongues will be cut out.' From Saxon England all the way through the Middle Ages, tongues were cut out as a form of punishment. Cutting out one's tongue has many meanings. The lying tongue, the proud tongue, the swift tongue, the cursing tongue, and the silent tongue are just a few of the many - Sins of the Tongue. If I had to make an educated guess, I would say this particular mutilation was one of the lying or the silent tongue."

"Okay Marsha. Let's say you're right," said Hines. "Then what would the killer gain by cutting out Gunderson's tongue after he was already dead?"

"It's probably symbolic. I would say it symbolizes power over the victim. A kind of self-satisfaction from knowing his victim would never be able to lie again about someone or something that happened to him, a friend, or possibly even a loved one. The silent tongue could mean just the opposite. Like Gunderson knew something from his past, but refused to speak up and someone else paid the consequences for his silence. Think about that for a moment. According to Proverbs 18:21, 'Death and life are the power of the tongue.' So maybe this murder isn't about the victim, but rather the life or death of someone else."

"You just lost me," said Agent Hines.

"Look at it this way, Patrick. Maybe the killer murdered his victim because of what he didn't do, instead of what he did. Are you following me?"

"I guess so. But what's to say this guy wasn't a crazy psycho? Maybe he cut the victim's tongue out as a souvenir or maybe he kills for fun and not revenge."

"That too is possible, Patrick. But as I said before, I truly believe the removal of the man's tongue was done to send a message."

"And what is that?"

"Well, let me think for a moment." Marsha paused for a few seconds and said, "Maybe it says he has silenced the man forever."

"Excuse me Patrick," interrupted an anxious Peter Dunn. "I have something that might shed some light on what Miss Hall is trying to say."

"Okay, go ahead Peter. Tell us what you've got."

"I spoke with Walter earlier today, before I left the crime scene, and I asked him to fax me a copy of Gunderson's complete military records. Shortly after that I went back to our office and ran a check on other recent crimes involving mutilation in the last couple of months, and I came up with an interesting bit of information. It seems another ex-Vietnam helicopter pilot was brutally murdered in Cross City, Florida just thirteen days ago. His name was Grayson Meeks. The killer strung him up by his arms using a hoist and let the helicopter blades slice him up like a Veg-O-Matic. When the authorities found him all that was left was less than half of a body. I understand the crime scene was morbid."

"That could be just a coincidence," said Hines.

"That might be true, but it also got me thinking. What if Gunderson and Meeks knew each other? So I cross-referenced their names and that's when things really started to get interesting."

"And?"

"And it seems that officers Meeks and Gunderson were both in Vietnam for eight months at the same time. And get this; they were both in the same squadron at Camp Enari in the Fourth Division at Pleiku from February until September of 1969."

"Wow," said Hines.

"Ditto for me," said Hall.

"And that's not all boss. I also searched for other Vietnam veterans who recently died, especially those who died mysteriously or were murdered. There was a man in Atlanta. His name was Roland Cummings and it was reported that he had committed suicide just one week before Grayson Meeks was murdered. Thanks to my inquiry, that suicide has now been reopened. There were also five other former Vietnam-era service members who had died recently. One of them was from the West Coast, so I ruled him out. Another died in a car accident and yet another was killed in a bar fight. The other two were known drug addicts and died from overdoses. None of those victims had ever been in the Fourth Division. But Roland Cummings, it seems, was in an infantry unit in Vietnam at the same time as our two deceased pilots. And get this, he was there at the same time as Meeks and Gunderson, and he too was stationed out of Camp Enari in the Fourth Division."

"This just gets stranger by the minute," said Walter.

"No shit," said Hines.

"And now for the icing on the cake. Drum roll please. Do you remember hearing about that federal judge down in Columbia, South Carolina who was murdered a few days ago? Well, as it turns out he worked for the CID in Vietnam. And guess what?"

"He was there at the same time as the other three," blurted out Hines before anyone could speak.

"You get the birthday present boss. I also learned that Judge Robert Foss used Grayson Meeks and Dave Gunderson as his escorts on remote interrogations."

Hines asked, "So is it time to blow out the candles, Peter?"

"Not quite yet. I also have another small bit of information. On Saturday, October tenth, a South Carolina highway patrolman was murdered along the side of the road. The patrolman had made a routine stop around three o'clock in the morning. He pulled his car up behind a disabled vehicle on Interstate 95, which runs from Florida to South Carolina. He then called in the truck's description, which was a blue Ford Bronco with Georgia license plates. He was never heard from again. Later that evening a motorist stopped and found the patrolman dead in the ditch. He had been killed with a knife."

"So tell me you've got more Peter. Like, has anyone gotten a description of the man?"

"Not exactly. No one has actually seen the killer, but I did obtain a report from the police department in Columbia where Judge Foss was killed. There was a statement in it from the victim's wife. She said the killer had tied her up in the bedroom before he went downstairs to confront her husband. The killer spoke to her several times while he was tying her up. She said the man's voice was definitely that of an Asian."

"Well Marsha, it's beginning to look like your profile is correct," said Hines. "An Asian man means the killer is obviously a male and it also adds credence to your theory that the killer is short, assuming most Asians are. I guess that ties everything together. I think you can put a complete profile together now, and we'll get it out to every law enforcement agency before the crack of dawn."

"Peter. Did you find out whom the truck was registered to?"

"It's a large company in Atlanta called Jordon Construction."

"What did they have to say about the vehicle?"

"I just got off the phone with one of the owners and he said the truck had been at a service garage getting the engine overhauled. It hadn't been reported missing until October twelfth. That was the Monday after the highway patrolman was murdered. They hadn't noticed it missing because no one called to tell them the work had been completed. I'm following up on that, but I don't think it will lead to anything. The company is real clean."

"Peter, check to see if they have any Vietnam vets working for them. And if they do, see if they happened to be in the Fourth Division at the same time as these other four."

Hines said to the group. "So let's recap. We have four dead Vietnam veterans who served in the same division at the same time and one additional highway patrolman. Of that group, two were known to have been possibly killed by a man driving a blue Ford Bronco and one was killed by an Asian man. And one of the veterans was suspiciously killed in Atlanta, the city where the Bronco was stolen. That's a total of five dead men in the past two plus weeks. Is everyone with me so far? So what does all this mean? Marsha? Walter?"

"Well," said Walter. "It's obvious to me that all of these people are somehow interconnected to one another. Now all we have to do is find out what the common element is that binds them together."

"I agree with you Walter. And as a profiler, I would say we have a serial killer on our hands. The person has some sort of vendetta against all these men, except for the patrolman who I believe was an unlucky victim. He somehow stumbled across some incriminating evidence and had to be killed."

"I concur," said Hines. "And I'm sure he is not done killing yet. We have two dead pilots. Correct? But only one dead ex-CID officer. Peter, I want you and Walter to find someone who worked with Meeks, Gunderson and the judge while they were in the Fourth Division in Vietnam. I want to know if the two pilots flew missions with other CID officers. The question is, did they fly as pilot and co-pilot or did they go solo? If they flew solo, then there is another possible ex-CID officer out there who is in grave danger of losing his life. He also could give us some much needed information on who he thinks the killer is. There has to be some connection that goes back to Vietnam. Also, see if you can find out anything these guys might have done to piss someone off. We need to hurry because more lives may depend on it. I'll have an APB sent out across the wire to all FBI regional directors to be on the lookout for a blue Ford Bronco with an Asian driver. Does anyone else have any thoughts?"

Peter Dunn said, "Maybe we should be looking for someone who lives in the Atlanta area. The one victim lived there and that is where the truck is from. I'm going to assume that Roland Cummings was our killer's first victim, so the man we are looking for is probably from that area. I'm going to go out on a limb and say that I believe this vendetta is being brought on by an ex-veteran. So that should narrow things down."

"Not necessarily, Peter," said Hines. "The killer could be from another city and stole the truck when he went to kill Cummings in Atlanta. He could also be the relative of an ex-veteran too."

"I thought the same thing boss, but it seems highly unlikely that a relative would go to such lengths. No, I'm convinced it has something to do with a person or persons from back in the war."

"There is only one hole in that theory Peter and this is it. Why would a vet wait this long to commit these murders? I mean, it's far easier to kill someone during a war than it is back here in the States. Everyone over there had a gun. Some of them even had illegal ones. So why wait so long? At lease get one or two over there and the rest back here."

"Maybe he did get a few over in Vietnam. Or maybe he couldn't get them because he or they were sent back to the States before he could get to them. These are all questions that need answers. I'll get on it the first thing in the morning."

Chapter 13

"So this is your office," said a very hot and seductive-looking Kate Rutan. "Very nice, and a great view of the city I might add. I stopped by to say hi and see if you wanted to take me to lunch?"

"I think I could do that. How does Moby Dick's sound to you?"

"Yeah right, nice try Ian. We'd both need a shot of penicillin to go in that place. How about we go to the Nankin? Chinese food sounds good to me. I've got a lot to tell you. I spoke to that friend of mine at the FBI and he told me some things you'll find interesting. He also wants to meet with you as soon as possible."

"You didn't tell him my name did you? I asked you not to."

"No Ian, I didn't, but after what has happened and what I've told him you knew, he wants to have a word with you to see if you can help them out."

"Let's not discuss this here. There are ears present, if you know what I mean. Let's go to lunch and talk about this while we eat."

I grabbed my coat and ushered Kate out into the hallway in the direction of the elevators. Two of my closest business associates were waiting there when we arrived. Both of them said hi as they give Kate the once-over. Billy Raff did the thumbs up and slapped me on the back as the four of us entered the elevator. We all rode it down to the fourth floor without saying a word. When the doors opened, two young women entered. They were discussing the tall redhead's date from the previous Saturday night. The redhead was openly telling her friend about some sexual act she and her boyfriend had done in a closet at a party in the Dinkytown area. It was definitely a conversation that was better off done in private. I believe I spoke for all of us when I say we were thankful when the elevator reached the Crystal Court. When the doors opened, Billy and Ben stepped to the front to hold them open so everyone could exit. I could sense that my two friends wanted to hang back to get a view of Kate's gorgeous set of legs. They were more than gorgeous, they were fantastic. I had run my cheeks up and down them many times; noting the soft, smooth texture of the inside of her thighs.

Kate and I left Billy and Ben behind and walked across the court to the exit doors on the northeast corner of the IDS Center. We then cross-walked Nicollet Avenue to Seventh Street and eventually wound up at the front door to the Nankin. The restaurant was a landmark in the downtown Minneapolis area. It had been there for sixty years and was soon to be relocated to City Center. There was no disputing the fact that the food was the best Asian cuisine the Twin Cities had to offer.

The gusty wind kind of blew us into the restaurant where we were met by a lovely, long-haired Chinese girl who led us to our table. She seated us in the far back of the restaurant and gave me a wink and a nod as she left.

"Beautiful girl, don't you think?" asked Kate.

"I didn't notice."

"Come on Ian, I saw how you followed her ass all the way to the table. She seemed to like you."

"How do you know that? Maybe she liked you. Maybe she's a lesbian."

"No Ian. I'm pretty sure she's not a lesbian. I know when people are flirting and believe me; she was winking at you and not at me. I think she has the hots for you."

"She does? Well, I'll have to come back and check her out some other time."

"Go right ahead. And then maybe I'll have a big surprise waiting for you after you go to sleep some night."

Why all of a sudden did I feel like I just had my testicles put in a jar? "I think you've made your point Kate. So tell me what your friend had to say?"

"First of all, his name is Ralph Yorkshire."

"Yorkshire?" I laughed. "That's a good one. The guy sounds like a dogcatcher."

"Ian..."

"Okay. Okay. Go on with your story."

"Anyway, Ralph and I had breakfast this morning because of a call he got at 5:00 a.m. The call was about a serial killer. He said the FBI is looking for a guy who may have killed almost a half-dozen people in the last couple of weeks. Among the dead are two helicopter pilots, that judge from South Carolina we heard about on the TV, and a highway patrolman. They also think that your friend from Atlanta may have been one of the victims."

"No fuckin' way," I said angrily.

"Yes fuckin' way Ian, and the guy's still out there. According to Ralph, the FBI thinks he is moving around the country trying to kill more people. Tell me something Ian, what did you get yourself involved in over there in Vietnam that has the FBI wanting to talk to you?"

"Well, let's see. I used to write the President some pretty interesting letters while I was over there. And I ran hookers in and out of camp whenever I had the chance. So maybe the White House wants me to be their new press secretary or maybe they want to arrest me for running a prostitution ring. You know, pimping!"

"I'm being serious Ian. Stop joking around. From what Ralph has said, and from what you have told me, I think you are connected to these murders."

"You mean you think I did them? I must be Superman."

"Again, stop with the fucking jokes. Can't you be serious for one minute?"

With a not so straight face I said, "Okay, but let's order first. What do you like on the menu?"

Kate replied, "I like just about everything and I'm about to order the Grand Duke for two. How does that sound?"

"It sounds great to me. The Grand Duke for two and hold the peanuts."

I smiled and placed our order, which included a couple of glasses of white wine. The food came in minutes and the two of us sat quietly eating what turned out to be chicken chow mein and beef and broccoli.

"This food is fantastic. Do you want to share?" I asked.

"I would love to try your beef and broccoli, but beware of the hidden peanuts in my chow mein," giggled Kate. "Now who's joking around? So let's get back to my question that you skirted a little earlier."

"Skirted? Why would you say that?"

"Oh. I don't know. Maybe it's because you gave me a stupid answer to my question. So once again I'm asking you, what were you up to over there that has you in this position now? You seem to be in the middle of a multiple-murder investigation, which I honestly believe you don't have anything to do with. So what gives?"

"Hey. Did I tell you this beef and broccoli is fantastic?"

"Okay Ian, if you don't want to talk about it we won't, but Ralph still wants to talk to you."

"That seems to be the problem. I don't want to talk to him or anyone at the FBI. I hate those assholes. They're the equivalent of the army CID, and no matter how you spell the agency's name they both wind up meaning the same thing -JAIL. Here's what I will tell you. There is someone out there who has a connection to Snake and me."

"Who the hell is Snake?"

"Oh. That was Roland's nickname back in Vietnam. He liked to go down spider holes. It's a long story...I'll tell you about it someday. Anyway, as I told you before, Snake and I witnessed two men posing as CID intelligence officers kill two enemy soldiers.

Now Snake is dead and so is Colonel Foss. So are the two pilots who flew the CID officers that day, to and from the village of Dak Sen Luc. That leaves only about a half-dozen people alive who know about the killings. One of them is me and the other is a high-ranking political figure in this country. I know this because I've seen his face on TV and read about his background in *Time Magazine*. His bio said he was an officer with II Corps during the Vietnam War. The other two men are my platoon buddies who were with me when we captured the Vietcong soldiers. They're probably dead by now for all I know." *That was a lie.*

"Didn't Snake's widow tell you there was an Asian man sniffing around before Roland was killed?"

"Don't you mean murdered? I think that's obvious at this point. Anyway, what does he have to do with this pool of dead people?"

"Just stop and think for a moment Ian. There was an Asian guy looking for Roland. There was also that Asian guy who was captured by your squad in Vietnam. That captured Asian guy then has two brothers murdered by fake CID men. That same Asian guy is one of those on your list who knows about the murders. Oh, I almost forgot to tell you something else that Ralph said. That South Carolina judge, he too was likely killed by an Asian man. So it makes plenty of sense to me that some Asian guy is right in the middle of all of this along with you."

"You've been reading too many cheap novels, Kate."

"I don't read novels Ian. I don't have the time. Think about it, that's all I'm saying. Logically there are no other explanations for what has happened."

"Kate, there's something else I haven't told you. Shortly after my platoon was nearly wiped out in Laos, I had a brief discussion with a colonel from the same II Corps that Foss and the other intelligence officers were from. I asked the colonel if there was a possibility we'd been sent on a particular mission with an outside chance of never returning. After all, we had witnessed two murders at the hands of two of his henchmen, and I thought the colonel might have tried to cover it up by having us killed by the enemy.

He stood there and glared at me for nearly a whole minute, then quietly said, no, that was not the case. But now I'm not so sure. Why you ask? Because the last living intel officer is about to seek higher office and he doesn't need any skeletons in his closet. Do you get my drift?"

"Yes I do. So who is this guy?"

"I can't tell you Kate. I need to keep it to myself in case you leak information to your friendly dogcatcher."

"Aren't you leaving out a part?"

"What part?"

"The one which includes you in this mystery. You seem to be front and center in this murder investigation, and even if I don't tell Ralph anything, it still leaves you vulnerable to being killed. Hell, I could be killed too if I happen to be around when the wrong person comes looking for you. Tell me, what are you going to do if this person does come looking for you?"

"I can take care of myself Kate. I've been hunted many times before and I'm still here. Now that I know the whole story I can better prepare for what might lay ahead. And you're right, Kate, you could be killed too. So maybe we better not see each other for a while."

"Fuck you Ian! You're not getting rid of me that easy. I'm not going to stop being with you. I love bear hunting. We'll just have to be careful and you'll have to be my bodyguard. Doesn't that sound like fun?"

"Listen to me Kate. This is not a goddamn game or a movie where the hero and his girlfriend escape unscathed. You have to understand that Kate. And if you want to be in the middle of all of this, then you have two choices. Either you stay at my place or we stay at yours. Yours is not an option. So that means you'll have to stay at mine, but let's play it cool for a couple of weeks. If something is going to happen, I think it'll be soon. I also have another thought about the killer."

"What's that?"

"It's quite possible he's someone who's been hired by the guy who's running for public office. The guy running for office might be trying to eliminate all those people who have something on him. He's doing it now because he has decided to push his political career higher, and something like murdering enemy soldiers would surely set off the buzzer in his game show. You know, I think it's time we head back to work."

We gathered our coats and I paid the bill. Kate and I then walked up the street as we headed back to the IDS Center. I stopped briefly in the middle of the Crystal Court to give Kate a little hug and a kiss.

Then I took the elevator to the tenth floor. I went directly to my office and sat quietly to think about my eventual encounter with the FBI and the killer. I knew I would have to talk to the FBI or they would eventually show up in my office and start asking questions. Talking to them would be easy as long as Kate kept her mouth shut. If that happened, as I expected it would, I could fill Mr. Dogcatcher with all kinds of bullshit. From my conversation with Kate, I knew the FBI would soon have me connected to the conspiracy. They would want to know what I knew and I would tell them exactly what they wanted to hear. I would fill them in on the capture of the three Vietcong soldiers back in 1969 and their subsequent interrogation and killing. I would tell them that Snake Cummings was in my platoon and say I was deeply sorry to hear he was dead. I would leave out the part about my phone conversation with Snake's widow along with the identity of the third intel officer and my other platoon members, those being Tom Wheeler and Paul Fisher. I would call those two men this afternoon and give them a heads-up on the situation. Tom might already know of the connection because he was a smart, young man. But he lived in a rural area in Iowa and news may not have gotten to him as fast as it did here in the Twin Cities. Fish, on the other hand, might be too stoned to even put two and two together. I was sure he didn't read the newspaper and probably never turned on the television unless it was to watch cartoons. Nevertheless, I would have to warn them to watch out for anyone looking suspicious.

My thoughts were momentarily interrupted by my two associates who had ridden the elevator down with Kate and me. They wanted to know how I had met my extremely hot lunch date.

"Ian," said Billy. "Isn't the hot chick we saw you with in the elevator the same girl who works at the information booth down in the Crystal Court?"

Ben Myers chimed in with, "Every single guy in our office has tried to hit on her. I think some married guys have too. They've all struck out. Nobody has even been able to get her phone number. So what gives? We want details."

"No," said Billy. "We want all the dirty little details. Like have you slept with her yet? And what is the real color of her hair? And does she like to do it on the kitchen table?"

"The kitchen table?" replied Ben. "Couldn't you have thought of a better place than that? I'm probably going to spend the rest of my life trying to get that vision out of my mind."

"Hey guys, listen up," said Billy. "I've got my fantasies and you've got yours. So, come on Ian and fill us in."

"Guys. Guys. You two are worse than a couple of old ladies. If I told you about Kate and me having sex in the shower, or in the front seat of my Porsche, or here on my desk in this office, then you would go around and tell everyone. And if I happened to tell you about our threesome with um, but I just can't do any of that. Instead, you'll just have to make things up in those tiny little minds of yours."

"Come on Ian, tell us," replied Billy.

"You two boys go back to work and forget about Kate and me. We've been having a great time, and neither of you needs to know about our sex life. I'll just say this; Kate is an old friend of my brother's and I knew her from when I was a kid. I just got reconnected with her, so go back to whatever you're supposed to be doing. Okay?"

Billy and Ben left the office with their tails between their legs. By the looks on their faces you would have thought they had just lost a new puppy. Children at work, I thought. It was obvious that neither of them had ever progressed out of the adolescence stage.

Getting back to my earlier thoughts, I figured I had a couple of ideas on whom the murderer might be. These were ideas I could only share with a couple of people and Kate was definitely not one of them. I also left out the names and identities of some other people who were there that day in Dak Sen Luc. There was also an interpreter and a third intelligence officer whose name escapes me. I left that information out on purpose because the less Kate knew the better. She couldn't give the FBI any information she didn't have. Besides, if Kate knew she would only be scared and she would never be able to grasp the idea of how I was going to handle the situation.

My first thought went back to one of the two remaining ex-CID officers whom I had told Kate about at lunch. One of them just happened to be Illinois Senator Randolph Wear. Wear obviously couldn't be killing all these people himself, but he could have hired someone to do it for him. He could have hired an Asian hit-man to throw people off-track. That made sense, but the theory had a lot of holes in it. A former CID cop, who was actually a CIA agent, would still have a lot of connections; but if he was the man behind the killings, he was sticking his neck out where it could easily be chopped off. A man of his status would never be able to hide a dark secret like that, especially if he should become the next President of the United States.

My second theory was the one the FBI had, the one about an Asian man who was doing all the killings. That one was a real mystery to me. If it was an Asian, then who was he? Where was he from? This one had me baffled. If it was a man set on revenge, then that meant it could only be someone who could be traced back to the surviving Vietcong we had captured. That seemed impossible from where I sat. No North Vietnamese farm boy could ever have traced all the men from Dak Sen Luc back here to their homes in the United States. No one, that is, except a man who had an accomplice who was an original citizen of this country. Could that be possible, I wondered? It was crazy to even think like that, but the more I thought about it the more I felt like that was the only explanation possible.

I decided I needed some more time to mill over these two theories and wait to see who would be the next person the assassin would go after. If it happened to be the senator, then he'd be ruled out because he'd be dead. But if it happened to be Tom, Fish or me, then I would have to step my game up and revert to a little jungle warfare to settle this like two opposing enemies.

Chapter 14

Chu was already three states away from New Jersey, but he still didn't feel safe. He was thinking to himself about how easy it had been to kill Dave Gunderson as he stood in the man's doorway. He put on the clown's mask and rang the doorbell. Chu said, "Trick or Treat," when Gunderson opened the door and Gunderson laughed and replied, "Aren't you a little early son?" Then Chu pulled the Beretta out of his bag and shot Gunderson squarely between his eyebrows. Yes, Chu thought it was the best trick of his life and one of the best treats for that matter. Still, Chu lamented on what he had done inside the man's house. He'd been reckless and had gone out of control. Shooting Gunderson should have been enough, but Chu wasn't satisfied with killing him. He had to make a statement. He had his reasons for doing what he did, but it wasn't necessary. It also left evidence behind and that was the first time he had done so since the murder spree began.

His reasoning for cutting Gunderson's tongue out went back to Vietnam. After he was jailed, an intelligence officer from II Corps came to him asking if he wanted to become a Kit Carson Scout. If he agreed, Chu would spend a short time training and be assigned to another unit which was stationed closer to the border. If not, he would rot in jail or be turned over to the Army of the Republic of Vietnam. Chu agreed and began his training. It was during this period that he overheard some stories about a couple of gooks who were killed in a small village to the south. The story tellers laughed at the killings as if they were a joke. Chu knew all too well they were stories about his dead brothers, Ho and Nye, because of the references of "shooting them in the head" or "dumping them out of a helicopter like some sack of shit."

Chu resented the stories and knew where they had come from. He thought of cutting Meek's tongue out before he killed him, but that would have meant the conversation would have been one-sided. No, he couldn't do that to Meeks, but he could do it to Gunderson. He did it because the two men gloated about the killings. Their tongues told lies about his brothers, and the only way to shut them up would be to kill them and remove their tongues. He had accomplished that in part, with the way he had handled Gunderson. He should have left well enough alone, but no, he just had to prove something to himself. And that meant there were bloody hand and foot prints all over the place that he didn't have time to cleanup. He had worn latex gloves, so there were no actual finger prints to connect him to the murder. But when Chu looked around after his act of violence, he saw a mess he thought needed to be destroyed. That's what led to the fire that hadn't worked.

Chu also knew his truck had most likely been identified by now because of the flat-tire incident back in South Carolina. The FBI would have put a number of things together and his truck would have to go. He was going to have to replace it quickly. He would do that tonight and find another vehicle. Chu had never stolen anything, except for someone's life. He had done that many times during the war and now here in America. And he was getting bolder with each kill. But he knew his next victim would be much more difficult to get to. It would take a very precise move to kill him. A senator would have protection of some sort, at least a couple of civilian and/or Secret Service men now that he was making a run at the presidency. They would shadow his every move.

Chu had been heading for Springfield, Illinois, but a conversation with his friend had changed that. He learned that ex-Major Randolph Wear was not there, but on a campaign tour that was presently halted in Chicago. Chicago would be a great place to change vehicles and hide as he stalked the presidential candidate. There were any number of places where he could get to Wear, but every scenario meant he would most likely have to take a couple of armed guards out before he killed him. That would be messy, not to mention almost impossible as Chu was fighting on their turf now. This was not Vietnam and it would not come under the cover of darkness or in a place where he could get him alone. No, Chu was going to have to find the perfect location to do what he had come here for.

Chu drove the Bronco to a mall in suburban west Chicago and left it. It was now 9:00 a.m. He thought it was better to leave the vehicle and go overland from there. The truck would eventually be found and processed by the FBI, but that would be far too late for them to stop Chu from killing the major.

He quickly hailed a cab and took it to the Palmer House in downtown Chicago where he got a room. It was expensive, but Chu felt it was the only real way to get close to Wear. Wear was giving a speech that afternoon in the ballroom, followed by a hundred-dollar-a-plate dinner for his Democratic campaign. Chu paid the man at the front desk and took the elevator to his twelfth-floor room. He opened the door and put a do not disturb sign on the knob outside. It was now eleven thirty. He put his bags on the bed and went to the window to get a view of the city. He could see the Sears Tower and Lake Michigan to the east. He was told the Navy Pier would be a nice release from his murderous activities if he had time to waste. There was a huge Ferris wheel in the park, which was something Chu had never been on before and he was eager to see it. The Navy Pier would also be a good place to hide in open site, as the park's many diverse faces would keep his hidden in the crowd. He wouldn't be looked at twice and it could be fun, but Chu didn't think he had the luxury of having fun at this point in time. Besides, Wear was only scheduled to be in Chicago for the day and then he was moving on.

Instead, Chu decided to relax by taking a shower to clean off the last two days of sweat. He started forming a plan as the hot, steamy water rolled down over his body. After numerous bad ideas, one of which included joining the Democratic Party, Chu settled on the old go-to of disguising himself as a maintenance worker. It had worked in Atlanta, so why not here. After a ten-minute cleansing, he dried himself and changed into clean clothes.

His next move was to head down to the main lobby, find the service elevator, and take it to the basement. The elevator was jerky and slow, and when the door opened he could immediately hear a hiss from one of the old boilers that heated the building. He took a left out of the elevator, but stopped when he heard men's voices coming from the hallway around the corner. So Chu went the other direction that led down a dark corridor of rooms marked A – F. He tried each one of them, but they were all locked. Finally he located a room that said maintenance personnel. He turned the handle on the door which opened into a room full of lockers. He checked them one by one until he located a uniform. He quickly dressed into the gray coveralls, but they were too large for him. He discarded them and looked a little further until he found another pair that seemed to fit him much better. He put them on, rolled the cuffs up, and repositioned his knife and Beretta to the front of the waistband in his trousers. He looked at the name on the coveralls; it said Mark. So now he was Mark Throng, a maintenance man for the Palmer House if anyone should ask. He took a deep breath and went to see if he could find Major Wear.

Chu walked up one flight of stairs to the main level, where he passed a couple of hotel workers on his way down a hallway that led to the kitchen. He felt the kitchen would be his best chance to gain entrance to the main ballroom. He opened the kitchen door and walked in. There was a lot of confusion going on. The staff was frantically trying to put together an extravagant dinner that was planned for later that evening. He noticed two men near the front doors of the kitchen which he assumed led to the ballroom. He could hear a man speaking into a microphone beyond that point and people applauding. He assumed the man with the microphone was there to introduce Wear. The men at the doors were dressed in black suits with white shirts and black ties, and held two-way radios. Chu was sure they were Secret Service men. He realized they weren't going to let him into the ballroom or anywhere near the major dressed as a maintenance worker. So Chu turned to one of the workers and said he had to fix a pipe in the kitchen staff's locker room. Could she direct him to the proper location? The woman told him it was out the door and down the hallway to the right. Chu felt he needed to change into a kitchen-staff uniform to get closer to Major Wear. He also knew he would blend in better if he was dressed in white.

At one twenty-two Chu was back in the kitchen running food for the chefs. He watched and listened as the afternoon wound down. The speech and ensuing handshaking were over by three thirty, which meant that now would be Chu's best opportunity to get Major Wear as he exited through the kitchen. He picked up an empty pot and carried it forward toward the ballroom doors. He wanted to conceal his identity the best he could. The doors suddenly flew open as several agents ushered Wear out toward the back hallway. Chu was in close pursuit as he unzipped his coveralls and went for his Beretta. He moved quickly with the group of men, and was about to pull his pistol out when he was blind-sided by a staff member carrying a crate of lettuce. The crate had shielded the worker from seeing Chu subsequently pushing him into another worker who was holding a tray of pastries. Things flew everywhere as Chu tried in vain to get to the senator, but all three men went down to the floor together and Chu's plan was foiled.

Now what am I going to do, thought Chu? He had almost made a mistake and gotten caught before he could kill the major. The man with the lettuce had damn near knocked the Beretta out of his hand and onto the floor. The opening to his coveralls had saved him from that. Chu recovered and got to his feet, but the opportunity had passed, and he had no other choice but to retreat to his room and regroup.

As he left the kitchen Chu couldn't help but overhear a Secret Service agent in the back hallway say, "I'll be glad when this day is over."

The second officer said, "Me too! And thank God he'll be leaving town tomorrow morning for that hunting trip."

Chu passed them slowly while the two men continued talking and walking as they followed him down the hallway. He again overheard the men speaking of the hunting detail they would be on the following day.

The first agent said, "Are you ready to go running around in the woods to shoot a couple of lousy grouse?"

"Hey, it beats wearing these suits day after day," said the other.

"That's true, but we don't get to shoot anything. Governor Chance of Wisconsin and the senator are the only ones who get to have any fun."

"Yeah, I guess you're right," said the second agent. "Where in the hell is this place we are going? I've never heard of it."

"It's a hunting camp called Buck Horns, about ten miles north of Tomahawk, Wisconsin. We leave bright and early in the morning, around six o'clock."

That was all Chu needed to hear. It made his heart leap with anticipation. In a day or two, Chu would have the major on his turf. This was going to be enjoyable.

Chu would go back and change his clothing and leave the hotel as soon as possible. He needed to find a cab driver who would take him to the nearest military surplus store so he could get a couple sets of camouflage fatigues and a compass. He laughed to himself as he took the service elevator to the main lobby, thinking how dumb those Secret Service men would look while running around in the woods in black suits. They sure as hell wouldn't be mistaken for Vietcong.

Chapter 15

I had just gotten off the telephone with Paul Fisher. Talking to him was like having a conversation with a mushroom. Fish had no clue that something dreadfully bad was going down. He didn't even know Foss had been killed. Paul was in his own little world that focused on drugs and wine. He said he was doing well and asked if I wanted him to come out to Minneapolis, so the two of us could "team up" and go after the person who was doing all the killing. Fish thought it would be grand fun. A "hoot" is what he had actually said...just the two of us going after the enemy one last time. I told Fish I didn't want him getting involved. I just wanted to make sure he was alright and for him to be aware of the situation. The conversation didn't last more than five minutes and I was happy when it was over. I figured the less he knew, the better it would be for all of us. I finished the conversation by telling him he shouldn't say anything to the FBI should they happen to contact him. Just act stupid is what I actually said. I figured that wouldn't be any problem for Fish to pull off.

The next call went to Tom Wheeler. Tom had been one of my radio operators during the war and I had gotten him transferred out of the platoon a short time after the killings at Dak Sen Luc. He was a nice kid who farmed the family homestead somewhere down south near Ft. Dodge, Iowa. I wasn't sure how Tom would take the news. He was a religious type and that was the main reason I wanted him transferred out of the platoon. He had seen enough death by the time Dak Sen Luc rolled around and I wasn't sure we could count on him because of his beliefs. What was it I had said to my old lieutenant? "Get Tom out of here before he quits on us."

"Hello Tom, this is Ian."

Before I could say another word, Tom shot back with, "What the hell is going on, Ian? I just got a newspaper article in the mail about the killing of Judge Foss. The headline reads; Judge Foss Murdered."

"Hold on Tom, you haven't even said hello."

"Okay. Hello. But what the hell is going on?"

"Well, there's a lot going on as you probably know from reading the headline in the newspaper you received. So tell me, where's the paper from?"

"It's from Columbia, South Carolina. It's called the *State*."

"And where was it mailed from?"

"It looks like it was sent from Columbia; at least that's where the postmark's from."

"Was there a letter along with it?"

"No. Not that I could see. But the headline had been circled in red pen and there was a line drawn from the circle with the words, Colonel Robert Foss of the CIA. Then below that was a note saying you and your buddies are next. I remember Colonel Foss, but I thought he was in the CID. He was the reason I got out of our old platoon. What's up Ian? What's going on? I'm assuming the - you and your buddies - means Paul Fisher, you, myself and possibly Snake. Is there anyone else?"

"First of all Tom, Foss was not in the CID. He only hid behind their insignia. He used them for his real cover, which was the CIA. You remember those guys don't you? They used to be the OSS in Vietnam with the French, back before the Americans got involved in the war. In those days they wore civilian clothes and hid in plain sight while working undercover as employees for import/export companies or oil companies. Some even worked for the

U.S. State Department. Then along comes the Vietnam War and they put on uniforms to play the good guys. Only they weren't good guys; they killed at will and it seems it finally caught up to Colonel Foss, or should I say, Judge Foss."

"And as far as what's going on, well, all I can tell you is this: a lot has happened in the last three weeks. I believe there's someone out there on a killing spree and so far he has managed to take Snake's life. He or them, I'm not sure about that yet, have also managed to kill the two pilots who brought Colonel Foss and Major Wear out to the field that day in Dak Sen Luc. As you probably read from that newspaper article, Foss was killed at his home during the night. Whoever is doing these killings is both bold and resourceful. He or they strike mostly at night or in remote locations, where you can't see them coming. The one pilot was killed in his helicopter hangar and the other one was shot dead as he opened the front door to his house. And you know about Foss from the newspaper article."

"I'm sorry to hear about Snake," replied Tom. "I liked the guy. He helped us out of a lot of tight situations. So what's your take on this Ian?"

"You know, it's funny you should say that about Snake. He always thought I saved saved his life that day in Fu Pin, but it was actually the other way around. If he hadn't had our backs, then the gooks would have sandwiched us in, and no one would ever have known what happened that day. We all would have died and disappeared, and people like you would still be guessing as to what happened to us. But that's then and this is now. So let's get back to your original question. I've got a couple of theories on what's going on, but first of all here is what I do know for sure. I have a woman-friend here in Minneapolis whom I go out with and she has a direct connection to the regional FBI boss. He's the link from which I have gotten all my information. And I've taken that information and used it to fill in the blanks about my theories. I've learned through my friend that an Asian man has been connected to the killings of all the American soldiers who were there that day with us in the village. The Asian has also killed a South Carolina highway patrolman who happened to get in the way. I also know that Major Wear is still alive at the moment. Did you know he was Senator Wear of Illinois and he's campaigning as the Democratic candidate for the presidency?"

"I might be a country bumpkin Ian, but I still read other magazines besides Farm Journal and Successful Farming. Yes, I saw he was trying to get on the Democratic ticket. Then I thought about what a bastard he was and hoped he wouldn't get the nomination."

"So you do know about Wear and the killing spree that's been going on. That's good. The killer or killers seem relentless in their pursuit for revenge. So here are my theories on what is going on. I have one that puts Wear behind the killings. I'm basing it on my belief that Wear can't have anyone around who can identify him as the killer of that Vietcong boy. And if he's behind the killings, then he must have hired an Asian to do the dirty work. That's a possibility, but the biggest hole in that theory is Wear would have had to kill everyone in the Montagnard village. That would mean he would have to kill an additional twenty-five to thirty more men. Give or take a few who were killed in the war or have died since. So, let's put that number at twenty for the sake of argument. I don't think that's possible. That would eventually point a finger right back to him and he could forget the presidency. If I'm correct, he's ruled out of theory number one. As a matter of fact, I'm going out on a limb and predict Wear will be dead within the next few days."

"Why would you think that?"

"Just hold that thought for a minute. I'm not finished. As I said, Wear can't have everyone killed, so that only leaves me with theory number two."

"And what's that Ian? There's a madman out there who has a short list of people to kill?"

"You got it. But first I want to refresh your memory about a few things. Let's go back to that day in May of '69 when our platoon captured those three Vietcong and brought them to the Montagnard village. We brought them in and called command,

and they informed us there would be someone out in the morning to interrogate the prisoners. Correct? That same platoon, except for you, went on a patrol three weeks later and you know the rest of that story. So, that means only four of us made it back to the States alive from that original patrol at Dak Sen Luc. Are you with me?"

"Yeah, so far. Go on."

"Well, add those four people to a list that includes the two pilots, the three intel officers, and their interpreter who came out to the village to interrogate the prisoners, and we have a total of ten people, assuming we exclude the captain and his men who ran the village. So, that short list of ten people is now down to six. I believe the interpreter should be crossed off the list because he was either taken care of during the war or is living somewhere in Vietnam. I truly don't believe he has anything to do with these killings. That leaves us with five possible suspects and soon to be four if I'm right about Senator Wear. And I am right about Wear because I've tossed out theory number one. That means the list will be down to four by week's end. I know I'm not the killer, and I'm positive you aren't, and that only leaves Fish and the other intel officer whose name escapes me."

"His name is Perkins. That was the name of the other intel officer. He was sent back to the States after he was shot when his convoy was attacked on its way to Ban Me Thuot. It was in early August, if memory serves me correctly. He was real messed up from what I heard, so I don't think he's a good candidate for your list."

"Okay, then he's more than likely to be on the killer's list. Then the list is down to three people. And let's face it. Do either one of us actually believe Fish is smart enough to do this?"

"No. I know he is not. So, then who does that leave?"

"Well, that only leaves Perkins. Or, possibly one other person, who I believe is the lone Vietcong who survived the interrogation. Or someone connected to him in some bizarre way. He also might have an accomplice."

"That's crazy Ian."

"I know. I know. Then you come up with a better idea Tom. I'm fresh out. The only other possibility is the killer is some kind of nut case."

"Are you sure about this Ian? If you're correct, then there are still a few of us who are in real danger of being the next in line."

"I'm positive Tom, and we better be ready. I've already notified Fish, and because of his location, he would most likely be the last one on the list. So we need to get ready for this guy. What's your status? Do you have a wife, kids, or parents? Who lives at your home that needs to be moved out?"

"God Ian, I don't know where I would begin if I had to tell my family about this. I have a wife and two small children. They wouldn't understand. My wife would want me to contact the police or the FBI. And speaking of that, shouldn't we tell the FBI about all of this and let them sort it out? At the very least, shouldn't Wear know that someone is after him?"

"We could, but that isn't going to stop the killer from eventually coming after us. And as far as Wear goes, he deserves whatever is coming his way. I'm sure the boy whom he killed wasn't his only victim of the war."

"I guess you're right. But if we get the FBI involved they might actually catch the killer and then we would all be in the clear."

"Let me ask you this Tom. Can you actually say you want to live in fear until that day comes? It could take weeks or even months. You would have to worry every single minute of every day about your family being victimized by this crazy person or persons. Not me. I've got a young daughter, and if I had to keep her away for something like this, then I would lose my visitation rights forever. I want this guy, and I know I'm capable of getting him, but I'm going to need your help."

"And what's that Ian?"

"I'll know more about it in a couple of days, if my theory holds water that is. In the meantime, I want you to talk to your family and see if maybe you could coax them into going on a short vacation to visit their relatives. Do your in-laws live near you?"

"No. My wife's family is from Nebraska."

"Great! Then ask her if she and the kids might want to go and visit them. It could be a fun Halloween for them. Tell them your old Vietnam buddy is coming down for a working vacation. I actually need a location to do some shooting for an agricultural commercial and maybe your farm would work well for that. Do you have clean corn and bean fields that we can use for the shoot?"

"I do."

"Good. Then I have a plan I think will work well. I'll call you soon with the details. Talk to you later."

Chapter 16

Chu was about an hour north of the Wisconsin border driving a newly stolen maroon Chevy Malibu with Illinois plates when he happened upon a talk radio station from Chicago. The reception was crystal-clear, much better than what he would have gotten if he still had the Bronco. Chu knew that listening to a call-in radio station would be the best thing he could do to stay awake for the long drive ahead. This particular station was broadcasting a portion of Senator Wear's speech from earlier this afternoon. The senator was going on and on about morals and the importance of being a good Christian. Chu got a chuckle out of hearing that. He thought Major Wear had no morals whatsoever. And as far as being a Christian, well that was something Wear had said to make the public think he was a devout man. Wear probably did go to church on Sundays, but it was purely for show. Chu was absolutely positive the major would never be able to get into his God's heaven when he left this earth. The only bad thing that would come out of Wear's death, he thought, was Wear would become a hero in the public's eye. He would leave behind a legacy of a good parent and wonderful husband, and no one would ever know the crimes he had committed against humanity. People would say he was killed by a crazy man. They had that right; Chu knew he was a crazy person. Just crazy enough to think he could pull off killing Wear without getting caught.

The speech rambled on for the next six to eight minutes until the station's DJ came on and cut it off. He said, "This is Nick Lick and we're back on the air. Now let's hear from our listeners. I want to hear from someone out there who has an opinion on Senator Wear's chances of getting the Democratic nomination for President of the United States. Call in now at 312-555-WKLZ."

Chu knew Wear's chances. They were absolutely zero and people would find that out soon. Political assassinations were a way of life all around the world. Dictators and politicians alike were being killed, and some of them, like Wear, had it coming.

The first person to call Nick was a young man named Bob, who had no particular political affiliation. He said, "Wear is no different than any other politician. He talks a good story, but then he says one thing and does another."

"What do you mean by that Bob?" replied Nick.

"It's like this. He says he is going to help people get off welfare by creating jobs for them. Then he says he has a plan to reduce income taxes for middle-income families. He said a lot of other crap too, but it's just the same old (bleep) that all the other politicians say. First off, how does he plan on creating new jobs if he doesn't give breaks to corporate America? That's not possible. So all he's doing is talking to hear the sound of his own voice. I say don't listen to him because he's never going to be elected."

Chu shouted out loud, "You're correct, Bob; Wear will never get elected because he's going to be dead long before he ever gets the chance to be nominated."

"Okay Bob," said Nick. "Thanks for your thoughts. Now we have a young college coed from Northwestern University. Are you with us Belle?"

"Yes I am Nick."

"So what do you think of Senator Wear?"

"My main concern with him is that he has been a one-term senator up to now and he wants to run the country. He hardly has any connections in Washington, no foreign policy, and almost no experience in running the government. He wasn't even a governor prior to the Senate, so what does he know about budgets?"

"Oh, so you're a Republican?"

"That's right Nick. But what does my political affiliation have to do with anything? If a person isn't fit for office, then they shouldn't be there. I'm not even sure he is a good senator."

"Okay Belle, thanks for your thoughts. Now let's try another listener. We have Jeffrey from the south side of Chicago on the line. Are you there Jeffrey?"

"I am."

"And what do you want to say to the audience tonight?"

"Well, first of all, I didn't hear Wear give his speech this afternoon, but I've read a lot of articles about the man and he does have some ties to the military. In specific, he was a former military cop in Vietnam. So, if Belle is still listening, I want her to know Wear does have connections in Washington. Only they may be the wrong kind. Might his affiliation with the CID mean he has strong ties with the CIA or other secret organizations within the government? I believe we need to check into the man's military records to find out more about him. I mean, we don't know anything about the man prior to1972. For all we know, Wear could have a dark side to him that would not be good for the country."

That got Chu's attention. He moved quickly to turn up the volume on the radio so he wouldn't miss a single word the young man was saying about Wear's connection to the military. Jeffrey was totally right; Wear did have a very dark side to him. Chu was delighted to hear Jeffrey speak out against the major. It was enlightening for him to know that people in this country could voice their opinions without the possibility of being thrown in jail. Back in Vietnam, Jeffrey would have become a political prisoner if he had spoken like he did. This was exactly what Chu needed to keep him going for the rest of the night. His adrenalin was flowing now, and he was more than ready to take on the challenge of the Secret Service and the rest of Wear's team.

Chu honked his horn with approval as he pressed on toward the town of Tomahawk. He had passed Madison awhile back and was staying on Interstate 94 until he hit Highway 51, which would take him all the way to his destination. He was planning on stopping only once on this final leg of his journey to get some gas and change the plates on his newly stolen vehicle. Chu estimated he would be at the hunting lodge by 7:00 a.m.

A light rain began to fall somewhere around Wausau and became increasingly heavier the closer he got to Tomahawk. The rain was a good thing, Chu thought. Heavier rain would probably delay the start of the day's hunt or cancel it altogether. Chu was hoping for the latter. He needed a head start on the hunting party. Actually he needed to walk the property to get a good idea of the lay of the land. After doing that, he would devise a plan that included escape routes. His compass would come in handy for that. Chu was positive there would be chaos the instant they found the major dead, and that would be a huge benefit to him, as he was planning on being long gone when that happened.

The next hour or so was uneventful, except for a deer that ran out in front of his car. Chu missed it by several inches, but still managed to keep the car on the road. He had driven the Chevy past a few small towns that were pitch-dark and locked up tight for the evening. If it weren't for the road signs, he would have blinked and missed them altogether. He passed a larger town called Merrill and headed toward Tomahawk.

He made it to the outskirts of Tomahawk at the brink of dawn. The first thing he encountered was a Texaco station that was open on the south side of the road as was the Badger Café, which was located next door. Chu had no clue as to where the hunting lodge was located, so he needed to find that out before the hunt began. He didn't want to make it obvious he was looking for the Buck Horns Lodge, so he had to do it discretely as not to draw attention to himself. Chu decided to wait for an hour or so when there would be more people milling around. That would be the time to ask.

The rain was still falling steadily at eight o'clock, which made Chu confident the hunting party would wait until it stopped. He had a notion these politicians weren't in any hurry to get wet. They would more than likely sit in the warm, dry lodge drinking coffee and smoking cigars until the sun came out.

Chu's next move was to stop at the bait and license shop in the center of town. There were four cars and a pickup truck out in front, which meant there were several people inside. He figured they wouldn't think twice about a man coming in to ask for information and directions. So he parked the car and walked in through the side entrance. The place smelled old and fishy. It had a half-dozen deer heads, one moose head, and several species of fish mounted on the wall that Chu was unfamiliar with. Once inside, he paused for a second to look for the sales counter. Chu saw it was ten feet up on his left by the display of duck decoys and hip waders, so he walked over to see if the attendant could be of assistance. The man working the cash register was a tall, burly-looking fellow with a thick brown beard. He stood there picking his nose as he watched the customers move about the store.

Chu walked right up to him and was greeted with, "How's it goin', chief?"

Chu took a long look at him, but didn't know how to respond. So rather than walk away he replied, "Okay I guess."

"So what do you need, chief?"

"I was wondering if you could tell me where the hunting lodges are at in this area. I'm looking for work and I was hoping you might have a brochure or something that might list all of them."

"Sure enough chief, but I thought you Indians knew all the hunting camps in the area."

Chu said to himself, so the guy thinks I'm an Indian. Well, I guess Asians do look somewhat like American Indians. But I'm too short to be one of them. Oh well, this may be just what I need to keep a low profile.

He replied, "I'm not from around here. I live far to the north."

"Oh," the shop owner said. "You mean like you're an Eskimo?"

"No. Not that far north. I'm from a village in Michigan."

"Okay, whatever you say chief. Here's a list of all the camps in the county, but the largest one is only seven miles northwest of town. It's called Buck Horns Lodge. If you take a left outside and go north out of town you'll run across RR6. Take a left on that road and follow it around Green Lake and past Mud Lake until you come to a sign for the lodge. The sign will be on your right, up near the entrance to the place. You can't miss it."

Chu bought a sweatshirt and took the printed material to be polite. He then thanked the man for his help and left by the front door. From there he got back in his car and drove north out of Tomahawk. Chu knew his conversation with the bait shop owner would eventually be retold to the authorities, but he was hoping it would lead them astray as they looked for an Indian instead of an Asian man. The shop owner didn't remind Chu of a brain surgeon, so the gaffe in identifying his nationality might actually benefit him in the long run.

It was still raining moderately hard when Chu exited his vehicle near the lodge. He had stashed the car a long way off the pavement on an old, unused logging road. He put on his rain poncho, grabbed his binoculars, and headed in the direction of the lodge. He had gotten within seventy yards of the lodge before stopping to settle into a crouched position. Through his binoculars he could see one state trooper car, a couple of colored sedans, a pickup truck, and another black vehicle with an antenna on the roof, which he assumed belonged to the Secret Service. Chu could hear dogs barking in kennels beyond the main lodge and see smoke bellowing out of the chimney from atop the roof. There were no guards posted at the front door, nor could he see any roaming the grounds. The security was lax, almost nonexistent. So Chu stayed low and dashed across a thirty-foot opening to a position around the side of what looked like a bird-cleaning house. From there he could see the back of the lodge. There were no guards there either, which made his job much easier. When he was positive the perimeter was clear, he took the compass out of his pocket and checked his location. There was no way he could have walked these woods and found his way back without one. He located north and headed down a road that was perpendicular to the lodge. He was going to walk the area to the east and work his way back. He would eventually make a full circle and wind up back at the lodge.

Chu spent two and a half to three hours scouting the property in a steady rain. He found thick woods of evergreens to the north, a few ponds and big meadows to the east, and several trails that seemed to go nowhere. He had gotten lost twice and thought he might not make it back to the lodge, but then he stumbled upon a landmark that seemed familiar and it put him back on course. He was glad he had this time to look around, even if he was getting wet and cold. He hoped the weather would break for the following day, and not get worse and turn to snow. Snow would have given him away as soon as the hunters saw his tracks. The Secret Service men would take the senator and governor back to the lodge, and they would call for additional men to sniff him out. He caught a break about one thirty in the afternoon, when the rain slowed to a drizzle and the skies began to break up. So he headed back to the lodge to make sure the party wasn't going to go out for an abbreviated hunt.

He finally reached the lodge a little after two. All the cars were still in the same place as they were when he had arrived, and no one seemed to be milling around the outside. Chu found a good observation place from where he would stay and play the waiting game until it got dark. If everyone was still in the lodge at sunset, he would go back to his car where he could get some dry clothes and rest for a while.

Tomorrow was going to be a long day; one that would make the American public stand up and take notice there was a serial killer on the loose.

Chapter 17

Dawn brought full sunlight and bright-blue skies to the region. It was a cool day. Chu could see his breath steaming from his mouth as he looked through his binoculars at the lodge. He had seen a man leaving the lodge at six thirty to go out to the kennels to attend to the dogs. Then at seven o'clock, a Secret Service agent stepped out to retrieve something from his car and have a brief smoke while he stood outside the main entrance. The agent had gone back inside after he finished his cigarette, and all was quiet until a quarter to eight. That's when a black Lincoln Town Car showed up with a driver and a man who Chu thought must be the governor of Wisconsin. The two men were greeted at the main door and led inside.

Chu continued monitoring the lodge from his position in the woods, nodding off a bit from time to time. He had been up a large portion of the night making a natural disguise out of pine boughs, sticks, and reed grass. His camouflage clothing was good, but he had learned back in Vietnam that adding foliage to it would allow him to move about the woods undetected. Chu knew from yesterday's scouting expedition that there were several open areas in the woods to the rear of the lodge. They contained forest on one side and open meadow on the other, with a pond thrown in here and there. He had scared up a couple of deer on his walk, so the sound of dead branches cracking under the hoofs of one of the large creatures wouldn't seem unusual or out of place to the hunters. He also saw several dirt roads that were cut through the woods in all directions, some even crisscrossed each other. Chu figured the hunters and the dogs were transported out on these roads to drop-off points where they would begin the hunt. They were probably left out there until it was time to return to the lodge for lunch or dinner. He had seen a number of human foot prints and deer tracks as well as many empty shotgun shells. The area had been heavily hunted over the past month.

About fifteen minutes after the governor arrived, the same man who fed the dogs emerged from the side door of the lodge and went out to fetch the dogs. He brought one Labrador retriever and two shorthair pointers around to the front of the lodge and put them in smaller cages in the rear of the pickup. He then went to the garage and backed out a white van that he parked at the main entrance to the lodge. When he was done, he went inside the lodge and said something to the hunting party. Chu couldn't hear what the man had said, but he assumed he told the party to come outside so they could begin the hunt. He saw the major, the governor, another man he assumed was the lodge owner, and a couple of government agents file out. There were six men in all, counting the dog handler.

The major was still drinking his mug of coffee when Chu heard the dog handler say to them, "When you're ready, I want all of you to pile in the van. I have your guns with me in the truck. Do all of you have ammo? If not, I've got plenty of extra boxes with me in the pickup. Mr. Vance, your host will drive the van out to the hunting site. Is there anyone out here who has to visit the bathroom before we leave? We'll be gone until noon, so go now or you'll have to wait until we get back. Or you can always go in the woods if you like. It's up to you."

Governor Chance replied, "Well then, I better take a shit before we leave. I hate wiping my ass with leaves."

The hunting party let out a hearty laugh at the governor's announcement as he excused himself and went back inside. The rest of the men milled around smoking cigarettes and drinking coffee. One of the Secret Service agents took a two-way radio out of his pocket and did a frequency check with the second agent. When they were finished, the second agent said, "I'm going to take a quick walk out to the main road to check the perimeter. I should be back in no more than ten minutes." Meanwhile, the driver for the governor came out of the lodge and said good-bye to the party. He got in his car and left.

Wear walked over to Mr. Vance and shook his hand. He said, "I want to thank you for the invitation to come up here and go hunting. It looks like it's going to be a beautiful day to bag a few grouse. And it's always great to get away from the campaign trail for a couple of days. I get real tired of feeding the American public shit day after day. I've kissed far too many babies over the last several months and have shaken so many hands that I think I've worn my fingerprints off. And you can't imagine what it's like sitting through donation dinners like someone had their hand up your ass making your vocal cords work. So being out here with nature is a welcome change of pace."

"Then we need to roust some birds for you to shoot senator. And then we'll bring them back and my wife will make them taste like chicken."

"Like chicken?" the senator asked. "I was hoping they'd taste like grouse. I've eaten enough chicken at those damn dinners to last me a lifetime, but if the governor doesn't get done with his shit soon, we'll be forced to eat those steaks we brought with us from Chicago."

Again the two men laughed and continued talking to one another. The agent who went out to the road was back and looking for the governor.

"Where's the governor?" he asked.

"What can I say, the man's full of shit," said a laughing Senator Wear as he made his way toward the transport van. "My God, didn't you hear his last state of the state speech?" At that exact moment the governor reappeared and Wear said to him, "Hell, I thought we were going to have to send a search party out to look for you."

"Well, all you would have had to do is follow the stink," chuckled the governor.

The dog handler said, "Is everyone ready now? If so, get in the van and follow me. We're going out about three-quarters of a mile to the east to an area that hasn't been hunted much this fall. I checked on the birds out there last weekend and they're plentiful. It's lucky for you guys the ten-year grouse cycle is at its peak."

The hunting party got in the van and followed the pickup truck. Chu immediately emerged from his hiding place as the van vanished into the woods. He knew it would be easy to follow the tire tracks after the rain that had fallen the day before. And three-quarters of a mile was a snap to jog for a former Vietcong officer, even in full camouflage. Chu checked the surroundings one last time to make sure there was no one else around who would blow his cover. When he was sure he was alone, Chu moved cautiously around the side of the garage and slid behind the dog kennels. He walked to the end of the kennels and looked toward the lodge. The backside of the lodge was filled with windows, and he wanted to make damn sure there was no one looking out in his direction. He saw no one, so he moved slowly out onto the exit road and shifted into tracking mode. He jogged along at a steady pace, stopping every couple hundred feet or so to listen for engine noise or human voices. He had been on the road for approximately seven to eight minutes when he heard a whistle blow. He stopped, went down on all fours, and crawled up to the next curve in the road where he saw the hunting party gathered near the van.

"Okay, listen up people. We're going to hunt this area in that direction for about two hundred yards," said the dog handler as he pointed to the woods up in front of him. "By that time you should be at the south edge of a large pond. We'll stop there and head west. Any questions?"

The Secret Service men had a question. They wanted to know where they should walk.

"Senator? Governor? Where do you want these two men?" asked Mr. Vance.

"I don't know," responded Wear. "Where do you think they should be, Lester?"

"I say we give them shotguns and let them hunt alongside us. They might as well have some fun as long as they have to be out here."

Wear said, "Sounds good to me. But keep your service pistols close, in case you have to use them. Okay?"

The two Secret Service men nodded and went over to the pickup to get a couple of twelve-gauge shotguns and ammo. The party started their walk when everyone was locked and loaded.

Chu moved swiftly to the vehicles as soon as the hunting party was out of sight. He wanted to disable them. The first thing he did was slash a couple of tires on each vehicle, then looked and found keys in the ignition of the van. He took them and tossed them deep into the woods. There were no keys in the pickup, so he popped the hood and pulled all the ignition wires from the distributor cap. Chu had made certain that no one was going to use these vehicles to go for help.

Chu was afoot again, cautiously following the hunting party while making sure he stayed a safe distance behind the group. He was walking through a heavily tree-lined area when he happened upon a small knoll. He started to inch his way up when he heard the flutter of wings followed by the sound of numerous shotgun blasts. That brought him to an abrupt halt. He then heard the handler say to the dogs, "Fetch 'em up." Chu used that time to crawl to the top of the knoll where he had total view of the party. He was so close that a fart could be heard. He watched attentively as the party high-fived themselves and began to move on toward the pond. Chu had drawn his weapon at the knoll, but he knew it was the wrong place to be taking a shot at the major. He could have easily missed with all the trees that were in the way. He knew he would have to wait for the right moment and place to do the killing.

The party continued on for the next hour shooting one grouse after another. Chu estimated they had eight to ten birds by now as they moved into a thicker wooded area. They were bunched together because of the terrain, which made an attack much more difficult. Chu checked his compass and saw the hunting party was heading in a southerly direction, back toward the lodge. It was ten thirty and Chu was getting antsy. He had hoped to have killed Wear by now and be on his way down the highway to his next stop, but that was not the case. So he decided to head them off at the next clearing to see what that would produce.

He was about to make his move when one of the dogs ran up to him for a sniff. Chu kicked the dog in the ass to make him go away. The dog let out a yelp, then headed back in the direction of the hunting party.

One of the Secret Service men said, "Did you hear that?"

The dog handler replied, "Don't worry. That happens all the time. The dogs step in holes every once in a while and they make that noise. Let's move on."

"Are you sure? I think I need to go back and check it out," said Agent Shawn O'Reilly.

"You can if you like," said Wear. "We'll move on and you can catch up with us later. But don't be gone too long. You don't want to get lost in these woods. You might not find your way back."

The hunting party moved out as Agent O'Reilly walked back to the wooded area where he had heard the dog let out the sound. Chu froze when he saw the man coming. He had no place to run, plus he would have been seen. It was time to form a plan, and fast. He made a quick decision to move back to a large pine tree that was a couple of yards behind him. From there he could kneel and watch as the agent approached. Chu spotted him walking no more than ten feet to his left and about fifty feet to his front. He held the Beretta in his right hand. He knew he would have to kill the agent if he got too close. He didn't want to, but he instinctively knew he had to or risk being seen. The agent continued to slowly make his way toward Chu. He would take a few steps, then stop and listen. Then another and another until he had cut the distance between the two in half. The woods were quiet, as if the agent had been in this situation before. Chu was beginning to wonder if the agent might have been his enemy at some point several years ago. He had gotten within ten feet of Chu when a huge ten-point buck came charging through the woods, running in the opposite direction of the two men. The deer startled the agent, sending him spinning around to his rear. Chu pounced on the opportunity to move around to the front of the tree where he took aim and shot the agent in the back of his neck. The bullet instantly shattered the agent's vertebra causing him to lurch forward and fall to the ground like a timber from a lumberjack's saw. The muffle of the silencer was almost nonexistent, which meant the only sound was that of the man's body as it crashed down onto the underbrush. Chu then rushed to the agent to see if he was dead. He put his hand to his neck and found a pulse. So he took aim again and pumped another round from his 9mm Beretta into the agent's skull.

Chu spent very little time covering the dead body with leaves and branches. He thought of letting the man live at one point, so the agent could walk away. But removing one agent was too inviting to pass up. It was time to move on and do it fast, as Chu needed to kill the major quickly now that one of the agents was missing.

It hadn't taken Chu more than ten minutes before he caught up to the main body of the party. From a short distance, he could see the dogs had retrieved a couple more birds while the party was taking a break at the edge of the woods.

The handler said, "Let's take ten here and then we'll hunt this meadow out in front of us."

Chu heard the lone Secret Service agent say, "I wonder where Shawn is? He should have caught up to us by now."

Wear puffed on his cigarette and replied, "Why don't you give him a call on your radio?"

The agent pulled out his radio and tried to contact the now dead Shawn O'Reilly, who was already starting the decaying process in the woods to their rear. He tried several times to contact O'Reilly without any luck. It was good that Chu had turned off

Shawn's radio and left it with him. The agent tried O'Reilly one more time and said, "Maybe I should go looking for him?"

Wear, stepping on his lit cigarette said, "I'm not sure that's a good idea. I don't know what's happened to him, but we need you with us just in case there's something wrong."

Governor Chance chimed in with, "Do you think we're in danger?"

"I don't think so," said Wear. "But I do feel we need to take precautions and hope Shawn shows up. Leave him one more message to meet us back at the vehicles or at the lodge, in case he's behind a hill or something and can't respond."

"No problem. Will do, senator," said the agent.

The hunting party milled around for the full ten minutes, which was just enough time to allow Chu to get in position in the meadow. Chu had crawled to the opposite end and took cover in the tall grass. He figured two-thirds of the way across the meadow would be a good ambush point to work from. There were several clusters of shrubs dotting the area and he found one to his liking. From that position he had the option of crawling from one cluster to another, which would eventually put him on a direct path with the major. It was the perfect hiding place. No one would be expecting him, nor would anyone walk through the scrubby thicket if they could walk the grassy area.

The assassin hadn't been in place more than two minutes when he heard the handler say, "I want the two of you to fan out about sixty to seventy feet from either side of me and walk this meadow in a straight line. There's a gravel pit up at the end near the tree-line and I think we'll scare up a few more birds somewhere around that point. I'll work the dogs up the middle with me. Is everyone ready?"

With the handler's command, the party moved forward. The senator was to the right of the handler and the governor to his left. The remaining agent and Vance went up to post the corners at the end of the meadow.

Chu was now semi-encircled in the center of the hunting party, and positioned no more than seventy yards in front of the major and about fifty yards from the gravel pit. He continued to move closer to the shrub and hung tight as he waited for the major to come to him. It wasn't long before one of the dogs found Chu again. It was the same pointer he'd kicked earlier and it was now poking him in the face with his wet nose. This time the dog did a quick retreat, seemingly knowing what the man had done to him the last time the two had met. Chu knelt in ambush shaking from the cold and the anticipation of a kill, while he listened to the approaching men as they talked to one another. He took a quick peek through the thicket and saw the major was in direct line with him. He was closing the gap fast. Chu turned his head back toward the gravel pit and prayed to Buddha to make this a successful kill. He heard the major approach as the sound of his legs moving through the underbrush got closer and closer. Chu glanced up from his position and saw the major had passed him and was now standing just three feet to his front. The major took one more step when everything exploded like he had stepped on a land mine. Birds flushed, shotguns went off, and Chu took aim and placed a bullet directly behind Wear's right ear. That one was for you, Nye, he said to himself. The major fell forward and was dead before he hit the ground.

Chu immediately started crawling to the west of the meadow as he began his escape. He knew it was best to go slow until the party located the major. By that time he might be over to the edge of the meadow and heading into the woods.

Governor Chance said, "Good shooting," as he looked right to congratulate Wear. "Where's the senator?" Chance yelled.

The governor and the dog handler looked around for a couple of seconds, while calling out his name. There was no answer, so the two men started to look for him. They eventually converged at a point where the senator had been walking and found him on the ground.

"He's bleeding," said Chance. "Someone must have hit him with some pellets when we shot at those last birds."

The Secret Service man was now running at full stride toward the men. He got to the senator about the time the dog handler said, "Half of his face is gone."

The agent stopped to look and see if there was an assassin lurking that might be waiting to kill them all. He went into an instant defensive mode and began a perimeter search. It wasn't long after that when he heard Vance yelling out, "Look over there in the tree-line to the east. There's a man in the woods." The agent immediately put his shotgun to his shoulder, took aim, and unloaded his gun. It was lucky for Chu that he was almost out of range and the fact that the hunting party was using birdshot. The pellets hit the trees around Chu, with some of them harmlessly catching him in the back of his right shoulder. They barely penetrated his clothing and never even knocked him off stride. The agent dropped his shotgun and drew his service pistol, emptying the side arm at the assassin more so out of desperation than anything else. But by that time Chu was deep into the woods and hidden in cover. The agent yelled, "Fuck!" at the top of his lungs. The scream was out of frustration at not using his pistol with his first attempt at shooting the assassin.

The agent looked back at the now smaller group of men and said, "Take the senator to the lodge, contact the authorities and tell them what has happened out here. I'm going after the assassin." The agent threw off his coat and began a full-out dash for the woods where the assassin had disappeared. The agent was bigger and most probably faster than the assassin, besides the assassin was loaded down with camouflage and clothing. And the assassin wasn't going to stop and disrobe; that would take precious extra time.

So the chase was on. The agent could hear crashing in the woods up ahead of him, but it was a long way off. He was gaining ground, but would it be enough to get to the assassin before he disappeared altogether. He stopped for a split second to listen for noise, but heard nothing. Then the crashing began again. The assassin had been listening for him too.

Meanwhile, Chu had stopped to catch his breath and check his compass. He was a little off course to the north. The one thing he didn't want to do was to hit the main blacktop and find out he was a long way away from where he had stashed the car. So he moved on steadily, trying to be quiet like he had been in the jungles of Vietnam. He had been chased many times by the enemy, but always managed to elude them.

He trotted for ten more minutes until he came upon a large clearing that ran northwest by southeast. It was at least fifty yards wide. The area looked as if it had gone through a tornado back two or three years ago, as trees were twisted and knocked down in a southeasterly direction. They were not going to be easy to maneuver over, but he had to do it before the agent got to the clearing. Chu had nothing but clothing on now and he was hot and sweating, even in this low forty-degree temperature. He dashed to the downed trees and started to climb over them like a monkey. They were easier than he thought to maneuver over. He was about four-fifths of the way over them when he heard a shot ring out behind him. The bullet struck the huge poplar tree next to his head as bark flew up in front of his eyes. Another shot rang out and then another and another, each one landing harmlessly in tree limbs around him. He was near the end of the storm-damaged area when he heard one last shot ring out and felt a sting in his left arm. A bullet from the agent had grazed him as he fell over the last branch of the downed timber.

"I got you, asshole," screamed the Secret Service agent. "I'm coming and I'm going to put another round up your ass before the day is over." The agent then rushed across the opening, leaping over downed trees as if he were a lynx running through the twisted mess. He was gaining a lot of ground on the assassin. The agent holstered his gun and began to climb over the downed trees as he watched Chu running in the direction of the woods. The agent had almost completely closed the gap between the two of them and was about to leap over the last log when he got his ankle caught in a branch. He twisted it, but he couldn't let that stop him from pursuing the assassin. He yanked his leg out of the branch and rolled over the last log as he fell to the ground. He then knelt on his good knee to check out the extent of the injury. It wasn't bad, but it was going to slow him down.

The advantage of the foot race was now with the assassin. The two men continued to move closer and closer to the blacktop. Chu was widening the distance between himself and the agent. Every now and then the agent would get a slight glimpse of the assassin and shoot at him in futility. The agent was losing his battle with the assassin, but he couldn't give up. He owed it to the senator and his fellow agent to keep up the fight.

Chu could tell he was almost to the blacktop from the sound of car tires on the pavement. They were just beyond the edge of the forest to his right. He stopped one last time to check his compass. He was heading in the right direction, but he wasn't sure where he was. That meant he needed to move to the road to get his bearings. It would be dangerous, as the road would expose him to the agent if he had flanked Chu and was moving up on it. It also meant he could be seen by passing motorists, and that was something Chu desperately wanted to avoid at all costs.

He decided to take a quick peek and then move back into the woods, unless he was already where he needed to be. Chu stepped out onto the blacktop, looking up and down the road in both directions. He didn't see the agent or any vehicles, and he also didn't have any idea where he was. He thought he was south of the car, but he couldn't tell how far. So he slipped back into the woods and began moving rapidly in the direction he thought the car was hidden.

He had traveled what he thought was about a quarter-mile and stepped out on the road again, at which time he saw a sign far up ahead that he thought read Buck Horns Lodge. Chu couldn't be sure if he was right, so he pulled out his binoculars and saw he was correct. There was little time to waste; he now needed to move up the road quickly to find his car, which was back in the woods about thirty to forty yards. He covered the distance quickly, staying to the inside of the tree-line. When he finally got to the correct spot, he ran across to the old logging road on the other side that led to his vehicle.

Finding his way to the car, he rapidly changed out of his camouflage jacket and into a red Wisconsin Badger sweatshirt he had purchased at the bait shop. He pulled out his ball cap, wiped his forehead with his sleeve, and said to himself…I'm home free. He put the baseball cap on and secured his weapons in his gym bag. He got in the car, backed it into the woods, and got the rear tire stuck in a rut. Chu exited the vehicle and saw the hole the tire had dug was not too deep, so he got back in the car and tried to rock it back and forth. That just made things worse. So he got out of the car once again and looked around for some old logs that he could put under the right rear tire. That took about three more minutes. He got back in his car once again and floored the vehicle. This time it bounced along a little and went forward toward the road.

Meanwhile, the agent had found the blacktop during the time Chu had spent trying to get the vehicle unstuck. He was limping along when he heard the car's engine whining. He followed the noise and found the logging road. He held up his service pistol to the firing position as he walked steadily down the dirt road. There were several tree branches blocking his view, but he still had a general sense the vehicle was up in front of him. He was still walking when he heard the vehicle coming in his direction as it crashed through the woods. So the agent stopped and got ready to fire at the oncoming vehicle.

Chu was heading out to make his getaway when he ran smack-dab into the agent at about twenty miles per hour. The agent went to the ground as his firearm discharged harmlessly into the sky. Chu felt the front axle bounce over the body and the undercarriage scrape something while dragging it along until the car hit the opening of the blacktop. The body dislodged at that point, causing the rear left tire to run him over.

Chu didn't stop to see if the agent was dead or if there was any damage to the car. He continued to head back toward Tomahawk. Chu figured if the authorities had been contacted they would more than likely think he was headed north. Going south was a calculated risk, but it seemed to hold logic. Chu was moving rapidly when he came upon the big bend in the road near Mud Lake. He slowed the car and looked for the next sharp corner at Green Lake. Once past Green Lake, Chu gunned the engine again. He was approaching Tomahawk when he heard sirens up ahead. He slowed the car to the speed limit as a state trooper flew by him doing at least a hundred miles per hour. That car was closely followed by a local cop and an ambulance.

Chu held his car steady to the thirty-mile-per-hour speed-limit as he entered the north side of town. He had to drive to the middle of Tomahawk before he could get to the intersection at County Road S. He drove slowly as more and more police and state troopers began to arrive on the scene. When he got to the intersection of Highway 81 and County Road J he took a right. He wasn't down the road more than a half mile when he looked in his rearview mirror and saw a roadblock being put up at the intersection he had just left.

Chu was exhausted, but he couldn't stop for fear of being caught. All he knew was he needed to put miles between him and the killings as fast as possible. He also knew he had to stop and check the damages to the front of the car. He had to make sure there wasn't anything that could connect his car to the presumably dead agent. When he was sure things had settled down, he grabbed the road map from under the gym bag and looked to find the best way to get to I-35W. Chu was headed to Minneapolis. He had an appointment with someone that was long overdue.

Chapter 18

I could hear the phone ringing somewhere in my subconscious. I had been out all night at the casino playing blackjack and drinking vodka with a contractor friend of mine who had done a lot of remodeling work in my house. I was presently in a state of mind somewhere between drunk and half-asleep when I rolled over and saw it was seven o'clock in the morning. I muttered to myself, who's the fucking asshole calling me at this time on a Saturday morning? Don't people know I don't get up until 10:00 a.m. on the weekends? Whoever is calling better have a good excuse for waking me up.

I picked up the phone and heard an overly excited Kate Rutan asking me, "Ian, did you see the news last night?"

"Hold on Kate. Take a deep breath and I'll be with you in a minute."

I got up, stretched and went to the bathroom to splash some water on my face. I needed a few seconds to get my bearings. "Okay, I'm back, and the answer to your question is yes, I did see the news last night and it was as I had predicted. So, now I suppose you want to know if the senator who was killed in Wisconsin was the same man I was referring to during our last conversation."

"I don't need to ask because I already know the answer to that question. That's not why I called. I called because I received a phone call from Ralph Yorkshire at six thirty this morning. He's pissed at me and wants to meet with you today as soon as possible."

I stood up and began pacing. I needed a distraction like a cigarette. The problem is I didn't smoke. Instead, I went to the refrigerator and went for a Coke. It gave me instant energy. I took a big gulp and said, "Did you say anything to him this morning or earlier this week? I really don't give a shit about the day; I just want to know what he knows. So tell me, did you say anything to him because I need to know what I'm going to be up against when I meet this guy."

"I've said nothing to him. Believe me Ian, I told him exactly want you told me to say and not a word more. He knows you're connected to the killings, so he needs information from you to help the FBI solve the murders. And what do you mean you predicted the killing? You never said that to me."

"Yeah, well about that. I spoke to one of my old platoon buddies and I must have said that to him. I do remember telling him I was sure Senator Wear would be dead by the end of the week. Presto, call me a fuckin' mind-reader, but I was right. I didn't tell you because you would've gotten more scared than you already are. Plus, I didn't want you to have any information that you might accidentally leak to Yorkshire."

I paused a few seconds to gather my thoughts. I didn't want to anger Kate, so I needed to use a little humor to lighten the situation.

"Forgive me?" I asked. "Dinner and drinks on me? How does that sound?"

"It's going to cost you more than food and booze, Ian."

"Okay then, we'll go bear hunting. That should fix things."

"Stop screwing around and listen to me. I need to call Ralph back with a time and place for the three of us to meet."

"Why all three of us? Why don't I meet up with the dogcatcher by myself? You don't need to be there."

"Yes I do. I'll need to be there to introduce you and get in between the two of you when you start strangling each other."

"Hey, even I know better than to get violent with an FBI agent."

"That's to be seen. Anyway, where and when do you want to meet?"

"Tell him to be at the Iron Horse at 11:00 a.m. today. I think I can get my story together by then. Does that work for you?"

"That'll be fine. Tony can watch the little ones or maybe I'll drop them at my folks. See you at eleven."

I slammed the phone back down and said Fuck! No, double fuck! I was hoping to slip past the dogcatcher and slide my way into Ft. Dodge without ever going one on one with him. Meeting with him was a waste of my time. What was he going to tell me? Nothing, because I already knew everything I needed to know, with the exception of whom the killer was. And now I was positive I knew the answer to that too.

I no more than got off the phone with Kate and was halfway through taking a piss when it started ringing again. This time the call was from Tom Wheeler. Tom wanted to know if I had seen the news and what I was going to do about it. I told him I had a meeting with the regional director of the FBI in less than four hours, and I would call him back after I talked to the guy. I hung up, finished my piss, and got dressed for what was sure to be an eventful day.

The dogcatcher and Kate were on time. They walked through the door at the Iron Horse at exactly eleven o'clock. I got up from my chair and hugged Kate. I gave her a small kiss on the lips to let her agent-friend know I was fond of her. I was fond of her, but that was more than likely to change in the next few days. I had let Kate be drawn into this mess and I needed to do something about that before she and/or her kids wound up like the senator.

Kate said, "Ian, this is Ralph Yorkshire."

We both shook hands. Then the three of us found a table and sat at the back of the bar. The place was nearly empty at this hour of the morning, but still I wanted to be as far away from the patrons as possible so no one would be able to hear our conversation.

Kate said, "Where were you last night? I tried to call you several times."

I cleared my throat to keep from getting angry and said, "I didn't know I had to check in with you every night. Are you keeping track of me? Anyway, I was with a friend at the casino. You don't know him. His name is Lane Moreland and he has wife issues. The two of them are separated and thinking about divorce, so he asked me if I wanted to go gambling with him for a while. I got home about four this morning and I'm real tired, so let's get on with this shit so I can go back to bed. Here's twenty bucks, go up to the bar and have a couple Bloody Mary's while Ralph and I talk."

"Is that really necessary?"

"It's best that we do it this way. I think Ralph would agree with me when I say you're better off not knowing what we're about to talk about."

Kate took the twenty and went to sit at the close end of the bar. She gave me the one finger salute and ordered herself a drink.

Looking intensely at the agent sitting across the table I said, "Okay Ralph, what's on your mind?"

"I think you know what's on my mind, but first of all would you mind telling me your last name and how you're involved in this mess?"

"I'm not sure that's necessary."

"Have it your way Ian, but all I have to do is run the plates on your car, and I'll know your whole life story five minutes after we leave this place. So let's stop fuckin' around."

"Oh, so you want to sweet-talk me, do you? Okay, have it your way. My last name is Christian and I knew all of the dead men, except for that highway patrolman in South Carolina. My association with the group comes from my tour of duty back in Vietnam in 1969. And that's about all I know."

"Come on Ian; let's stop all the bullshit right here and now. You can feed me all the crap you want, but remember, I've done a lot of research on these murders. I've also been in contact with the bureau chief in Washington D.C., and I have a lot of information in this file in front of me that says you're lying."

He pushed a confidential file across the table to me, but kept his hand on top of it to prevent me from seeing its contents. Then he said, "I'll let you see the file under one condition."

"And what's that?" I asked.

"You can see it if you promise to end your relationship with Kate. She got hurt once a long time ago and I don't want that to happen to her again. Besides, we're not just talking feelings here. She's in real danger if the two of you continue to see each other. As of the moment, I believe whoever is behind these killings knows nothing about Kate, as the two of you just started your relationship in the last month. Would you agree?"

"First of all, fuck you, Ralph." I always liked to bond with a person right off the bat. It solidified relationships so well. "And yes, I do agree she could be in danger, especially after that murder in Wisconsin yesterday. But I don't think the person who's behind all of this shit knows of Kate. And as far as the file goes, I don't give a goddamn what's in it." So I smugly slid it back to him and said, "You can shove this up your ass. I don't need it."

"Are you sure about that, Ian? Maybe there are one or two small details in it that you could use."

"Use for what?"

"To pursue this man. That's what you want, isn't it?"

"I'm not sure I understand the meaning of your question."

"Come on Ian, it's obvious to me you want to take this man down as much as we do. You want him because he killed a friend of yours, and we want him because he is a serial killer. I don't much give a shit which one of us puts him in a body bag. But if you're thinking about doing it, then you have to end your relationship with Kate. Or I'll see that you wind up in jail. The only question is how bad do you want him?"

"I want him bad, but I'm in favor of the FBI doing it for me. So, don't expect me to get involved in your mess."

"Okay, have it your way Ian. But listen to me, I have reliable information about the killer that you might find, shall I say, helpful. I only need to fill in a few holes and we can go from there."

"Holes?"

"Yes, like who else besides yourself is involved in this. There must be at least a couple more people. Tell me their names and we'll protect all of you."

Well kiss my fuckin' white ass. The dogcatcher doesn't know about Tom and Fish. And I don't think he knows about the killer or the other intel officer who was there at Dak Sen Luc. I think he's fishing for answers and the asshole is using Kate as bait. So I said to him, "Then you know about Johnson and Phillips, my two old platoon buddies?"

"Yes we do."

"And about II Corps Colonel Wellington, the head intel officer behind the person who is doing all the killing?"

"Colonel Wellington," he stuttered as he wrote the name down on a small notepad that he took from the inside of his jacket. "Yes, we know about him too."

Now I knew he was lying. Two of the men I had just named were fictitious and the third was that colonel who sent my platoon into Laos to be killed. He was grasping at straws. The FBI really did need my help in solving these murders and that was the one thing I was going to make sure didn't happen. This changes the playing field, I thought to myself. I can lead the dogcatcher in all sorts of directions from here on out and it's going to be fun. And to top it off, Colonel Wellington is now going to be taken into custody and have a hot cattle prod shoved so far up his ass his tonsils will glow. The day just couldn't be going any better if I had planned it this way.

"So, what can I do to fill in those holes of yours?" I asked with a huge smirk on my face.

"Why don't you start at the beginning and we'll go from there."

"The beginning," I replied. "What beginning? Do you want me to start from the incident in Vietnam or from the time that Cummings was killed in Atlanta?"

"So you know Cummings was killed?"

"Of course, that's obvious at this point. He was there when all this began. And that's what got him killed."

So, I took Ralph back to that awful day in 1969. I told him the story about the capture of the three Vietcong and their subsequent interrogation. I said there were a couple of intel officers, those being the now dead Judge Foss and Senator Wear, who surfaced that day at Dak Sen Luc. They were transported to the location by the now dead pilots, Grayson Meeks and Dave Gunderson. There was also a South Vietnamese interpreter who was on one of the two helicopters whose name I did not know. The only other people who observed anything were the two men I mentioned before, those being Johnson and Phillips. I purposely left out any information about Perkins, the third intel officer who was there that day. And I said nothing about talking to Snake's widow, as she didn't need to be dragged into this and start the hurting process all over again. I also told him nothing about Wheeler or Fish. I figured I had him going in circles, and he would need another three or four days to figure out I was lying about the other names I had given him. I could use the time to develop a plan that would put a resolution to the situation.

"Is that all you know, Ian?"

"That's it. Are you going to show me the contents of this file now?"

"Are you going to stop seeing Kate?"

"No." I said. I was going to end it with Kate, but I wasn't going to give him the satisfaction of knowing that.

"So where do we go from here?" asked Agent Yorkshire.

"What do you mean, we, Ralph? There isn't any we in this scenario. I'm going back to work at the agency on Monday, and you're going to catch a killer. Isn't that how it's supposed to work?"

"Yeah that's right, but I think the FBI needs to put all of you under protective custody until this whole thing blows over."

"You mean like have someone ride to work with us or shadow us for the next decade? No thanks. I saw how well that worked for Senator Wear. Didn't he lose his life and his complete security detail? You can't protect me or any of us forever. Only I can protect me. If the killer sees someone hanging around, then he'll most likely kill that person. And that will continue until you're all out of agents. So, I suggest you find the killer's name and a picture to go along with it and capture him before you have a pile of dead agents lying around."

"And how do you suggest we do that?"

"How the hell should I know? You're the fuckin' FBI. You figure it out. Go back to your files and find the addresses of Johnson and Phillips and talk to them. Maybe they know something I don't, or maybe they might want you to put a protective detail on them. But not me, I don't want anyone hanging around my workplace. I'll tell you what you can do. I'm leaving on a trip to Dallas the early part of next week to talk to one of my clients. And logic suggests the killer is on his way to Minneapolis to find me. So why don't you put a couple of agents on the inside of my house after I leave town and see if the killer tries to break in. If he does, you've got him and this whole thing will be over. How does that sound?"

"That's a plan we can work with. But why don't we put a man outside your house until you decide to leave."

"That's a dumb idea Ralph. You'll just scare him away. He won't come around unless he thinks I am at home alone. And for the next day or two I'll be staying at Kate's place. *I said that to piss him off.* So, you can post a detail outside her apartment if you'd like. As a matter of fact, why don't you lead that team? I think Kate would love knowing you were outside her place watching over her and the children. I'll leave the key to my place with her and you can get it on Monday morning."

I could see I had gotten to the man from the grimmest look on his face. His reaction said it all. I had won and he had lost, but I didn't have time to gloat. I needed to go home and pack for my trip. The one I was making to Ft. Dodge, Iowa.

Chapter 19

The early part of the day had gone far better than I had anticipated. In the end, I had totally outsmarted one of Uncle Sam's top cops, and in the process gained valuable time to lure a madman into my trap. Knowing I had just beaten the dogcatcher at his own game almost made me want to pay my fair share of taxes. Yeah, like that was ever going to happen. Sometimes a person needs to win for the sake of winning and I had just won the lottery.

There was a lot to be done before I could head to Iowa. First of all, I had to talk to Jack Evans on Monday morning and let him know I was going down there to scope out some farms for a John Deere photo shoot. Then I would have to call Avis to rent a car to drive down to see Tom Wheeler, and somewhere in between all of that I needed to pack a couple of revolvers that my uncle had left me when he retired from the police force. He had given me a .357 Smith & Wesson magnum and a snub-nose .38 with an ankle holster. The two weapons would come in handy if and when I ran into the killer.

I was almost home when I turned onto Yalta Street, the road that ran from Constance Boulevard to the front door of my house. I looked in all directions for any signs of a vehicle that was new to the neighborhood or anything that said there was a crazy man out there who was looking to kill me. I didn't see anything I thought was out of the ordinary, so I pulled up to the mail box, took out the contents, and drove the Porsche up the driveway and into the garage.

I parked the car and went into the house, stopping briefly when I entered the door to the back hallway. I wanted to make damn sure there wasn't anyone waiting for me. When I thought the coast was clear, I moved down the hallway and into the kitchen where I set the mail on the countertop. I was sifting through the pile when I looked down and saw a large envelope with a Minneapolis postmark. It had yesterday's date and no return address. I instinctively knew who had sent it. I almost didn't need to open it because I already knew what was inside. And I was correct. The package contained the front page from Friday's *Minneapolis Tribune*. It had the day-old story about the killing of Senator Wear and his two Secret Service agents, and a little note from the killer. It read, "Catch you in Iowa." That was the extent of the message. I looked for more, but there wasn't anything else that would fill me in on the puzzle. Just - catch you in Iowa - which could only mean one thing. The killer was trying to coax me into going to Iowa where he thought he could kill two birds with one stone. He didn't have to send me an invitation, as I was already onboard with the reunion that wasn't going to end well for him.

"Hello Tom," I said. "I just got back from my meeting with the Feds and I think I'm going to be coming down to Iowa on Tuesday morning. Can you clear your slate for the rest of the week and send your family to visit their relatives?"

"I was hoping you would call with better news, but yes, I can do that. I've already talked to my wife and she likes the idea of taking the kids over to Nebraska for Halloween. She said it wasn't a real holiday, so she was fine going there without me. She also thought it was a good idea that I got together with one of my army buddies to reminisce for a while. So what are your plans, Ian?"

"All I can tell you for now is I will be leaving on Tuesday and driving down to Iowa. I'll get a room at a local motel when I get to Ft. Dodge and then I'll call you. I have an idea on how we can draw the killer out, but it will be risky and it involves using your farm. Are you alright with that?"

"I guess I'll have to be, but we're still going to try to capture him aren't we?"

"If we can we will, but if not, I'll have to take him out. The agent here in Minneapolis sort of gave me the impression I had carte blanche to take the killer down. He was actually trying to bargain with me."

"What do you mean bargain with you?"

"It's an odd situation Tom. The agent, his name is Ralph Yorkshire, has a thing for my girlfriend Kate. He tried to strike up a deal by using her as the bargaining chip. He wants me to end my relationship with her and all but assured me he was willing to turn his back on everything if I did that. I believe he's lying. I think he wants me to leave Kate and then fuck me in the process. Again, it's a long story, and I can tell you more when I get down there."

"The question is do you want to get rid of Kate?"

"Yes and no. I'm wavering on the issue, but I'm leaning toward the yes, if only for her sake and her kids' too. She got caught up in all this by mistake and she doesn't deserve to get hurt. But let's get back to the plan. Where's your farm located?"

"It's approximately twelve miles south of Ft. Dodge, not too far from the little town of Otho. I have seven hundred and eighty-eight acres of land and only a small percentage has been harvested at this point."

"And what does the property look like that surrounds the house?"

"The usual stuff. There's the house, of course. And behind that is a barn with an attached tool shop, a couple of silos, some cattle and hog pens, various implements, and a small grove of trees to the south side of the house. I also have a large number of round hay bales beyond the cattle pens."

"And what about the crops? You said you had corn and bean fields. Is that right?"

"Corn and bean are all we do. There's a large soybean field beyond the trees to the south and corn to the north. We also have corn behind the barn and across the road."

"And do you have any farm dogs?"

"As a matter of fact I do. I've got an albino German shepherd named Omar. Why do you want to know that?"

"Dogs are always good to have around to help with first alert. Does he like people?"

"He's friendly enough to those he knows. Once I introduce you to him he'll be fine."

"Let me ask you this. What's he like if he doesn't know you?"

"Well, there is a good chance he'll bite or attack you, but I'm not too sure of that because everyone around here knows him."

"And where do you keep him at night?"

"I usually put him in the barn, unless I know there are coyotes in the area. Then I let him run loose. But I could keep him in the house if that's what you are asking."

"Good, I think we can use him. We'll talk more about that later. So here's what I want you to do. I need you to go out and clear all the corn behind the barn for no less than an eighth of a mile. And you might want to take down the first ten to twenty rows across the street too. You're also going to have clear the corn on one side of the house, but don't worry about the bean field. He won't be coming from that direction. It doesn't afford him any cover. Do you think you can get all that done in the next four days?"

"I think so. I'll call my brother-in-law this evening and see if he can come over and help me with the grain wagons. What do you have in mind Ian?"

"Well Tom, I'm not completely sure until I see your farm. But our main focus will be to force the killer to come at us from the main road. I want him to walk up to your farmhouse and knock on the front door."

"You're kidding, aren't you?"

"Yes, of course I am. I don't actually expect him to come knocking, but I wouldn't put it past him to do something like that. This guy is slick and very dangerous. He's also bold, as he has killed in broad daylight and at the side of a major highway. And if you've been watching the news, you know he killed the senator right under the noses of two Secret Service men. That's why we need to have a great game plan. We also need to stay calm and be able to communicate with each other at all times, which reminds me I need to stop at Radio Shack before I leave town."

"Ian, you said you were going to stay at a motel in Ft. Dodge. Why not just come and stay at the farmhouse with me? There's lots of room."

"No Tom, I have to stay in the shadows for a couple of days before we meet. I need to get a feel for the area, so I'll drive around for the first day to check all the routes that run into and out of your property. I want to check out the neighbors too."

"There's something else I haven't told you. I got an envelope in today's mail. It contained the front page from yesterday's Minneapolis newspaper. There was a message written near the headline, just like the one you received. It said, catch you in Iowa. And I think I know what he meant by that. I believe the killer wants me there to be with you, and I'm not going to let him have that opportunity until we're good and ready. I know he thinks he's baiting me and I'm going to let him think we're hungry fish. "

"Are you sure about all this Ian? I hate being the target of a madman and have something drastically go wrong, so my wife and kids are left without anyone to take care of them. I mean, we still can call your agent and have the FBI come down here to catch the guy."

"And what are they going to do Tom? Bring down a bunch of cars and trucks full of surveillance equipment. Put down hundreds of footprints for the killer to see while they try to hide and wait. That would be a surprise, wouldn't it? No Tom, we need to lure him in and do it ourselves. I believe I have a plan that will work just fine. I'll see you in a few days."

Chapter 20

"Tell me you're not going to do something stupid," said an angry Kate Rutan.

"Okay, I'm not going to do something stupid. Although some may call it crazy and others might even say it's insane, all I know is I have to do this on my own. If I don't, the guy behind all these murders will get away and possibly never be caught. Or he'll go to jail for the rest of his life. And I can't let either of those things happen. I owe it to Snake and those other men he has killed to take him out, even if I don't really give a shit about the senator or the judge."

"But why does it have to be you? Odds are the police or FBI will shoot and kill this guy when they eventually find him. I can't believe the killer will let the authorities take him alive."

"I agree with you Kate."

"Wait a minute; you're agreeing with something I've said. That's a first. So why can't you let this go?"

"It's like this. I've killed a lot of people in my lifetime because I had to or they deserved it. God is never going to forgive me for what I've done to all those people, so doing this isn't going to change a thing when I finally sit down and have our little chat."

"That's just plain idiotic."

"Whatever. It's just something I have to do. Let's change the subject. Have you heard from the dogcatcher?"

"Yes I have. He has positioned some of his people outside in the parking lot. I understand there are two agents out there and a couple more in a vacant apartment on the third floor. He said he would call in the morning to see if everything was alright. He gave me a number to call if we should need help in the meantime."

"So, is he one of those people up in the vacant apartment?"

"I think so, but he didn't actually tell me that. Why do you have such a problem with him?"

It took every ounce of restraint in my body to not tell Kate about Ralph. I wanted to tell her that he wanted me out of the way so he could fuck her. Instead I said, "Oh, I have my reasons. But it seems to me the guy has something for you. Down deep he cares for your safety, and that says his desires go a lot deeper than what you see on the surface."

I had no intention of telling Kate that the dogcatcher had tried to bribe me this afternoon. She would have hated him for doing that. Nor did I want her to think I was giving her a line of bullshit about him. So I decided to stay impartial on the issue of his feelings for her. If she thought we were cutting cards for her she might blow up and tell me to get out. And I wanted to make sure that didn't happen because I needed to be here in case the killer showed up at her doorstep. Those cops could pretend to protect her, but I knew differently. Besides, I still wasn't sure what I was going to do about Kate. That decision would have to wait until this situation was over.

"Tell me Ian, aren't you even a little bit afraid of what might happen?"

"No. I'm Superman. Or did you forget that? And later on tonight I'll show you my super powers."

"Now you're starting to sound like the old Ian."

"No, the old Ian is something of the past, Kate. I've transformed myself. Or maybe I should say I have transgressed myself back to an image of someone I like to call Sam the Nam man. Either way, I've stopped being the person you met back at Duffy's. I'm feeling and acting like I'm back in the war again because that's exactly what this is. It's a war against an enemy. I have to feel that way or I'll lose my edge. I can't afford not to be serious right now because I have to catch a killer and put an end to the terror he has brought to my friends and us. I know you probably don't understand what I'm saying, but you need to believe in what I'm doing. You need to do this for yourself and your children."

Kate stared at me for the longest time with one of those, are-you-for-real looks and said, "Sam the Nam man?"

"Forget that, Kate."

"Okay, then is the old Ian ever going to come back?"

"God, I hope so. I've worked hard over the last thirteen or so years to get my sanity back. You probably can't understand what I'm trying to tell you because you've never been where I have. You haven't had to kill people to feel safe, but that's what I've had to do. Just trust me Kate."

"It's hard, Ian. It's real hard, but I just don't know what else to say."

"There's nothing more to be said on the subject. But there is something else I want to discuss with you and that is whether or not I can still trust you to keep quiet about all this. By that I mean, do you still promise to keep everything I've told you to yourself?"

"You know I will, Ian."

"Good. That's important because the whole city of Minneapolis is going to be crawling with Feds come Monday morning. And I don't plan on being around to talk to any of them. I'm leaving town on Tuesday morning, and I probably won't be back for a week. Now listen to me. I told Ralph I was flying down to Dallas to see a client. That's a lie. I'm actually getting a rental car and driving down to Iowa to meet up with one of the guys from my old platoon. He's one of two remaining men who are still alive from that patrol back in '69. I'm not going to tell you where he lives or his name, should you get tempted to tell the Feds what they want to know."

"Believe me Kate, I understand the FBI completely. I had a major encounter with their military counterpart back in Vietnam. They wanted to put me in jail for murder. Their idea of justice was guilty until proven innocent. It took everything I had to get the situation resolved. They finally let me go after I told them everything they wanted to know. And they weren't going to do that until I gave up the killer. They're an extremely complex group of people, and they're seldom paranoid because they know they have the law on their side. They work you hard to make you think they're in this to help, but what they really want is the power over you. And they don't give a damn if they hurt you in the process. Most of these guys are lawyers, and when have you ever seen a lawyer who doesn't talk out of both sides of his or her mouth? Hell, FBI agents wouldn't tell the truth if the pope was standing next to them giving them absolution. So don't believe any of the bullshit they're going to feed you. Just tell them what I told you to say – I'm flying to Texas. Do you understand me?"

She nodded and said, "But…"

"No buts, just repeat what I said. You need to stay to the plan or else my friend and I might wind up dead. Okay?"

"Okay."

"I need you to help me because I need the extra time to work on my plan. I think I can lure the killer into a trap, but that won't happen until possibly Halloween night. A very ghoulish plan I might add. Anyway, I can't have the Feds around because they will contact the local authorities in Iowa, and even you can understand what that will mean. I could be dealing with the likes of a Barney Fife, and he could fuck things up so bad he'd get Tom and me killed."

"I understand. So what do you think Ralph is going to do?"

"I'm sure he ran to the nearest secure phone after the three of us met this afternoon and called his boss in D.C. The Feds are probably forming some sort of task force as we speak, and I believe they will be here tomorrow afternoon or Monday morning at the latest. And that's when they're going to want to talk to me, but I'll have vanished by that time. So, when they find out

I'm gone they'll stick you in a room and pump you for answers. That's why you have to stay calm and act dumb. Just tell them I've left town for Dallas and you don't know when I'll be back. Tell them I specifically didn't want to tell you anything for your own protection. They'll buy that, especially Yorkshire. By the way, make sure he's there when the Feds talk to you. It will take them awhile to check over all the flights to Dallas before they realize I didn't go there."

"They also need time to check on the two men in my platoon who I said were with me in Vietnam. I gave the dogcatcher phony names, but I'm assuming they will dig pretty deep into the army files and come up with the right two guys within a day or so. And by that time I'll be deep into my plan. I need a minor distraction, and you're the right person to set that in motion. If they need a bone, throw them this one. Tell them you remembered me saying that one of the men in my platoon lives somewhere in the Dallas area and I planned on seeing him when I went down there. That should fuck them up for a while and keep them reeling."

Kate sort of smiled and slightly nodded her head in agreement. She put her fingers to her lips and gazed at me with an expression of love for what I was doing and said, "What else do you want me to do?"

"Well, I want you to stay close to the phone all week long. Tell me, do they have one down where you work in the Crystal Court?"

"Yes they do." Kate went to a kitchen drawer to get some paper and a pen and said, "Here, I'll write the number down for you on this piece of paper."

"No, I'd rather you write it down on this business card the dogcatcher gave me. That way I don't have to be searching all over the place when I need to make the calls. I plan on calling you, and then you can contact Ralph if I ask you to do so. Or I can call him directly, but that leaves a phone number that he can trace. Either way, I might need both Ralph's and your assistance, so be aware that I might be getting in contact with you throughout the week."

"God Ian, is this the kind of stuff that my ex-husband went through when he worked for the CIA? If so, I need to feel differently about him than what I do."

"I would assume so. Only Bill probably didn't have the luxury of knowing someone had his back. Foreign espionage is a lot different than domestic terror. At least I know where I can go for help or a safe place to hide. He had neither one of those. No, most of the time he was out there on an island all by himself. At least I know I have you and my friend in Iowa to help me."

"Thanks Ian. That was a nice thing to say about me." She came over and gave me a hard kiss on the lips and said, "I feel a little better now knowing I'll be of some assistance to you."

I wasn't going to let her think otherwise. I needed her on my side, and if she thought she was an asset, then so be it. That was a good thing for both of us. I could count on her keeping her mouth shut, and I also made her feel like she was an important part of what I was trying to accomplish. "There's something else Kate. I think you should keep Yorkshire around for a while. Have him drive you to and from work every day. That will also keep him close to you in case I need to contact either one of you. Just keep him by your side; at least until I tell you I have the situation under control. That might not be easy, but do it for me and for your children."

"So Ian, does this mean you're going to tell Ralph or someone in the FBI that you've killed the guy when this is all over?"

"Hell no! That would be pure lunacy. The government doesn't give anybody a free pass, especially when it comes to killing someone. They don't forgive people for killing serial killers, even if the bad guys should happen to be Charlie Manson or Ted Bundy. They'd probably stick me away for a real long time, maybe for the rest of my life. No, I'm going to dispose of the body where no one will ever find it and come home and deal with the Feds. I'll eventually sit down in a room and tell them I went to Iowa to look at some places to do a photo shoot and got a little rooster hunting in while I was there. I'll tell them I didn't like the idea of them putting a tail on me, so I gave them and you false information about my whereabouts. That's not a crime unless I'm a suspect, which I am not. It's that simple, Kate, and they can't do a damn thing about it. And when they're done with me, they'll continue to search for the killer, and he'll be on the FBI's Ten Most Wanted list forever. The best part of all of this is I can eventually go into any post office whenever I like and see a picture of the guy, and know he's dead and gone forever. And I can have the satisfaction of knowing I put him there."

"That doesn't seem right to let the government waste their valuable time on a ghost," said Kate.

"You know I kind of like that thought."

"What thought?"

"Well, that's exactly what I'm planning to do to this guy. Make him a ghost. And what makes it even better is I'm planning to do it on Halloween night. You know Kate, sometimes I crack myself up with all the shit that goes around in my head."

"So you do plan on killing this guy? Are you positive you don't want to bring him to justice?"

"What justice? You mean leave it to the politicians or the lawyers who will say the killer was getting justice for his brothers? Shit, unless the state that prosecutes him actually has capital punishment, he'll just sit and rot in jail until he dies. And I don't want that. I want him to pay for his crimes with his life and I'm the only one who can guarantee that will happen."

"But what if something should happen to your friend who's helping you?"

"He knows the risk and I'll be there to protect him like I'm here to protect you."

"What do you mean by that?"

"Wait a minute; you didn't think I came here tonight with the thought of throwing a toaster or a rolling pin at the killer if he should happen to show up. Did you? Or did you think all you had to do was call the dogcatcher if the killer should happen to get by the agents out in the parking lot? No, I don't think that's how it works. You don't go into a gunfight without a gun and that's why I brought a couple of Smith & Wesson pistols along with me to make sure both sides are even. As a matter of fact, I almost want him to come after me tonight, but not with you here. You mean a lot to me Kate. And I wouldn't have come here tonight if I thought the kids would have been home. That would have been too risky, but I wasn't going to come over unless I was sure I could protect you. Is that okay with you?"

"It's fine with me Ian. My ex-husband had all sorts of guns around the whole time I was married to him, so they don't scare me."

I replied, "So we're good then?"

"Yeah, we're good. And speaking of being good; isn't it about time you show me those super powers you were bragging about earlier?"

"I forgot my cape."

Kate turned around and went to the second drawer near the kitchen sink and returned with a long, white dishtowel. She took out a colored marker and put a big red "S" in the middle of it and tied it around my neck. "Now you have one, so show me what you've got," she said with a laugh.

"I tell you what, why don't you open a bottle of wine and we can watch Saturday Night Live. And after that, I'll show you the real reason why they call me the Man of Steel."

"I have a better idea." With a wicked look in her eyes she said, "Why don't we play bad doctor and dirty nurse instead of watching television? And I'll give you one guess as to which one of us is going to be the dirty nurse."

I replied with my best Groucho Marx impression, "It can't be me because I don't look good in garter belts."

"But I do!"

"Ohhhhhhhhhhhhh Kate! You must have read my mind. And do you have a nurse's outfit too?"

"Well, sort of. I used to work in a dental office and we had to wear a white uniform. Will that do the trick?"

"It sure will! And do you have all the accessories that go along with the uniform to make me feel like we're in a real examination room?"

"You actually had to ask me that question? Ian, I think you're losing your touch. Yes, if course I do. And I have just the right undergarments to tie the whole outfit together. And guess what?"

"You want to invite the dogcatcher in so he can watch."

"No stupid. Try again."

"You want to play Monopoly so I can use my card."

"I really do think you're stupid sometimes. I would've thought you would've remembered that everything falls right off without…"

"Oh, yeah! Déjà vu. Dorothy, I think I've been here before. So, why don't you get dressed up and I'll show you the big red weasel? Isn't that how Dan put it the night we met at the bar?"

"Yeah, I think it went something like that. But somehow I think your red weasel will be much more satisfying than his ever would."

"That's me. I aim to please."

"So you don't want to watch Saturday Night Live or have a bottle of wine?"

"Later. Much later."

With that she pulled me into the bedroom and said, "Get in here Ian. I need to warm up your stethoscope before it gets cold."

Chapter 21

MONDAY, OCTOBER 26, MINNEAPOLIS, MN

As planned, I left my house key with Kate at her apartment when I left at six forty-five on Monday morning. I told her to give it to the dogcatcher on their way into work. That way he could have his men positioned inside my home by sometime in late afternoon in hopes of catching the killer. I knew their odds were damn near nil, but I had promised them access to my place and I wanted to uphold that part of the agreement. Plus, it was one less reason for the FBI to go looking for me before they decided to take me downtown to their office for questioning. If I could just put them off for the first three hours of the day, then I would be gone and they would be left standing around with their dicks in their hands.

My plan was to drive my car to work and park it in the Dayton's ramp for the week, instead of my normal underground spot in the lower section of the IDS Center. From there I'd walk the half block to the IDS building and check in with Kate at the information desk. I wanted to make sure Yorkshire saw me enter the building and watch as I took the elevator up to tenth floor. I also had one other thing to do in the court prior to that, which would come in handy in the upcoming days.

Entering the building by the Eighth and Marquette entrance, I stopped briefly by the payphones, then walked directly to the nearside of the court to get a can of Coke from a shop vendor whom I knew as Fahad. I also got a morning paper to make it look like I was going about my daily routine as if nothing out of the ordinary was happening. After that I stopped at the information desk to say hi to Kate and the dogcatcher, then made a beeline to the elevator. No one else got on it with me, so I figured I was still on my own for a couple more hours. The Feds had not yet decided to follow me which was something I'd been counting on.

When the elevator stopped at my floor, I walked out and went straight to my office without stopping to say hello to my assistant Evelyn. I laid my newspaper on the desk, opened it to the sports section, and popped the top on my can of Coke. The first thing I noticed was the red light flashing on my phone, indicating I had messages to retrieve. So I picked up the receiver, punched in my code, and listened to the cold-hearted voice of what I assumed was the killer. In a muffled tone he said, "Where the hell are you Mr. Christian? I've been waiting for you. I'm extremely disappointed you didn't come home this weekend, but I'm sure our paths will cross sometime soon. Iowa, perhaps?" That was all he said. The voice sounded like it was muffled through a handkerchief or something like that. I wasn't sure it was Asian, but the masking mechanism he was using could have accounted for that. By the sound of the message it seemed like he had given up on the idea of getting to me here in the Twin Cities. But that might have been done to get me to let my guard down, and I had no intention of letting that happen until he was dead.

Turning my attention back to the sports headlines, I saw the Vikings had another good day on Sunday beating the Green Bay Packers in overtime at Lambeau Filed. That was good to see. I hated the Packers; they won far too much for my liking.

I took a few more sips of my Coke and picked up the phone to call Jack's assistant. "Hello Judy, this is Ian. Is Jack in? I need to come down and talk with him about some travel plans. He's there? Great, I'll be down in a couple of minutes."

Jack was on the phone when I entered his office and held up two fingers indicating it would only be a few minutes before he was done talking. In the meantime, I sat and looked at the lone picture on his desk. It was of Jack and his wife. The photo was encased in a gaudy, silver-plated frame, and it must have been at least a quarter of a century old. The woman in the picture was beautiful, but she looked terrible now, mostly from being an alcoholic since the mid-sixties. I guess he simply wanted to remember the young woman he had married or he didn't want others to know she was actually beastly-looking these days. Jack eventually hung up the phone and I said, "Nice picture of the two of you."

Jack looked down his nose at me, but didn't reply. Instead he said, "What's on your mind Ian? I'm in a hurry this morning. I have a budget meeting in fifteen minutes and then I'm going down to DeKalb to talk to them about an advertising campaign for their new seed corn verities. I need to be on the road by ten o'clock."

"This won't take long Jack. I've decided to go down to Iowa to look at some farmland for a John Deere photo shoot. I'll be gone the rest of the week. I'm planning on doing some pheasant hunting on the weekend, so I probably won't be back until midmorning on Monday."

"Not a problem Ian. I'm driving down to Illinois and probably won't be back until Friday. By the way, how are you doing on the Gustafson account?"

"Good. I've got the art department working on some storyboards which should be done by the middle of November. We can show them to Gustafson when we go down to Dallas next month." "Great! Then I'll see you sometime next week. Don't forget to leave a phone number with your assistant where you can be reached. I may need to call you to toss a couple of ideas your way."

"Okay, I'll see you in a week."

I beat a hasty retreat and headed back to my office. On my way in I passed Evelyn's desk and told her to follow me as there was something I wanted to talk to her about. It was now nine thirty and I needed to wrap things up in a hurry if I wanted to vanish before the Feds got to me.

"Take a note Evelyn. I'm going to leave town this afternoon and fly down to Dallas. I need to talk to the Gustafson people.

I'll call you with a number where I can be reached when I get there. I may stay at my brother's place; I haven't decided yet, but I'll let you know as soon as I can. I spoke to Jack and he knows I'm going. If anyone else should call, tell them I'm in Texas. Did you get that?"

"I did, but a man called while you were talking to Jack and asked if you were in. I told him you weren't, but I expected you to be back soon."

"Did he say who he was?"

"Yes, he said his name was Ralph Yorkshire. He left his phone number and said I should tell you to call him as soon as you return to your office. Here's the number."

She handed me the message and asked if everything was alright.

"Yes, why do you ask?"

"Well, the man seemed agitated that you weren't here."

"How so?"

"Oh, I don't really know how to put it exactly, but he was rather abrupt with me and said it was extremely important that you call him. Then he repeated it a second time like I was a child and asked if I understood him."

"Not to worry Ev, he's always that way. He doesn't know how to talk to people. I'll make sure I call him, but from now on take messages until I come back. Remember, I'll be in Dallas."

That fuckin' Yorkshire was hot on my trail. I was kind of surprised he hadn't come up to my office to talk to me, but I assumed Kate had stopped him from doing that, seeing she knew I was heading out of town as fast as I could. I didn't have any time to waste, so I reached for the phone and called Avis. I wanted to make sure my car would be ready when I went there to pick it up. They said it was and wanted to know if I needed them to drop it off. I told them no, I was going to grab my things and walk over to their office. It was only three blocks away, and I didn't want to risk having someone see me get in the car.

With no further ado, I grabbed my coat, said good-bye to Ev, and headed down the elevator to the second floor. When the doors opened, I took a quick right into the skyway and headed for Dayton's department store. I knew I could escape through the skyway system if need be, as long as the Feds hadn't put men there to watch for me. I figured the dogcatcher would be looking for me to come down the elevator and leave by the Crystal Court. Instead, I went through Dayton's and took their store elevator to level D, which was where my car was parked. I retrieved my bags from the trunk of the Porsche and headed for the Avis office.

There was an attendant waiting for me when I got there. I signed the necessary paperwork and asked if I could use their phone to make a call to my office. The attendant said yes, and handed me the receiver and punched in the number that I gave him. The phone rang twice before I heard the familiar voice of Kate Rutan. She said, "Hello, this is Kate at the IDS Center. May I help you?"

"Yes, it's me, but don't say anything unless I ask you to. Are you alone?"

"Yes I am."

"Good, where's the dogcatcher?"

"He was here, but he left no more than a minute ago to go up to your office. He got tired of waiting for you to return his phone call, so he went to find you. Where are you now?"

"I'm still in town, but not for long. I'll be at Lane Moreland's place later this evening. I'll call you at nine o'clock tonight and we'll talk further. Okay?"

"Okay."

I hung up the phone and got the keys to my rental car. From there I drove out to the suburbs to have a couple of cocktails with an old bartender friend of mine. I knew the dogcatcher would be on my ass by midmorning, but was he after me to talk or take me in to regional headquarters for questioning? I guess I wouldn't know the answer to those questions until I spoke to him and that wouldn't be for a couple of days.

The late-morning traffic on Highway 12 was lighter than expected. It only took me twenty minutes to take it and Highway 100 to the city of St. Louis Park. I was looking for Bunny's and a guy named Crazy Johnson. Steve, or Crazy as he was known by his close friends, was an old college buddy from St. Cloud. We went way back to a time before the Vietnam War, and I couldn't wait to see his stupid-ass face.

"Hey Crazy, give me another Stoli martini. I'm dry," I said as I looked around the nearly empty bar. It was slightly past eleven fifteen, and there were no other customers in the place except for me and two businessmen who were sitting directly across the bar. They were in a heated discussion about something and they let it be known to anyone who was within listening distance. I guess that was okay, seeing that Crazy and I were the only ones who could hear them.

"That's your third Ian. Were you intending to drive after that one?"

"Need I remind you Crazy, I helped you out of a jam back in college, so keep 'em coming. And the answer to your question is no, I'm not driving. I plan on staying to have some lunch and maybe then I'll have another drink. Who knows, maybe I'll catch a cab or call a friend to pick me up."

I continued sipping on another cocktail as my old college friend placed a food order for me. It was a mildly delicious lunch, as much as fettuccine Alfredo could be from a bar. I ate in silence as I thought about how absolutely mad the FBI must be at me. The people who were in from Washington were probably reaming the dogcatcher's ass about now. I imagine they were asking Ralph how it was possible that I could have given him the slip. If they thought giving Ralph the slip made them mad, then I only wished I was a fly on the wall when they learned the names that I'd given him were fakes. That would more than likely piss them off enough to throw me in jail. That was fine by me. I wanted them mad as hell and for them to waste their time looking into my past. I knew at some point I would have to talk to Yorkshire, but I wanted to make sure I had all my ducks in a row before I did that. Ralph would come in handy at some point down the line, and I had plans for him that included helping me with the killer.

I sat around for another two hours talking to Crazy while I drank free Cokes from the bar. The time was spent making small talk about the Vikings and what they needed to be champions once again. Crazy and I both agreed it would take a new coach and lots of help on the offensive side of the line. The players were getting old and they needed to be replaced, just like Bud Grant. It was around that time that the after-work crowd started to filter in, and Crazy didn't have any more time to talk to me. So I paid and tipped him and left to meet up with Lane.

My eyes squinted as I opened the door and looked out into the parking lot. It was mostly filled to capacity with cars and trucks, but not so full that my crappy, green Chevrolet Cavalier with the ugly Avis sticker on the rear bumper didn't stick out like a bum on a street corner. The car was a piece of shit. It had two speeds, slow and slower. Either way, I was going to have to push the car hard in the morning if I wanted to make it to Ft. Dodge by 2:00 p.m. tomorrow.

Lane had almost finished unpacking his work trailer by the time I pulled the rental beast into his driveway. He stopped when he saw me and offered me a beer, which I gratefully accepted. I stood there patiently drinking from the bottle of Bud and watched as he finished removing the last of the floor tile he had bought for a job he was doing next week. When he finished, the two of us headed in the house where we could relax and work on the rest of his twelve-pack.

Lane took a chair and I settled in on the couch.

"So tell me Lane, why does your wife want a divorce?"

"She's got a boyfriend, and he wants her and my daughter to live with him or he wants to move in here. It's one or the other; I'm not sure at this point. Either way, he's going to fuck me. Can you imagine that? He wants to ruin my life by taking my daughter away from me, just so he can have my wife. I mean, he can have the bitch. I don't give a shit, but I don't want to lose my daughter. Lilly means the world to me and to complicate things, she really doesn't like being around my wife Linda. The two of them get along like oil and water. If the truth be known, I'm the one who really takes care of Lilly. Linda only pretends to be a mother. Actually, the best way to describe her is that she is a real motherfucker."

"That's a good one. I like that," I said. Then we clinked our bottles together in a mock toast to his wife's motherly instincts. "And I suppose she wants half of everything you own?"

"Half," he said with disgust. "Hell, she wants almost everything I have, including the house. I'll be damned if she's going to get that, just so her new boyfriend can live in it with her and Lilly. I'll burn the place down before I let that happen."

"Hold on Lane, you might want to stop and think about that. I believe the beers are starting to talk. I'd sleep on that idea for a couple decades before taking any action. I tell you what. I'm going to be gone until next Monday, but when I return I'll have a word with our corporate attorney. He specializes in advertising law, but he belongs to a very large brotherhood of people who get paid tons of money to fuck people over. So I'm sure he'll be able to recommend someone for you to speak to that can handle this properly. I know he'll be honest with me and get you a good divorce attorney. I'll tell you this; Linda isn't going to toss you out of this house that you built. You put too much of your time and money into this place before you ever met her, so I think you'll be the one who'll be staying here. It's going to cost you, but what's money to a gambler like you?"

"God I hate you Ian. You always seem to make me feel worse by the time our conversations are over. I should learn not to tell you a damn thing."

"You know me, I aim to please. But really, who the hell else would you talk to? You don't go to church, so you can't talk to a priest. You don't have a shrink, the card dealers at the casino don't give a shit, and now you don't have a wife to talk to either. So who does that leave? Your sisters, your brother, and little old me, that's who. And I'm not family, so drink up and tell me everything. I don't have all night. I have to call Kate by nine o'clock."

Chapter 22

"Hey Tony, is your mom there?"

"Yeah, wait a minute Ian and I'll get her."

Kate sighed, seemingly exhausted by the whole ordeal. She took the phone from her son and said, "Where are you calling from Ian?"

"I'm in a phone booth, in case the Feds decided to tap your line. And if they're listening all I want to say is, fuck you, cocksuckers. I hope you have fun looking for me. Anyway, how did things go today?"

She took a deep breath and said, "Not bad. Ralph was back and forth to my desk a lot, and there were half a dozen agents swarming the place looking for you. As crazy as it was, I just had to laugh, even though I felt bad for Ralph. His boss is real pissed at you for not calling Ralph back."

"Good. Someone needs to put those bastards in their place. You wait until tomorrow when they have the airport crawling with agents and I'm nowhere to be found. They'll be even more pissed than today. So what have you heard from the dogcatcher?"

"He called me tonight around seven o'clock to ask if I knew where you were. I told him I didn't have any idea where you were staying. I said the last thing you told me was that you were heading to Dallas on Tuesday morning."

"Good job. Did he say anything else?"

"Only that your house was broken into over the weekend. I understand whoever did it went in through the basement. The intruder left quite a mess from what I've heard. The guy must have been looking for something. The Feds aren't sure what it was, but they've secured the place, and they're going to stay for a couple more days in case he returns."

"They're wasting their time; he's not coming back. The killer is more than likely watching my office to see where I'll go next or he has moved on. Say, the next time you speak to Ralph tell him to have someone go over and clean the place up, and then tell him to send the bill to the government. He'll get a kick out of that."

"Yeah, like that's going to happen. So tell me Ian, what do you think the killer was looking for?"

"My first thought would be that he was waiting for me to come home so he could kill me, and when I didn't show up on Sunday night, he became enraged and trashed the place. Then there is another possibility, and that would be he was looking for something. Like information telling him where the third intel officer is. He might have thought I had the guy's name written down somewhere after talking to some of my old army buddies. I'm thinking the killer doesn't know who the third officer is. And now he's pissed because he may never be able to kill everyone that's involved. I'm sure he'd like to get his hands on me, so he could try and beat the answer out of me. That makes me think he doesn't want to kill me yet. He needs me or one of my other two platoon mates so he can gain access to the last element in his little game."

"So what's your plan?"

"I've got a lot of thinking to do. I need to sleep on everything for the night and get a good start in the morning. I'm meeting a friend tomorrow night, and that will be the beginning of the end to all of this. I just need to decide how I'm going to lure the assassin into believing he can come after me at any time and any place. I need him to think I'm letting my guard down. I have a pretty good idea on what I'm going to do, but I need to see the playing field before I make any final decisions.

"And where are you going to stay tonight?"

"I'm going to have another drink and hole up where no one can find me. Then I'm heading out early in the morning to take care of business. You stay close to the phone until I tell you otherwise, and watch yourself. I don't think the killer will come after you, but you never know what a madman might be thinking. Quite honestly, the dogcatcher and I don't think the killer knows you exist. At least that's our theory. Plus, if the guy really wanted to get to me, he would have grabbed you by now and used you as leverage. But that hasn't happened, so I think he's on his way down to find me, and hopefully that won't happen until I've set my plan in motion. I'll see you when I get back in town. Bye."

I was sure that Kate's phone hadn't been tapped at her home or her office, not yet anyway. The Feds might get to that by midweek, but they needed a judge to sign the warrant and that would take a day or two. So I was pretty confident anything I'd said was still between her and me. She was a real trouper. As of tonight, she hadn't said she was worried for me, nor had she said she loved me. That would have been the wrong thing to say to me at this juncture in our relationship. She also hadn't said to take care or to watch my back, as she probably knew I was the one person in this entire mess whom the killer should be afraid of. It wasn't the police or the FBI. No, it was me because the killer must have known by now that I've been one step ahead of him for quite some time. And I, just like him, was the one person who didn't play by the rules. I would just as soon cut the killer's throat or gut him like a pig, as take him alive.

That very thought created a huge dilemma; was it blood or jail? It was definitely blood! I needed to kill this guy so Benita Cummings could have some peace of mind. She and Snake deserved that, even though Roland was no longer on this earth to revel in the outcome. Whoever this guy is better be looking over his shoulder because Sam was back and he was looking for revenge.

Chapter 23

What was the curse that made motel managers so incompetent they couldn't give you a wake-up call when you asked for one? My plan was to be long gone by 7:00 a.m., so I could be at my destination by later this afternoon.

A very late start and a short detour had put me several hours behind schedule. It was now almost eight thirty in the evening as I entered the east side of this broken-down little town. On my right was the Lamplighter Inn and just before that was a roach-infested-looking place I wouldn't have let my dog sleep in if I actually had one. As I drove further into the center of Ft. Dodge, I began passing a lot of old dilapidated two-story office buildings, a couple of pizza parlors, some boarded-up shops, and an abnormally large amount of bars. It was as if I'd been transported back in time to the Old West; all that was missing were the cowboys and their six-shooters. Even the town's name seemed to fit the surroundings.

It was now too late in the evening to do anything but look for a room for the night. My intentions were to get here early, so I could locate the Wheeler farmstead. That way I could drive the roads and see the land that surrounded his place. I also wanted to see if I had been made and if anyone was following me. I had kept a close eye on the rearview mirror for any indication that someone might be tailing me. I saw nothing to indicate otherwise as I continued my drive down North Ninth Street. I wasn't sure what I was looking for, but when I found it, I'd know.

I had almost made it through Dodge when some flashing lights and the sound of music caught my attention. I looked just beyond my front bumper and saw a place on the left called the West End Bar. The marquee outside read; Topless Women and Dollar Drinks – 9 PM to closing. This was my kind of place. It wasn't home, but it would suffice for the moment. I took the next left after the bar, drove around the block, and parked my car at the curb. I sat and watched for ten minutes to make sure there wasn't a car following me. When I thought the coast was clear, I drove the Chevy around to the alley and parked it at the rear of the bar.

I then walked around to Ninth Street and entered the place by the front door. There was a partition to my immediate left as I entered, which I assumed was there to keep people from stopping to gawk at the strippers on stage. Some of the locals seemed to switch their attention to me as I made my way through the crowded, smoke-filled joint. Small-town people had a knack for knowing the new guy when they saw him, and I was as out of place here as a tiara on a pig. The locals soon switched their focus back to the slinky brunette on stage with the gazelle legs, melon breasts, and a titanium ass you could crack walnuts off of. My paranoia was getting the best of me, so I quickly moved to the bar where I found an empty stool. I sat my ass down, ordered my old stand-by Stoli martini, and took a long sip while watching the stripper do some things with a pole that I thought was humanly impossible.

The girl on the pole couldn't have been much more than twenty-five to twenty-six years old. She had a wonderfully seductive routine that kept the drunks howling for more. What more could they want, I wondered? She was down to her G-string and that wasn't coming off until they changed the laws in this state. The lovely young woman was grinding her ass to the beat as if the song had been written for her. She had precision movements that were very erotic, so much so that she had the entire male audience, and a few female patrons, standing and applauding her every move.

I was even getting aroused myself. She kind of reminded me of Kate, but with much longer legs.

Kate could do the bump and grind too, as she had demonstrated for me one evening before bedtime. She wasn't quite as talented as the girl on stage, but I would have thought she could have held her own with this crowd even though she was in her later thirties. Kate, too, had a stripper mentality. She was all about sex, just as I suspected the stripper was.

I could be wrong, but if you're provocative enough to flaunt your body for everyone to see and let people stick greenbacks down your crotch, then you more than likely were a major sex monster.

I looked away from the stage and ordered another martini from the bartender with bushy eyebrows. The second Stoli went down even faster that the first. I tried a couple of times to ask the bartender where there was a good, clean place to stay for the night, but his preoccupation with the customers and the stripper made it seemingly impossible. He, like all the others in the West End, had sold out to the babe on stage.

Ten o'clock was swiftly approaching, and all I had accomplished up to this point was three great martinis and the urge to call Kate and talk dirty to her. That wasn't going to happen as it might have given away my location. The next thing I knew, I would be having a conversation with the dogcatcher. He'd be sitting next to me at the bar with handcuffs in one hand and a warrant for my arrest in the other. No, there would be no late-night phone sex call to Ms. Rutan or any other call to the Twin Cities for that matter. I was saving that for tomorrow, when I would place a call to Yorkshire.

The music stopped promptly at ten o'clock. That's when about two percent of the patrons decided it was time to leave, others thought it was a good time to hit the bathroom, and those who were left either sat in their chairs waiting for the next set, or they moved to the bar to get another drink. I was looking to my right to get the bartender's attention when I heard a seductive voice from behind me ask if the seat next to me was open. I shifted around on my stool to put a face to the voice and realized it was the stripper. She was on break and asking if she could take a load off of her feet and sit down to have a drink.

Without hesitation I said, "Yes, the seat is open if you'd like to sit down. I was trying to get the bartender's attention to get another drink. Can I buy you one if he ever gets back to me?"

"Oh, you mean Floyd. Let me help you with that," she replied. "Girls like me get what they want, while others have to wait their turn. If you know what I mean."

I think I knew what she meant. Baring her tits and humping a pole was all that was necessary to get whatever she wanted, whenever she needed it.

I said, "You mean having a great personality like yours is the key to success with bartenders?"

"It's something like that," she replied with a wink and a smile. "I also have a B.S. degree in Psychology from the University of Minnesota, and that helps more often that you might think. Here, let me show you how it works. Excuse me Floyd, but have you been working out lately. Wow, you really look like you've been hitting the weights. How about you get me a Cuba Libre and a drink for my friend? By the way, what is your name? I didn't get it."

"That's because I didn't give it to you," I said. "But if you insist, it's Ian, Ian Christian, like those people who were sacrificed to the lions back in Roman times."

"So tell me Ian, am I getting a history lesson or do you want to fuck me? And you can call me Mitzy," she said as she slid her room key down the bar top in my direction.

The awkwardness of her invitation and the passing of the key didn't go unnoticed by several of the locals who were sitting next to us and those who had gathered behind. I could tell these individuals were somewhat perturbed by her invitation, and at me, for being in this establishment where I wasn't wanted. If looks could kill, then the assassin would definitely have to wait his turn. I could sense their contempt for me, even though I hadn't yet replied to her question.

Then I said, "That depends."

"On what?" she replied with some confusion.

"Well, I need a place to stay, and I'm going to be in town for at least five or six nights, so does this offer extend to the whole time or is it just for the night?" I replied with all the confidence of a rock star. "I usually don't make a habit of getting picked up in bars, but I've been known to make exceptions."

She snickered and replied, "Oh, so you have rules, do you?"

"Of course I do. Don't you? Like how far am I expected to go on a first date?"

She gazed back at me with one of those you-must-have-just-climbed-out-of-an-alien-spaceship looks and said, "You know Ian, you drive a hard bargain. But I think I can fit you in for the full stay. I mean, I can as long as you're not some sort of crazed maniac or killer. And you aren't either one of those are you?"

How in the hell was I supposed to answer that question? I wanted to say I was in town in pursuit of a crazed maniac killer, but that wouldn't have flown. So, instead I thought about how I could answer her truthfully without being told to hit the road. As far as being a killer, well yes, I had killed many people in my past. Then there was the assassin whom I was definitely going to kill this coming weekend when I had my chance, so I guess the answer to those questions is…"No, I'm none of those things. And I bet you another drink that I'm the nicest guy you'll meet in this bar tonight."

This time she let out a full-blown laugh as she spilled her drink on the bar. Floyd, the ever so attentive bartender, was right there to give her a refill as she stepped down from her stool. Mitzy, regaining her composure, stopped for a couple of seconds to rub her breasts up against my bicep and to toss down her drink. She set the glass down gently on the bar and said, "I need to go back and do my next set. In the meantime, why don't you go out and get us some Cold Duck to drink for later on. It's my favorite. They don't serve it here at the bar. You can either come back later to catch the rest of my act and stay until I get off at one, or you can go to my room, and I'll give you an encore show later. The room's upstairs. Don't lose the key. It's the only one I've got."

She was about to leave when I stopped her to ask, "Pink or white?"

"Pink or white what?"

"The Cold Duck."

"Oh yeah, surprise me."

She lit a cigarette and off she went to say hi to all the horny, dirty old men as she worked her way back to the stage. The bouncer was in close pursuit, making sure none of them put their grubby little hands on her. That, as I had just learned, was reserved for me.

I turned my attention back to Floyd to ask where I could find an off-sale liquor store. He told me there was one about a half mile to the east and a block north on Fifth Avenue. It was right next to the VFW. I couldn't miss it.

"By the way Floyd, how do I get to the room upstairs?"

"Oh that's easy. You take the stairs on your right just before you exit the back door. The room is at the top of the stairs. Or you can get to it after hours by going up the back steps. Use the key Mitzy gave you to either door, but I'd lock them behind you, if you know what's good for you."

"Thanks for the tip Floyd. Maybe I'll see you later."

I was halfway down the rear hallway when I noticed I had entered into a rugby scrum. I was about to go for the door handle when some men pushed me from behind, using my face as a door opener. The group sort of stumbled out into the trash area located directly behind the bar. When I turned around I saw three men staring me down.

After a few exhausting seconds the tall skinny guy in the middle said, "What in the fuck do you think you're doing? You don't belong here taking our women."

I, being the usual cordial individual that I am, replied, "Just to set things straight, I'm actually here to be with one woman if memory serves me right. And she doesn't belong to anyone as far as I can tell."

The fat guy to his right said, "Are you trying to make fun of us?"

"No, not at all," I replied. "You're doing a great job of that on your own. I just wanted to make sure we had the numbers straight and we're talking about Mitzy the stripper inside. I don't actually think she's a local from what she has indicated to me. And she seems a lot smarter than the women you guys might tend to be with."

That last statement got me to thinking I might have overstepped my bounds with these Neanderthals. So I stopped running my mouth to size up the trio and to look for any type of weapon that could be used to fend off what looked to me like the second coming of the Three Stooges. I saw four trash cans to my immediate left, three with covers. There were also a couple of old mops by the side of the door and a milking stool I figured was used as a place of rest for employee smoke breaks. Outside of that, all I had was my two fists, my feet, and the .38 special that was strapped to my ankle, which I really didn't want to use.

We all just stood there as the three of them tried their best to figure out if I had insulted them. Then finally the skinny guy with the curly hair, whom I tabbed as Larry, came at me. I reached over and grabbed a cover off one of the trash cans and held it up to my chin, just as he threw a right-cross at my face. His fist hit hard against the cover and glanced off my cheek. That, in turn, led to a very jackal-like scream from Larry. I had managed to sidestep him in the process while placing my knee firmly into his nut sack. He went down in a lump as he held his injured hand to his smashed balls.

Curly, the fat, short-haired one was up next. He charged me with all the agility of a blind rhino, as I quickly turned the cover sideways and caught him with a wicked blow to his throat. That essentially ended the fight with blubber boy. He immediately went to his knees as he clasped both of his hands around what I expected was a cracked or broken Adam's apple.

That left one last person to contend with. The guy was short and not very well built, but as Mark Twain once said, "It's not the size of the dog in the fight; it's the size of the fight in the dog" that counts. No sooner had that thought popped into my mind when

Moe pulled a nasty-looking hunting knife from his hip. He slashed it back and forth at me several times as I defended myself. It was on his fourth or fifth try that he made a classic street-fighting mistake. He thought I was going to deflect the knife with the cover. Instead, I attacked him with a bull rush as I slammed the cover through the knife and into his face, breaking his nose. He dropped the knife and staggered back as he held his nose with both hands. I could see blood squirting out of both nostrils as it began running down the front of his arms and neck. His shirt was stained bright red as he coughed blood from his throat.

I should have left well enough alone, but Sam was beginning to come out like the Incredible Hulk does when he's over the top. I pulled the Smith and Wesson from its holster and shoved it down the open mouth of the now standing guy I called Larry. I grabbed his privates with my other hand and noticed that he had pissed his pants. I said, "Are you kidding me asshole? Did you really have to do that?"

Then I said to the group, "This didn't have to go down like this boys, but you just had to push it. I tell you what fat man; you'd better go out and eat a basketful full of hamburgers before you come at me again. And you, little man, the next time you pull a knife on someone, you'd better be ready to go to the hospital. Now I want all of you to listen to me. This is what we're going to do. You, skinny boy with piss in your pants. I want you to get all three of your drivers' licenses together and give them to me. Then you're going to leave and not come back to this establishment for at least a week. I have business here in town that will take me through the first of the month, so stay away if you know what's good for you. And remember, I now know all of your names, and where you live, just in case you're thinking of going to the police. I also have an FBI friend named Ralph. He'll be here in a couple of days to give you back your licenses, and if I'm in jail, he'll get me out. And then the three of you are going to be in some serious trouble because I'll find you and make sure each one of you squeals like a pig. Do we understand each other?"

The three of them nodded yes without saying a word, as Larry handed me their licenses. I looked down at their names and laughed as one of them was actually named Larry.

"Okay boys, it's time for you to leave and go home. I suggest you take the alley as you don't want to suffer any more pain and indignity than you already have. Being laughed at by your friends back in the bar would be pretty embarrassing, I should think. So get moving, and I'll be watching you all the way around the corner. Bye."

I waved and watched as they disappeared around the corner into the night. The three of them "took quite a licking, but kept on ticking," as Timex says. They all went down, but none of them went out. I took a deep breath and thought it was good to get a preliminary fight out of the way before I made my way to the main event. I got some of the old kinks out, and I had used my gun on someone for the first time in a couple of years. It felt great. I almost felt superhuman. Maybe I actually was a hybrid between the Hulk and Superman. That was something that had yet to be proven, and I believe it was just a matter of days before I would know if that was possible.

Chapter 24

There was a knock on Mitzy's door somewhere around one thirty in the morning. I wasn't sure if it was her or if the boys had come back for round number two. So I got up with my revolver in hand, walked to the door, and asked, "Who's there?"

An agitated voice from the other side said, "It's Princess Kay of the Milky Way. Who in the fuck do you think it is?"

"Then go away and come back when the lady of the house is home."

"Okay Ian, if you want some of this, then you'd better open the door fast. I'm freezing my ass out here."

I put the revolver back in my bag and opened the door to see a completely naked Mitzy standing there with two wine glasses in one hand and her skimpy outfit in the other.

"By all means come in," I said. "And I noticed that you're freezing your tits, too," as her nipples were standing erect and pointed in my direction. As she made her way inside, I looked down the stairs to make sure the Three Stooges or some of their friends weren't lurking in the shadows.

I closed the door and locked it. Then I looked at Mitzy in all of her splendor and said, "Doesn't being naked to begin with go against all the principles of being a stripper? I mean, isn't it your job to take your clothes off so I can get aroused? That's the main purpose of being a stripper isn't it? And you're naked. That kind of takes all the fun out of it for me."

She pushed me aside, walked on by, and said, "Are you saying you don't like what you see, because you can go jerk yourself off, and I can go to bed if you like. Or we could have some champagne and do some kinky stuff. Your turn."

"Oh, we're playing tag are we? If it's a game you want, then I can banter back and forth like this all night and still have wood come morning."

"Good," she said. "I was hoping for something like that or I wouldn't have given you the key to my room."

"That brings up a good point. I told you I was going to be here until maybe next Monday, so you better get another key. I'll probably be coming and going for the better part of the next two days. If that's okay with you?"

"That's what I was hoping for," she said with a smile as she kissed me on the cheek and went to open one of the bottles of Cold Duck. "I see you got pink and white, and a red mark on your face since we last saw each other. Have a little run-in with one of the locals on your way to the store, or did you trip and fall on somebody's fist?"

"How did you know I had a misunderstanding with some of the rural boys who seem to have fallen a bit short of their GED?"

"No one told me. No one had to. The farm boys around here are either after my pussy, or they want to make sure no one else gets to it. They just swing that way down here."

Tapping my foot I said, "Or maybe you wanted to see if I might get my ass kicked just for laughs."

"No Ian, I'd never do that," she said as she poured me a glass of the cheap champagne. "I thought they might try to scare you, but I didn't think they would get violent."

"And what don't you understand about good ol' farm boys? They like to drink beer and see who has the biggest dick. Then they pick fights for no reason at all, and when one of them falls, others pick up the slack until someone gets hurt. And all three of them are someplace now whimpering like whipped dogs."

"Really Ian, I don't take any pleasure in hearing you were jumped or that someone was hurt. The only pleasure I want tonight is with you. So why don't we stop the arguing and do what we came here for. Here, give me your hand. I want you to explore every part of my body, and then we'll take turns." She then took my hand and placed it on her crotch. "Now tell me, how does that feel?"

She was right. It felt great! And this was no time for bickering. It was time for her to put her clothes back on, so she could give me a proper encore of her show. Then, after that, we'd see what direction this expedition was headed.

Chapter 25

I was lying on my back, staring at the ceiling fan when I heard the distant sound of Mick Jagger's voice. It was hump day and the distinct sound of the Rolling Stones was coming from somewhere downstairs in the bar. I assumed it was either Floyd or some cleaning person who was playing the music. The song was low and muffled, but I was sure it was *Jumpin' Jack Flash*.

I turned to my side and looked over into the face of one of the most unpretentious and free-spirited women I'd ever met. She was still asleep, looking more like an innocent child than the vivacious, erotic dancer that she was. As I looked at her, I thought about what she had said to me last night at the bar…the thing about girls like her got what they wanted while others have to wait their turn. That statement had come from the mind of an intelligent woman and a cock-teasing stripper. Both of those traits stemmed from a manipulating personality, yet for some reason she didn't seem to fit the mold. She was sharp, smart, and extremely beautiful, but there was also a dark side to her. *Who was I to talk; I was so dark at times that I could have been mistaken for Hannibal Lecter on holiday.* Yes, Mitzy was warm and giving, she had shown me that several times last night. She was also very confident, yet she danced around on stage as if she needed the crowd's reassurance that she was both, wanted and desired by all.

She opened her eyes, blinked several times, and yawned. As she pulled the hair back away from her face she said, "That sure was some evening Ian. It was everything I pictured it would be when I first saw you back in Minneapolis a couple of years ago."

"What are you talking about?"

"What did you think? That I'd give a key to my room to a complete stranger? Hell no, that would never happen, even to Jesus Christ himself. You probably don't remember this, but I saw you when I danced at the Bull Pen in Hopkins. You were there with your wife talking to Mary Ye. After that you came back alone to talk to her on several occasions. I always thought the two of you had something going. Then one day she told me you only came there to talk about your wife. Mary said you were hoping she could spend some time with your wife to help her work out some of her problems. I understood your wife wasn't normal. I always thought you were handsome, but you were married, and I didn't want to get myself involved in a mess like that. And when you walked in the door last night, I recognized you immediately. I could hardly wait for my set to be done so I could come over and sit with you. I didn't see a ring and well, here we are. By the way, I haven't seen Mary since I last worked in Hopkins. She disappeared off the face of the earth, and no one has seen or heard from her since. Do you know what happened to her?"

"I understand she took a long trip and won't be coming back to Minnesota." *Actually she was at the bottom of Lake Superior, but that's a story for another time.*

"I'm hungry," she said. "Are you?"

"Yeah, I didn't eat last night."

"You drank your dinner if I remember correctly."

"That's true. And as much as I'd like to have breakfast with you, I have to go out and make some calls. Then I have to go visit a friend's place this afternoon. So, why don't you get another key for the room, and we'll meet downstairs at five o'clock for dinner. How does that sound?"

"I have a better idea. Why don't I go with you and we can spend the day together? We could grab some breakfast on the run."

"You know I'd like nothing better than that, but what I'm doing this afternoon is real boring and I might have to get muddy in the process. So I think I'd better go solo for now and we'll catch up later. Okay?"

"Now that you mention it, I don't like playing in the mud unless I'm getting paid for it. So you go have fun and I'll see you for dinner."

We spent another hour in bed, then I showered, dressed, and headed down the outside stairs to find my pea-green rental car. The day was bright and sunny as I moved out into the clean, country air, but that would change later in the day as there was a slight chance of rain around four this afternoon. As a matter of fact, the weather forecast for the week was supposed to be warmer than average with some possibilities of severe weather on or around Halloween. I wasn't sure I liked that, as bad weather tends to unnerve me. It also creates a multitude of difficulties at a time when I'll need to stay focused. One way or another, I knew the battle ahead was going to be brutal. Whether it was rain or shine, hail storm or tornado, someone was going to bleed, and someone was going to die.

There were no policemen waiting to arrest me as I approached to unlock the Chevy. I think I had sufficiently put the fear of God in those three idiots last night. They weren't going to the police, nor were they going to show their faces around the West End for quite some time. I was sure of that.

My plan for the day was to drive out to the interstate to call the dogcatcher on a public payphone. I'd stop at Casey's General Store to get some food and a shit-load of quarters for the phone. Then I'd call Kate at work to make sure Ralph was by her side. I'm sure he was getting a little nervous by now, not knowing where the hell I was. I figured he'd jump at the chance to be my backup down here. After all, his ass was in a bind, and coming down to aid in the capture of a serial killer was probably good for his career, especially after he had fucked up his latest assignment. I was counting on him to still be open to the idea of letting me do what I needed to end this killing spree. And a man in the shadows would be infinitely better than a boatload of agents running around scaring off the man we needed to bring to justice; my kind of justice, that is.

I found a Standard Oil station at the exit of I-35W and Highway 20 and went inside to see if they had a payphone. The attendant said there was one down the back hall near the restroom. I found it and called Kate. The operator said I needed to deposit a dollar twenty-five for the first three minutes. I did what she asked, and the next thing I heard was Kate's voice saying hello.

"Kate, this is Ian. Is the dogcatcher there?"

"Yes he is."

"Good, then give him the phone."

Kate did as I requested and handed the phone to Ralph. "Is this Ian?" he asked.

"Yes it is Ralph, but I'm only going to be on the line for the next thirty seconds, so you can forget about tracing the call. What I want you to do is hang the phone up when I'm done talking and go to the second payphone from the left on the bank of phones in the lobby. Go there now and wait for my call. I'll call you back in exactly sixty seconds. Have you got that?"

"Yes."

"Good, then get your ass going. I'm not calling back a second time."

I had a small amount of time to waste, so I went out to the vending machine and bought myself a Coke. God, I loved the taste of Coke almost as much as alcohol. I rarely had one during the war, and I just couldn't get my fill of them now that I was back in the States. I purposely let the clock tick a little, so Ralph could sweat awhile longer. I wanted him to know I was fucking with his head; maybe let him think I wasn't going to call him back at all. Seven minutes had gone by before I decided he'd waited long enough. I dialed the number I had gotten when I went in the back way to the IDS and deposited another dollar twenty-five into the phone.

He answered, "This is Ralph. Is that you Ian?"

"Yes it is Ralph. And now that I have you on a phone that isn't tapped, I want to have a heart-to-heart talk."

"Hold on, where the hell are you?"

"Fuck you Ralph, and shut up. I'm going to do all the talking, and if I run out of quarters before we're done, then you're SOL. Got me?"

He realized he had no trump card to play, so he said, "Okay, start talking."

"First of all, gumshoe, I don't like you. Never did, never will, but for both our sakes I'll look past my distain for the FBI and try to work with you. But it has to be you and only you. If I even smell another agent in the vicinity I'll pull the plug on this little adventure and we'll all be back to square one. Will that work for you Ralph?"

"I can make that happen."

"Good. Then I want you to swear to me you'll be coming alone to meet up with me."

"I promise. I'll come alone, but I'll have to tell my superiors something. I just can't go running off without letting them know where I am."

"TFB Ralph. I understand your predicament, but you work out the details with them and meet me down here later tonight."

"And where is that?"

"Hold on, you're getting ahead of yourself. This is what I want you to do. You'll need to go out and rent a car from Avis, preferably one with a big-ass sticker of the company on the rear bumper. That way I'll be able to identify you with no problem. Plus, it won't have one of those cell phones in it that you could call your boss on. Then I want you to drive south on 35W until you come to Highway 20 in Iowa. It's about seventy miles south of the Minnesota border. I'd say it shouldn't take you any more than four hours to get here. Don't waste any time Ralph, because if you aren't here by two thirty this afternoon, I'll be gone. When you get here go to the Standard station on the southwest corner of the intersection and wait at the payphone inside. I'll call you there."

"What if I can't make it there by then?"

"Get real Ralph. You're a fuckin' FBI agent, so drive as fast as you want, and flash your badge at the highway patrol if they should happen to stop you. Have you got all this down on your notepad?"

"I think so."

"You better hope so. Now, do you have anything for me?"

I was interrupted by the operator, who wanted another dollar twenty-five for three more minutes. I put the money in the slot and asked Ralph again if he had anything else to tell me.

"Yes I do Ian. I have a couple of things. The most critical one is that your friend, Lane Moreland, was found dead early Tuesday morning. He died from a gunshot to the head. We're not sure at this point if his death has anything to do with the assassin or if it's unrelated. It could be a suicide or possibly a murder. The local police and the FBI are looking into that as we speak. And, as you might suspect, the FBI wants to talk to you about his death ASAP, as you were the last person to see him alive. The other thing has something to do with the killer's identity, but I'd rather we talk about that when we meet. It's the one thing I have that you want, and it assures me that we will meet this afternoon. And that's it. I have nothing else. We'll talk more when I get there."

"Okay, but can you do something for me?"

"What's that?"

"I want you to make a call to your buddies at the main office, and tell them to take a good look at Lane's wife for the shooting. I don't think the assassin would have killed Lane just to spite me. No, that wasn't the work of our killer. That was someone else. I'm telling you; look into the wife's whereabouts at the time of the murder. I left him at eight thirty on Monday night, so she would have had ample time to go over to his house and kill him."

"I'll make the call and let them know what you've said."

"Thanks Ralph. I'll see you by no later than two thirty. And make sure you're alone."

I stood still for several minutes and thought; oh my God, Lane's gone. Then I punched the wall. There's no way the assassin followed me and took his frustration out on him. It has to have been someone else, like his wife or her boyfriend. Either one of them could be possible suspects. I hated myself for thinking I had anything to do with Lane's death, but I would make it my life's quest to help the authorities find his killer and bring him or her to justice.

Now I'm involved in multiple murder investigations. The day started out so well, and from there it's been all downhill. I went from making love to an angel to making an agreement with the devil, all within two to three hours of each other.

Chapter 26

"I know. I know. I need to deposit a dollar twenty-five in the phone. You don't have to tell me twice." This was beginning to sound like a broken record.

"Hello Tom, it's Ian. How are you doing?"

A hesitant Tom Wheeler replied, "I thought I would have heard from you before now."

"Yeah, I thought so too, but I had a little problem last night when I came in town. I ran into an interesting individual, and the evening just got away from me. But I'm here now, out on 35W at the junction of Highway 20. I just made a call to the FBI in Minneapolis, and the agent whom I told you about is going to meet me here in about fifteen minutes. He's going to be our backup. I felt his help was needed, and using him gets me out of a whole lot of shit. I wanted to touch base with you to see if you had cleared all the fields like I asked. Did you?"

"They'll be done by the end of the day."

"Great. And tell me, have you seen any suspicious vehicles around your place in the last couple of days?"

"Now that you mention it, I have seen a guy driving a maroon Chevy Malibu. He has gone by the place at least four times that I know of, twice yesterday and twice again today. He may have been by more times than that, but those are the only times that I've noticed him."

"That's him, Tom. That's our killer. Be very leery of him, and if he should pull into the driveway, stop what you're doing and go in the house immediately. Do you have any guns there at the farm?"

"Yup. Got an old 30-40 Krag rifle and three shotguns. Why?"

"Well, load up the shotguns and use one of them if you have to. Keep one close to you at all times, even in the cab of your tractor. As I said before, if the killer pulls in your driveway, go in the house and get your shotgun, and run the guy off your property. He's probably not going to stop in broad daylight and pull a gun. He's more than likely going to stop and ask for something normal, like directions, and then he could do anything from driving away to killing you. I don't think he wants to get to you yet. I believe he's waiting for the right moment when we're both together. That's when he'll strike. Also keep that dog of yours with you. It's just about time for me to meet the agent, so I'm going to have to get off the phone. But there's one thing I need to ask you before I have to leave. Can you meet me for breakfast tomorrow morning in a place that's open and visible to the world? If so, do you have any suggestions?"

"Yup, there's Hanson's Truck Stop out on 169. It's just south of Dodge about a half mile out of town."

"Excellent. I want you to meet me there tomorrow morning at eight thirty and again on Friday at the same time. Drive slowly and make sure you're followed if at all possible, especially if it's that maroon Chevy you've seen driving by the house. We need to let the assassin know we've made contact with each other. He already knows where you live, but he doesn't have any idea that I'm staying above the West End Bar. And I'm not going to let him find that out. Now go out and finish your work, and stay at your brother-in-law's or your dad's place for the next few nights. Take Omar and make sure that you're not followed."

"Okay Ian, but when are you coming out to the farm?'

"I'll be around after dark tonight to look things over, and then I'll follow you back to the farm on Saturday morning. I think by Halloween we'll have our man right where we want him. See you tomorrow morning."

Good, that takes care of Tom. Now all I had to do was locate the dogcatcher, and everything would be moving in the right direction. I glanced back across the intersection from my position inside a phone booth at the Texaco station to see if Ralph had arrived. He was late, but I was sure he'd show up at any moment. And I was right. No less than three minutes later I saw another ugly Avis rental car drive up and stop at the gas pumps. Ralph got out of the car, looked around, and went inside. He stayed there, as the attendant went outside to refuel his automobile. I took the opportunity to call him at the station. When I heard the phone ring, I saw Ralph head toward the back hallway, and within seconds he picked it up and said, "This is Ralph. Is this you Ian?"

"It is," I replied. "So how was the trip? Quick I presume."

"You damn straight it was. I almost pissed in my pants trying to make it here on time. Only made one stop to go the bathroom and here I am."

"Is there anyone following you, because you know our agreement? If I even think I smell a cop, then I'm gone, and you won't get credit for any of this."

"Don't worry Ian. I had to do some fast talking, but I managed to leave without incident. I actually slipped out unnoticed like you did back in Minneapolis. Now where do we meet?"

"This is how it's going to work. I want you to leave the station and drive west on Highway 20 toward the city of Ft. Dodge. When you get there, stop at Casey's on the east side of town and go to the payphone on the outside of the store. I'll call you there. Have you got that?"

"I do. And then what?"

"You just worry about finding the store and we'll go from there."

I saw Ralph pay the attendant, and grab a soda and some chips as he made his way out of the station. He drove west like I told him, while I followed at a safe distance. I hadn't noticed any unusual vehicles trailing behind us, so I felt pretty confident about the two of us being alone on this stretch of the highway. He could have had a homing device in his car, but I ruled that out because I thought he was kind of a glory hound; and he wanted to solve this case as badly as I did. I figured he was living up to his end of the deal. It took about thirty minutes to drive the stretch from the interstate to Casey's. It normally would have been quicker, but the detour made the drive a little longer.

I watched as he pulled up to the convenience store and got out of his car. He went right for the phone. He checked his watch; put his left hand in his pocket and stood there looking around like some misplaced city-slicker. Meanwhile, I pulled my car around to the back of the station and parked it. Ralph was waiting patiently by the phone when I walked up behind him and put my hand on his shoulder. He turned around and seemed a bit astonished to be looking at me face-to-face.

"I thought you were going to call me on the phone?" he said.

I laughed and said, "What the hell, did you think you were the only crafty person in this world? I can be sneaky too. You Feds don't have the market cornered on that. Here's what I want you to do. There's a small motel back down the road just before the Lamplighter. It's called the Resthaven. I want you to go there and get a room. I'll find you after you've checked in. I'll get us some beers and meet you there in half an hour. Got that?"

"Yeah."

I really shouldn't have made the dogcatcher stay in such a cesspool, but I hadn't gotten to the point yet where I was willing to let bygones be bygones. He had pissed me off royally, and I was still feeling some payback was necessary for his smug attitude. Besides, what were a few bed bugs and roaches amongst friends?

I knocked at room number four and handed Ralph a six-pack of Hamm's Beer.

"Here you go, the beer refreshing from the Land of Sky Blue Waters," I said with a laugh that he understood immediately.

He took it from me and said, "You shouldn't have. If I'd known you weren't going to splurge, I would have bought some real beer."

"What can I say; I only get the best for a good friend." *A good friend...that was stretching the truth a tad bit.*

"I guess that pretty well sums up our relationship," said Ralph. "It's been shaky at best. Let me be the first one to say I'm sorry for how I've acted. It's just that agents have learned to be cold and I've sort of been that way toward you. I guess it's because of Kate. I've always liked her, and I've been jealous of you from the very beginning."

Cold? That was an understatement. "I understand, Ralph. Kate makes men act foolishly. And I want you to know I've decided I'm not going to see her anymore after this is all over. And I'd like it if you would ask her out on a real date someday. I believe if you give it some time, she'll eventually warm up to you. Don't be so stiff. She seems to be attracted to rich guys, but I believe she'll gravitate toward you after everything that's happened. So just try to be more human and I think she'll like you. Okay?"

"Sounds good. All I can say is I'll try."

"Good. Now tell me what you have."

"Well, we do know the assassin is Vietnamese. He came to this country on the basis of political asylum. He left South Vietnam before the end of the war because he was a Vietcong who'd been turned. His name is Chu Throng. He was that lone captive who wasn't killed in Dak Sen Luc. He must have come over here with distinct intentions of killing everyone that was involved in the murder of his two brothers. That includes you and your fellow platoon mates. By the way, what are the real names of those other two guys? We know their names aren't Johnson and Phillips."

I chuckled to myself and said, "One of them is Paul Fisher from California and the other is Tom Wheeler, the guy I came down here to meet. He lives near a small town south of here. You won't get to meet him right away, but you will see the two of us together, and I'll have you on his farm on Saturday night. I want you to stay in the background for now, so Chu doesn't know you're here. Does that make sense to you?"

"It does, but how am I supposed to get in position if I don't know where Wheeler lives?"

"You'll learn that after we have breakfast tomorrow. I'm going to meet up with Tom in the morning and again on Friday morning out at Hanson's Truck Stop on 169. It's just a little south of Dodge. Tom says you can't miss it. Be there a little before eight and be on the lookout for this guy. Get a table and order breakfast like any other normal person would. Have some coffee and read the newspaper. Do what you guys do best at a stakeout. Then you can follow Tom home and see his place after he and I are done talking. And Ralph, if Chu should show up, let him be. This guy is mine and if he has an accomplice we'll lose both of them if we act too soon. Is that a deal?"

"It is."

"Good, so tell me the rest of what you know before I drink up all this good Minnesota beer."

Ralph then spent the next hour briefing me about the case. And when he was finished he let me see the contents of the confidential file. It actually did have some stuff that I didn't know about, like profiles and other pertinent information about the person who sponsored Chu's move to Atlanta. And he actually knew about Perkins. There were FBI agents protecting him and his family in Phoenix as we spoke.

"Now Ralph, tell me about Lane Moreland. What does the FBI know about his murder?"

"First of all, I want to extend my condolences to you. I know Lane was a good friend of yours, and you obviously must miss him. His death is a shitty thing to happen in the midst of everything else that's going on, but mark my words, we'll find out who killed him. I spoke to the ME and he said there were no fingerprints on the gun, so we believe he was murdered. And seeing that the assassin probably didn't know of him makes us believe he didn't have anything to do with Lane's death. All the experts agreed the assassin wouldn't have chanced blowing his cover or have left a gun that could be traced, so we're taking your advice. We're looking at the wife or her boyfriend for the murder. We don't have much more than that at this time, but we'll keep you posted."

"Thanks. I appreciate it. I suggested the wife, not only because of what Lane told me about her, but also from what I know of her personally. Linda is a mean bitch, who has a devilish temper and a bad attitude to go along with it. I've witnessed her firsthand and it's not pretty. I could be wrong, but I believe she has the capabilities of doing something like this, or at the very least she is manipulative enough to get someone to do it for her. After all, she stands to gain a lot from Lane's death. The biggest thing is the house the Lane built before the two of them ever met. He worked nights and weekends to get that place built. And the place is paid off. They don't owe a penny on it. And Lane received a large inheritance from his mother after she died and that will go to the bitch too. So don't waste any time looking elsewhere. She's got motive and opportunity to do something like this."

"I'll pass the information on to our Twin Cities office when we all get back to Minneapolis. But for now you need to put that in the back of your mind and focus on Chu. Don't take him lightly; he's killed a lot of people. He's very dangerous, so proceed with caution or you'll wind up like Lane."

"I hear you. Now let's talk about something completely different. I'm staying here in town above the West End Bar at the far end of North Ninth Street. It's a small room above the back of the place. And I had a confrontation out back of the bar the other night with three local farm boys. I might have sent one of them to the hospital. I took their drivers' licenses away and said you would be returning them tomorrow or the following day at the latest. Here they are. Just flash your badge and give the boys back their licenses. That will put the fear of God in them and make them think twice about trying to jump an outsider the next time one comes to town."

"There's something else I think you should know. I'm staying with a woman in the room. She's an old friend whom I happened to run across and she invited me to stay with her while I'm here in town. It's a good hiding place. It keeps me from being seen at one of these crusty motels. So, if you should happen to see us together at the establishment or out on the town, you'll know I'm supposed to be with her. Any questions?"

"Does she know why you're here?"

"No, I haven't told her anything. She thinks I'm down here because of my job."

"And is this woman the reason you got in a tussle the other night? I see someone planted one on your cheek."

"She would be the reason. She, shall I say, is a very talented dancer, and a few of the locals took exception to my connecting with her. It was their loss and my gain."

"Wow! Three farm boys and all you got was a bruise on your face. What the hell did they teach you in the military?"

"They taught me how to survive Ralph. And that's exactly what I intend on doing. I've got to go. I'll see you tomorrow morning, sort of, that is."

All in all, it was a good late-afternoon talk. But I had to get back to the bar to meet up with Mitzy for dinner, so I said good-bye to Ralph and headed to the West End.

Chapter 27

I was trying my best to keep my identity hidden by entering the West End through the rear entrance. The place was about a third-full, but no Mitzy and no Asian. I was nervous, my right eye was twitching. I felt a drink would help settle my anxiety, so I bellied up to the bar and said to Floyd, "Quick, give me a Stoli martini." I took a couple sips and asked him if he'd seen Mitzy lately.

"Yeah, she was in here a while ago and left to do some shopping. She gave me this key to give to you and said you could go up to the room and rest or wait down here for her. By the way, word has it three of our local boys got their asses kicked out back last night. You wouldn't happen to know anything about that would you?"

"No, my night was uneventful."

"Then how did you get that mark on your cheek?"

"Oh that? It's nothing. Mitzy and I were fooling around last night and I fell out of bed on my face. Just make me another drink Floyd, and quit asking questions that you seem to already know the answers to."

Floyd poured me a second martini while I sat at the bar quietly thinking about what tomorrow might bring. I hadn't seen a single Asian person since I got in this godforsaken town and for now, that was fine by me. I was positive he would find me soon enough, so tonight would probably be the last time I had a chance to relax and get a good night's rest. Yeah right, who was I kidding? Mitzy was a sex monster and I probably would be lucky to get two hours of sleep.

I had about half of my second martini down when I felt a tap on my shoulder. At first I thought it might be another one of those pesky local boys wanting to call me out for kicking the shit out of one of their own. But I tossed that thought aside because they would have jumped me by now without any warning after what I had done to their buddies. So I slowly turned around on my stool to find myself gazing eye to eye with Mitzy. I almost didn't recognize her. Her long brunette hair was on top of her head, and she was wearing a pair of gold pierced earrings that draped down her slender neckline. Her dress was skin-tight, which truly accentuated her rather long figure. It showed more than enough cleavage to peak one's interest. The high heels were jet-black and the lipstick was a pale shade of red. She didn't look anything like a stripper. She was radiant and way too elegant for an establishment like this.

"So, you're speechless are you Ian? As you can see, I can dress like a lady when I want to. So how do I look?"

She made a quick three-sixty turn and came to a stop between my legs.

"You look absolutely dazzling, my dear. And I can't wait to get you out of that outfit."

I stood up and ever so slowly slid my hand down her backside until I reached her mid-thigh, and noticed she was wearing stockings with a garter belt, but no panties. My heart skipped a beat as Little Ian was beginning to be Big Ian again. I took one step back while holding on to both of her hands. I slowly twirled her in a pirouette to once again get the full view of her stunning beauty. I was amazed at how fabulous she looked and so were the patrons. I wasn't sure if the locals realized that Mitzy was the same woman who was preforming on stage later tonight. It was almost a shame for such a gorgeous woman to bare it all for these lowlifes. She belonged in a room where she could be a one-person show. And I intended on making that happen right after we got back from dinner.

"Now that you've gotten all dressed up, I think we need to go somewhere nice to have dinner. You don't want to waste this on these people."

"I agree," she said.

"Floyd, is there a country club around here where we can go to have something good to eat?"

"Yeah, it's called the Nineteenth Hole out on Route 13. Go back up North Ninth and you'll see the road on your left. It's out maybe three miles."

I took Mitzy by the hand and off we went to have dinner at a place where she wouldn't be on display. That was probably a slip of the tongue because looking like she did meant she would definitely be on display. Only this time it would be with her clothes on.

The country club actually had a nice supper club attached to the pro shop. Mitzy was way overdressed for the place, and I, on the other hand, could have used a shave, shower and a sports coat, but that would have made us look like a couple of yuppies which we definitely were not.

The hostess was in the process of seating us when Mitzy abruptly let go of my arm. That confused me, so I turned around to see why and noticed she had stopped directly in front of a table with a good-looking couple, both seated to one side. I heard her say, "It's nice to see you Paul. Is this your lovely wife? Hi, I'm Mitzy. Did you know your husband is a great tipper? I'm sorry; I didn't mean to interrupt you. Go back to what you were doing. And Paul, stop by some night and I'll give you a free dance."

She then slipped away before anyone could say a word and came back and took my left arm as I continued to escort her to our table. The hostess had seated us next to a cozy, wood-burning fireplace. It was hot, but not as hot as the woman at the table that Mitzy had just left. I could tell by the tone of her voice and her finger wagging that she was irate with the man who I assumed was her husband.

"What was that all about?" I asked.

"Oh, just some off-the-cuff dinner humor. That's all. Paul, the guy sitting back there, comes in the bar whenever I'm in town and gives me twenties with the hope that I'll go to bed with him. He's really full of himself, but a tip is a tip, and I don't discriminate, even if you're the world's biggest asshole. I saw he was with his wife, so I had to stop and thank him for his generosity. I don't think I'll be getting any more of those Jackson's in the future."

"Are you sure you wanted to do that?"

"You're paying for dinner. Right? Then I damn sure wanted to do that because I'm going to make it up on you tonight. This place looks like it's going to cost you at least four or five of his visits." Then she laughed and said, "Where are our drinks?"

"I hope you're happy with yourself for spoiling that woman's dinner tonight. But I think you made the right decision, even though it's going to cost me."

"Hey, he's always wanted to get his hands on me, so I thought I'd send him a message. That's all there was to it. If he doesn't tell his wife he goes to strip clubs, then that's his problem."

With that in mind, we toasted her little act of revenge with a clink of our glasses.

"Here's to us and getting naked," I said.

"You know Ian, I don't think we'll be able to make it back in time for you to undress me, but I'm sure they have a bathroom somewhere around here that we could visit for dessert."

"Dessert? Oh God, you have no idea how I love dessert!"

"Are we talking about the same thing Ian, or am I missing something here?"

"No, it's a long story. I just happen to refer to sex as dessert."

"I can hardly wait to find out what that means."

"So tell me, why is a beautiful young woman like you stripping for her livelihood? I mean, you have a degree, beauty, and intelligence from what I can tell. So what gives? Is it the attention you crave? Or maybe it's the psychologist in you that says you like the power it gives you over men? Which is it?"

"It's none of the above. I do this because it pays for my education a lot faster than waiting on tables. I've been going to school off and on for the last three years to get my master's degree in psychology. All I have left to do is write my thesis and I'll be done. I've been working on the paper and a girl has to eat, so this is what I do. I want to be a licensed therapist someday. Actually, I want to work with sex offenders, and I think what I do will give me great insight into their deviant minds. To see the lengths that men go to get me in bed is astonishing. I've even had a couple of women who've tried."

"So how did that work out?"

"I'm totally straight if that's what you're asking. You didn't get that from our encounter last night? If not, you really do need dessert. By the way, have you ever had sex at thirty-five thousand feet? I have and it's exhilarating! I think you'd like it if you ever got the chance. Maybe I can give you a taste of what that's like after dinner."

"Oh," I smiled and said, "There you go talking about dessert again and we haven't even ordered dinner. So when do you think you'll be done with your thesis?"

"Probably in a few weeks if knuckle down and get to it. Then I'll go out and find a real job. And if I find a company that offers tuition reimbursement, I might go after my doctorate."

"That would he something. Then you could go out and do a little stripping every once in a while under the name of Doctor Debbie or something like that, and do some research at the same time. Tell me, do you ever work at the Bull Pen anymore?"

"No, I quit doing anything in the Twin Cities area when I started on my master's degree. I want to put some distance between that and my career. Now I only work in places like the West End where no one knows me."

"You mean like me?"

"Yeah, like you. Actually, you had no idea who I was until I told you this morning, so in reality I could still be a stranger and you wouldn't be any the wiser. Let me ask you this Ian. Did you want to order dinner or would you like to take a trip to the sky-blue yonder? By the looks of the place, it's dead, so I don't think we'll get interrupted. Are you game?"

"I see no reason to wait. Let me order a couple of drinks first and I'll meet you there. Okay?"

She leaned over and whispered in my ear, "I'll be the one in the bathroom with no panties on in case you get confused."

I quickly ordered the drinks and wasted no time in meeting Mitzy in the ladies' room. To my chagrin, the place was empty. I checked both stalls, but she was nowhere to be found. Then I thought for a moment, and I wondered if she meant to meet her in the men's room. No way. Why would she do that? But yet it would be just like a stripper to want to do it in a place like that where it posed more of an adventure and less of a chance of having someone run to the manager. So I went to the men's room and sure enough, she was sitting there on the sink with her legs crossed and her dress hanging over the bathroom stall. She was right. She was pantiless. I went to lock the door and she said, "No, don't do that. It takes the thrill out of what we're about to do."

I looked back at her and said, "And once again you're naked. You know you're starting to take all the fun out of this. Besides, I thought we were going to do it in the stall, like they do on airplanes."

"What makes you think they only do it in airplane bathrooms? Someone has been feeding you the wrong information. Do you know how easy it is to do oral sex up there? And for you to find out the answer to that question, you'll have to take me on a trip someday. Now drop your pants, and get over here before I start without you."

Dinner was certainly entertaining after that. We laughed and giggled as we hand fed each other cracked crab and lobster. As she wiped off the butter that had dripped down her chin she said, "Now I know how Jennifer Beals felt in *Flash Dance.*" Then she slipped her right shoe off and began to tickle Big Ian back to attention. And when the waiter came around with the dessert menu, Mitzy and I looked at each other and burst out laughing.

The poor, young waiter left with a rather perplexed look on his face, as did the few customers who were still eating. Everyone seemed a little bewildered as the two of us carried on like a couple of animals in heat. I couldn't remember the last time I had so much fun at dinner.

Chapter 28

I was sitting in a booth near the front window at the truck stop sipping my favorite soft drink when Tom Wheeler pulled up and exited his truck. It was 7:55 a.m. and I was a bit hung over. The caffeine from the Coke was badly needed, as I only had a few hours of sleep the night before. Damn that Mitzy for having to work so late and me, for being so stupid to think I could outlast her in a fuck marathon. I looked around and saw a highway patrolman and a local cop sitting two tables to my left. They were having coffee. The rest of the place was filled to near capacity with truck drivers and local businessmen. Ralph was positioned at a table across the room reading the morning paper as Tom walked in the front door. He recognized me immediately and came right over to the booth. I stood, and the two of us hugged and slapped each other on the backs as would be expected of two old friends. We were more than friends, we were former comrades-in-arms and we were about to be that once again.

"How in the hell are you Tom?" I asked in a voice so loud the whole place could hear. I glanced back across the room and noticed Ralph had dropped one side of his newspaper to get a glimpse of the man I was there to meet. He then got up, left a ten on the table, and walked outside where he stretched and lit a cigarette. As I sat in the booth talking to Tom, I kept a close eye on Yorkshire while he checked out the vehicles and their drivers.

"So Ian, life looks like it's been good to you. You seem fit. Any lingering effects from that explosion back in Nam?"

"No, my neck's okay for the most part, but I still have a hard time turning to the right. I get the finger quite often from motorists when I'm out on the road, but outside of that I'm doing fine. I work out now and then, mostly with my sensei at the karate studio near my house. He keeps me limber and coolheaded which is great for times like this."

"I guess that's true. So what have you heard lately about the guy we're looking for?"

"I don't want to say too much in here, but he has been identified. His name is Chu and he was the lone Vietcong who didn't die that day. I guess our government brought him to this country, and he's been living in Atlanta for the last six to seven years. I can't say much more than that right now."

"That's good to know. At least it confirms your theory. And we do believe he's somewhere here in town. So, the only question I have is how do you expect to get him to waltz up to my place and say howdy?"

"I'm hoping he takes notice of our get-togethers. He knows where you live, but he hasn't found me yet. At least I don't believe he has. And when he does he'll strike, as he doesn't want to stay around this town too long. Because the longer he stays, the more apt he'll be caught. The FBI has his description and a photo of him has been circulated to every law enforcement agency in the country, so it won't be long before they catch up to him. I understand the picture of him is rather old, so maybe he's a little heavier and his hair might be a little longer, but an Asian around these parts sticks out like corn smut."

"If the Feds have his name and photo, then why don't we get them in here so they can take care of him?"

"It's a little complicated Tom. Trust me. We'll have this over by no later than Sunday. By the way, did your family make it to Nebraska?"

"Yes they did."

"And have you heard from them yet?"

"Yeah, they called last night and I spoke to Loren. She said her parents were thrilled to see the kids, and they were going out today to find costumes for the boys to wear for Halloween. Tommy Jr. said he wanted to be a pirate and Timmy, the little one, is too young to know what's going on, but they thought they'd still get him something to wear for pictures."

"Good, I'm glad they're safe. And did you get everything cleared like I asked you to?"

"Yup, we even got the bean field done. I wanted to make sure nothing got destroyed in case this guy decides to run his car through my fields. It worked out well. Now I can help my brother-in-law next week. We alternate harvesting our crops in case the weather gets bad. You just never know when we could get a rain or snowstorm, so it's better to be safe than sorry."

"My sentiments exactly! That's why I decided to bring down the agent I was telling you about. If you look slowly over your left shoulder you can see him standing over by the gas pumps. He's just a tad bit over six feet tall with short brown hair and he has a Jakes Seed ball cap on."

"You mean the guy in the blue jeans and denim jacket?"

"That's him. He's actually not such a bad guy. He apologized to me yesterday afternoon for being such an ass. I guess it's in their blood, the FBI that is. He'll be in the background the whole time. Don't speak to him until he comes out to the farm. Okay?"

"Gotcha."

"And now to our plan. I want to spend the next two mornings having breakfast with you. Saturday we'll do it later, say ten o'clock. Let's do that one at the coffee shop downtown on North Ninth. I think it's called Val's. Do you know the place?"

"Not off hand, but I'll find it."

"I want you to park out front of the restaurant, and make sure you can be seen by anyone who may be walking or driving by. I'm hoping he finds us before that, but if not, we might need to take a little walk up and down the main drag and display ourselves. I had a chance to go out and look at your place last night after dark. I had some observations. Is the light out on the lamppost in your backyard?"

"You know, I think it is. I'll go home and replace it today."

"Good. We need a well lit area back there. I also want you to back your John Deere with the cab into the tree-line so it's facing the rear of the house. Outside of that I think we're doing fine. Tell me Tom, are you still okay with what we're doing?"

"I think so Ian, but I've got to tell you I'm a little scared."

"I am too, Tom."

"I've never seen you scared Ian."

"I was scared shitless on a number of occasions back in the war. I just didn't show it for the sake of the squad. And you weren't there the two times the platoon was nearly wiped out. I almost shit my pants when we ran into those Red Chinese in Laos. No Tom, I get scared just like you do, but I tend to channel it. I think the karate helps me with that. So, if you don't have any more questions, I think we're done here for today. Ralph is going to follow you when you leave. He'll do it at a safe distance until you get back to the farm. Drive slowly and don't lose him. He's going to be in a blue, four-door Chevy with Minnesota plates. It has a big Avis sticker on the rear bumper. Ralph and I want to see if Chu is waiting out there somewhere, so he can follow you home. Ralph should have a good idea if you're being followed. But there's always the possibility Chu is already out at your farm waiting for us to show up. By the way, where's Omar?"

"He's locked up in the house."

"Not a bad idea, but I'd rather have him with you. Got that loaded shotgun in your truck?'

"I do."

"Okay, then keep the dog close to you at all times until this is over. I have my reasons which I'll tell you later. So take off and be extremely cautious. I think Yorkshire might drive past your farm on the way out, but he'll turn around and come back and probably pull into your driveway. When he shows up, shake his hand and introduce Omar to him. Act like he's just another farmer-friend who stopped for a visit. I suggest the two of you check the farm out for Chu, just to be on the safe side. Bring Omar with you and act like you're showing Ralph around the place. Now get out of here. I'll see you tomorrow."

This time the two of us stood and shook hands. I watched from the inside of the restaurant as Tom got in his truck and drove away. I saw Ralph follow him a minute after that.

There were a number of things I wanted to do before I met with Ralph later in the day. I needed to purchase some new batteries for my two-way radios, buy a Bowie knife, and take a short nap. I knew if I went back to the West End I might not get much sleep, so I decided I'd get a room at the Lamplighter Inn as a diversionary precaution and take a nap. If Chu should happen to run across me today he'd think I was staying at the motel. That would keep him away from the bar and Mitzy. I had already gotten one woman involved, and I was going to make damn sure that didn't happen twice.

Chapter 29

I made the Town & Country hardware store my first stop on the drive back into town. The storekeeper seemed quite knowledgeable about knives and asked what I was going to use it for. *I'm going to use it to cut a serial killer's throat.* I thought twice about saying that and let the question slide without responding. The cashier, on the other hand, wanted to know if the knife was sharp enough for all my needs. *A dull knife would be more fun to use to slash the assassin's throat as it would cause him greater pain and a slower death.* That was the actual truth, but then I would have felt obliged to tell him my intentions, and that might have raised an eyebrow or two. In the end I paid the man for the items and headed to my car.

    I couldn't have been more than twenty feet from the rental when I saw a maroon Chevy Malibu with Iowa plates drive right by me. I wasn't able to see the driver, but I was sure he'd seen me. I needed to make sure he saw me, so I milled around on the sidewalk for a couple of minutes before I went to get in the car. As I approached the driver's door, I stopped and fiddled with my keys for thirty seconds more while I waited to see if the Malibu came back for another peek. I had just gotten in the car when I looked left and saw the Malibu pass me going the opposite direction on North Ninth. My pulse heightened and my chest got tight as our eyes locked for a moment or two. That split second meeting had been a complete adrenaline rush, as it brought both relief and rage for the man who had killed my friend. Good! He knows I'm in town. Now all I have to do is lead him to the Lamplighter. I started the engine, turned on my signal, and watched for him in my side mirror. When I saw him approach, I pulled out into traffic and headed north to the motel.

There was a warm wind in the air, and I could tell by the sky there was a storm coming. I rolled down the window and adjusted my side mirror to make sure the assassin was still following me. Just for shits and giggles I took several lefts and rights as we both drove in tandem to the outskirts of the city.

I drove past Casey's, pulled into the motel, and found a parking spot in front of the manager's office. I got out and went inside to register. I looked over my shoulder as I entered the office and saw the Malibu pass slowly by the motel, then speed up as it headed out of town. The manager gave me the key to room ten. I drove down and parked in front of it. I quickly entered the room, closed the door, and immediately pulled the curtains almost all the way close. I stood there peeking from behind a small opening until I saw the Chevy drive past, headed back in the direction of the city.

The first thing I did was call Tom's place, but no one answered. He didn't have an answering machine, so I couldn't leave him a message. The next thing I did was call Yorkshire to leave a message with the manager of the Resthaven. I said, "The eagle has been spotted, and we should get together later to talk about it." I also wanted to know if he had returned the licenses I had given him. After that there was nothing else to do but take that long overdue nap. I set the alarm for 3:00 p.m., locked the door, and put my knife and guns on the nightstand.

The tinny sound of the alarm woke me out of a deep sleep. I'd been dreaming that Lane Moreland was alive and trying to tell me his wife had poisoned him. Poison or gun, it didn't really matter because Lane was lying on a cold slab in the morgue, and I was sure his wife was tits deep in his death.

I looked outside to see if the Malibu happened to be anywhere in sight. It wasn't, but I was sure it or Chu was somewhere close. I showered, called Ralph again, but he still wasn't in. So I tried Tom's phone and he answered.

"Hello Tom, it's Ian. I assume by now you've realized you weren't followed out to the farm this morning."

"How did you know?"

"Because Chu found me as I was exiting the hardware store. It wasn't long after our meeting at Hanson's. He followed me out of town to the Lamplighter. I've got a room here. I want him to think I'm staying here. It'll actually work to our advantage. I just need to give him the slip when I go to the West End. Did you get to visit with Ralph?"

"Yeah, we had a nice talk. I think he admires you for what you're doing and that you were going out with a hot babe whom he seems to have a crush on."

I didn't put credence to that comment, but rather decided to let it pass as I was presently putting the wood to a much younger woman who was equally as beautiful as Kate.

"You know Tom, sometimes we have a tendency to misjudge people, and I think that's what happened with Ralph and me. So everything's okay?"

"So far, so good," he said.

"Then I think you're fine for the moment, but leave before it gets dark, and lock the place up as tight as a jail. Windows, doors, the refrigerator; lock everything that has a handle or knob. It will be easier if you do that when you get back and check the place in the morning. And don't forget your shotgun and Omar. Where are you staying tonight?"

"At my parents' place. It's a couple of miles from here."

"I suggest you keep the dog in the house just in case. I'll see you for breakfast in the morning."

I hung the phone up and tried Ralph's number one more time. This time he answered.

"Ralph, it's Ian. Did you get my message?"

"Yes, I just got it. I was about to call you when the phone rang. I saw your car as I passed the Lamplighter on my way here. I must say it looks like you have better accommodations than I do."

"It really doesn't matter because I don't plan on staying here. It's too easy to be shot through the front window. At one point I thought of getting the room next to yours, so we could collaborate. But then I decided it would have been too risky to have cars from the same rental company parked side by side. Here's what I want you to do. I'm going to sneak out after dark and walk down to your place through the woods. I'll call first. You can pick me up around the back of your motel, and we'll head into town. I believe Chu will be on the west side of the Lamplighter, parked somewhere between it and town. I'll stay low in your backseat until we think the coast is clear. Talk to you in about an hour and a half. Bye."

It was waiting time once again. I pulled an old wooden chair out from beneath the desk and put it directly in front of the slit in the curtains. I sat down, rested my arms on the chair's back, and continued to look for the assassin. It seems we were back at the game once again. I was sitting in wait, hoping the enemy would cross my path. It wasn't Vietnam, but it was close enough to an ambush to make it feel that way. The hunter and the hunted; we had taken a step backwards in time and shifted into primeval mode. The only question was, who was the hunter and who was the hunted?

It was beginning to get dark when the phone rang. It was Ralph. He said he was outside his room having a smoke when he saw the Malibu drive past heading toward the interstate. I must have dozed off for a moment and missed it when Chu drove by. Ralph suggested this might be a good time for me to exit the room and meet him out back of the Resthaven. I quickly gathered the weapons and left with my tote bag in hand. It took me about ten minutes to fight my way through the saplings and the bright-red sumac to reach his motel. Ralph was waiting with his engine running, exactly where he said he'd be. I jumped in the back seat and lay down just low enough to see out of the window.

Ralph said, "Where to?"

"Just head into town, and I'll watch out the back to see if we're being followed."

He laughed and said, "Isn't that supposed to be my job?"

"Well maybe you were trained for that, but it's my head he's after, so drive on, Rochester."

Ralph put the car in drive and off we went. I looked for the Malibu until we reached the center of town, but Chu was nowhere in sight. That kind of surprised me. I had been looking on both sides of the road, and I thought I would have seen him by now. Or maybe he had seen me in Ralph's car and put two and two together and realized I wasn't in this alone. Yet Chu was mostly a jungle warrior and not used to playing this cat-and-mouse game, so we may have eluded him altogether.

"Did you see him Ralph?"

"No, did you?"

"Nothing. Oh well, he knows I'm here so that's all that matters. Drive up to the end of town and take a left at the corner when you pass the West End Bar."

"What are we going to do there?"

"We're going to have a couple of drinks. You're going to get jealous, and I'm getting laid."

"Oh, is that all?"

"You want more? Okay, then you can leave at ten o'clock when I get a beautiful female visitor and drive out to Tom's farm to see if Chu is there."

The two of us walked in the back door to the West End and found a table in the corner. Mitzy was nowhere to be seen, but Floyd was in his usual place behind the bar.

"Tell me Ralph, did you get a chance to give those licenses back?"

"I only had time to stop and see one of the kids. You fucked him up pretty bad. He has two black eyes, one which is completely bloodshot, and he has a broken nose. His dad gave me some shit when I started talking to the boy, so I pulled out my badge and he clammed up real fast. First he looked at the badge and then at me, and then asked his son what kind of trouble he and his buddies had gotten into. I thought the kid was going to shit his pants right there in the kitchen. The kid just shrugged his shoulders and said nothing. I assured the old man that his kid wasn't in any trouble. Then I told the kid he was lucky he had gotten off with just a broken nose. I don't think the kid will be going to town any time soon. I asked the kid where I could find the other two boys, and he said one was still in the hospital, and the other one lived out on Route 6. I had to laugh as I rode away. The badge does put the fear of God in people, even more so than one from a regular cop."

"Are you going out to deliver the others tomorrow, or would you like to go out to the hospital tonight so we can do that together?"

"I think you should stay put. The less we're seen together the better. Lest you forget, there's a killer out there who wants to put a bullet in your head. And I don't think he cares if he kills you and Tom together or individually. Now that you're here it doesn't make any sense to take you both on at the same time."

"I disagree. I believe he still thinks he has the element of surprise. And killing us individually would put an end to that. The guy also has a huge ego, and he's starting to believe he's invincible, so I think he'll come after Tom and me when we force him to. Tom is safe with relatives for now. And I'm going to do my very best to drive Chu crazy as he tries to find out what my next move will be. Saturday will be his best chance, and I'm sure he'll take his shot on that night."

I looked up and saw Mitzy coming toward us with refills. She was wearing a Catwoman costume with a black mask. I could tell it was her from the form-fitting outfit she had on. There was no way she could hide those breasts; they were magnificent.

Ralph saw her too and said, "Look how our waitress is dressed."

That was a split second before Mitzy made it to the table and said, "Meow," and planted a big kiss on my lips.

I caught my breath and said, "Good God, the women in this town sure are friendly."

Ralph, the analytical genius that he was, had figured out by now that this was the lovely woman whom I said I was staying with.

I introduced Ralph by saying he was friend of mine who was down here looking at some farmland to purchase. I told Mitzy we had talked a couple of weeks back and he decided to come down this week when I was in town. My other friend, the one who lives south of town, asked us to go pheasant hunting with him and his brother-in-law this weekend, so I informed her we'd be out there Saturday and Sunday.

"Oh that's a shame. So you're not going to be here this weekend to see my grand finale?" She seemed hurt that I wouldn't be around to see her, but that wasn't in my original plan, and I wasn't about to change it to satisfy her.

"No I'm not, but I'll be returning Sunday night, and we can get together then."

She seemed okay with that and turned to Ralph and asked, "So, what do you do for a living Ralph?"

He hesitated and said, "Oh, I'm a cop. I'm just about ready to retire, and I want to buy a small hobby farm that I can run and have some peace and quiet."

Real smart Ralph. Way to blow your cover.

"So do you have your gun and badge with you?" she asked. "I've always wanted to see a real badge and hold a big, steel gun. It turns me on. Meow."

I could sense that Mitzy had embarrassed Ralph, but he took it in stride and said, "No, I left all of that back in Minnesota."

Mitzy joined us for drinks and dinner. We spent the majority of the time having a lively conversation about the world of stripping. And in the end I think Ralph thought better of her line of work. An FBI agent probably thought all strippers were either in the business because they had no real skills or they were prostitutes on the side, but after a while he started to warm up to her when he learned she had a degree and was about to add another one to her resume. Maybe it was the drinks, or maybe it was her outfit, but he certainly seemed to like what he saw. She left at eight thirty to go up to the room to change into another outfit for her show, while Ralph and I continued on with our conversation.

When her set was over at ten, Ralph excused himself and left to do a little snooping on his own. Mitzy and I talked for another fifteen minutes, and then I went off to bed. I told her I was tired, and I would see her after she was finished for the evening.

We were in the middle of act two when I heard pounding on the door to the back steps. I heard a voice say, "Ian, are you in there?" It was Ralph, and he seemed real agitated about something. So I got up and put my shorts on, and told Mitzy to put on a robe. Then I went to the door and let him in.

He said, "Excuse me for the intrusion, but someone put several shotgun rounds through the window to your room at the Lamplighter about forty-five minutes ago. I went over there when I heard the shots. The police were there shortly afterwards and I spoke to them. They wanted to know who I was and what I was doing at the scene. I explained who I was to try and stabilize the situation. I think everything's okay, but they want to talk to you ASAP. I told them I'd pass that on to you the next time we got together. Now I know why we didn't see Chu or his car. He was going to try to eliminate you tonight and deal with Tom later on. See, I told you so. He wasn't going to wait for the two of you to get together and gang up on him. So what do you want to do now?"

Mitzy asked, "What the fuck is going on here Ian? Who did what to your room? And you have another place outside of town where you're staying? Who's Chu? And did Ralph say someone tried to kill you a little while ago?"

I knew I owed her an explanation, but I wasn't quite sure how I should handle it.

"Just hold on for one second, Mitzy." I looked back at Ralph and asked, "Did anyone follow you here?"

"No, I made sure I wasn't followed. Besides, whoever shot your place up wouldn't be waiting around to make sure you were dead. He'd have had to leave in a hurry and God knows where he's at now. You're actually lucky you're staying here. The police found six or seven empty shell casings. The shooter was using 00 buck shot. They really pack a wallop. The place was pretty torn up, and you wouldn't be alive if you'd been sleeping in the bed."

"Okay, somebody better tell me what's going on," demanded Mitzy. "And I mean right now, or I'm going downstairs to call the police and tell them you're here."

"First of all, I want to say I'm sorry you've been involved. I was positive you wouldn't ever find out any of this. I am who I said I was and so is Ralph. Only he's an FBI agent and ..."

Ralph interrupted me and said, "Ian, I don't think you should..."

"Stop right there Ralph. I think she deserves to know what's going on because her life could be in danger. Look at me Mitzy. As I was saying before Ralph interrupted, we are working together to track down a serial killer. I'm filling you in so you can decide if you want to let me stay or tell me to hit the road. Are you okay with that, Ralph?"

"I guess so. It's your neck and your plan. So let it fly."

"Listen to me for a minute Mitzy. Things have changed and so has our plan. I now need to lie low for the next twenty-four hours while Ralph makes sure my friend is okay. I need to stay here in the room with you until Saturday morning. Can I do that?"

Mitzy was shaking uncontrollably. She stood there looking at me with her mouth wide open and said, "A fuckin' serial killer! Are you guys for real? Let me see your badge Ralph." He took it out and showed it to her. "Okay, I see that Ralph is who he says he is, but are you Ian? I truly hope so. Now, the only way you're going to stay here is if the two of you swear I'm not going to be hurt. Can you do that?"

"What do you think Ralph? Are you good with that?"

"Yeah, I guess I am. I'll head back to the Resthaven and sleep with one eye open for the rest of the night. But what's next Ian?"

"Well, seeing that I told Tom specifically not to go home tonight, I'll need you to go to the truck stop in the morning to make sure he's okay. I'll also need an emissary to deliver a message to him. Mitzy, do you think you could do that for me?"

"Wait a minute. You want me to deliver a note for you? I don't think that's in my job description. I'm a fucking stripper, in case you forgot!"

"I know it's not, but all you have to do is slip him the note as you pass his table. You don't even have to speak to him. What do you say?"

She hesitated for a long time, then finally said, "I guess I could do that, but how will I know what he looks like?"

"I've got that covered. Here's a picture of us back in 1969." I pulled a photo of the old platoon out of my bag. It was tough to look back at all those dead guys, especially the one of Snake Cummings. "Tom hasn't changed much from this picture. He's about a hundred and a half, with light-brown hai,r and he'll most likely be wearing blue bib overalls with a DeKalb ball cap. So what do you say?"

"I guess so. I need a little more adventure in my life," she said with a very straight face.

"Thatta girl. I knew Catwoman would be up to the task."

I sat down and wrote Tom a note telling him what had happened, and to be very careful and to meet me at Val's at ten o'clock Saturday morning. Then I slipped the piece of paper between Mitzy's cleavage and told her to hold it for safe-keeping.

I turned back to Ralph and said, "I'm not going back to get my car. I'll use Mitzy's if that is okay with her. Tell the police to keep things under wraps, and I'll explain everything to them next Monday morning. Also tell them to have my car towed to Hanson's Truck Stop and to leave the keys with you. That should further convince Chu that I'm dead. For now, let's let Chu think he's killed me, and let him focus on going after Tom at the farm. Actually, we've got him right where we want him. We're going to bed now. I'll meet you back here tomorrow night at six o'clock."

"Okay, I'll be here. Good night Mitzy and thanks for your help. You two watch your asses."

"No problem. From where I'm standing, hers looks pretty good, and I've got nothing else to do but keep an eye on it until tomorrow night. See you then."

Ralph left by the back stairway, and I watched him from the doorway as he disappeared into his car and drove away. I hadn't seen any other headlights go on, so I figured we were alright for at least another day or two.

Mitzy said, "Wow, all that excitement has got me hotter than a porn star. Let's get back to where we were, and you can tell me more about what's going on in the morning. By the way, do you have a gun too?"

"Yes, I have three of them; two in my tote bag and another one in my shorts. That one is loaded and ready for you, which brings me to the next question. Are you ready?"

"I was born ready," she said. "Let's get down and dirty. This may be your last chance to have some of this, and I wouldn't want you to waste a minute thinking about anything else."

Chapter 30

Mitzy left bright and early the following morning to deliver my message to Tom Wheeler. I sensed by her smile she was having fun playing the liaison between Tom and me. She was an extremely bright and gutsy young woman, but I didn't want her involved any further than delivering a message for me, which would be the last thing I asked her do until this whole thing blew over. She was in danger, even if Ralph and I had said things to the contrary. That would especially be true if Chu had followed Ralph here last night, or he had seen me come in the bar earlier in the evening. But I was confident Chu wouldn't go after Mitzy unless he needed her as a hostage or for trade bait. If there was no additional contact with Chu by later in the day, then I'd go downstairs and watch her until she finished her final set to make sure she was alright. And tomorrow I'd leave, and that would be my last contact with her until this was over. But for now I needed to lie low and wait for her to return.

It was a little before 9:00 a.m. by the time Mitzy made her way back to the West End, along with a hearty Iowa breakfast of pancakes, sausage, scrambled eggs, and two pieces of apple pie. Getting breakfast was a good cover for her rendezvous with Tom. It made it believable and removed any assumption that she was there to meet up with him.

"So did everything go according to plan?"

"Smooth as silk," she said.

"You didn't happen to see an Asian man or a maroon Chevy Malibu while you were there, did you?"

"No, I didn't. And I also didn't see anyone with that description follow me back here. I even drove the long way around to make sure. You know I never asked you why you were after this guy. What's the story?"

"Did I tell you how good the sausage and pancakes were? And you know how much I like dessert, so let's leave it at that and go back to bed and forget about this mess that I've gotten you involved in."

"No Ian, as much as I like fucking you, I want to know what this is all about. After all, I've stuck my neck out and I think I deserve to know why."

"Okay. Do you want the whole story or the abbreviated version?"

"Just tell me what you think is necessary, and that will probably be enough for me."

"Well, you remember the photo I showed you last night? That was a picture of one of my old platoons back in Vietnam. Anyway, almost all of those men are dead now. They were killed during an ambush. The others made it back to the States, and then one more died at the hands of the man we're after. His name was Roland Cummings, and he was a good friend of mine. He saved my life once, and I'm here to repay that debt. That's why we've set up our own ambush for this guy, and we're hoping he walks into it tomorrow night at Tom's farm. We captured him and his brothers one night during the war and turned them over to the CIA. The CIA in turn tortured and killed his two brothers, and he blames me for letting that happen. At least I think he does, and that's why he has gone to such lengths to try to kill me. In between the time he killed Roland and now, he has managed to eliminate seven more men."

"Wait a minute. Is this the guy I keep hearing about on the news; the one who killed that senator and his two security guards?"

"I believe so. Why do you ask?"

"As you might suspect, I've got a lot of time to waste during the day. I read the newspaper and watch a lot of television. This guy has been all over the five and six o'clock news this week. They've even released a picture of him with information linking him to crimes all across the country. I think he's been reported to have killed a dozen people or more. What gives?"

"I'm not sure. I'll have to speak to Yorkshire about that. But I suspect the Feds are blaming everything they can on him. The Feds tend to bunch a lot of murders together when they can't find the real killers and bring them to justice. What exactly do you know about this guy?"

"So far I've seen his picture and learned that he has killed a judge and senator, some Secret Service men, a cop, I think, and some other people. I'm not real sure how many men in all, but I do know they say he's a serial killer. One station said he was last seen in Minnesota and was thought to be headed to California. I kind of didn't give it a second thought, as it never occurred to me that he would be coming in this direction. I mean really, Ft. Dodge, Iowa? Who would have guessed it?"

"I for one. And none of this was supposed to have gotten to the press. I need to talk to Ralph. I hope what he's done hasn't compromised our situation. Can I use your car?"

"Sure. Where are you going?"

"To find Ralph. He has a lot of explaining to do."

I took her keys and went downstairs to make a phone call. I dialed the Resthaven and asked the manager to ring Ralph's room. There was no answer. Where was he, I wondered. Then it dawned on me that he was probably returning those last two drivers' licenses. I had no clue where the one kid lived, but I did know that the second one, the fat boy named Larry, was still in the hospital. I got directions to the place from the cleanup guy, and off I went.

I entered the hospital parking lot at five minutes after ten and drove up and down the lanes to find a car with that ugly Avis sticker on the rear bumper. And there it was, sticking out like a tick on a hound dog. I parked three cars down from Ralph's, walked directly to the hospital's entrance, and straight to the information desk. You could tell it was getting close to Halloween as there was a plastic pumpkin on the desk filled with all sorts of candy for the taking. I picked out a cherry sucker because my mouth was beginning to get dry and asked the receptionist if a man had come in here in the last half hour looking for a patient named Larry something. The guy's name was Ralph Yorkshire.

She said, "Yes, a man did come in here, and I directed him to Larry's room."

"Good. And could you be kind enough to tell me what room that is? I'm a close friend of Ralph's. It's urgent that I speak to him immediately."

"Well, I'm not supposed to give out room numbers unless the person asking has the patient's full name or he's a relative. And you're not a relative, so I'm not sure I can do that."

"I understand, but I have a dilemma. I need to talk to Ralph because I'm supposed to be leaving town in the next fifteen minutes, and we need to speak. It's about the guy who put Larry in the hospital. I know who he is, and I need to convey that to Ralph. So could I please have that room number now?"

"Oh, in that case I guess it would be alright. Larry Peck is in room 312."

"Thank you so much."

I went straight for the elevator. When the door opened, I punched in the number three on the wall and went up to find the dogcatcher. The rest of what was going down in the next two days depended heavily on what Ralph had to say. For his sake, I hoped he was in a better mood than I was. I went to 312 and stopped just outside the door. I didn't want the Peck kid to see me. After all, I had put him here, and I didn't want to scare him by getting in a shouting match with Ralph while the three of us were in his room.

I could hear Ralph talking to Peck, but there was no reply from the kid. I must have messed him up real bad, which I was truly sorry for. I could have probably put him down another way, but he was big boy, and I knew it was going to take something extraordinary to stop him. A karate chop to the throat might have been just as effective and less harmful, but in the heat of the moment I did what I had to. Ralph finally said good-bye and exited the room.

When Ralph turned the corner, I immediately grabbed him by the collar and pushed him up against the wall. "Okay asshole," I said. "What did you tell your boss, and how did the press get the information on Chu? If you weren't a cop I'd kick the shit out of you right here and now."

"You might want to take your hands off of me Ian. After all, I am an agent, and I could arrest you right now and finish this myself. Is that what you want?"

"Fuck you Ralph, you can't arrest me for diddly-shit, and you know it. Let's take a walk outside. I want some answers."

The two of us walked down the hospital stairwell together and went outside. The atmosphere was overcast, and the wind was beginning to pick up. I felt a few raindrops hit my face as Ralph and I headed to our cars. I stopped at mine and said, "Get in." We both entered the pea-green Avis at the same time and I said, "Okay Ralph, start talking."

He hesitated, I assumed to make sure he said the right things to appease me. He knew I was pissed because he had sort of broken our agreement. When he finally spoke he said, "I had to speak to the D.C. bureau chief in order to come down here on assignment. I needed to give him something or you'd be here alone. It was decided, after a long conversation, that we'd leak a little information to the public. That way they'd think we had a concrete lead in the case. We published his picture and some information like we often do in cases like this. We let out false information to let the killer think he has us fooled. Ian, we want him to think he's free and clear to do whatever he wants. That's not to say he isn't a little more paranoid than he probably has been, seeing that his picture is all over the news. And now he has to keep a lower profile, especially during the day. That's it Ian. That's all there is to it.

I left Minneapolis saying I'd call for help if I thought we needed it. And so far that hasn't happened. Especially now that Chu thinks you're dead. And he'll be going after Tom as soon as he finds out he's back at his farm. I spoke to him in the bathroom at the truck stop before we left and told him not to go back to his place until sometime around midday tomorrow. I also told him I thought it was still a good idea that he has breakfast at Val's on Saturday morning. I told him to walk around town and let his face be seen, then drive out to the farm and act like nothing was wrong. He gave me a key to his place, and I figured we would go out there tomorrow while he was in town."

"So there are no other Feds in town as we speak?"

"That's right."

"So tell me more about your plan."

Ralph said he had the opportunity to look over Tom's farm when he visited him yesterday. There were several entry points that Chu could come from to gain access to the farmhouse. But Ralph said he could cover the back by concealing himself in the large, round hay bales that were beyond the cattle pens. That way he could see anyone coming from the east side of the property. There also were several other places I could hide myself from view, now that Chu thought I was dead. Ralph and I would be the biggest elements of surprise, and that would be a huge advantage to us. He said Tom was ready and willing to do his part, so all we had to do is show up at the farm and position ourselves.

"Sounds good to me Ralph, but I have some other ideas as to how we can plan this ambush. I need to personally see the farm during the day so we can tie up some loose ends."

"So where are you going now Ian?"

"I'm going back to the West End and spend the afternoon with Mitzy. I want to make sure she's safe and protected. Mitzy, like Kate, was probably unknown to Chu, but who knows if I'm correct in that assumption. I'll talk to you later."

Yorkshire got out of the car and headed for his. I was halfway out of the parking lot before he even got in his car and started his engine. I headed to town with one thing in mind. That was to keep Mitzy from the killer.

Chapter 31

It was Friday night, the day before Halloween, and many of the patrons at the West End were already in the spirit of Día de Muertos. I wasn't Spanish, but tomorrow would be my day to celebrate the holiday of the Day of the Dead. I had it set aside to honor my old friend Snake Cummings and reserved for killing the man who had taken his life. I believe it was Shakespeare who coined the phrase "Everything comes full circle," and if you waited long enough, that seemed to be true. At least in this situation it did. Yes, tomorrow night was going to be a horror show of real life, one that Wes Craven would have paid millions to film. It was going to be bloody and brutal, but most of all it was going to bring closure to a mystery that had origins that went back nearly fifteen years.

Looking around I noticed over half of the bar was in costume, which had me a little worried. What if Chu was in costume and in here looking for Mitzy? He might see me. He'd know I was alive. That would end the element of surprise and make tomorrow's event less cryptic. But there wasn't much I could do, even if he was hiding in this mass of humanity. I simply had to sit and watch as Mitzy dazzled the crowd.

It was show time, but I, unlike the others, already knew what she was going to be wearing. She had modeled all three outfits, if you could label them that, for me throughout the afternoon. And I must say I've never been so entertained or aroused in my entire existence. She was going to begin her first set with an angel costume, which I thought was sacrilegious for a bar, but then a G-string and some wings would definitely fly in a place like this. After that, she was going to entertain the crowd as Wonder Woman, an outfit she could definitely pull off in more ways than one. She had a body that rivaled Linda Carter's, and it was uncanny how much she actually looked like the real starlet. The red, white and blue costume with a cape would transcend her from a celestial being to the actual heavenly body of the crime fighter she was trying to portray. And in a certain sense she was trying to be that for me, as she had demonstrated this morning by delivering a message to another crime stopper of sorts. She was going to follow that up with the Catwoman outfit she had worn to the bar the night before.

It had been strange sitting there with her last night, without anyone noticing who she really was. Her masked costumes blended well with the others, and that was the only reason why we could share the time together without being hounded by drunks and lustful men who wanted to lay claim to this adorable individual.

As the night wore on I spotted and analyzed every male in the room wearing a costume with a mask. There were eleven of them in all, and most of them were either too tall or too heavy to match the criteria for being Chu. There was also a person dressed as a transvestite, so I couldn't tell if it was a he or a she. I ruled him or her out for being too weird for an Asian immigrant to pull off. All in all, there were two men who fit his description, but one of them was sitting with a woman, and they seemed to be together, as he was all over his partner every time Mitzy did a bump and grind in front of his face.

That left one man at a table by the bar. He was alone, sitting quietly and didn't seem to be into the show. It made him a perfect suspect. I watched and waited for him to make a move, but he sat patiently sipping what I thought was a glass of pop. He hadn't moved from his chair for over two hours and a quarter. Then he got up unexpectedly and headed in the direction of the rear entrance. I got up and followed him all the way into the men's room. I was right behind him as he made his way to the urinal. He unzipped his pants and began to piss. I moved in quickly and grabbed him by the back of his neck, and told him to finish before I slammed his face into the wall in front of him. He began to shake; his body, not his penis, as he zipped his pants up. He turned toward me and asked what I wanted.

I said, "Take that mask off. I want to see who you are."

He did. And there stood a little old man in his late sixties, trembling in fear. He thought I was going to hurt him. Then he said the funniest thing, "Am I in trouble with my wife?"

I stood there with my mouth open, unable to speak. Finally words began to come out that were a mixture of incoherent nonsense and apologetic babble. I wasn't able to begin to explain how embarrassed and sorry I was for what I had just done. Fear and stupidity go hand and hand sometimes, and this was one of them. I cleared my throat and said, "No, I don't believe you're in trouble with your wife."

"That's a relief," he said. "She's kind of old and wrinkly. I don't get turned on by her anymore, so I come down here every Friday night to get pumped up. Then I go home and pretend she's the woman whom I've been watching all night long."

My embarrassment turned to laughter, as I wondered how many of these men were actually fantasy-fucking Mitzy when they went home at night. This little man had just provided me with a better understanding of why the Three Stooges had jumped me the other night. They weren't actually mad I took Mitzy home, but rather brokenhearted over the fact that I had destroyed their individual fantasies. I told the old man to put his mask back on and go out and enjoy the rest of the show. If I didn't think Mitzy would have thought I was weird, I would have asked her to put on a private show for him after hours. That wasn't going to happen, so I sent him off to get all the jollies he could for the rest of the evening.

I went to the sink and splashed water on my face. I couldn't look at myself in the mirror because I had almost done the unthinkable. Chu was getting to me more than I would admit, and I needed some fresh air to clear my head. I went out the back door where I found one of the cooks sitting on the milking stool having a smoke. I looked at him and said, "Nice evening."

"Yes it is," he replied. "But tomorrow is going to be a different story. It's going to storm and get uglier as the day progresses."

I turned and went back into the bar without saying a word, thinking to myself that he was completely correct in his assumption. Tomorrow was definitely going to be ugly.

Mitzy found me in her room later that night. I'd been sitting on the floor with my back pressed up against the wall drinking a beer when she entered the room. She was Catwoman and she was on the prowl. "Meow. Meow. Meow Ian. A penny for your thoughts," she said.

I replied, "You know, I've got a lot of emotion going tonight."

"I was hoping you did, and I'm ready to help you release it."

"No, that's not what I mean. What I'm saying is I've been sitting here for the last hour waiting for an epiphany to happen, and I keep coming up empty. I've been thinking to myself that everything I've done up to this point will have some sort of resolution by this time tomorrow night."

"Yeah, so what's the problem?"

"Well, when this thing with Chu is over, I'll have to go back home and start rehabilitating myself all over again. I've spent well over a third of my life getting back to being normal, and I'm worried that tomorrow might rocket me back to the starting line. I can't go through that again, but I can't let go either. Do you understand what I'm going through?"

"As a psychologist, well almost a psychologist, I understand your torment and I recognize your agony, but I don't have any real training for something like this. I guess I would say you need to follow your heart and do what you think is right. Then sit back and say what you did was for the betterment of mankind. And that way you might feel a little better, like a policeman does or the soldier that you were, about the significance of your accomplishment. Make it meaningful and not criminal, and I think you'll come out of this okay."

She switched off the lights, slipped under the covers and said, "Come to bed when you're ready, and I'll try to help you resolve everything that's troubling you."

Chapter 32

The cook's prediction had been right; the day was starting out dark and dreary. From where I was standing on the back deck above the West End, I could see clouds swiftly passing overhead as the wind from the west was blowing in some precipitation. It was exceptionally warm and humid for the last day of October, and I wouldn't be a bit surprised if we got some severe weather along with this rain. A storm with rain could put a damper on our plans, but like the postman's motto says, neither rain, nor snow, nor sleet and blah, blah, blah can stop me from what I was about to do. Actually, it was Herodotus who wrote that, but no one knows who the fuck he was. And he was right. Nothing was going to stop me from my quest, even if it meant being hurt or killed in the process. I was focused today, in much the same manner as I was during my days in Vietnam. When I walked out into the farm tonight, I'd have my game face on and ready to do battle.

Mitzy chose that moment to walk out onto the deck with a robe covering what was left of her Catwoman outfit. She handed me a Coke, touched my arm and said, "Don't you want to come back inside and play awhile before you go?"

"I can't. You know how much I love your vagina; it's like a lifetime of candy bars, but the time for playing is over. It's time to face the music and do what I came here for. Ralph and I have to head out to the farm and get ready for whatever is coming our way. It's been great fun Mitzy, way more than I expected for this journey I've been on. And if everything goes according to plan, and if he shows up tonight, I'll see you back here tomorrow morning."

With that I gave her a kiss on the forehead and went back inside to gather up my things. We hugged for the longest time, and then I vanished down the stairs to make a phone call to agent Yorkshire.

Ralph was in his room when I called, which was a good thing. It meant he was alive and we hadn't been made. I had no way of contacting Tom as he was already at Val's having breakfast. And I squelched the urge to go down and see if he was sitting at a table in the front of the coffee shop. Instead, I made plans with Ralph to have him pick me up at the West End in ten minutes, and then we would head out to the farm. It was going to be a long day and the intensity was beginning to mount. I already had sweaty palms and my stomach was telling me that diarrhea might be right around the corner. I was nervous, but I had to stay focused.

All the signs were there; they indicated it was time to get out of Dodge. I walked out the rear door to the bar and got in the car with Ralph. The last thing I did was to wave good-bye to Mitzy and the West End. It was now ten thirty-five.

"So tell me Ralph, did you resist the urge to drive by Val's to see if Tom was having breakfast, or did you succumb to the temptation and sneak a peek?"

"I did, take a peek that is. Tom was there with another man sitting in the front window."

"Good, he made it, which means he's still alive too. You know, we've done a great job of concealing our plan and I want to thank you for all your help in case I forget or don't get a chance to tell you."

"Glad we could be of service."

"What do you mean by we?"

"Oh, I meant the bureau and Tom. The bureau let me come down here, so I guess they get a thank you too."

"Yeah, I see what you mean. Did you get the keys to my rental car?"

"I did. Here they are."

Ralph handed me the keys and I safely tucked them away in my tote bag. He then asked what I had for weapons and I said, "I bought a large Bowie knife at the store the other day and I've got a .357 magnum and a .38 special that I keep in an ankle holster."

"Did you go out and buy them too?"

"No, my uncle gave them to me awhile back. He used to be a cop like you."

Neither Ralph nor I spoke for the rest of our ride as we proceeded to head down to the Wheeler farmstead. We began by traveling south out of Dodge past Hanson's Truck Stop. I looked to my right to see if my Avis rental car was parked by the service garage. It was there. We didn't stop. We continued driving down the highway, keeping a close eye on the traffic to see if the Malibu was following us. We checked behind billboards, alongside buildings and down side roads for any sign of Chu and his car. They were nowhere in sight; not on the road nor anywhere off the road from what we could tell.

We were about five miles past Hanson's when we hit County Road P59. Ralph took a left over the railroad tracks and continued driving south toward the little town of Otho. The town consisted of about fifteen buildings with one gas station on the north end. I thought I saw Chu's car parked around the corner to the town's only side street, but maybe that was my imagination getting the best of me. We didn't stop to take a look. Instead, we pressed on toward Tom's farm that was three and a half miles further down on a narrow strip of blacktop.

Ralph took a left into the property upon arrival, drove down the gravel driveway, and stopped next to the house. We both took a moment to look out from the inside of the car at the old, two-story farmhouse. It was painted white, but it looked more like a pale shade of gray. There was a faded, red barn directly ahead that was also badly in need of some paint. We needed to stash the car. I said to Ralph, "Pull up in front of the doors to the barn and stop while I get out and open them. And when I do, drive in and park the car so it's hidden from Chu." The place was exactly like I had pictured it in my mind. There were four or five old, rusty implements set at the edge of the woods and a small kids' pool filled with leaves off to the side of the yard. It looked like it hadn't been cleaned or used for a number of years. All in all, the place was badly in need of repairs. From the house to the pens, the place needed some looking after.

Meanwhile, back in Dodge, Tom and his brother-in-law Willard were having breakfast at Val's. The diner was very fiftyish, right on down to the red, vinyl-covered counter stools and the black-and-white square floor tiles. The waitresses were all dressed in costume, and Silvia, a sharp young woman in a duck hunter's outfit had just set down their food order. As she left she said, "Make sure you boys leave room for today's pie special. It's pumpkin." Tom looked away from Silvia and back at his brother-in-law, thinking that having breakfast with him was a good idea. It seemed like the thing friends or relatives would do on a Saturday morning, plus it gave Tom someone to talk to while they ate. Willard had asked him on the ride in why they hadn't stopped and eaten in Otho or at the truck stop out on 169. Tom told him that he just wanted to get away from the small-town atmosphere for a while. And besides, he needed to stop at the John Deere distributor on their way back so he could pick up some parts he had ordered for his tractor. Willard was none the wiser to what was going on and Tom planned on keeping it that way.

The two of them were sitting there finishing their second cup of coffee when a strange little person in a clown mask came up to the window and peeked in. He put his hands to the window and stared directly at them. The clown didn't move. He continued to stand there as he studied the two men.

"Will you look at that," said Willard.

"You mean the clown?" asked Tom.

"Yup, don't you think that's a little strange?"

"I guess so, but maybe he's looking for a family member in the restaurant."

"I don't think so. He hasn't moved his head or his eyes. He seems to be staring directly at you and nobody else."

The clown stayed there for a full five minutes before Tom stood up and went outside to see what was going on. The clown took off in a sprint as soon as he saw Tom coming. By the time Tom had gotten outside, the clown was already halfway down the block. Tom watched him the whole time until he disappeared around the corner. When he was gone, Tom walked back into the diner and sat back down with Willard.

"Where did the kid go?" asked Willard.

"He ran down the sidewalk and vanished out of sight. But I don't think it was a kid. I think it was a grown-up. Are you done with your coffee? I think it's time we go. I've got some work to do in my tool shop this afternoon."

The two of them left Val's and drove toward the dealership. Tom saw the Malibu follow them out of town and pass by when they pulled into John Deere. He watched as the car continued south out of town toward the city of Otho. From that time on, Tom watched the road closely as they made their way to the farm.

When Tom arrived at the farm he told Ralph and me about the clown he and Willard had seen in town. He thought the person's behavior was rather odd. "It was as if he was looking right at me the whole time. He didn't seem interested in my brother-in-law or anyone else."

Ralph said, "I believe you were looking into the eyes of our killer, Tom. Chu can't risk being seen in the daylight, so he conveniently put on a clown's mask to hide his identity from you."

"I think you're right, Ralph," I said. "And I think we'd better stay well hidden until it gets dark."

"I don't think you have to worry about that," said Tom. "I don't think he followed us."

"That makes sense. He already knows where you live. But let's play it safe and stay in the house until later."

The three of us then sat down at the kitchen table to discuss our plans for the evening. "Tom," I said. "Do you have a large tarp to throw over Ralph's car in case Chu slips past us and makes his way into the barn?"

"Yes I do."

"Good, then go out and put it over it when we're done here. I see you have the tractor over on the side of the house. I need you to reposition it in the woods, so the cab is facing the middle of the backyard between the house and the barn. Try to tuck as much of it in the trees as you can. And where's that Krag you told me you have?"

"I've got it behind the door in the back bedroom."

"Good. Get it for me when you've got the time."

"What are you going to do with that?" asked Ralph.

"I'm going to take it with me when I go up to the loft in the barn. That's going to be my position for the evening. I plan on keeping the loft door open so I can have a one-eighty view of the front of the property. I'll be able to see anything that's in front of me from that perch. I want the Krag in case I need to take a long shot at someone. It's a precaution. Besides, neither of you can use it from where you're going to be."

Tom handed me the Krag and I checked it for bullets. It was completely loaded. I said, "Here Tom, take my .357 magnum as a backup to your shotgun."

He replied, "Are you sure you want to do that?"

"No problem. I've got my .38, my Bowie knife, and that Krag. I think that's more than enough. And Ralph, I suspect you're adequately protected?"

Ralph opened his jacket and smiled. He had double holsters of government-issued semi-automatic Glock pistols. "I think these will suffice," he said.

After I spent a little time going over incidental items, I went to my bag to retrieve the four two-way radios I had purchased at Radio Shack. I put them on the table and told each man to take one. "I want both of you to take new batteries and put them in your radio. I want to make sure they'll last the evening. And later tonight I want Tom to take one as he eventually makes his way to the tractor. Ralph, you're going to be in the hay bales back beyond the pens with a second radio. I'll be in the top of the barn with the third one. Let's go check them now and be done with it. I want to make sure we have good reception at all three locations."

We were all back in the kitchen in less than fifteen minutes. The radios had worked like a charm. I told everyone to place them back on the table for safe-keeping. Ralph looked down and said, "Hey, there's only three of them, where's the fourth?"

"Ah, you noticed. Good observation Ralph. I purposely left one in the loft to be used as a decoy."

"How so?" asked Ralph.

"I'm going use it to fool Chu. My plan is to coax him up the ladder to the loft to look for Tom. He'll be expecting Tom because he'll be hearing his voice from the time he enters the barn. Instead, Tom will be down in the tractor talking to himself on his radio." I looked over at Tom and said, "I want you to act as if you're looking for something. Just a little jibber-jabber to make Chu think you're up there. Only you won't be there. I will. And that's where I'm going to take him down. How does that plan sound to the two of you?

Looking befuddled Ralph said, "Not bad, but how do you plan on getting him up there?"

"You leave that to me. I plan on leading Tom through the house and out the back, exposing just enough of him for Chu to get a glimpse. Remember, I'm going to be in the loft, and I'll be able to orchestrate the whole game plan from that position. Okay, let's get to work and finish what we need to do. We still need to eat something. It's going to be a long night."

I stood and watched from the kitchen window as Tom backed the John Deere into the woods. It was now in perfect position for him to watch and be ready for when I needed him.

Meanwhile, Ralph was sitting over at the table. He had picked up the newspaper article that Tom had received in the mail, the one about the murder of Judge Foss. He saw the writing above the headline and began reading the article. He was about halfway through when he said, "This Chu guy is crafty. He attacked the judge at night. He seems to like doing that a lot."

"Yeah, that's one of his traits. He killed Cummings, Gunderson, and the judge in the dark of night. He also killed the patrolman at night, but I don't think he meant to do that. And now he's coming our way under the cover of darkness. Only this time we know he's coming, and it won't be a surprise."

"Have you forgotten something? Chu thinks you're dead, so he'll be the one being surprised this time."

"True, but we can't be sure he hasn't seen me. We'll just have to wait and find out the answer to that."

"After reading this article and seeing the file, I'm beginning to think Chu is a real psychotic individual."

"You don't have to tell me that, Ralph. He doesn't just kill his victims; he tortures them both mentally and physically. At least that's what he did with the judge and the first pilot. But one thing I do know is he didn't make Cummings stand at the edge of that Atlanta office building before he was pushed off."

"And how do you know that?"

"Well, I actually got a call from Roland's widow around the first of this month and she told me he had vertigo. So it was virtually impossible for him to stand there before he fell to his death."

"I see," said Ralph. "So there is a lot of information that you haven't told me. And I can see by the note on this front page that the killer has been in contact with Tom for some time too. Did you receive anything like this?"

"As a matter of fact I did. I got something similar to that in the mail the day I returned from our first meeting. Only mine said, 'Meet you in Iowa.' That's how I knew the killer was heading in this direction. I only gave you the key to my house as a distraction, so I could slip out of town. By the way, did you fix my door and have the house cleaned?"

"Yes and no. We put a piece of plywood over your back door, but we left the place as we found it. Sorry. Uncle Sam doesn't shell out tax-payer dollars for housecleaning."

"I figured as much. So I guess we're even?"

"How do you figure that?"

"Well, I've held back from telling you everything I knew, so you've kind of repaid me by leaving my place a mess."

Tom came in the kitchen door as Ralph and I were finishing our conversation. He fixed dinner, and we sat and ate without any more discussion on the "are-we-even issue." I was feeding Omar a few table scraps when I heard the rumbling sound of thunder in the distance, as the warm weather was causing the moist air to form small patches of fog on the road out front. It was misting by five fifteen, creating a classic Halloween farm setting for the evening. All that was missing were the jack-o'-lanterns, ghosts, and goblins. It was bewitching to say the least. And I, for one, was excited to get the horror show underway.

Chapter 33

The three of us spent another halfihour after dinner going over the plan to make sure everyone knew what was expected of them. I looked at Tom and said, "It's imperative that you keep moving at all times and keep Omar with you every step of the way. The dog's your trump card in case Chu attacks you. And under no circumstances are you to put your life in jeopardy. *Don't play hero. Just lead Chu to me. That's all you need to worry about.*"

I sincerely hoped my speech had been inspiring enough to keep Tom from doing something stupid. I knew Ralph was a veteran of this kind of work, but Tom was not. Tom had been in his battles during the war and survived them all. But this was a different situation. This was a cat-and-mouse game, not your typical military operation. Still, I wondered if somehow he might possibly wind up dead before this was all over. And that was it; the talking was over. We were as ready as we would ever be. All we needed to do now was grab the radios and make our way to our appointed positions.

I arrived in the loft by six thirty, far too early for someone to come charging in to kill Tom Wheeler. But Ralph and I needed to be in place; somewhere out of sight where we could monitor the situation. As I stood in the doorway to the upper loft, I felt a nasty westerly wind blowing in rain that was becoming more than just a drizzle. My senses had become acute again, much like they were back in Vietnam. I could hear the droplets of rain as they fell from the farmhouse rooftop, down two stories and into small puddles by the door to the rear of the house. The rain was something that Tom didn't want and we didn't need. It created problems in more than one way.

The fog hadn't lifted; it was still moderately thick. And the air was getting warmer with every passing hour. There was a storm on the rise. A real storm…one that would make people run for cover. Yes, the night was beckoning Chu, and I was ready and willing to make sure his killing spree ended here and now. I had promised myself days ago that it would go no further than the Wheeler farm, and I intended to keep that promise. And to do that, I had to stay alert, believe in Tom and Ralph, and be ready for anything. But before I did that, I needed to check in with Tom and Ralph. My next step was to get on the radio and ask if anyone had heard or seen anything.

"No I haven't," said Tom. "I've been watching the news and the weatherman says there's a severe storm heading our way…lots of rain and hail, along with some high winds. The storm's going to be here by nine o'clock, and all those in its path should seek cover."

"Ralph, did you get that? Maybe you need to come inside with me," I said.

"Yes, I heard you, but I'm staying here. The storm is going to wreak havoc on our little party, so keep your eyes and ears open because this is only going to help our intruder. I'll see you guys later."

"Okay. But if it gets real bad, head for the back of the barn and stay out of sight. I agree the weather is only going to get worse from here on in, so use extreme caution. And I also think it's time we go to radio silence. No one is to use their radio unless I communicate with them. And keep the volume low. Is that understood?" The two men answered yes and the airways went silent.

Ralph was right. The advantage was now on Chu's side. *Damn it!* Tonight was a mirror image to the one in Vietnam when my platoon captured Chu. There was fog and rain that night too. At first it aided him, and then it switched back to us. I'm sure that's on his mind tonight and he'll not make the same mistake twice. He'll wait 'til the last minute for the worst weather and then he'll attack. The weather won't do him much good inside the house, unless it knocks the power out. And if that happens we're all in deep shit. I hadn't planned on a blackout. That would make things real difficult, especially up here in the loft. If I couldn't see him, I couldn't fight him and I definitely couldn't kill him. And that meant my size and martial arts skills would no longer be an advantage. Chu could shoot me and that would leave Tom and Ralph to deal with him. And let's face it; Tom was no match for Chu.

The rain was continuing to come down in buckets and the wind's velocity was soaring. I was no weatherman, but I thought the gale-force winds were approaching fifty miles per hour or more. It was almost impossible to stand in the doorway, let alone see anything inside the house. The rain was damn near coming down sideways. I heard a crack and then a limb fell in the driveway, just to the left of the John Deere. Debris was sailing all around the yard. I knew deep down that Chu was going to use the storm as a cover to attack the farmhouse. He wasn't in line to win the brother-of-the-year award, nor was he even up for honorable mention, so I knew he was out there waiting to pounce on us at the worst possible time.

That was all right by me, as I had prepared a little surprise of my own. I had stacked several bales of hay to the far side of the loft, directly across from the ladder that led up to this level. Then I put the fourth, two-way radio on a bale behind the stack and kept mine in my jacket pocket. And for decorative purposes, I put a pitchfork to the left side of the stack. It extended beyond the top bale by a little more than eighteen inches. I felt the pitchfork might come in handy if I needed another weapon. I wasn't sure what I was going to do with it. Maybe I'd skewer Chu and toss him out the loft or use it on him as a final act of insanity. Either way, it was there if I needed it. The hay bales looked natural, and the area behind them was the right size for me to sit and wait for Chu to come to me once he reached the loft.

I looked down and checked my watch. It was eight fifty-eight and still nothing was happening, except for the weather which was quickly approaching disaster potential. The road out front was nonexistent. And the front yard was barely visible, but I was sure I would notice a car if it came down the road. I was beginning to worry. Not for me, but for Tom. He was out there in a well lit house with a target on his chest. Chu would definitely be able to see Tom easier than I could.

Another half hour passed and I still hadn't seen anything, except the flickering of lights from inside the house. *Where is the little bastard?* The light inside of the loft had also gone on and off several times in the last fifteen minutes. I vaguely saw Tom get off the couch and go into the kitchen around nine fifteen. He opened the rear door and let Omar out to piss. The dog was back in the house in less than two minutes. Then, about nine forty-five, I saw headlights through the fog and rain from a vehicle on the road. The weather was so thick I couldn't see the make or model of the vehicle. For all I knew it could have been a truck. It passed by slowly without incident and drove on.

I contacted the two men and told them I had just seen a vehicle pass by the front of the house. Tom said he saw it too. His voice was crackly and hard to hear, but at least I'd received his reply. The storm was definitely interfering with our communication. We both figured it was more than likely Chu because no sane person would be out on any road tonight under these conditions. *No sane person would be in a loft waiting to kill someone either.* So, for the betterment of Tom's welfare, I told him to go out and turn off the light on the front porch. That would make it a lot more difficult for Chu to see inside, but it also sent him an invitation to come knocking. After that I said he needed to turn on the backyard light; the one located on top of the tall lamppost.

Another ten minutes passed, and then another ten minutes, which eventually became half an hour. The clock was tick, tick, ticking…and there still was no sight of Chu. On the brighter side, the rain had slowed, and the wind had calmed down just enough to see the shadows of the corn stalks in the field across the road. I wondered aloud if this was the calm before the storm.

Then, around ten thirty, I saw another set of headlights pass by the farmhouse. This time I heard the distant sound of squealing brakes and saw the faint glow of red brake lights beyond the woods to the south. The vehicle had stopped. I didn't hear a door shut, but I assumed someone had parked the vehicle and gotten out, and was now headed to the farmhouse.

I stepped back into the shadows and contacted the two men once again. I said, "I think someone got out of a vehicle about three to four hundred feet to the southwest of the house. I think he's just beyond the edge of the woods. Tom, did you get that?"

"Yes I did."

"Good. I can hear you a little better now. Is Omar acting like he hears something?"

"No, he's lying quietly on the floor in front of me."

"Okay, so he hasn't sensed anyone yet. Is the front door unlocked?"

"Yes."

"Hold tight, I'll call you back if I see anyone."

My heart was pounding, and frankly, I was getting a little tired of the waiting. I knew in my bowels the person in the vehicle out front was our killer, but he hadn't revealed himself yet. Twenty minutes passed and I still hadn't seen him. He was waiting for something. My best guess was he was staying in the woods until the weather got worse. He needed that. I moved out of the shadows of the loft and got closer to the opening of the door. My binoculars weren't of any use anymore, as the thickness of the night had rendered them useless. From here on in, I had to go on instinct or get closer to the farmhouse. But moving now could give away my position, or I could miss the killer altogether. I simply had to hold tight and hope for the best.

It wasn't long before the winds began to pick up again. This time it wasn't accompanied by rain, but the wind speed was back in that forty-five to fifty mile per hour range. Ten more minutes passed, then eleven, then twelve, and finally on minute thirteen I saw the silhouette of a man as he began to creep through the woods on the south side of the house. The winds were getting worse. They were quickly approaching sixty miles per hour and climbing. The door to the loft suddenly began to bang against the outside wall of the barn. I peeked out around the corner and saw the intruder turn his head to look up in my direction. He was trying to see where the noise was coming from. It was loud and drawing attention. When he realized it was a door, he looked away and continued to move toward the farmhouse. What was left of the loose hay on the floor was now in the back of the barn. And the wood floor was exposed and wet for the first fifteen feet. It would be slippery and dangerous in a fight. I had to remember that in case we got close to the edge during a struggle. I looked again and saw the silhouette was actually a small man and he was almost halfway across the driveway. I frantically tried to contact Tom, but there was a crackle in the connection like before, so I wasn't sure he could hear me over the interference. The only thing I could do was whisper and hope he got the, "You have a visitor. So move quickly to another room and take Omar with you."

Tom must have received the message because I saw him grab the dog by the collar and head to a room in the lower back hallway. It wasn't more than a split second after that when I saw the man walk up to the side of the house and peer in through the glass. He scanned the place, and when he couldn't find anyone he moved toward the back of the farmhouse. A flash of lightning lit up the skies and the crack of thunder bellowed out directly overhead. The thunderous roar caused the intruder to jump then fall to his knees. My heart damn near leaped into my throat at the same moment as the storm moved closer and closer to being on top of us. He was clearly visible now. It was Chu. He was standing once again and on the move. He was wearing camouflage, and he held a gun in one hand and a knife in the other. Another round of lightning and thunder struck, causing the lights to flicker on and off, and back on again. Chu stopped momentarily when the lights went out. Then he moved again around the corner to the back of the house after the lights came back on. He looked up again at the loft opening, then turned his attention back to the rear door. He went for the knob. It was locked. He tried again, but this time he used his body to try and force the door open. The door won; it was stronger than he was.

That hadn't worked, so he stepped back five or six feet and saw there was a stairway that ran from the northeast corner of the house to a landing on the second level. He wasted no time in ascending the stairs. When he got to the top, he looked out to the back of the property through the opening between the silos and Tom's tool shop. Then he switched his focus to the north. The wind was now topping seventy miles per hour and I could hear the roaring sound of what I thought was a tornado. Chu hunched down near the base of the door and kept looking to the north. Maybe he was looking for a tornado or maybe he was looking for Ralph; either way I was getting scared or paranoid, or maybe a little of both. Again, he moved his vision from the north back to the opening in the loft. I think the constant knocking of the door against the barn was distracting his attention from the purpose at hand. He stared at it for what seemed like an eternity before moving his attention back to the house. I thought for a minute he might have seen or heard me, but that notion quickly faded when Chu tried to turn the knob on the upstairs door. It too was locked. Chu stayed there for five full minutes trying to use his knife to cut between the door and the jamb so he could get at the deadbolt. He quit after realizing not only did he have to get through the deadbolt, but he would also have to jimmy the door lock too. He eventually gave up on gaining access to the house from the second story and headed back down the stairs.

The wind immediately blew him to the ground when he got to the bottom and stepped off. He struggled to get to his feet. He couldn't, so he crawled back to the steps and used the railing to right himself. It looked from my vantage point that he had lost his knife when he fell to the ground. And I was right. I saw him crawl back to where he had fallen to dig around in the mud with his hands until he came up with the knife. He put that, along his gun away for safekeeping and headed back toward the front of the house.

The wind was getting stronger as Chu felt his way along the crumbling painted siding of the house. It was a little more sheltered on that side, and he was making steady progress toward the front. He eventually turned the corner and was now around the front of the house. I assumed he was about to enter the front door, so I called Tom and told him to quickly move to the upper level as fast as he could. I then heard a screen door slam, followed by an explosion from a transformer on a power pole in the backyard. The electrical box lit up like a thousand sparklers on the Fourth of July and caught fire. The house went instantly black. And that's when I heard the sound of a freight train roaring through the cornfield to the northwest. It was a tornado. And it was ripping off shingles and tossing lawn furniture around the backyard like tinker toys. I saw a gnome fly up and hit the side of the barn just to the right of the opening in the loft. I ducked, out of instinct. I was lucky it hadn't passed through the opening or I may have been gravely hurt or dead on the floor. Glass was shattering and farm animals could barely be heard over the sound of the tornado as it passed within a quarter of a mile of the house.

Meanwhile, Tom was running up the stairs to the master bedroom on the second floor. Chu could hear his footsteps and that of the dog's paws as they ascended the single flight of wooden stairs. The house was completely dark. Chu couldn't see past his nose, so he had to feel his way across the entryway and into the living room. He took three steps into the room, fell over a hassock, and landed chin first onto an end table. He eventually wound up on the floor. The hit had stunned him, but not enough to keep him from going after Tom. He shook his head twice to clear the cobwebs and quickly scrambled to his feet. He continued feeling his way until he found the opening to the upper staircase. From there he quietly tried to climb the steps, but the floorboards to the old farmhouse were dried and creaky.

I whispered, "Tom can you hear me? If so, close the bedroom door, and go out the back and down the steps. Make sure you leave that door open and let the screen door slam so Chu can hear it. Then run to the tool shop. Did you get that?"

"Yes, but I hear him downstairs. He must have fallen over something. He'll find his way up here in no time, so I've got to leave."

Tom had to slow the killer down. A small man like Chu couldn't break down a solid oak farm door, so he jammed a chair under the handle and headed down the back steps.

Chu wasn't fooling anyone at this point. He ran up the last two-thirds of the stairs as fast as he could. He was on the upper landing now, and he was trying the doors to the rooms on that level. The first one he tried was the bathroom. He opened it, moved inside, and threw open the shower curtain. He stepped in, but one was there. He then tried a second room, but it was blocked. He immediately knew he had the right room, so he put a shoulder to the door and on the third try it burst open. He couldn't see anything in the room because it was completely black, but he remembered hearing a screen door slam and the door to the back steps was open. That he could tell from the dim light that was coming from the backyard. He quickly felt his way across the room to the open door. That's when he heard the sound of a door closing on a building directly down below and across from where he was standing.

I could see him standing there on the upper level, watching and listening. I could have shot him from where I stood, but I wanted him to come to me. I felt the need to have a little talk with him before I broke his neck or cut his throat.

A light came on in the tool shop down below. I could see it reflecting out through the glass and onto a puddle on the ground outside. Chu saw the light too. It was moving around in circles, like the person holding it was searching for something.

"Tom, it's me again. I can see Chu standing on the top of the stairway. He's looking down at the tool shop. Do you have a light on in there?"

"Yes, it's a flashlight. I'm trying to get to the emergency backup power system to the house and the barn. There's a lot of crap in the way. I haven't used it for a couple of years. Let's hope the batteries still have enough power to run it. I've almost got it reset, but it won't come back on for another fifteen minutes. The system needs to regenerate before the lights will come on again."

"You better hurry your ass up. Chu is almost at the bottom of the steps, and he'll be there in less than half a minute. Leave now and go out the back door. Call me when you get inside the John Deere."

That was the last I heard from him. I was praying that he escaped. I didn't hear a struggle or a gun shot, so I figured he made his way out the back door and was now headed for the tractor. It seemed like an eternity as I waited for him to give me a call back.

In the meantime, I heard Chu rustling around in the shop below. He must have been feeling his way around the room, trying his hardest to get his hands on Tom. And he wasn't being quiet about it. I even heard him yell out. He said, "You might as well come out because I'll eventually find you." And, as I had hoped, Tom was not there. He was in the John Deere and calling me back at this very minute.

"Ian, I'm back in the tractor. What do you want me to do?"

"Just sit tight and wait for me to get back to you. At some point I may need you to turn on the tractor lights."

Now it was my turn to draw the assassin into the trap. I began to cough and drag my feet across the floor. I banged my fists on the wall a couple of times and rattled some chains I had found earlier in the evening. I stopped and listened. There was no sound from the tool room. So I called Tom to ask if Chu had come outside.

He said, "No."

That's when I heard someone at the side door to the barn. The rusty, old hinges squeaked loudly as the door was being opened and closed. That was followed up with the sound of footsteps as they slid across the concrete floor below.

"He's in, Tom. Start whistling and talking, but not too loud that you can be heard from inside the tractor."

Tom's voice was the next thing I heard. It was coming over each speaker and it was sporadic, just the way I wanted it. Not too loud, but not too soft either. I turned the volume on my radio down, so I could use his voice to guide me in the general direction of the hay bales. I needed to get back to them in the dark without tripping over my feet or slipping on the wet floor. The bales were at least fifty feet to my front and to the right.

I was slowly making my way toward them when I heard someone climbing the ladder. I froze in my tracks. I knew I couldn't rush over and find my hiding place before he reached the top. That would have given away my position. Instead, I turned up the volume on my radio and whispered to Tom to quit talking. I then set my radio on the floor and froze again as I heard someone's hands feeling their way across the opening of the landing. It was Chu. I could feel his evil presence. He was breathing hard and most probably now in an upright standing position. He knew I was there. And I assumed he knew I knew he was there.

I suddenly had the urge to sneeze. It must have been the hay. I held my hand over my mouth and nose and fought it back. I was getting it under control when I heard Chu move a couple long steps to his right. I waited and listened for him to do it again. Then I moved when he moved. Then we would stop and do it over again. This happened four or five times. Either one of us could have let out a shot, but that would have given away our position. No, neither one of us was willing to do that. Then suddenly out of nowhere came the rattling of chains on the wall about fifteen feet to my front and left. I knew exactly where he was, so I used the opportunity to make a dash for the hay bales. Two shots rang out from his pistol as I dove for cover. The bullets missed, whizzing behind me by several feet. I still hadn't reached the bales, so I stayed on my knees and crawled the last few feet. At the same time I looked back over my left shoulder toward the opening in the door, hoping Chu might have gotten careless and stepped out into it. There was just enough light to see him if he should happen to do that.

I was finally safe for the moment, tucked behind the wall of hay bales. *Where's the fuckin' lights Tom?* All I had to do now was stay calm and wait for Chu to make his move or for the lights to come back on. We waited. I assumed he must have thought I was Tom and I didn't have a weapon or I would have used it by now. Yes, the game was in full stride. The mouse or the rat in this case, was looking for the cheese. He was on the move again. I heard the chains rattle once again and the shuffling of feet across what was left of the hay that hadn't been blown to the back of the barn. A voice from directly in front of me said, "Why don't you come out sergeant? I know you're there. You aren't fooling anyone. As a matter of fact, I've been playing your little game all evening long. I knew your friend was leading me on a wild-goose chase, but I assumed it would eventually get me to you. So come out sergeant. Come out and we'll settle this like two men."

The place went silent again. No wind, no loud breathing; just two men standing like guards at the palace gate. There was no doubt in my mind that he was trying to bait me into talking, so he could take another shot at me. He also knew I wasn't going to give away my position. He probably figured I was waiting for him to get close enough so I could rush him. He was taking a calculated risk by talking, but by now he was more than likely convinced either I didn't have a gun or I didn't want to use it at this time.

The lights slowly began to come back on. They started out dim and kept getting stronger with every tick of the clock. The backup system was finally on, but it took time for the lights to be fully illuminated. I looked through a small hole in the hay bales and saw Chu had moved two or three more steps to his left. He was now about fifteen feet to my front. His figure was still a bit sketchy. He was making his way toward the bales as the lights reached half power. He was now ten feet away, but still too far for me to rush him. He continued to inch closer and closer to the bales as the lights reached full power. He was now directly in front of me on the other side.

I reached out slowly and put my hand on the pitchfork. I grabbed it firmly with my right hand thrusting the knob end forward into Chu's mouth as the wall collapsed on top of him. His gun went off harmlessly into the hay bales as he fell backwards onto the wooden floor. The gun went flying across the room, hitting the wall to his backside. I leaped over the fallen bales, and was standing over him with the pitchfork in hand when I looked down and saw I had knocked out at least eight to ten of his front teeth. He was bleeding heavily. He looked up and spit blood and teeth in my direction. I held up the pitchfork and said, "Get the fuck up asshole!"

He looked straight back at me and then to his right, presumably looking for his gun. It wasn't there. So, the only thing he could do was to get to his feet and use his knife. Looking directly into his eyes I said with a laugh, "Are you kidding me? You think you're going to hurt me with that? I could put a hundred holes in you with this, and you'd never even get close enough to do any damage. No, first we're going to talk. I have some questions that need answering."

"Then what?"

"Then we'll dance!"

He looked strangely back at me as if he didn't understand what I'd said. He blinked twice and replied, "What do you mean dance?"

"Well, it's like this. I'm going to put this pitchfork down and take out a real knife. Not a little toad-sticker like that one, but a real knife like this one." I stuck the pitchfork in a bale next to me and pulled out my Bowie knife with the fourteen-inch blade. His eyes got as big as silver dollars at the sight of the knife. It must have looked like a sword from where he stood. "Yes, we'll dance and when we do I'm going to cut you just a little bit each time that we go 'round and 'round. Not enough to kill you, but in the end you'll be wishing I had. And now to the questions. Did you kill my friend Lane back in Minneapolis?"

"Who?" he asked. "I don't know anybody by that name. I killed no one back in your home town."

Good. That means Lane's wife is in on the hook for his murder. "That's one for you. For that I might take your life a little quicker.

And now on to the next question. You killed my friend Roland Cummings in Atlanta, did you not?"

"Yes, that one was me. He didn't suffer like my brothers did. His death was swift."

"Oh well, now we're back to square one. Do you see how this works? We dance around for a while and you get points for not killing my friends. Then when I learn you've killed one of them, I deduct points. Now I'll have to kill you a lot slower. I'm afraid you're going to bleed all over the place before you beg me to kill you. So tell me. Why did you go through all this? Revenge is one thing, but to waste your life over a tragedy of war is downright idiotic."

"It's not stupid. I owed it to my brothers and my ancestors to avenge them."

"That's total bullshit. You could have come to this country and had all the men responsible for your brother's deaths brought up on charges. You found Roland, Tom, and me, and we could have testified for you. We had nothing to lose by telling the truth. That way the true criminals would have gone through a war crimes tribunal and more than likely found guilty. If nothing else, you would have ruined their lives forever. They would have been shunned by society, and that would have been your revenge."

"No, that would not have been good enough. That would have meant I wouldn't have been able to do anything about you and Roland and some of the others."

"That's correct, asshole, because we didn't do anything wrong to you or your brothers. You have a delusional mind. It says kill everyone and let God sort them out. Do you know what the media is calling you? They're calling you a serial killer. And you know what that means don't you? It means you're a fucking moi."

"I'm not a savage!" he screamed back at me.

"Yes you are, Chu. You and the rest of your fucked-up Vietcong buddies were all mois. There's an old saying in this country: a leopard can't change his spots. And that's you Chu. You're the leopard. You're the animal or savage that just can't let things go. And for that you're going to die like an animal."

He looked back at me. I think his jaw was clinched, but I couldn't tell as I had joyously dislodged nearly half of the man's teeth. He was still bleeding. Blood was running down each side of his mouth. *Alice Cooper you have a twin.* And the look in his eyes said it all. He was gone. I could tell he had passed over to the dark side, and now we were both there together. Ready to dance and head down a path into the abyss.

He chose that moment to rush me. He leaped over one bale and tripped on the next as he tried in vain to slash at me. His knife missed way wide as he fell harmlessly to the floor. I looked at him lying there and laughed in his face and said. "That was a poor attempt. Come on Chu, show me a little more than that." I let him get back on his feet so he could try again. This time he came directly at me and tried to come over the top with his knife. I blocked it with my arm and karate kicked him in the chest. He went flying to my right. This time he stayed down. He needed to gather his breath, as the kick had temporarily knocked that out of him. He eventually got to his feet and tried a frontal assault once again, only this time I stopped him with my left arm. He got lucky and cut through the leather sleeve on my jacket as I sliced a large portion of his left ear off. He went down; this time he held his hand to his ear. Looking down at his hand he saw it was covered in blood. The knife was so sharp that the ear was gone in a split second, and that's why he hadn't actually felt the slice. That and the adrenaline had kept him from screaming out.

I looked down at him once again and said, "Hurts, doesn't it? And that's just the beginning. You got lucky with that last cut Chu, but it won't happen again." I put the Bowie knife back in its sheath and picked up the pitchfork. "Get up moi; it's time for you to bleed."

I took five steps to my left to get to open floor. I wanted to make sure I could maneuver without worrying that I might actually trip over one of the bales of hay. "Come on moi. It's either time to fight like a man or run like a dog. Which one are you?"

"I'm not afraid of you sergeant." He looked to his right and saw his pistol lying on the floor not more than five or six feet away.

He was being obvious, so I said, "Go for it. It'll make things more interesting."

There was no need for an invitation. He hardly hesitated as he made a dive for the gun. I followed in close pursuit with pitchfork in hand. He grabbed the gun, went to one knee, and turned to fire. The pitchfork caught him in the middle of his forearm and went clean through before he could get the shot off. He screamed and screamed again as the pitchfork stuck in the wooden wall to his backside. Chu was still wailing away when I kicked the gun from his hand. I then knelt down beside him and began to strangle him with my left hand while holding on to his loose arm with my right. I was eyeball to eyeball with him now and I could see he was slowly dying right there, four inches in front of my face. But I wasn't done with him yet. He needed to stay alive for few more minutes, so I could ask him one more question. I let go of my grip and watched as the color returned to his face. He looked awful. There was so much blood that he could have been mistaken for a corpse, but the heaving of his chest changed that perspective.

"Look at me Chu," I said. "I'll kill you quickly if you tell me where your partner is."

He mumbled and replied, "Go screw yourself."

"What's that you say? Go screw myself? No, I think it's the other way around." With that, I pulled the pitchfork out of the wall and tossed it behind me. I picked him up and bashed my fist into his face. Blood went spurting in all directions. He was still alive, just barely. So I stepped back and told him to get to his feet.

He got up and said to me, "Why don't you kill me?"

"Not yet. I'm not done with you." I grabbed him by the neck and said, "I'm going to toss you out the door and see if you can fly." And that's exactly what I did. Out the door he went. I heard him hit the ground down below, followed by a deep groan. Then I yelled to Tom to turn the tractor lights on so we could see him.

Chu had gone about ten feet when the lights hit him. He was hobbling along. I was sure his left ankle was broken along with his spirit. I couldn't let him go, so I took the Krag from the back room, rested it against the door opening and let one round off. The twenty-three-hundred-feet-per-second round entered through his back and exploded his heart in a hundred pieces. He took one step and fell face first in a puddle. *That one's for you Roland.* He was dead. Chu would never again kill another living soul.

Tom got out of the tractor, and he and Omar went over to the body. "He's dead Ian. I thought you were going to bring him to justice."

"Hold that thought. I'll be right down."

It took me a few minutes to get down and to think about what I was going to say to Tom. I had used him for my own revenge and placed his life in danger at the same time. And now I was going to have to explain myself and ask one more favor of him. I walked up to him and all that would come out was, "I'm sorry Tom, but I just couldn't let Chu live. He was psychotic, just like Ralph had said he was."

"Speaking of Ralph, where is he?" asked Tom.

"He's probably still out there watching the perimeter to make sure Chu was acting alone. He'll be here soon enough. In the meantime, I need you to help me get rid of the body."

"What do you mean get rid of the body. Aren't we going to leave that to the FBI?"

"No, I can't do that now that I shot him in the back while he was trying to get away. I'll get tossed in prison forever if they find out. And that's why we need to move fast before Ralph gets here."

"I don't know Ian. I didn't sign up for burying a body. I mean, I'll always know it's here somewhere. What if someone should find it someday?"

"Well, then we better find a place where that will never happen."

"No Ian, I'm not doing this."

"Okay, then I'll do it. Just point me in the right direction. I'm sorry I made you an accessory. And I promise you, Ralph will never hold you accountable for any of this."

"But this happened on my property and I went along with the whole thing. So where does that leave me?"

"It leaves you a true champion of justice. It means you saved my life, yours, and probably Fisher's too. Not to mention your kids' and wife's. They're safe now; you'll never have to worry about them for the rest of your life. Chu was a monster. As a matter of fact, I told him something to that affect in the loft. I called him a moi. He didn't like that, so he charged me with his knife and tried to kill me. From that point on I just lost it. And shooting him was pure instinct. I hope you understand."

"I guess when you put it that way I have to agree with you. But where are we going to bury him?"

"First of all, get a tarp, so we can wrap him in it. And then get a couple of shovels and bring your truck over here."

"Then what?" asked Tom. "We still have to put him in the ground somewhere."

"I've got that figured out. Is there a large pile of fieldstone anywhere around here?"

"There are quite a few places like that around here. Why do you ask?"

"Just drive us to one that's off the road and where we can't be seen by anyone. Now get those things and get the truck over here. We need to move fast before Ralph shows up and changes his mind."

Chapter 34

Tom seemed quite distant as he drove his pickup down a narrow dirt road that connected the blacktop with Chu's final resting place. I'm sure he was deep in thought about what had happened back at the farm and what he was about to do. Being a religious man with a conscience separated himself from people like me. In a sense, I was no different than the man I had just killed. I had taken someone's life without a sliver of remorse and lied about it to an old friend in the process. I was sure this would damage our friendship for life. It wasn't as if I was going to keep in touch with him every month or even once or twice a year after this was over. Hell, I hadn't talked to him more than a handful of times in the last fourteen or so years, so nothing that happened here was going to change that routine. Yet, I felt closer to the man now than I ever had during the whole time we were together in the war. And that meant mending our friendship would be much more difficult to handle after the wedge I had driven between us.

"So where are we going, Tom?"

"This road will take us to a small hundred-acre field that my cousin owns. He leases it out to a guy in Otho. It's probably the safest place I can think of to put the body. Tell me Ian, were you ever thinking of taking Chu alive or were you feeding me a line of shit to use my place for your benefit?"

"I guess the answer to the first part of that question is no, I never had any intention on taking him alive. I planned all along to kill him for what he did to Roland, his wife, and son. They're the biggest losers in this whole goddamn mess. I also did it to keep Chu from killing you, me, Fish, and all of our loved ones. When I first found out what was going on, I wasted no time in making my decision. And when I realized who the killer was, I knew he would be coming after all of us. That included you and maybe your family. So I decided I would be the one to stop him. Maybe it was an ego thing, I don't really know. But one thing I do know is I was the most logical person to take him down. Let me put it this way; this isn't my first encounter with a killer. I have some history of doing things like I did today. I knew you couldn't pull the trigger, even if it meant your life. So I stepped in and did what I had to. I hope you see this and forgive me for what I've done."

"I can forgive anything Ian. That's not the problem. The problem is you've involved me, and now I'm on the hook along with you. You gave me no choice, and I'm worried how this is going to affect me for the rest of my life."

Tom continued driving down the road filled with potholes and puddles until we finally stopped under a small grove of dying elm trees. It was beginning to rain again…slow, but steady in waves. The air was clean, unlike my blemished soul which I seemed to have sold to the devil. At least Tom thought I had, and who knows, maybe I had.

"We're here Ian. So what's your plan?"

"I suggest you park the truck right here and leave the headlights on so we can see what we're doing. Is that the fieldstone you were talking about?"

"Yup, that's it."

There was a large pile of rocks to my front, way more than we needed to stack on top of Chu's grave. They would conceal his body nicely and no one would be the wiser. Well, Tom would, but he'd just have to forget Chu was there and move on with his life. Tom left the engine running and we got out to remove Chu's body from the truck bed. I got the shovels and we began to dig the grave. The task ahead wasn't going to be easy. We had to dig in the mud and rain, and that was going to take some time. It was now 1:45 a.m., and we had to work fast to get the job done before the sun rose.

We hadn't been digging for more than ten minutes when I heard noise from behind the truck. It couldn't have been more than thirty seconds later when a man in a black hooded sweatshirt stepped out from the shadows, walked up next to the truck, and crossed over the front left headlight. The man stopped directly in front of the hood ornament with a gun in his hand. He said, "I see you've taken care of Chu for me. That was nice of you to do."

Tom said, "Who's there?"

Staying calm and steady I said, "I'm surprised you don't remember his voice, Tom. It's the ghost of James Wilson."

Tom froze; he couldn't believe his eyes or his ears. It couldn't be Wilson. He was dead. At least that's what he was told. Tom stuck his shovel in the ground and said, "How in the world did you get here?"

I cleared my throat and said, "That's a question I'd like answered too."

"Just hold on boys. We'll get to that in good time," he said as he pushed the hood off of his head. "It's good to see you Tom; you were on my side the last time we spoke. But as for you Christian, I can't say I'm happy to see you again. You make my stomach crawl to think you're alive, but at least you're here where I can kill you. The last time I saw you I was flat on my belly, looking up at you and Fisher as the two of you retreated from Fu Pin. Do you remember that day Ian? That was the day you put three bullets in my back and left me for dead."

"How could I forget; you ran like a coward from the fight as I predicted you would. I told Lt. you'd never hold your ground in a firefight and I was right. You got several other men killed that day. They didn't have to die. You could have taken your head out of the ground and supported them. And maybe you and some of the others would have escaped with Snake, Paul, and me. I wasn't proud of what I did, but when Lt. died, I was the highest-ranking person left in the platoon. So I judged you and sentenced you to death, right there on the spot. As you know, soldiers can be shot for cowardice during times of war. And that's exactly what I did. I shot you with the intention of killing you, and my only regret is I didn't finish the job."

"That was not your job to do; judge and sentence me that is. That was for a court to decide. Do you have any idea how much I suffered after that at the hands of the Vietcong?"

"I can only imagine. Yet, it was nothing by comparison to what happened to Lt. and the others who died that day. They died and we never recovered their bodies. So tell me, how is it that my bullets didn't kill you?"

"I always wore a flak vest on patrols. You must have forgotten that or in the heat of the battle you missed it. Anyway, you shot me twice in the back and a third round caught me in the shoulder. By the way, in case you wanted to know, those vests don't completely stop bullets. And when the firefight ended they took me prisoner. I had to live in a tiger pit for over four months. I was beaten by the Vietcong daily. It was horrible. The only thing that kept me alive was the thought of killing you one day."

"Well here I am. Take your best shot."

"Not so fast. We've got plenty of time. But first you two need to get digging. Only now you'll have to dig a hole big enough to fit three people. Sorry Tom, I hate to have to kill you, but I can't leave behind a witness. So keep digging boys."

I looked at Tom, and the only thing I could think of was I had failed him. I never meant to get him killed, but shit happens, and now we were about to be buried here forever with a man we both despised.

"What are you looking around for Ian?" said Wilson. "Is it your friend the FBI agent? I believe his name was Ralph Yorkshire. That's whom you're looking for, isn't it?"

"What do you mean was?" I asked already knowing what the answer would be.

"I'm sorry to have to burst your bubble, but he's dead. Ralph had his speaker on too loud in the hay bales, and I heard it all the way back in the cornfield behind him. I waited for the storm to get brewing and I went up and shot him. He never saw me coming. I would have come after you with Chu, but you outsmarted me. You made Tom keep the dog with him. You knew how terrified I was of dogs. That was the main reason you had me replaced walking point near Fu Pin. It wasn't that I was scared of the Vietcong. No, it was because I was scared of the scout dog."

"Wait a minute," said Tom. "Are you telling me Ian knew about you all along?"

"Why don't you answer that question Ian?"

"That's right Tom. I've known about Wilson for the last four days. Ralph told me that bit of information when we met in his motel room. The FBI knew Chu and James were working together. Actually, Chu wanted all of us dead, but I'm assuming James's only interest was killing me. Or am I wrong about that James?"

"No. You're absolutely correct. But I was willing to let Chu kill you, only that didn't happen. I was pretty sure you were going to kill him; therefore, I had to have a backup plan. And this is it. Kind of clever don't you think?"

"Clever?" asked Tom.

"Yes, getting Ian to kill Chu, so I or the authorities didn't have to do it. I needed him dead at some point to keep from being implicated. Now you're here digging a grave for all three of you. I'd say I was clever. You two are wasting time. Keep digging."

I looked over at Tom and knew we were profoundly fucked. The only possible thing I could do is throw a shovel full of mud at Wilson and go for my .38 that was strapped to my left ankle. It would come at a price. It would mean Tom or I would most likely get shot in the process. Maybe not an immediate mortal wound, but one bad enough that one of us wouldn't make it to the hospital before we died. We just needed to dig slowly and keep talking to Wilson. Maybe we'd get lucky and get a distraction.

"So tell me," I said. "How'd you get away from the Vietcong?"

"That was none of my doing. I got lucky one day when Chu walked into the prison camp I was being held in. It was directly across the border in Cambodia from Fu Pin. I recognized him right off as one of those three men whom we captured and took to V81. I'd been working in the fields when I caught sight of him. I got his attention and he came over and spoke to me. That's when I learned how badly he hated you. At first he wanted to kill me when he learned I was one of the men in the patrol that got his brothers killed, but I talked him out of that. Instead, I said I would help him get to the States if he helped me escape and get me back to an American base camp."

"How did Chu manage to do all of that?"

"Chu was a double-agent. He could come and go in the jungle as he pleased. He actually made a deal with the prison commander to let me go. I'm not sure how he worked that out. I never asked him and don't know the answer to that to this day. I was just thankful he got me out of that hellhole."

"How did Chu explain you to the American authorities?" asked Tom.

"He didn't have to. He led me to the base at Kontum City and told me to walk up to the gates and tell them I'd been a prisoner of war. They believed me, and from there I was sent to a hospital for two months. And by the time I made my way back to Pleiku, you were gone."

"Why didn't you tell them I'd shot you?"

"I figured they wouldn't believe me. Plus you were out of the army, and they couldn't do anything to you if they wanted. You hadn't killed me, so they probably didn't give a shit. Besides, I was planning your death for a long time. I wanted to be the one who nailed you."

"You're telling us that you got Chu out of Vietnam?"

"No. I couldn't do that. I just gave Chu my address and the name of one of my father's businesses in Atlanta. I told him when he applied for political asylum he could use our names and we would sponsor him here in the States. My dad gave him a job, and we worked together for five or six years, during which time we planned our attack on the people we hated the most in life. I had the time and resources to locate everyone except for the third intel guy."

"So that was you who broke into my house looking for a way to find him?"

"That's right."

"And was it you who killed my friend Lane Moreland?"

"No. I don't know anything about that. Who the hell was he?"

"It doesn't matter. *Fuckin' asshole could be lying.* Then who was it who tried to kill me the other night in the motel? Was that you?"

"No, that was Chu. He planned that all by himself. Actually, I haven't spoken to him but twice since I left Minneapolis. I told him to do whatever he thought was necessary to take care of you. I only furnished him with the truck he used, some cash, and weapons. He was happy with that."

"Did your dad know anything about what you two were planning?"

"That's not important. Keep digging or we'll still be here when the sun comes up. And I can't dig because of the bullet you put in my shoulder. I was in that tiger pit for too long, and my shoulder wasn't properly looked at, so it got infected. If Chu hadn't come along when he did I might have died."

"But you didn't," said Tom. "You made it back here, so why risk going to jail for killing us?"

"I think that went out the window when I shot Yorkshire. And I've been thinking about this day for nearly fifteen years, so I'm not going to let my dream slip away."

I said, "If your father doesn't know about this, then what does he think you've been up to all these weeks?"

"Again, that doesn't matter. But if you insist on knowing, he doesn't care what I'm up to. When I got back to the States after the war I went to the VA. They learned that I was a POW, and they gave me a hundred percent disability without blinking an eye. The money I get from the government and what my father gives me is all I need to live really well. And my dad thinks I'm a little crazy from my captivity, so he lets me be unless I want to work or I need some additional cash."

The rain was coming down harder now, which got me to thinking. Maybe I could use it to our advantage. I saw Wilson wipe his face and eyes a couple of times during our conversation. It didn't take him long, but those few seconds could be all I needed to make my move. I could also see he was getting sleepy and fed up with all the question-and-answer bullshit. And that meant I didn't have much time before he got pissed off and shot the two of us. The only other thing I had left was to try and bluff him. So I said, "You must have seen me with a woman back in Dodge. She knows we're out here, and she knows all about you and Chu. I filled her in before I left."

"You're lying!" he shouted back.

"No I'm not. Do you know whom I'm talking about or did you completely miss the two of us?"

"I didn't miss anyone," he said angrily.

"You didn't? Then where were the two of us staying? We certainly weren't at the motel."

I could see that I was getting to him. *Bastard.* I had him confused and angry. I had learned this little tactic back when I was playing sports. You get your opponent mad and that confuses him. He wouldn't think straight and that is when you could attack.

"What are you going to do now James? You don't know who she is or where she's at. So you can't cover your tracks. Someone else knows and now you're fucked."

"Shut up! Shut your fuckin' mouth for one minute. I need to think."

"Think about what James? What her name is? Where we were staying? Or how you'll be able to find her if I'm dead?"

"Shut up, I said!"

"Okay, let's think about this for a minute. If you kill me, you'll never know whom I'm talking about because you now know I was staying someplace else besides the Lamplighter. You missed that didn't you? And it probably became evident when you saw me at the farm. I'm not lying. And you know it."

"Okay. Let's say for one moment I believe what you're telling me. What's keeping me from killing Tom to make you talk?"

"Go ahead and shoot Tom. He doesn't know where I was staying or whom I was with. He thinks I was staying in the motel. Besides, killing Tom now won't get me to talk and that leaves only me to dig. That'll be one trump card down and only one to go. Are you sure you want to risk that?"

"Wait a minute. I don't want to be used as a pawn in this game the two of you are playing," said Tom.

"It doesn't matter Tom. He's going to kill us anyway."

"That's right," said Wilson. "But let's get back to this mystery woman you've been talking about. Where is she?"

"She's safe where you can't find her. But she has instructions to call the FBI if I'm not back by noon today. We have a lunch date and if I don't show, your picture will be all over the TV by nightfall. Are you willing to risk that?"

"You're bluffing!"

"Try me."

Wilson leaned back against the truck and wiped the rain from his forehead. I could tell by the look on his face he was contemplating things. He was torn between killing us and going to jail. Being in a tiger pit for four months was one thing, but being in a prison cell for life was another. He was sure I wasn't bluffing, but he couldn't let me go now, after all he'd done to get me to this point.

Minutes went by and then he said, "None of that bullshit matters. I'll be long gone in a couple of days where no one will ever find me."

He was pacing now, back and forth between the headlights like a caged animal. He was barely paying attention to either of us. I decided it was now or never. I was about to toss the shovel at him when I heard someone on a bullhorn say, "This is the FBI, drop your weapon and put your hands on top of your head."

Wilson jerked his head in the direction of the bullhorn, ducked down behind the hood, and began shooting. I pushed Tom behind the rock pile and went for my gun. I had it out and almost in a firing position when Wilson looked back for me and took a wild shot. He thought I was still standing in the same place as before and missed me by a foot and a half. I raised my gun and fired as he turned and ran toward the woods. My first shot from the Smith & Wesson caused him to lunge forward as he headed into the darkness. *I hit the little fucker.* I unloaded the other five rounds in his direction as he disappeared behind the truck and into the woods. Then I looked over at Tom to see if he'd been hurt.

"Tom, are you okay?"

"I'm fine," he replied.

"Good. Stay down. We'll wait for the Feds to come to us."

Both of us stayed hunched behind the rocks for two or three minutes. I looked down at my watch. It was not yet three o'clock, and that meant Wilson would have a good head start on the Feds before they could launch a full-scale search. It would take hours to get dogs out here and for the sun to rise high enough to get a manhunt underway. By that time, Wilson would be long gone. He said he had resources. I'm sure that's what he said. If so, one of those resources must have been his father. Wilson was somewhat reluctant to talk about him, so I'm wondering if he would use his dad to help him disappear. One thing I knew is he was on the run, and if the Feds didn't locate him in the next twenty-four hours he'd be gone.

The next thing I saw was a man standing near the front of the truck. He was checking to see if we were alright. Looking at us he asked, "Is one of you Ian Christian? If so, then I'm Special Agent Devlin Cotch of the FBI's Domestic Terrorist Division."

"We're okay," I replied. "But I'm afraid James Wilson has escaped." *I missed killing the fucker a second time. He wouldn't get a third chance.*

"Don't worry, he won't get far," said Cotch.

That's what he thought. Wilson was like a cat, he had many lives. He was on the run and even a black man in Iowa could somehow vanish with the right assistance and money.

"How did you know we were here?"

"We've been in daily contact with Agent Yorkshire ever since he came down to Ft. Dodge. He called us the minute he got to his hotel room, and we moved in right after that. We actually saw you leave his room that first evening. There has been an agent following your every move since Wednesday night."

"I guess we should be grateful to him for that. *Ralph had blown the whistle on us after all. Good man!* Then you must know he's dead."

"We do. We went looking for him as soon as we saw you pull away from the farm. He had been in contact with us until yesterday morning. The last time we talked to him he told us he was going to take up a position in some hay bales at the back of the farm. And that's where we found him. Actually, we've had the farm covered from all sides since yesterday afternoon. Wilson must have slipped past us in the fog. We saw him leave the farm in Throng's stolen vehicle and follow you to this place. Sorry we didn't get here sooner, but it took us a little time to locate you."

"No problem. We're just fortunate you knew we were here."

"Ian, I'd like you to come with me to Ft. Dodge. I'll have someone take Tom back to his farm and make sure he is protected in case Wilson comes back to go after him."

"I wouldn't worry about Wilson coming back. He'll try to get as far away from here as he can. I'm the one he wants. But Tom knows James killed Ralph, so I think some protection would be a good idea until Wilson is caught. Do you mind if I have a few words with him before we leave?"

"No, go right ahead."

It was time to make amends with Tom. I'm not sure that would be possible, but I thought I'd give it a try.

"Tom, I'm sorry I hid things from you and lied about a number of stuff, but…"

"Just hold on for a second Ian. You don't have to say anything. I've been thinking about what you said to me earlier, and after listening to what you and Wilson discussed, I realize now you had me covered from all angles. You knew James was petrified of dogs and that's why you wanted Omar to be with me. You knew he wouldn't attack me as long as I had the dog around. And you made sure Ralph had our backs. That left you to handle Chu and Wilson. The only thing that went wrong was you believed Ralph would come to our rescue. And thank God he lied or both of us might be dead right now. I also saw you push me aside to protect me from Wilson's bullet. That's the kind of man you've always been. I saw it in Vietnam several times and here again tonight. You've always put your life on the line for others, and that's all I need to know. We're still friends Ian, but don't ever call me again to get me involved in another one of your crazy schemes. I'm not a good crime fighter."

He laughed and then we hugged again like we had at the truck stop. There would be no dead bodies buried on or around his farm to worry about, and the secret he'd been hiding about Chu and his brothers would no longer haunt him. He was free of that stigma and so was I. We both could breathe a little easier now that Chu was dead. But Wilson was still out there, and he needed to follow Chu into the after-life.

Chapter 35

Special Agent Cotch extended his hand and said, "The agency wants to thank you for your assistance Ian. We know how badly you wanted these men, but it came at a stiff price. Ralph is dead, and I'm going to have a ton of explaining to do to the people in Washington."

"Thanks. I understand the length and risk you went to so I could run this thing my way. I know it was unconventional, but I felt I knew those two better than anyone else and I could get the job done. *I failed.* By the way, what have you heard from your men back at the farm?"

"I got a call five minutes ago from Gavin Marsh. He informed me they have tracking dogs out at the site this very moment. They're going to start the search within the next half hour. I've been told they found blood at the scene. You must have hit him with one of your shots."

"Too bad I didn't kill him. *The next time he'll die!* He's crazy you know. He won't stop until I'm dead. I can guarantee this isn't over. At some point we'll meet again."

"I sincerely hope that doesn't happen. He's more than likely on the run and looking to get you is the furthest thing from his mind. Usually, people like Wilson want to go and hide so they can regroup. He may come back for you at a later date when things quiet down and the dust settles. But in the meantime, we'll be around to protect you."

"How are you going to do that? Put a guard at my door?"

"We don't need to talk about that here. We'll discuss it when we get back to Minneapolis. There are a lot of options, but let's talk about that after the funeral. Okay?"

"Alright, but I want to be able to be with my daughter, so you need to keep my name out of the media. If my ex-wife finds out I've been involved in this there will be hell to pay. I can kiss my ass good-bye to ever seeing my daughter again."

"I've got that covered. Your name won't show up on any report. Now tell me what you and Wilson talked about. Did he say anything that might be of help to us?"

"You know, he didn't say much. He mostly spoke of his relationship with Chu and how Chu had gotten him out of a POW camp in Cambodia. He also indicated he might have gotten his father to help sponsor Chu here in the U.S. There was one thing that stuck in my mind and that was his reference toward resources. My guess is he was talking about his father. Do you know what he does for a living? Wilson said he owned a number of companies."

"His father does own a lot of different companies: commercial construction, transportation, shipping and off-shore drilling to name just a few. He's part-owner in Jordon Construction, the company we traced the truck to that Throng used when he killed the South Carolina patrolman. We didn't make the connection at first because we talked to his father's partner. And neither Throng nor Wilson was on the payroll at the time because they quit about six months ago. Can you remember anything else?"

"Yeah, there was one other thing. He said he was going to kill us and disappear where no one would ever find him."

"What do you think he meant by that?"

"Your guess is as good as mine. But if I had to make an educated guess, I'd say he's thinking about relocating to a place where the majority of the population is black. Like a big-city ghetto perhaps. Or maybe a country whose people speak English, but doesn't have extradition? I don't know. He could be headed anywhere. If his dad is into shipping, then he could wind up in Africa for all I know."

"Yeah, it's a big world out there. I'll make sure our Atlanta office talks with Wilson's father, and I'll let you know what he has to say."

"Speaking of Atlanta, I have a favor to ask. Would you contact the Atlanta Police Department and tell them you have concrete evidence that Roland Cummings was murdered? Chu told me that before I shot him. And visit with his widow and tell her the same thing. Now Roland's life insurance can be paid and his wife, Benita, can have some closure. She knew Roland didn't commit suicide. She's been distraught over this whole thing, and now she'll be able to feel better about her husband."

"That'll be the first thing I do when I get back to the Twin Cities."

"I also had a conversation with Ralph about the death of Lane Moreland. I believe his wife murdered him or had someone do it for her. Let's meet with the local police in the Twin Cities and talk more about that after I get back home."

"Okay, we'll do that too."

"Is there anything else you want to talk to me about? Otherwise, I need to visit with a friend here in town. She's probably worried about me by now."

"You mean Mitzy?"

With a look of surprise on my face I said, "Yeah, you know about her?"

"We do. We've had her and the West End under surveillance from the time Ralph told us you were staying there. We made sure neither of these criminals would get to either of you."

"That's comforting to know. I appreciate that. I guess that only leaves one more question."

"What's that?"

"Am I going to be in any trouble for shooting Chu?"

"You mean Throng? He was killed in a shoot-out in the woods near the Wheeler farm. That's the official report. Don't worry.

As I said before, your identity will be kept secret. Now go see that friend of yours. I'm sure she's wondering what's happened to you."

Leaving the police station was a major relief. I wasn't going to be arrested for killing Chu. Agent Cotch said he would explain everything to the local authorities about the motel incident, and my name would be kept confidential. Cotch was a very cool guy. He was a lot more flexible than Ralph was. I felt I could trust him to keep my name out of the papers and to be of assistance if I needed him.

The long walk up the back steps to the West End took me forever. Each step was harder than the one before, as if my legs were filled with lead. I was completely exhausted from the ordeal, and yet I felt the need to tell Mitzy about Ralph. It wasn't going to be easy. She was probably expecting to see Ralph and me again. Unfortunately, that wasn't going to happen. I eventually made my way to the landing. Taking a deep breathe I went inside and knocked on the door to her room. It opened and there stood Mitzy, wide-eyed and smiling. She threw her arms around my neck and kissed me several times as she pulled me inside.

Still breathing hard she asked, "Are you okay? You're bleeding. It looks like you've been cut. I'll go and get something to take care of that." Then she kissed me hard on the mouth and retreated to the bathroom. She returned in seconds with some towels and bandages and asked, "How did you get this cut?"

I just stood there. I really didn't want to share the details with her. After not speaking for nearly two whole minutes I replied, "Chu got lucky and took a slice out of my arm. It doesn't hurt. *I was numb. I felt nothing.* It'll be okay in a week or so. Just wash it off and put a bandage around it."

"You should go to the hospital. This needs stiches."

"I'll get to that later. First I need to have a talk with you."

"Why are you being so serious Ian?"

"I have some sad news to tell you. Ralph's dead."

She put her hands to her face and said, "Oh my God. What happened?"

"Chu's partner killed him last night."

"Chu had a partner? Did you know that?"

"Yes he did. And I knew about him. He was a guy I thought I'd shot and killed back in Vietnam. His name is James Wilson. You'll be hearing about him on the evening news. He's still out there somewhere, but he doesn't know anything about you. I found that out when I talked to him."

"You spoke to him? And one of you isn't dead?"

"That's right. And Tom and I would be right now if it wasn't for Ralph and the FBI. It's a long story that I'll skip for now. Anyway, Tom's okay and back at his farm with a shit-load of FBI agents."

"And what happened to Chu?"

"Well, let me put it this way. I eliminated him late last night. He's no longer a threat to anyone."

"He's dead then?"

"Yes. Dead like road kill."

"That must have been awful?"

"No, I rather enjoyed it. I was thinking of my friend Roland the whole time. And now he'll never be able to hurt anyone ever again. The man was pure evil. He was bent on revenge and he needed to die."

"Ian, I'm so glad you're alive. What are you going to do now?"

"Now I'm going to get drunk. Can we stay here tonight and leave in the morning?"

"That's not a problem. I'll talk to the owner."

"Good. Now let's talk about you. I involved you in this mess, and I can't tell you how sorry I am for doing that, but you can never repeat anything about what happened this week. I don't care if you want to tell someone about meeting me. That's okay, but nothing else. No names, no FBI, no Chu or Wilson and definitely nothing about anyone dying. My name is not going to be mentioned in any report nor is the media going to find out anything about me. We need to keep it that way. Are you okay with that?"

"I am. Honestly, I'd be too afraid to tell anyone about this week. Who'd believe me anyway?"

"Good. Then let's go to the hospital and come back here and open the bar downstairs. You drive. My car's still out at the truck stop."

Chapter 36

MONDAY, NOVEMBER 2, THE HIGHWAY HOME

The long, sullen ride home was exactly what I needed. It gave me adequate time to reflect on the insanity of life. I thought the war had ended for me in 1969, but this week changed all that. It brought back monsters from my past, as well as deeply suppressed thoughts of people and things best left forgotten. Plato once wrote, "It's only the dead that see the end of war," but I'm not so sure he was correct. The war was as real today as it had been fourteen years ago. And it wasn't over yet, not by a long shot. There was still a man out there connecting me with Vietnam and that wouldn't go away until he did. Memories are said to be sweet, and yet, all I wanted to do is block them out of my mind, the bad ones that is.

The day was sunny and bright, a stark contrast from the week gone by. The overcast skies, rain and tornadic past had given way to a warm and inviting November sun that was shining on me through the windshield of my car. The delightful day was helping me deal with my ghastly feelings for Chu and Wilson. I knew Chu was dead, but Wilson survived, and now I would have to set up new defenses when I returned home. But for now I just wanted to relax and remove all thoughts of the past week from my mind.

As I drove along I began to think about the two, wonderful women who had ventured into my life in the past month, neither of whom would be there in the future. There was no way I could go forward with a relationship with Kate or Mitzy. They both had seen the good and the bad side of the real Ian Christian. I was a man deadlocked with my past, but frantically trying to pick up the pieces of a fragile existence and move on to the future. Kate knew me as the loving father and witty guy who enjoyed gourmet cooking and red wine. Mitzy, on the other hand, saw me as a liar and sexual freak. And together they had knowledge of the dark and murderous side of a man whom they actually didn't know at all. They had no idea of my checkered past that included the Apostle Islands, Washington D.C., and the farmland of Iowa to name but a few. I was a detriment to them if Wilson came back, and for that alone I had to forget both of them.

The further I drove, the cloudier it became, like the tangled mess I had created in this awful October past. A few snowflakes were falling and the further north I drove the whiter the ground would become. I hadn't gotten any of my yard work done, and now I'd have to go home and clean up the mess left behind by Wilson. The lower door would need to be replaced as soon as possible to keep any intruder from entering. That included people like Wilson. Then there was work. I had to go back tomorrow to keep everyone from wondering what was up. If I missed more days than one I'd have to explain myself and that was something I couldn't and wouldn't do. I was sure there would be questions about why the FBI was looking for me, but I could handle that. After all, I was a good liar. I could spin a tale better than most, and that's exactly what I'd have to do. It was fortunate for me that I had a long drive ahead so I could put a story together for each and every individual. That included Kate and the local police.

I wished my journey to the Iowa midlands had been more successful. I was hoping the outcome would have been more like the conquests of Julius Caesar, a man whom I admired for his ability to be triumphant over countries and continents. He traveled far and wide to say, "I came, I saw, I conquered," but in the end I was no Caesar. Hell, I wasn't even a Caesar salad. I hadn't accomplished anything. All I did was to go down to Iowa, get a man killed, damage a friendship, and expose my dark side once again. Sam the Nam man was back, and he wasn't going anywhere while Wilson was still alive.

Chapter 37

It was eight forty-two on Tuesday morning when I got a call from Judy Hartshell. She said Jack Evans wanted to see me right away in his office. I told her I had a couple of things to do before I could get there, so I'd be down shortly.

"That's not good enough Ian. Jack wants to see you now," she said with some urgency. "Drop what you're doing and get down here."

Goddamn Jack Evans was on my ass and it wasn't even nine o'clock yet. I'm sure he's pissed I didn't come into the office yesterday, but I needed more time to get things straightened out and to go to Lane's funeral. On top of that the Feds and the Coon Rapids police wanted to have a chat with me. With hesitation, I dropped everything and went down to the ninth floor to see Jack.

"Sit down Ian, we need to talk," said Jack with a harsh tone to his voice. "Why in the hell didn't you leave a phone number with your assistant like I asked? I needed to get ahold of you last week to talk some strategy. The people at DeKalb want us to do all their advertising and trade show development. Do you know what that means? They'll be this company's largest account, and I'll be in the driver's seat to make vice president in a year. They wanted me to give them a date when we could start to produce their projects.

I needed to have a conversation with you to inform me when you could get a team together and begin. I couldn't get in contact with you, so I had to put them off."

"I'm sorry, but things got out of hand down in Iowa. *Jack... ass.* I was in the middle of working out some details myself when a tornado came through, *Chu and Wilson*, and all power and phone lines went down. What else can I say? I was in no man's land for a couple of days, trying to dig my way out of shit." I had never told a truer lie than that in my entire life.

"Oh yeah, I guess I did hear a tornado had gone through Iowa, but I didn't realize it was anywhere near you. Was anyone hurt or killed?"

How in the hell was I to answer that one? Hurt? Killed? Shit, there was a lot of that. "Well, let me think, Jack. Nope, no one that I knew of, but Tom's farm was hit and his fields are a total loss. I don't think we can go down there and shoot any video for that John Deere commercial. His corn is twisted and flat, so I'll have to look for another place to do a photo shoot. We were lucky to get out with our lives as the twister went within a quarter of a mile of his house. I had to hide in the barn when it came through." God I loved telling this story. It had such a double entendre that I had a hard time keeping a straight face. "And when it was over, we had to start putting things back together. The authorities helped us do some of that."

"Wow. It sounds like the situation was quite scary."

"You could put it that way."

"I take it you didn't get in any hunting?"

"Actually we did. Tom took us to his cousin's place where we got some shooting in."

"And how did that go? Did you get your limit?"

"Yeah, all but one."

"I'm glad to see that you weren't hurt. Let's get together after lunch and talk about DeKalb. We have a lot of work ahead of us. If you could put your thoughts together between now and lunch, I'd be grateful. Do you think you could do that?"

"I think so."

"Good, then let's turn the discussion in another direction. I heard the FBI was here looking for you after I left for Illinois. Is that true?"

"Yeah, I heard that same thing from my assistant Evelyn. I guess the Feds wanted to talk to me about a friend of mine who was murdered. I spent the evening with him the night before he was killed, then I went home. I got up the next morning and drove to Ft. Dodge. I didn't know anything about it until I got back Sunday night. There was a message on my machine asking me to call the Coon Rapids police. They told me I needed to come in and meet with them and the FBI as soon as I could."

"Murdered," he said surprisingly.

"That's right. The guy's name was Lane Moreland. I went to his funeral yesterday; that's why I didn't come into the office."

"Did you talk to the police yet?"

"No, I haven't had the time. I'll need to do that. Maybe I can give them a call later today to set up a meeting. Lane was a real good friend. I'm thinking his wife had something to do with it. Don't really want to talk about it. Probably shouldn't have said what I did. I'll see how it plays out and let you know."

"Wow. A murder. That's something that doesn't happen every day, at least to people you know."

"I should think not. I'm just glad I'm not involved. I'll keep you posted."

"You do that and stop back after lunch so we can go over the accounts."

That was an easy one. Jack did all the leading and all I had to do was follow. He was a good dance partner.

I was nearly home free when I ran into Billy Raff exiting the elevator on the tenth floor. He said, "Hey Ian, Jack told me you were in Ft. Dodge, Iowa last week. Did you know the FBI shot and killed that serial killer down there?"

"What serial killer?"

"He was the one on the news all last week."

"Where did you say that happened?"

"Ft Dodge. Isn't that where you were?"

"No, I was in a small town south of Ft. Dodge hunting with an old friend of mine. The craziest thing I saw all week was an albino pheasant. Outside of that it was pretty dull. A serial killer huh? I must have missed that. What happened?"

"I heard about it on the Sunday night news. The reporter said the FBI trapped the killer in some rural area and shot him dead in a gun battle. One guy got away and an agent was killed. They showed a picture of the killer and his accomplice. That's all. Kind of wild don't you think?"

"Wow. I'm glad I wasn't there. I would have shit my pants."

"Yeah, can you imagine that?"

"No I can't. I'll talk with you later."

That Raff was like an old lady. He loved to gossip. And Jack was no better. He should have kept his mouth shut about where I'd been and there would be more work getting done around here. I think I needed a vacation from all this. Maybe I should go out and see Fish for the weekend and leave all this behind.

I was three steps from the door to my office when I heard the phone ringing. By the time I reached it the person on the other end had hung up. Impatient people, that's what this industry was all about. They'd call you ten times a day, but only reached you once or twice. And they would leave you the same message the other eight or nine times. They thought you were dodging them if you didn't call them back right away. There was no message. Good, must not have been important.

I was barely into that timeline project for Jack when the phone started to ring again. It was Kate and she wanted to have lunch with me. I said, "I can't do it today. I've got a lot of work to do. Let's talk at Ralph's funeral on Friday."

Puzzled she asked, "Don't you want to get together with me before then?"

"No Kate. I think we need some space. All of this shit with Chu and Ralph has me thinking."

"About what?"

"About my time with you and my life going forward. Iowa wasn't a walk in the park. It was brutal. And Ralph died when he didn't have to. Let's just leave it at that. I'll see you Friday." And I hung up.

If the death of two friends in separate altercations, the FBI and police wanting to question me, and Jack Evans being on my rear end wasn't enough, now I had Kate calling wanting to cozy up again. I didn't have time for all this bullshit. I wanted to leave and go visit Crazy Johnson so I could drink myself into oblivion. That, off course, was not the answer. I had to knuckle down and get back to work.

As I sat in my chair another thought crossed my mind. Where was Wilson? And was he in hiding or was he out there in the suburbs waiting for me to come home. That was the big question. If I let my guard down and thought Wilson was in hiding, then he could sneak up on me and I could be visiting Ralph and Lane shortly. With that in mind, I picked up the phone and called Agent Cotch. I told him I needed someone to watch the house and would he please make an appointment to meet with the police tonight so I could be done with both cases. He said he would and told me he'd call back later with a time and place.

Chapter 38

The mortuary parking lot was full by the time I arrived. There were several marked and unmarked police cars parked out front in the no-parking zone. *Go figure.* The entourage, I read, would include the governor, the St. Paul police chief, and several important agency personnel from the Midwest and Washington, D.C. FBI offices…a virtual who's who of law enforcement. The funeral was highly publicized in both the Minneapolis and St. Paul newspapers.

It was in stark contrast to Lane's wake where police officers seemed to be nonexistent. Well, none in uniform anyway. It had been a cold and dreary day last Monday, just like the atmosphere inside the funeral home. The Moreland family was on one side and the Stark family on the other. It was the equivalent of the Hatfields verses the McCoys. Each side was giving the other the cold shoulder, and the only ones in mourning seemed to be Lane's relatives.

Night was beginning to fall on what was a cold and clear day. I parked my car on the side street and walked up to the front entrance, only to stand outside for several minutes before going inside. I needed some extra time to compose myself and get my story straight as to how I knew the victim. I eventually made my way inside. The only familiar face I recognized was that of

Agent Cotch. He had been standing to the left of the door when I entered. He said hi and told me to see him before I left for the evening. He had something he wanted to talk to me about.

From there I made my way through the mass of people to the viewing room where I met the grieving ex-wife and her two teenage children. I offered her my condolences and told her a lie that I had worked in the office for a short time with Ralph. I said I wasn't a field agent and I didn't know him very well, which was true, but I liked him and was proud to have known him. Again, another truth. At this rate I'd lose my liar image; pretty soon people would start to think I was actually a nice guy. She thanked me for coming and I moved on. It was short and sweet, just as I had planned. There was no reason to tell her I was with him in the end, which I was not, so I left well enough alone. Any explanation would have caused me to open up about my involvement and that was a bad idea.

Kate looked up from across the room and caught my attention while talking to someone who I thought might have been an agent. She waved me over. I figured there was no time like the present to have my conversation with her. If she began to cry, then people would take it as a grieving friend and they wouldn't think twice. I moved in, gave her a hug, and said, "Isn't this a pity?"

"It sure is," she replied. "Ian, I'd like you to meet Donald West. He was an old friend of Ralph's and my ex-husband's. He works out of the D.C. office."

We shook hands and he said, "Kate told me you were with Ralph when he died. Is that true?"

"I think you should talk to Agent Cotch about that. All I can tell you is that I was in Iowa last week, somewhere near where Ralph was killed. I don't know anything else. And that's more than I want to divulge, if you get my meaning."

"Yes. I understand," he replied. Then he turned to Kate and said, "It was nice talking with you. Maybe I'll see you later. Ian, it was nice to meet you. I'll leave the two of you to talk. Bye."

I looked over at Kate and said, "You can't go around telling people I was down there with Ralph. It's not in the official report, and I can't afford to have my name in the newspapers. Got that?"

"Okay. Okay. I thought it was alright to say something to another FBI agent. I didn't know you'd been kept out of the ordeal."

"Well I was, and Agent Cotch has gone to great lengths to make sure it stays that way. We all need protection. That includes you and your family. Chu had a partner and he's still out there. Didn't you see his picture on the TV?"

"I saw his picture in the newspaper. I was wondering why there wasn't any mention of you in the article. Now I know. You could have explained all of this over the phone or come over to see me so I would have known. What gives Ian, why are you being so standoffish?"

"As I said to you on Tuesday, I need some time to heal. And Chu's partner, Mr. James Wilson is still at large, so I can't spend any more time with you. I could have gotten you or one of your children killed, and I'm not going to go through that again. I couldn't live with myself if that happened, so we're going to end this here and now. I told you when we first met that this wasn't going anywhere. It was strictly for fun. I never wanted it to become a relationship. And that's what it has become because you want or see it that way. I'm not ready for a family, and I believe the only thing we have in common is friendship and sex. Kate, we're not going to make it in the long run, and I'm not willing to take a chance that I'm wrong. Does any of this make sense?"

"Yes, some of it does. The threat of someone out there who could hurt my children or me says run. But the good times we've had together tells me I want to continue to see you. It doesn't have to be about love. It could be about friendship and nothing else."

"Listen to yourself; you're trying to talk yourself into believing this crap. More than anything you want a husband to help you with the kids. And I'm not that guy Kate. I've got too much of a dark side for that to ever happen. Listen to me when I say this: I've had a thing for you since I was a young kid and that thing is over. You were like a new drug to me. And once I had it I wanted more. But in the end I knew I had to quit it or I'd be hooked on something that wasn't good for me."

"So, what you're saying is I was just a fling to you."

"Yes, that's what I've been saying all along." I took the Monopoly card out of my wallet and handed it to her. "Look at this. You gave it to me the night we met. What does it say on the back? It says, 'What's mine is yours and I hope you take everything soon!' That's all you really wanted. You liked me, and you wanted me to take you home to do whatever I damn well pleased. So let's not be angry with each other. Let's just walk away now and stay friends."

"You mean like friends with benefits?"

"No. I mean like friends who say hi when they run across each other or have a drink now and then to see what they've been up to."

I saw tears forming in the corner of her eyes, so I held her in my arms and told her things would work out. "You'll be fine," I said. Then I turned and walked away. It was the right thing to do even if it felt wrong. She had been the woman of my dreams, but it just so happened she came along during a nightmare. And that nightmare was all about revenge without the worry of any remorse.

Visitation was concluding, meaning it was finally time to go and see what Agent Cotch wanted. I saw him in the back hallway, towering well above the crowd. He was talking to a tall brunette in a sleeveless black dress. The woman had her back toward me, and I couldn't help but think she looked vaguely familiar. She had the same gorgeous body and long slender legs as Mitzy. The closer I got the more I was sure it was her. And just before I got to them I saw Cotch nod in my direction. Then the brunette turned around and smiled at me. It was Mitzy. I was actually happy to see her, for no other reason than to thank her once again for helping me out during a very difficult situation. I navigated through the last ten people or so and found my way to her side. Smiling I said, "I'm surprised to see you. What possessed you to come here tonight?"

"Something inside me said I needed to come and pay my respects. Besides, I only live a mile away, and I wanted to say good-bye to Ralph. I didn't get that opportunity, and I felt it was important. After all, he had people watching over me and I didn't even know it. He also did the same for you. "

"Will the two of you please excuse me?" asked Cotch. "I've got a couple of people whom I need to talk to before they leave. Ian, I'll catch up with you in a half hour if that's okay?"

"Sounds good. I'll see you later." I then turned back to Mitzy and said, "You're looking marvelous, my dear. You've done something to yourself. You changed your hair."

"Yes, I had it cut. Last week was a life-changing experience and that got me to thinking. Maybe I needed to make some changes too. So, I got a haircut and applied to the university's doctoral program. I can start winter quarter if I get my paper done by the end of this month."

"That's great! I wish you all the success in the world. I really mean that."

"Thanks. I came here hoping to see you. I wanted to tell you my plans and let you know you're the person responsible for getting me off my ass and back to work on my thesis."

"Wait a minute. I liked you on your ass and in other positions too. The very thought of you will get me through the cold winter months ahead."

"There's also another reason I wanted to see you."

"Don't tell me. You're pregnant and the kid is mine."

"You'd be so lucky. No, that's not it. I stopped by because you never finished telling me why you loved my vagina. I think you said it was like an all-day candy bar."

"No, I believe I said I loved it because it was like a lifetime of candy bars."

"So what did you mean by that?'

"What I was saying was I like having an unlimited supply of candy bars. I could eat one today and know there would be one there tomorrow and one every day after that for the rest of my life. It was sweet, just like you. And if there ever was a woman who had a box of Bit-O'-Honey to fill, it would be you. But this just isn't the right time. I actually had a conversation similar to this, no less than ten minutes ago."

"Was it with that woman you were talking to in the other room? She seemed upset."

"Yes, that was Kate. The woman Ralph had a thing for. I was seeing her before I left for Iowa, but decided it was over on the drive down."

"So I was a rebound?"

"I don't think so. I wasn't rebounding from anyone. She was a good time, much like you were. The only thing I was looking for in Ft. Dodge was the man who killed my friend. And I found him and more. You were a wonderful distraction, on and off stage. Like I said before, you were a box of Bit-O'-Honey, and I was more than willing to get my fill of it."

"You know if a guy would have ever used that line on me I would have probably gone to bed with him. It's funny how things work out. Another time, another place, and the two of us would be lovers forever. But as it is, I understand where you're coming from. I guess it's the psychologist talking in me and not Mitzy the stripper."

"By the way, what is your last name? I never asked."

"She took out a slip of paper and wrote something on it. Then she handed it to me. She said, "My real name is Carol Ann Miller. I wrote it down there along with my phone number. Call me sometime and maybe we can get together for old times' sake. Or if you like, I could offer you some free therapy." She kissed me on the cheek and left.

I watched her all the way as she vanished into the night. When she was out of sight Agent Cotch walked up and said, "So how did that go?"

"Much better than the one before. Kate wasn't taking no for an answer."

"I don't know what you've got, but telling two gorgeous women to hit the road in the same night takes some big balls. It has to be some kind of record and at a funeral nonetheless. How do a couple of consolation beers sound?"

"Lead the way."

Cotch and I left the funeral home and drove east on Highway 36 to a small bar in North St. Paul. The place was called Newmann's.

"This place seems quite old and dumpy. Why did you bring me here?" I asked.

"Ralph and I came here often over the years to discuss business. Two cops in suits were a strange sight in a place like this. One day a couple of the bikers decided to ask us to leave. So Ralph and I stood up and opened our suit coats, exposing our guns and badges. You should have seen those two exit the place. They got on their motorcycles and probably never returned. That's just one of the great memories I have of Ralph. He was actually fun for a guy with such a cold personality. Anyway, we liked coming here to talk. We knew the people who frequented the place were a bit shady, but they weren't the kind of people we were after. Mostly drunks and some low-level pot dealers. We could sit and talk and not worry about who was listening. I'd like to think we helped change the element in here. Did you know this is the oldest bar in Minnesota? It's almost a hundred years old."

"From the looks of the architecture and the decor, I think you're right. Then the sign over the door saying it was established in 1887 confirms that. It was a pretty easy guess, even for a drunk, I'd say."

"You got me."

"So let's talk. What did you want to tell me that couldn't wait for another day?"

"It's about Wilson. He escaped the net we cast over Webster County down in Iowa. He fled the scene with plenty of darkness to make his getaway and broke into a farmhouse about five miles from where you shot him. The farm was owned by an elderly couple. Wilson tied them up and stole their car. A motel owner outside of Tulsa said a man with Wilson's description driving a car with Iowa plates paid cash at his place on Sunday night. That same car was found abandoned by the docks in New Orleans on Wednesday."

"Are the old couple all right?"

"Yeah. Wilson only took their money and some food. The couple was scared, but okay by the time their son found them the day after Wilson left. The son said his parents told him the ordeal was the most excitement they'd had in the last twenty years."

"Oh well, that's what they get for living their whole life in Bumblefuck, Iowa."

"You got that right!"

"Did you talk to Wilson's father?"

"I did. I flew down to Atlanta yesterday to talk to him. His name is Donavan. He painted a picture of a tormented son. Said the kid came back from the war and worked when he wanted to. Sometime Donavan would have to bail him out of jail for drunken and disorderly, and at other times he'd be paying for the kid's rehab. He seemed to be telling us the truth until I asked him if he'd heard from James lately. The older Wilson said he hadn't heard from his son or seen him in a couple of weeks. Then I asked him to explain why there was a five-minute phone call to this office from the younger Wilson's motel room at 10:00 a.m. on Monday. Donavan couldn't explain it. He said the kid must have called and spoken to someone in the office. Said he'd check into it and get back to me. I could tell he was lying by the look on his face."

"Did you check with the office staff?"

"They weren't any help. No one remembers talking to him."

"So why do you think he called?"

"I believe he was looking for shipping schedules. His stolen car was found near a freighter that belongs to one of the companies his father owns. It left for Puerto Rico sometime on Thursday. It was a cargo ship with parts and equipment for offshore well drilling. For all we know he's holed up at some rig waiting for things to cool down. And we couldn't touch him even if we did know he was there. We have no jurisdiction in international waters."

"But I do."

"Nice thought Ian, but I wouldn't recommend it. Let's wait for a few days and see if he gets off the ship when it reaches San Juan."

"So then what?"

"Then I'll see what I can do to bring the boy back home for prosecution."

"I have a better idea. Why don't you tell me where he is when you find him, and I'll go down and settle the score."

"Wow, you're asking a lot. I could lose my job for doing that. And you could spend a very long time in a Puerto Rican jail. Do you really want to do that?"

"They'd have to prove I did it. And believe me, no one would ever find his body. I'm pretty resourceful."

"I'll call a friend of mine tomorrow and see what I can do. I can't promise you anything."

"Just remember what he did to Ralph and see if you can find a sympathetic ear that will listen."

We finished the last of our three beers and departed. Devlin said have a nice weekend and he'd talk to me as soon as he had any information to share. I wasn't any closer to Wilson than I'd been when I woke up this morning, but wheels were beginning to turn, and I had a good feeling about Cotch. If anyone could do it, he would be the one to put me face-to-face with Wilson, so I could carve it up like a pumpkin.

Chapter 39

The evening was chilly. I had just lit the fireplace and sat down with a glass of my favorite cabernet to watch the evening news. The local anchor was commenting on last week's record stock market increase when the phone rang. It was Devlin Cotch with some news for me.

"Ian, it's Devlin Cotch. I received a phone call from a counterpart of mine in the CIA. We don't usually work together, but he and I go way back. He told me the Puerto Rican and American authorities were waiting for the cargo ship when it docked in San Juan. They checked it from stem to stern and it was clean. There wasn't a trace of Wilson on board. So they checked the manifest and saw the ship had dropped off some cargo the day before in Ponce, which is located on the bottom side of the island. It wasn't a scheduled stop and no one was looking for him down there, but they got lucky. One of our operatives in Ponce said he talked to a dock worker, and the man identified Wilson from a photo. He's in or around Ponce right now. I'm going to give you my friend's number. His name is Colin Green. Call him in the morning."

"Thanks. I'll let you know how things work out."

"I don't want to know. Just be careful and watch your back. How's your Spanish?"

"Old and rusty. I still remember some words, but I haven't spoken it for a long time. I never used it much after high school. My French is much better. I spoke a lot of that during the war."

"Good luck, and I hope you find what you're looking for."

I hung the phone up and went back to watching the news. So Wilson had made a successful escape from the States and was now in one of our commonwealth countries. He could be extradited from there quite easily, or he could be conveniently found dead on a beach. I was pulling for the latter. I knew Wilson wouldn't hide on an oil rig; that wasn't a place for anyone to live. No, he needed to be where the fast life presented itself, and Puerto Rico was exactly that kind of place. But I didn't expect him to stay. It was too dangerous and close to home. He was heading much further away. And if I was right I'd have to move fast to catch up with him before he disappeared off the map. I only hoped Colin Green would let me do that.

I let my thoughts of Wilson pass and turned my attention back to the TV. A weatherman was on now and he was reporting that the thermometer in the Twin Cities was going to dip down low tonight. It was going to get to the freezing point and stay cold for the next week. I predicted the weather was going to get warm and sunny, about seventy-five degrees and hot. So hot in fact, that Wilson would feel me breathing down the back of his neck in no time.

Chapter 40

A man with a heavy smoker voice answered the phone and greeted me by saying, "Hello, this is Agent Green. How may I help you?"

"Agent Green, my name is Ian Christian and a mutual friend told me to give you a call. Can we talk now?"

"No, I'm busy. I'll have to call you back in a few hours. What number can I reach you at?"

I gave him my office number and said I would be here all morning long. I didn't have any appointments, so he could call me back at his earliest convenience. He said he would and hung up.

It was ten thirty by the time I got a call back. Agent Green said, "I'm sorry Ian, but I couldn't talk to you earlier. I had to finish up what I was doing and leave to get on an outside line. They tape all of our conversations inside the complex, and I can't have anyone knowing what I'm about to tell you."

"I understand."

"Good. Then you'll also understand you can never repeat anything I tell you. My job's on the line if anyone should find out we spoke. I wouldn't do what I'm about to if I didn't owe Cotch a couple of favors. Okay?"

"Okay."

"I believe Devlin told you the target was spotted in Ponce on the south side of Puerto Rico. He's been seen by a contact of Agent

Ramón García, living in a small house in the mountains above the city. The contact has been watching him for the last thirty-six hours. I know this is short notice, but how soon can you get down there?"

"I think I could leave the first thing in the morning, but I'll need to take care of a couple things around the office before I can do that. Who will my contact be down there?"

"García. I'll notify him you'll be arriving in San Juan sometime tomorrow night. Call and give me your flight information. If I'm not here, just say it's Ian and leave the information on my answering machine. Nothing else. Have you got that?"

"Yes, but how will I recognize García?"

"He'll give your name to the authorities in San Juan and pick you up as you pass through customs."

"What will García supply me with?"

"Anything you want. Just ask him." And then he hung up.

It was going to be a rough morning. I had to lie to Jack Evans and tell him my mother was in the hospital, and I needed to go and be with her. He was going to be pissed, but what could he say. I had to make up something like she might need surgery, and it could be a week or so before I could come back to work. He would need to go down to Dallas and make the Gustafson presentation by himself, so I had to make sure I called my brother to cover for me in case the two of them had a conversation.

The last thing I did before I went to bed was call the airlines and book a round-trip ticket to San Juan. The flight left at 6:45 a.m., which meant I wouldn't get more than five hours of sleep if I was lucky. My adrenalin was rushing so hard that I doubted I'd sleep a wink all night. So I popped a valium with my last glass of wine and went to bed.

Chapter 41

The last leg of my exhausting flight, the one from Miami to San Juan, was a turbulent one. The cell we were passing through was tossing the fully booked Bowing 747 around like tumbleweed in a windstorm. If it hadn't been for an extremely attractive red-headed stewardess, the flight would have been downright unbearable. Her name was Naomi, and she had hovered over me the entire flight, like a hummingbird looking for nectar. And by midflight, I knew she wanted to be more than just an attentive stewardess. Her inquisition had been so obvious that it would have made the late Cardinal Richelieu blush. It began with small talk. Like, where do you hail from? And are you working or visiting in Puerto Rico? *It's both...I'm working on paying a visit to someone that I'm going to kill.* By the way, are you staying long? After that she went to a more direct approach. Do you need someone to show you the town? *Yes, Ramón García.* And for the final knockout punch she said, "I'm staying in town for the night at the Old San Juan Hotel. Would you like to meet me there later tonight?" The more times she stopped the friendlier she became, and each time she passed she left a free drink courtesy of the airlines.

I was in the process of finishing my last cocktail when the captain came on the intercom. He said, "We're making our final descent into San Juan. The crew will be coming through the cabin to collect any miscellaneous items that you want to dispose of. The seatbelt sign is now on and we'll be landing shortly. On behalf of myself and the crew, I want to thank you for flying Continental Airlines. We hope to see you on another flight soon."

That was Naomi's cue to stop by one last time to remind me she would like to hook up with me later to see who looked better naked. It was no contest. Without a doubt it would have been her. She handed me a slip of paper with her full name and the address of the Old San Juan Hotel. I took it out of courtesy and put it in my shirt pocket. I smiled back at her saying, "While I would love nothing better than to spend the evening with you, my agenda won't allow it. I'm not staying in San Juan. I'm leaving tonight for another part of the island." She dropped her lower lip like a pouting child and gave me that sad puppy-dog face, probably because no heterosexual man had ever rejected her in that manner. But I had things to do, and the warmth and promise of a sure thing wasn't going to stop me from getting to Wilson.

"That's really too bad," she replied. "I'm positive we would've had a great time. If you're ever in New York look me up. I live in Manhattan." Then she took the slip of paper out of my pocket and added her home phone number to it. Delicately, she slid it back in the pocket, tapped it with her fingers and said, "Don't lose that, my number is unlisted." She smiled, winked, and walked to the front of the aircraft.

She would have definitely made me forget about Wilson, but work is work and there was no time for play. I had to get off this plane as soon as possible and find my contact.

I cleared customs with a wave of the hand and was met by Ramón García all in the same motion. We introduced ourselves as we left the terminal and walked outside into the warm evening air. It was hot and humid; probably seventy-five degrees just like I had predicted. I was thinking to myself it was going to get way hotter in the next day or so when I finally met up with Wilson.

"Tell me," I asked. "Do you still have Wilson under surveillance?"

"Yes, my cousin Rafael has been watching the house he's been hiding in. I spoke to him earlier tonight, and he said Wilson hasn't left it since he arrived, but suspects he'll be on the move shortly."

"Why do you think he said that?"

"Neither of us thinks Wilson intends on staying in Puerto Rico. If he's caught here, we'll send him back to the United States for prosecution. And he knows that, so we think he's heading down deeper into the Caribbean. It's hard to say. He could be thinking of going to one of those Dutch or French islands. Both of those countries have extradition, but the government officials down here are so corrupt they could be bought off easily. That means he could stay on one of the islands indefinitely and slip away at any time. My guess would be he's looking to settle in Jamaica. That country is very large and Kingston is an easy place to get lost in, especially if you're black. But let's not get ahead of ourselves. Let's drive down to Ponce tonight and see if we can't corner him before he makes his move."

"How long will that take?"

"Most of the night. You can sit back and try to relax. Get some sleep if possible. I'll drive and wake you up before we get there." With that, Ramón tossed my bag in the back of the jeep and we were off.

I tried to get some rest, but I kept thinking about Wilson and how mentally deranged he had gotten over the past fourteen years. In a sense he was a lot like me. Both of us had suffered terribly, and we were paying the consequences of a nation that really didn't give a shit about their veterans. In essence we had been let out to pasture to graze like a couple of old horses. And as long as we didn't create a stink the government would let us be. I had it in my mind to hate Wilson, but then I thought about all he had been through, and I almost began to feel sorry for him. After all, I had tried to kill him twice, and he did spend some months in a prisoner of war camp. Then there was his unattended wound I was responsible for and a second one from our encounter in Iowa, so maybe I should have felt some shame in what I was about to do. Then the thoughts of Roland and Ralph came back, and I was hyped to kill him all over again. Hate or forgive, that was the question of the hour. Some would say there was no excuse for what I did to him in Vietnam, but Wilson was a coward, and he caused the deaths of many men who otherwise would be here today doing what I was about to do. I guess I wasn't just looking for revenge for myself, but for others that James Wilson had turned his back on and let die.

I stopped thinking about Wilson for a moment and changed my attention to the night air. It was quite warm, even up here at this this time of night at this elevation. I was feeling clammy and fairly ill from going up and over so many mountains. I would say it was the combination of the lack of air-conditioning and the mountain terrain that had me feeling like I did. Ramón looked over at me around 2:30 a.m. and noticed I wasn't doing well. He took the opportunity to help me by pulling over and stopping at a small town in the middle of nowhere.

"Where are we?" I asked. "There isn't a light on as far as the eye can see."

"It's called Huacca. The place isn't located on any map. But I know a family that lives here where we can get something to drink." He restarted the jeep and drove down past the town's only food store. He took a right at the store and went down a couple of side streets that looked more like goat paths than roads. We were on the second goat path when he turned off the vehicle's headlights and pulled up in front of a small house with two windows and a single door. He kept the engine running and said, "Stay here. I'll be back in a few minutes." I watched as he disappeared inside the front door and returned almost as quickly as he had entered with a large bottle of water. I never saw a light go on or off. It was as if he was never there, which got me to thinking maybe Ramón wasn't always a cop.

"Here, drink some of this," he said. "I think you had too many cocktails on that plane. You need to get rehydrated. The heat in this country isn't very friendly to those who drink a lot of alcohol."

"How did you know I had a lot to drink on the plane? I wasn't drunk."

"It was just an educated guess. I knew it was a long flight and you looked a little green around the gills when we went around that last road on the edge of the mountain. Have a little more and we'll get back on the road. I want to be in Ponce by dawn."

I washed a handful of aspirins down with some more water and ate what was left of a candy bar as Ramón got back on the road. I felt better, but not to the extent I wanted to be on the move again. I quickly learned that the second half of the trip was going to be worse than the first half. Ramón must have thought I was doing better, so he put the pedal to the metal and got to Ponce as the sunlight was peeking over the mountain top.

"Isn't she beautiful," said Ramón. "I've driven here many times, but I've never entered it at this time of the morning. Puerto Rico is such a lovely place once you get out of San Juan. The hillsides and beaches are like no others in the Caribbean. You Americans always spent your vacations in Cuba until your government closed it down to travel. You should've come here instead. The women are just as beautiful."

I agreed and said," But your cigars aren't."

Ramón laughed and nodded his head in agreement. "You know, I'm glad the agency allowed you to come down here. It's about time people understand that revenge is an important part of one's life. I know I got in this business because I wanted to get back at some Haitian fuckers who killed my older brother."

"Wow that sucks. What happened to him, if you don't mind me asking?"

"His name was Miguel. Dealing drugs was his business, and he got involved with a bunch of bad hijo de putas. Do you know what I mean?"

"Sí."

"Good, Then you understand Spanish?"

"Un poquito."

"That's good to know. Anyway, he made a deal with some Haitians he didn't know, and they killed him along with three other men during a drug deal that went bad. All four of them were found dead in the hull of an old ship, hacked up by machetes. I got crazy and went after them. I followed them all the way to Port-au-Prince and that's where I lost them. That motivated me to come back to this country and enter the police academy. And five years ago the Americans recruited me into their organization. I jumped at the chance, if only to help me find my brother's killers."

"Did it work?"

He smiled at me and took his index finger and ran it from ear to ear. I took that as a yes, and thought this was a guy you didn't want to fuck with if you wanted to stay alive. At this very moment I was glad he was on my side. He cleared his throat and said, "Let's stop and eat. I need to make a phone call."

I wasn't really hungry, but I didn't know where or when we would have another chance to eat, so I ordered something Cuban with eggs as Ramón went into the back room to call his cousin. He reappeared in a matter of minutes, sipped his coffee twice, and said," Let's get moving. The rabbit is on the run."

"What does that mean?"

"That means you better eat your food fast because Wilson's leaving town. He left by car no more than five minutes ago. If we leave now we'll be able to catch up with him before he jumps on a cigar boat or a water plane. My guess is he's leaving the island and he doesn't want to do it from Ponce in case people like us are looking for him. Are you ready?"

I took a couple quick bites of my food, grabbed the can of Coke off the countertop, and left some money on the table for the uneaten breakfast. Everything was happening so fast I didn't have time to relax and take a breath. We both jumped in the jeep, and Ramón drove to outskirts of the city where we found Rafael waiting for us next to a Spanish billboard that advertised Ron Rico Rum. In Spanish, Rafael told Ramón to stay close and follow him down Highway 52. He suspected Wilson was heading east down the coastline. Ramón pointed the jeep in that direction, and the three of us took off for the port of Salinas. The two men drove without fear, hugging the cliffs like a child in its mother's arms.

I was sure at any moment that Ramón and his cousin were going to launch our vehicles off the road into a ravine where we would die and never be found. But the two men knew how to drive these roads at a high level of speed. I could tell they had done this before. They were veterans of this terrain and they seemed to know where each piece of road was broken or washed out. It went from blacktop to dirt in a blink of an eye, without any sort of sign to indicate there was trouble ahead. I couldn't tell if we were gaining on Wilson or losing him. Then suddenly Rafael hit his four-way flashers, indicating there was something going on up ahead. There was no break in the road, so I assumed he had spotted the rabbit's vehicle. We slowed down to an average speed and followed Rafael.

Ten minutes had passed when we began to make our descent down the mountainside. I could see from my window we were entering a port on the coast. I asked, "Ramón, is that Salinas down there?"

"Yes it is. And if we're lucky, we'll corner him somewhere down there. The city is fairly large. We'll have to be careful. I don't want any civilians getting hurt. The men helping Wilson are bad hombres and they'll shoot at anything that moves."

The beautiful Caribbean Sea was directly beneath us, along with the city of Salinas. From what I could see the city was spread out about a mile long by a half-mile wide. There was a dock at the west end holding a ship that workers were unloading. The town seemed alive with traffic, which I assumed would be a detriment to our cause. Rafael and Ramón traversed our way down the mountainside as we entered the city. It was good to have Ramón's cousin in the lead vehicle as it kept Wilson from accidently spotting me. He would have had no reason to think I was following him, so an attack on them would be a surprise when the right time came.

Patiently we followed Wilson and his thugs through the streets of Salinas. Then, at a controlled intersection, Wilson's car sped off back in the direction of the mountain highway. The driver must have noticed something suspicious in his rearview mirror and the chase was on. Rafael and Ramón followed in hot pursuit as they honked their horns at pedestrians to move out of our way. A policeman blew his whistle and motioned us to pull over, but the two men ignored him and continued on. We followed the lead car out of town and back on the highway heading east.

As we followed I was sure we would draw gunfire from Wilson's car, but that was not the case. The driver was more interested in loosing us than he was at trying to kill anyone.

"What's happening, Ramón?"

He replied, "I think the car up ahead recognized Rafael, or they got a little jumpy and took off to see if we would follow them. I don't think they ever intended on stopping in Salinas. They just used the town to check us out and see if they could lose us. Now they know and there's not going to be any element of surprise when we get to the final destination."

"And where do you think that will be?"

"It could be anywhere. My guess is they're heading to the small port city of Arroyo. It's coming up in less than a half an hour. We should know soon. And if that's the case you'd better be ready. Do you have a weapon?"

"No. Not unless you consider my Bowie knife a weapon."

"I do, but that won't do you any good today, my friend. When we stop, get a gun from my cousin. He has an arsenal in his trunk."

Within minutes of the city of Arroyo, we saw Rafael's brake lights come on as he took a sharp right into town. All three cars moved quickly and dangerously down the streets filled with people and stray dogs. The lead vehicle was honking at people to get out of their way. He even went up on the sidewalk to avoid hitting a street vendor. Then suddenly and unexpectedly he took a left turn down a back street, and Rafael and Ramón had to stop and back up to follow. They were almost a block ahead of us now and moving at accelerated speed. We could still see them, but they were putting distance between themselves and our vehicles.

"They're headed for the beach," said Ramón. "We need to gain some ground or they'll be gone before we get to them."

At that exact moment Rafael locked up his brakes and stopped his car in the middle of the block. The car he was chasing had stopped in front of him and was now situated crossways in the intersection up ahead, barricading it from any car getting through. He exited his car and went around back to open his trunk.

"Get out Ian and go up there and get what you need."

I hurried my way out of the jeep and kept low as I made my way to Rafael. He handed me a vest with the single word POLICIA on the front and back. "Póngaselo," he said. Then he asked me what weapon I wanted.

I put the jacket on as he requested, and took a quick peek in his trunk where I found an old friend. It was an M16. I took it along with a couple magazines of ammo and went into a doorway next to Rafael's rear bumper. I drew instant fire. Bullets were going all over the place. Some of them were ricocheting off the stone wall above my head. I could feel small portions of rock or mortar fall on my head. I brushed it off and thought, holy fuck it's Vietnam all over again. I hugged the wall and returned fire as Rafael and Ramón got into position. I saw Wilson make a dash for the beach as his two henchmen returned gunfire. They had both ends of their vehicle covered and showed no signs of giving up. I looked over at Ramón who was standing behind a wall on the other side of the street and said. "I'm going through this house on my right. I'll go around until I get to the rear of their car." At that same instant I saw Rafael take a round to his shoulder and fall to the ground behind the trunk. He said he was alright and motioned me to keep going. I nodded back and left to see if I could flank Wilson's hired gunmen.

I went through a couple of houses, then a business or two, before I got to a walkway. It was small and tight, just wide enough to walk through without touching either side with my shoulders. I knew I needed to move quickly as Wilson had a six to seven minute lead on us. The further I got down the alley the louder the gunfire became. I stopped at the end, just short of the street and saw I was directly in back of the assailant's car. I fired once and shot the nearest man in the leg and put a burst of fire over the other man's head. They both stopped shooting and put their guns down. I had no intention of killing either of the men. I only wanted Wilson.

Ramón and his cousin moved up quickly. Rafael covered the two men as Ramón and I moved down to the beach.

"Did you see which way he went?" Ramón asked.

"Yes. I think I saw him go up the beach that way," as I pointed to the east.

We both made a dash for the water when Ramón said, "Stop for a moment. Look there. Those are his footprints in the sand."

"How can you be sure of that?"

"Look at the footprint. It's has a deep impression in the toe area and pushed up at the back as if someone was in a hurry. If it was someone walking, the print would be flat. No, it's him, and he's running down the beach. Let's go."

I followed closely, ready to shoot anyone with a gun, especially if it should happen to be Wilson. The next thing I heard was the roar of an engine from one of those fast boats that Ramón had spoken of. We turned the corner of a rock wall and saw the boat speeding away toward a seaplane that was out on the water about a quarter of a mile off shore. Wilson was escaping, and all I could do was stand there and watch him get away. Ramón shot several times at the speeding boat, but never once did it waver from its destination. I saw it stop and watched as Wilson stepped up on the bow to get into the plane. Just before he entered, he turned and gave me a mock wave, then the finger, I suspect, as he disappeared inside. My hopes and dreams were dashed as I watched the plane take off going southeast.

"Now what do we do Ramón?"

"We go to the nearest phone and notify the air force. I saw the plane's tail number through my binoculars. They'll scramble a fighter jet, and we'll know where they're headed before nightfall. I wish we could have gotten him. Let's go and see how my cousin is."

I walked back to the jeep with little belief I would ever see James Wilson again. I told myself he was lost forever, and I'd just have to go home and deal with it.

Chapter 42

"Ian, I spoke to my boss and he said an American Air Force jet intercepted Wilson's plane and watched as it landed outside of Fort-de-France, the capital of Martinique. I can get you on a commercial flight tonight and you can be there in less than two hours. Going down to Martinique will be dangerous. We won't be able to help you if you should get in a jam down there. It's up to you if you want to go, but if you don't he'll vanish and you'll probably never see him again. Do you still want to go?"

"Yes, of course. Are you going with me?"

"No, that's not possible. The French don't like us poking our noses around in their country. I'm actually not welcome there after an incident that happened last year. I went down to bring a French fugitive back to Puerto Rico who had escaped one of our jails. The guy had ten more years to serve, so we were going to smuggle him out when we were caught. They told my partner and me to leave the island, and the fugitive stayed. But on the bright side, I do have a good contact down there I can call. The only problem is you'll have to go into the city and locate him. You said your French was pretty good."

"It is."

"Good, then let's head to the airport and get you on that plane. We don't have a lot of time to waste."

Ramón filled me in on the details of my contact as we headed for the airport. He told me I was to go to the Café Axes in Fort-de-France and ask for an Algerian named Armand Pluvierre. He was a French Interpol agent.

"Armand is quite a character. He's somewhat devious, but you can trust him as long as you're truthful. Don't tell him any lies or you might find yourself dead with your throat cut. He works all the French islands in the Caribbean and has a lot of connections. He'll definitely be the man to find Wilson."

"What then?" I asked. "What will he let me do if I catch up with Wilson?"

"He'll let you take him out. You'll just have to do it discretely. Tell him the truth. Tell him Wilson killed a couple of your friends and has vowed to kill one of your family members, so you're there to make sure he gets what he deserves."

"But that's a lie. He didn't threaten my daughter."

"Armand doesn't know that. And he'll have no way of finding it out. He could check up on your friend and Agent Yorkshire, but that would take time, and time is something you don't have. Just be straight with him and you'll be okay."

"Are you sure that will work?"

"Trust me; the French are big on family. They all love their mothers and children. Now get going and stay safe."

Chapter 43

The Martinique flight was relatively quick, but very rough as one of those late-season hurricanes was blowing some severe weather in from the Atlantic. All totaled it took no more than two hours from terminal to terminal. Arriving in the wee hours of the morning had its benefits, as it meant I would pass through customs in a matter of minutes. From customs I caught a cab for the capital to see if I could still meet up with my contact. It was late and I was running on fumes. My brain was working overtime to tell me to pick up my feet and put one in front of the other. I hadn't slept more than seven hours in the last three days, but I had to forge on no matter how tired I was. The window to Wilson was closing fast, and if I didn't locate him soon I'd lose him quicker than a hand in a lion's cage. My ace in the hole was Armand. I was betting on the premise that he was a nighthawk and he would be awake and at the café.

Things were still hopping when I arrived in the downtown area. People seemed to be coming and going at will. The casinos were open, and shady-looking characters were going from bar to bar looking for some excitement. My first impression of the city was that it seemed like a filthy, stinking barberry town with lots of modern-day pirates. Martinique was nothing like the travel brochures. It was more like the underbelly of the world than the beautiful vacation spot that I had once read about.

I told my cab driver to drop me off at Café Axes and not to wait. I said I was going to meet up with a friend and stay the night. I paid him in American dollars, which he readily accepted, and went to look for Armand. I entered the café and walked up to the bar so I could set my bag on a stool. I visually surveyed the place and saw seven men sitting or standing in various places around the bar, any of which could have been Armand. Each and every one of them was with a distinctively tattered-looking woman. One woman could have passed for a man, which truly might have been the case. I think she had an Adam's apple. The patrons didn't give me much more than a glance as I stood at the bar. I wasn't sure Armand was in the room. And no one made an immediate attempt to come over and talk, so I got the bartender's attention and ordered a glass of red wine. As I sipped the wine, I looked around to see if anyone was giving me the once-over. If Armand was here, I figured he would eventually stop what he was doing and make contact with me in his own good time.

Twenty minutes passed and I was still seated at the bar drinking my second glass of wine. That's when the bartender asked me, "Cherchez-vous quelqu'un, monsieur? Une prostituée peut-être ?"

"Non, je cherche un homme qui s'appelle Armand Pluvierre. Est-il ici?"

The bartender shifted his eyes to the far side of the bar and nodded at a man seated at a table with a woman in a pixy haircut. "Oui. Il est là-bas avec la femme qui porte la longue robe noire, et elle a la cheville tatouée avec un papillon."

I thanked him and told him to send a couple of drinks over their way. "Dites à Armand que ce sont des compliments d'Ian."

I watched as the bartender delivered the drinks. He whispered something in Armand's ear and then looked back at me, tilting his head in my direction. Armand turned and looked at me and tipped his finger as to say thanks. It wasn't long after that when he came over and sat down on the stool beside me. "Bon soir, Ian.

Je m'appelle Armand. Bienvenue à Martinique. J'entends dire que vous cherchez un Noir-Américain qui peut-être vient d'arriver ici par hydravion. C'est ça ?"

"Qui. C'est ça."

"Je vais faire une petite investigation, et au matin, nous pouvons avoir un rendez-vous. Restez ce soir dans l'hôtel, et demain nos prendrons le petit déjeuner vers dix heures au restaurant d'à côté. D'accord ?"

He then went over to his table, kissed his companion on the cheek, and left the bar. Turning back to the bartender, I asked if I could get a room upstairs like Armand suggested. I was informed one was available for sixty-five francs a night. I finished my wine, paid the bartender, and went up to take a well deserved and needed sleep.

I was sitting in the café restaurant eating a tasty ham and cheese quiche with a heavily buttered croissant when Armand walked through the front door. I could see him better now in the daylight than I could last night in the dimly lit bar. He was tall and as dark as described, but Ramón had left out the part about the scar that ran from Armand's left ear to the bottom of his jaw. And the fact that he only had three fingers on his left hand. The man was downright scary looking. If he hadn't been my contact, I would have steered way wide of him from the get-go. He approached the table, via a waitress and sat down. "Bon jour, Ian. Préférez-vous parler en anglais?"

"Yes, that would be much easier. My French is rusty and not very good."

"Nonsense Ian. Your French is very good. I have to admit that it's much better than most of the vacationing assholes that come to my island. They try to speak to us as if we were slow children. They rattle off a question or two in bad French, and then they look at us like we're speaking a foreign language when we answer them. I think most of the people who think they can speak French can't. The real problem is they never learn the language. Do you know what I mean?"

"Yes. I agree with you. I learned my French in Vietnam. And it's always good to know the answer to one's question. Which brings me to the point; what did you find out about the man I'm looking for?"

"We'll get to that in a minute Ian; I haven't even had a cup of coffee. First of all, I want to know if your quiche is any good."

"It's excellent. Why? Haven't you eaten here before?"

"Of course I have. I just wanted to know what you thought of it. You see, I own this place, and I want to make sure people enjoy the food as well as the service."

I scratched my head and said, "How does an Interpol agent come to own a place like this?"

He leaned into me and said, "It was available at a very cheap price after the former owner died unexpectedly."

"Unexpectedly? *Somehow I didn't believe that. I figured he died conveniently more that unexpectedly, but who was I to question Armand.* That sure was lucky for you."

"It was, and to think I owe it all to a hurricane. Ah good, here's my coffee. Would you like some?"

"No, I never drink the stuff. It leaves a bad taste in my mouth." *Just like you.*

"Oh well, to each his own I suppose. The French live and breathe coffee in the morning along with cigarettes. Do you mind if I smoke?"

"No, go ahead. Just blow it the other way."

"Ah," he chuckled. "A man with a sense of humor. I like that. You've got to have one if you're in our line of work."

"Our line of work? And what would that be?"

"You know. The extermination business."

"I think you've got me all wrong Armand. I'm not a hit-man or a murderer. *Well, that might be splitting a few hairs.* I'm here to take down a murderer in the name of justice and revenge. I've never killed anyone for money or anyone who didn't deserve it, excluding the war that is."

"I see. And I want to thank you for killing those cockroach Vietcong who sent some of my relatives to see the blessed Savior. They're a ruthless bunch."

"You're welcome, but let's get back to why I'm here."

"And why is that exactly?"

"I think you know. To find a man called James Wilson."

"And then what? You'll kill him and go home and start life over again? That's not possible Ian. If you have a conscience, you'll turn around and go home before this man destroys you."

"He already has destroyed my otherwise pleasant and serene life. You see, I have a small daughter and she will always be in danger as long as this man is alive. Wilson has threatened to kill her, and I can't let that happen. As long as Wilson is alive, there will always be a chance he could come after me and kill my daughter in the process. It could be a year, five or ten, but he'll do it. I can guarantee that."

"I see. So eliminating him is your only way out. Well then, we better get on with it. But first of all, you must know something about the justice system here. If you're caught killing this man down here you'll pay a stiff price. They'll send you back to the mainland, and you'll live the rest of your life in some dark and dreary French prison. They're nothing like your country club jails in the States. The French prisons are made for breaking people, and you'll die there a forgotten man."

"I would go to prison for killing a wanted man?"

"That depends on how he's wanted."

I took a piece of paper out of my pocket and handed it to Armand. "Look at that and tell me what you think."

He unfolded the paper and read it. "Oh, Mr. Wilson is wanted dead or alive for murder, aiding and abetting in several murders, and attempted murder. The man's been busy I see. This totally changes things. You're a bounty hunter then? So, are you in this for revenge or is it the money that drives you?"

"It's definitely not the money. For all I care you can have the reward if we get him. I'm doing it because the man I'm after had his partner eliminate a former Vietnam buddy of mine. And then he killed an FBI agent I was growing fond of. They were both friends of mine, and the revenge part is what has brought me to this place."

"I can tell you one thing. The local government frowns on bounty hunters, and if they catch you with any weapons you'll be in trouble. Do you still want to go forward with this?"

"I wouldn't be here unless I did. Nothing is going to stop me."

"Okay, we'd better get moving. There's a hurricane coming our way. I'm not sure how close it will come to the island or if it will even hit land, but time is of the essence. I've learned the man you speak of is trying to get a boat to take him to St. Lucia."

"Why St. Lucia? Why not stay here?"

"Martinique, if you haven't noticed, is a French island. Most of the people here speak French, and he would stick out like a priest in a whorehouse if he stayed here. He probably wants to go to St. Lucia because it's British and the spoken language is English. He would fit in quite nicely there, and it has a lot of places to hide, especially if you have money. Does he have money?"

"Money? I believe so. He has a large government pension thanks to me and his father is worth millions."

"Okay. Go grab your stuff and meet me out front in half an hour. I'll have a car and driver waiting for us. We're going to get wet, so brace yourself for the wind and weather. The conditions are going to make the trip much more difficult than it normally would."

"Where are we headed?"

"Cap Chevalier. It's the closest point between Martinique and St. Lucia. It's on the southern tip of the island."

I got into an older-model Mercedes diesel with Armand and his driver around eleven fifteen. The driver was a French islander who spoke a language that was French in origin, but a dialect that was difficult to understand. That meant Armand would have to translate every conversation between the three of us. And Armand was right about the weather. The rain was coming down in sheets like it did during monsoon season back in Vietnam. The further we traveled, the more intense the storm became. We weren't but a few miles outside of Rivière-Pilote when we came upon some downed trees. They were stretched across on the road, which meant our driver would have to turn around and head in another direction.

"Where are we headed now, Armand?"

"We'll have to retrace our steps at bit and go to the town of Sainte Luce. From there we'll head to Cap Chevalier. It will take some extra time, but we don't have any other choice."

"But what about Wilson? He may be gone by the time we get there."

"I wouldn't worry about that. If he hasn't left the island by now, he'll still be there when we get to Cap Chevalier."

"Are you sure he's there?"

"It's the only port on this end of the island with fast boats. Yes, he's there. I can almost guarantee it."

The Mercedes trudged along on at a snail's pace. I looked at the speedometer and saw we weren't traveling more than twenty kilometers an hour. At this rate we wouldn't get to our destination until early in the morning. And that might be too late to start asking questions. Oh well, I was trapped in this car with a man who spoke no English, an enigmatic foreign agent, and a storm that was breathing down our necks.

Time was passing far too slowly for my liking. My two travel partners chain-smoked nonstop, and I couldn't open my window to get any fresh air for fear of being drowned. I guess I was exaggerating a little, but the rain was heavy and I was sure the inside of the car would become a bathtub if I decided to go that route. The closer we got to the coast the lighter it became, or maybe that was my imagination. It was too early for the sunrise, but I was sure it was getting lighter out. That's when I heard the driver say something to Armand as he pointed out the windshield. Armand turned to me and said, "We're here. It's Cap Chevalier."

So that was it. It was the lights from the town that made the evening brighter. And with that, my spirits were lifted higher than some of the mountain tops that we had traveled over.

"Armand. What's our first move?"

"I think we should get a room and wait for morning. That gives us four hours to sleep. I'll wake you when I find something out. Now get some rest and leave the worrying to me. Okay?"

Armand woke me around seven thirty. He said he had checked around, and a man matching Wilson's description had been in town for a day or so. No one could tell him Wilson's exact location, but speculation had it that he could be found down in the cove where all the fast boats were docked.

"So what are we waiting for?"

"The rain to stop or slow down so we can see in this weather. I don't want to risk either one of our lives. We need to wait out the storm. It's tracking north, so I expect we can head down to the cove around noon. Get something to eat and meet me in the bar at eleven thirty."

It was noon in the bar, but Armand was nowhere to be seen. And still no Armand at twelve thirty. Finally, at five minutes to one he burst into the bar and told me to follow him. He had located Wilson on the Witch's Eye, a red cigarette boat that was in the cove and ready to move. The sea swell was still quite high, but the word that someone was looking for Wilson had gotten back to him, and he was about to make his move.

"Let's go Ian. There's not much time to waste."

Our driver, who I learned was Freddie, was waiting out front. The rain was still falling steadily, but the winds had subsided. I could only see a hundred to a hundred and fifty feet in front of me, but I was sure I could spot Wilson if we got close enough to him. Freddie stopped the Mercedes short of the cove, and Armand and I exited the vehicle.

"Here, take this gun Ian. I'm sorry we don't have any high-powered weapons, but in these close quarters that Glock will work just fine and draw less attention. Stay low and follow me. I don't think the men operating the boat will give us any trouble; they aren't rogues."

I followed in Armand's footsteps as he led me to the cove where the boats were docked. And as we came upon the Witch's

Eye, it fired up its engines and headed to the high sea. The boat disappeared into the mist in a matter of seconds. We hardly even got a glimpse of her.

"Goddamn it!" I screamed. Then I kicked the pillar next to where I was standing. I had gotten so close and never even got off a shot. That was twice in a row, and I was no closer to killing Wilson than I had been back in Iowa.

"So what do I do now, Armand?"

I suggest we call your man in San Juan to see if he has any contacts in St. Lucia that might be able to locate Wilson. If we work fast, maybe someone can locate him as soon as he makes landfall."

"How will you know where that will be? And how am I supposed to get over to St. Lucia?'

"First things first, my friend. Let's call the CIA office in Puerto Rico and get hold of García. Then we'll get you a seaplane when the weather breaks. Until then be patient and stay calm."

Chapter 44

I was positive I was going to toss my cookies a number of times on the ride to St. Lucia. The only thing stopping me was the threat of death from the pilot and the fact I didn't have any time to clean up the mess once I hit the island. I needed to be afoot as soon as I hit the coast. I had one last contact to meet, and he was going to be in the city of Castries.

The rain was still coming down as we approached the coastline, but it had subsided some from what it had been on Martinique. The storm that hit the island had veered north and was now pushing its way through the Eastern Caribbean. We were on the water now, taxying into a dock area on the calm side of the island. I was told to jump off at the dock because the water was still too rough to tie up the plane.

The man at the dock grabbed my arm and ushered me up the hill to a waiting taxi. From there I was driven to a local hotel where I met a man named Bobby Cogan. Bobby was what you'd call the local man with all the answers. He would find out anything you needed for a price. And finding Wilson would cost me two hundred fifty dollars up front and another two-fifty when he came back with the information. It seemed like a lot of money, but Ramón García didn't have any kind of government contact on this island, and I didn't have time to waste. So Bobby was my only choice. He told me to sit in the bar and have a drink while he went out to gather information.

I'd been waiting for almost six hours when Cogan finally arrived with the news that James Wilson had entered the island sometime late last night or early this morning. The boat he'd been on docked at Gros Inlet, and from there he took a cab to the old capital city of Soufrière.

"Where's Soufrière?" I asked.

"It's on the south end of the island. It's not far, but the weather may cause some road problems. I suggest you stay here the night and go down there in the morning."

"I don't have time to waste, Cogan. I need to get there as soon as possible. I've lost this man twice in the islands, and this may be my last chance to get to him."

"Why is this guy so important to you?"

"It's better for the both of us if I don't tell you too much. I will say he is wanted for murder by the American authorities."

"Then you're a government agent?"

"Something like that. *I lied.* I've been given authorization by my country to bring this man in. *Officially I could bring him down in Puerto Rico, but here, like Martinique, I was flying by the seat of my pants.* And it's imperative that I get to him before he gets lost in the landscape. My biggest fear is he will get down to Soufrière, find a house in the mountains, and disappear."

"Well I can tell you from living here for over ten years that that won't happen overnight, unless he has a contact down here."

"That's the problem. His father is very wealthy, and I figure he has already purchased a place for him to live. Or at the very least he has set up a connection for his son."

"Then I've changed my mind. I think you should get a taxi and go down there tonight. Slip in under the cover of darkness. There's a small hotel downtown on the beach in Soufrière. It's old but adequate. You can stay there as long as you want. It's run by an old German couple. They keep it clean, but it's barebones at best. I've forgotten their last name, but just tell your cab driver to drop you off at the Downtown Hotel. Catchy name, huh?"

"Yes, real catchy. And how can I find a cab driver I can trust?"

"Give me five minutes and I'll have one at the front door."

Cogan left, and sure enough, he was true to his word. He had a driver out front and I was on my way in less than ten minutes. The driver said he was a friend of Cogan's and he would drive me all the way to the other end of the island for a price. He obviously was a friend of Cogan's. He told me the drive would normally take an hour and a half on a good day in the light, but tonight it might take us three hours or more, depending on the road conditions.

"Sometimes the rain washes out the road and we can only go five or ten miles an hour," he said. "And if there are any downed trees we'll have to sit and wait for a truck to come along to pull them out of the way. But I'll get you there safe and sound."

That's what I wanted to hear. Safe and sound was music to my ears. I hadn't felt that way for over a month, and I would revel in the thought once I had accomplished the task at hand. Wilson had been slippery throughout the Caribbean, but if I was quiet and slid in undetected I might be able to corner him. I'd have to be careful when I ask around about his presence. Otherwise, I'd give myself away, and he'd vanish like he had done so many times before. I had to be creative in my investigation. I couldn't use the direct approach, so I decided I'd get a room at the Downtown Hotel, ask the proprietors if a man with Wilson's description was staying there, and get some rest. If he wasn't, then tomorrow night I'd go hunting and look for him. It would be much like Vietnam. I'd hide in the shadows and keep a low profile. If Wilson was here and he had his guard down, I'd find him in a restaurant or bar. More than likely it would be a bar, where he would be celebrating his newly found freedom in paradise.

St. Lucia, from what I could see, was much like Vietnam. It had a lavish tropical landscape, rugged mountains, and waterfalls that cascaded down from rivers all over the place. Wilson would feel right at home here, and that's what I was hoping for.

The driver dropped me off at the hotel and I got a room for the night. I wanted to ask the night person if Wilson had taken a room here, but he was a local, and I didn't want to push the issue. I figured it would be better if I asked the German couple in the morning. They more than likely wouldn't spread the word I was here looking for someone. So here I was, walking down the hallway in a hotel that might be harboring the fugitive I was here to kill. For all I knew, Wilson might be sleeping in the room right next to me. That was a very exciting thought that I'd have to sleep on.

Chapter 45

I woke at the crack of dawn, ready to do battle with my adversary. Wilson was somewhere in this town, and I had to locate him before he found out I was here. My first thought was to get some breakfast, right after I asked someone at the front desk about Wilson. I opened the door to my room and peeked down the hallway. I saw no one, so I slipped out and headed down to registration. I was greeted by a lovely elderly woman who must have been one half of the German tandem that owned this establishment.

"Good morning," she said. "You're a new guest. I see that you came in last night. Did you have a good rest?"

"Yes I did ma'am. I got here a little after midnight and went straight to bed. I slept better than I have in days. I have a question. Do you have an American man staying here named Wilson? He's a black man about five feet eight. I would think he's been here for a day or two."

"No, I don't believe we have anyone by that name or description staying here. We have one American couple, but they're both white. I could ask around if he's staying in one of the other hotels if you'd like."

"No, don't do that. I'm here to surprise him and I would like to keep it that way."

"I understand."

"How many other hotels are there in town?"

"There are four; two very expensive ones and a couple of moderately priced ones. The two expensive ones are Ance Chastanet and Ladera. Then at the top of the hill is La Haut. It's nice, but not too expensive. And there is one more down at the other end of the beach called the Hummingbird Restaurant and Resort. The food there is very good if you're looking for a place to eat dinner."

"Thanks, I'll check them out. And how about bars?"

"There's but a handful of them. Most of them are down the street from the police station. They're pretty rough places. I wouldn't suggest you go there unless you're with a local. And that's probably not such a good idea either. Most of the locals are pretty docile, but they change rapidly once they get to drinking. What's your friend like?"

"He changes from day to day. I'd say he was secretive."

"Then I'd suggest looking at La Haut and the Hummingbird. And as far as bars go, I'd checkout the Anchor. It's three blocks down the beach from us and two doors this side of the police station."

I thanked her and went into the restaurant to get something to eat. I figured I'd be safe inside this establishment as long as Wilson wasn't staying here. There was no sense in doing any recon today, as all I would do is get wet and possibly expose myself. I'd wait the day away here in the hotel, then go out and purchase a cap and start looking for Wilson as soon as it got dark.

At half past seven I took a cab and started looking for him at the furthest point from the city. That was the La Haut Resort. It was positioned on top of the hill overlooking Soufrière. It didn't seem like a bad place to hide from the masses, but too far away to be anywhere close the action. I inquired about Wilson and was told the same thing as the old lady had said at the Downtown Hotel. No one by that description was staying there.

That left three other places to visit. Then I started thinking, would Wilson be staying in very expensive four and five star hotels, or would he be in a less expensive and less conspicuous place like the Hummingbird? My gut feeling was he would be at the Hummingbird if he was anywhere here in Soufrière. But walking into a hotel and showing my face was risky. I had to do it another way. I went back to my hotel and made a call to the Hummingbird. When I called, the person at reception told me they had no one registered under the name of James Wilson, but they did have a black American male staying there under the mane of Lewis Brown. That had to be him. It only made sense. Wilson could no longer be using his real name. He had to have gotten a new passport under an assumed name. After all, no one could register in a hotel without a passport. That was the law in the islands, like it was in Europe, Asia, and the rest of the world except for the United States. It had to be Wilson, and there was no other way to find out without going there to check it out.

I left the Downtown Hotel and walked the quarter mile or so to the Hummingbird. I wasn't sure how I would locate him. I figured I could start knocking on doors and wait for him to answer. But then what? Attack him in his room and have someone summon the police? That would only get him arrested and he'd still be alive. No, I had to hide and wait for the right moment to pounce on him. Or I could go out and check the bars to see if he was in one of them. I decided that was the best plan.

It was 10:15 p.m. when I made my way to the first bar. The Mango was a half block from the corner police station. I stood across the street, pulled my cap down over my forehead, stuck my hands in my pockets, and looked into the bar. This was actually a great option as all the bars in this town were open and accessible to the eye from a great distance. I could see everyone in the place from my location, but no one could see me. The Mango was a bust. No Wilson or any American from what I could see. And by the looks of the place I could see why. It was one step up from being a toilet.

The next bar was fifty feet from the Mango and it too was a dive. No Wilson, but I did see a couple of white men and a white woman sitting at the bar. All three looked like hippies, with long hair and dirty clothing. The woman did a shot of something and kissed the guy on her right. Then did another shot and kissed the guy on her left. I wasn't sure what the arrangement was, but I can say for positive I wouldn't have wanted to be either of the men after seeing what the woman looked like. But who knows, maybe she was the best of the trio.

That interlude led me to the third bar. It was the last one on the side street and it was right next to the police station. I had to walk to the middle of the street to see inside this place. It had a much smaller front door than the prior two did. The place was much quieter and I could see from first glance that Wilson was not there, unless he was in the bathroom. It was empty, except for two guys who were sitting at the bar having a light discussion.

That made it three bars and three strike outs. I wasn't doing so well. There were only two places left, both of which were on the street facing the beach. I was leaving them for last because they weren't as accessible to the eye as the three on the side street. Plus I was hoping to find him in one of those other three bars because the street was dark and it would be easier to take him down in an area like that.

The rain was more like a heavy mist by the time I made my way to Front Street. I was soaking wet, but I couldn't let that bother me. And once again it was like Vietnam. I was soaked to my socks looking for the enemy. I continued walking past the police station and out toward the beach. I went seventy feet or so and circled back toward the bar the German woman had suggested. The Anchor was in the middle of the block, and if Wilson was in there he'd have to leave and pass right by the police station to get to the Hummingbird. I got to within twenty-five feet of the bar entrance when I stopped in my tracks. I froze like an ice sculpture as I looked into the bar and saw Wilson sitting between two men who looked like local thugs. The three of them were drinking with a woman who was standing next to Wilson. One of the men said something to the group and all four of them laughed so loudly I could hear them out here in the street. Finally I had found my man. Happy birthday to me! Literally, I was thirty-four today and I couldn't have asked for a better present than this asshole.

It was time to hide and wait. I decided the best place for me to do that was to the north of the police station, just off Front Street on the other side of a small river bridge. If I positioned myself there, Wilson would have to walk right past me to get to his hotel. There was no other way to get to the Hummingbird unless he circumvented the bridge and walked a couple of miles out of his way.

It was getting close to midnight, and I figured it wouldn't be long before he headed home for the night. I was standing at the north end of the bridge when I saw Wilson and his two friends exit the Anchor and start to walk my way. One of the men was holding a medium-sized bag and staggering a little. As a matter of fact, all three of them looked a little drunk. *Thank you Lord!* I watched as they made their way up the street.

There was a narrow road to my right that ran between a construction company lot and the cemetery. It looked like a good place for an assault, so I ducked down and watched the men from behind the stone wall as they inched their way toward me. They were taking their sweet time walking down the road. Suddenly one of the men, the one without the bag, stopped to urinate on a parked car. He laughed and stumbled as he caught up with the other two. They were almost to the far side of the bridge when they stopped. I heard one of the men suggest they go back to the bar and have another drink. Wilson said, "No, let's go up to the Hummingbird, and I'll buy you guys a couple of drinks there."

That seemed okay with them, so they turned toward the Hummingbird once again and continued to walk that way. They were finally on top of the bridge, which made me feel like a troll waiting for the men to cross so I could make them pay the toll. Wilson's toll was his life and probably the other two if they didn't leave when I asked them to. I couldn't leave any witnesses behind who could tell the police that I outright killed Wilson. That wouldn't fly in a court of law.

I waited until all three men made it to my side of the bridge. Then I walked out from behind the brick wall and staggered toward them like I was drunk. I bumped into the first man and excused myself. Then I came down hard on Wilson's ankle with a stomp from my right foot. It was so hard that it turned his foot almost ninety degrees sideways. Wilson let out a scream and said, "Look what you've done, you drunken son of a bitch."

I stepped back a couple of yards, removed my cap and said, "It's nice to see you again James. I thought this day would never come."

He was stunned to see me, or maybe he just couldn't believe his eyes as he stood there holding himself up with the aid of one of the men. He was wincing in pain on one leg and trying to stand at the same time. Being drunk didn't help, and the sight of me terrified him. His chest heaved a couple of times, and then he vomited in the street. Wiping his mouth with his arm he said, "Take him boys."

The man with the bag opened it and took out two machetes. He handed one to his friend, and they took a step or two toward me. Machetes. Fuck, I hated machetes. They were just long knives, but they could do some major damage. The two men stopped as Wilson hobbled around them heading in the direction of the Hummingbird. They shielded him as he limped past, and when he was a safe distance behind them, they began their attack.

I said, "Hold on a second. You two guys don't have to die here. You can walk away now and live to see another sunrise."

"That's pretty big talk coming from someone in your position," the man with the bag said.

"What are you going to do? Talk us to death," laughed the other man.

"No. I'm going to stick my knife in one of your chests and watch you die here on the pavement."

With that I pulled my Bowie knife out from underneath my raincoat and threw it directly into the man's heart who had laughed at me. He staggered back a couple of feet, dropped his machete, and looked down at his chest in disbelief. He made a vague attempt to pull it out and fell backwards. He was dead before he hit the pavement.

The other man raised his machete over his head and was about to charge me when I said, "Think again asshole. I've got a gun and I'll shoot you dead where you stand. I don't want to make any noise, but I'll use it if I have to. It's up to you. Do you feel lucky?"

He looked back at me and said, "You're bluffing."

"I don't think so. It's your choice. Again I ask, do you feel lucky?"

He hesitated a second to think the situation over. He must have decided he was too quick for me and I couldn't get to my gun before he could cut me in pieces. Plus, he knew I had to kill him or he had to kill me, there could be no witnesses. He was wrong about being quicker. And he was no challenge either. He came over the top trying to slice me in half with his machete. I easily side-stepped him and drove his nose into his brain by thrusting the palm of my right hand into the bridge of his nose. In one swift motion he flew backwards and fell dead alongside his friend.

I wasted no time in retrieving my knife and replacing it with one of the machetes. Then I made a couple of cuts with the other machete on the leg and arm of the man who had his nose somewhere in his brain. I took off my bandanna and wiped my prints from the handle of the machete and took the other one to find Wilson.

He wasn't hard to spot. He had only managed to make it about a hundred feet or so past the now dead bodies of his henchmen. He was hobbling along and looking over his shoulder. When he saw me coming, he tried to put pressure on his twisted ankle and run, but it was of no use. He stumbled and fell forward on his face. He rolled onto his side and started crawling as he saw me coming down the street. I didn't even run up to him. I walked slow and steady, letting him suffer every step I took. As I approached, he held up his left arm and begged me not to kill him.

"Wait. Wait a minute Ian. Please, please don't kill me."

"Give me one good reason why I shouldn't."

"Because I've suffered enough. And I promise, if you let me go, I'll never come after you. I'll leave your family and friends alone."

"Not nearly good enough James," I said as I dragged him by his collar into the cemetery. "You've ruined too many lives to keep on living. You have to pay for your wrong-doings."

"No. No. You don't understand. Vietnam is the cause of all my problems. You must know what I mean."

"I do. I too suffer the after-effects of the war, but I haven't gone around killing innocent people or having someone do it for me. I got help, and I was almost okay until you came along. And now I've taken a couple of giant steps backwards, but I'll come out of this doing fine in no time. But you James, you have no excuse. So sit up and take it like a man for once in your life. I said sit up!"

James came to a sitting position and once again begged me not to kill him. This time he put both hands in the air to protest, but I had already made my mind up. I took the machete and with great force came down on top of Wilson's head, splitting it halfway down like a ripe watermelon. There was a popping sound followed by silence. James never said a word after that. He fell backwards with eyes wide-open and stared directly to the heavens. The rain, which had returned, instantly began to wash the blood from his face and in a short period of time he almost looked recognizable. Stupid, but recognizable. I stood over him while I removed the wanted poster from my jacket pocket. Unfolding it, I placed it on his chest and stuck it there with the aid of my Bowie knife. A blade in the head and one to the heart…that was a good way for all of this to end. I wanted everyone to know James Wilson was no longer a member of the world order, and he would never again be a menace to society. He was dead and that was all that mattered.

I stood looking down at Wilson one last time and thought how peaceful he looked lying there on the ground. He had said to me the war was the cause of all his problems and now they were over. His pain was gone, but mine was just beginning. I wasn't going to get over this in a short period of time, like I had said. No, it would take years if not the rest of my life to accomplish that.

I turned away thinking how much I had enjoyed what I had just done, and knowing that I was now walking the same path as Chu had. My transition was complete, I had moved to the dark side. I too was a serial killer as I had just added numbers three and four to my list of victims.

Epilog

I was sitting in my favorite chair in the family room watching a comedy I couldn't name when the phone rang. It was Agent Cotch. He wanted to say hi and let me know the authorities had found the body of James Wilson on an island in the Caribbean.

"Ian, it's good to talk to you. By now you probably know James Wilson is dead. He was found in a cemetery with a wanted poster attached to his chest. I read the police report. It said two local men had been seen drinking with him in a bar. They probably identified Wilson as a wanted man and after a night of drinking they took him down the beach and killed him. The report speculates that the two men then got into an argument, probably over who was going to get the reward and they killed each other. You wouldn't happen to know anything about that would you?"

"Not offhand, but if I did, I'd say it was an appropriate place for him to die. Tell me, is there still a reward being offered?"

"That depends."

"On what?" I asked.

"On whether or not someone can prove who killed him."

"In that case I can definitely tell you on good authority that the person responsible for his death is Benita Cummings. I can vouch for that, and you can send the money to her."

"Well Ian, that might be difficult, but I'll look into it. You take care and keep in touch."

"You too Devlin. You too."